# The Rabbit Hole

## Weird Stories Volume 1

A Writers Co-op Production

Compiled and edited by Curtis Bausse, Atthys Gage and

G.D. Deckard

Cover design by Ian Bristow

http://iancbristow.com

*"Oh, how I wish I could shut up like a telescope! I think I could, if only I knew how to begin." For, you see, so many out-of-the-way things had happened lately, that Alice had begun to think that very few things indeed were really impossible.*

# Table of Contents

## Preface

Following Alice following the rabbit down the rabbit hole is fun. To those willing to rush headlong into a wonderland of intriguing and haunting adventures, welcome!

You are in good company. Readers and writers alike share the same imaginative spirit when questing for the weird because weird means more than strange. Weird is destiny. It is that moment when life turns. Such a moment in any story, yours, mine, or those herein is strikingly odd. There is an uneasy sensation and a suspicion leading to a certainty that life has just changed.

When the call went out for content for *Weird Stories Volume One, A Writers Co-op Production*, the response was strong, frustrating and heart-warming. Strong, because many stories were submitted, frustrating because there were more excellent stories than one anthology can reasonably present and heart-warming because so many authors agreed to have their proceeds donated to charity. Half a million people die each year and 400 million fall ill from Malaria. Unnecessary, of course, in a world where mosquito nets can make the difference. Proceeds from the sale of this anthology will assist the Against Malaria foundation, againstmalaria.com, for the purchase of mosquito nets.

The Writers Co-op exists as a forum for members of the writing community to showcase their work. It is my honor and privilege to have been a part of creating our first anthology. *The Rabbit Hole* is the cumulation of efforts by editors Curtis Bausse and Atthys Gage working with a select group of writers from around the world. Here are their stories. May you enjoy them as much as we have.

GD Deckard, July 2018

# Ruby

by Jon Michael Kelley

The day Ruby went missing was occasioned appropriately with sodden skies and a dreary, almost forlorn disposition; a grayness that extended all the way downward to the gutters running fast and full along the Institute's sea-blanched facade. And so shocked was I that when initially calling out for my assistant, only a papery gasp issued forth. Successive attempts eventually produced a hoarse but hearable plea, and Miss Petticourt appeared forthwith, wide-eyed in the doorway.

She'd stopped just short of fully crossing the threshold, reticent to venture farther until the situation was assessed, and the safety of her progression guaranteed.

"Ruby's gone," I said, fighting back tears.

Miss Petticourt fixed her attention immediately upon the room's two hundred-gallon aquarium. Her expression turned from frightened to utterly annoyed. "Escaped? Again?" she said, then shook her head. "Crafty little cuss, that one." Then suddenly remembering the recent safeguards I'd finally employed to staunch such occurrences – she looked at me, astonished. "But sir, *how?*"

"Not an escape this time," I assured her, "but a larceny!"

Miss Petticourt looked quite taken aback. "Who, pray tell, would want to abscond with your bloody, ill-tempered octopus?"

Ruby was not, as my daft assistant alleged, "ill-tempered". Ruby was just… patiently determined.

The octopus's name came by way of a popular American song made famous by Kenny Rogers and the First Edition. The song, if you'll indulge me one moment, is about a paralyzed war veteran and his woman, Ruby, stepping out on him, and not for the first time; *taking her love to town*, if one is to believe the lyrics. And while Ruby the octopus hadn't acquired her name because of such lasciviousness, her previous attempted jailbreaks were no doubt to satisfy such desires. A sad little note, but most female octopuses successfully mate only once in their lifetimes, then die.

Better odds, I might add, than I give Miss Petticourt.

But to finish explaining the reason for naming her as I did: On the second day of her captivity, that folksy album happened to be on the phonograph, and when that aforementioned song began playing the shy octopus finally eased out from under her rocky shelter in the aquarium and attached two pairs of appendages to the facing glass, while allowing the other two pairs to buoy unconcernedly in the water, as if she were 'channeling' the music, the tempo, and swaying accordingly. Then she began blushing with the rhythm, an arterial redness pulsing across her otherwise whitish skin, and in perfect cadence with the beat. Whether she was purposefully imitating the true color of a ruby, or was passionately empathizing with the song's enraged protagonist, I can't be certain. You see, I stopped thinking octopuses as merely clever creatures years ago, and have since come to realize them as being highly intelligent and uniquely cunning.

There again, the pulsing redness could have simply been a deimatic display, something cephalopods do to ward off predators, though I hardly think myself or Kenny Rogers and his band threatening enough to encourage such a demonstration.

And while we're there, I should note that Ruby was quite adept at mimicry, as are most octopuses, putting to shame even the most practiced chameleon. In fact, Ruby's gift at imitation surpassed her species' customary levels and approached something I would call, if I were so inclined to use the term, supernatural.

Not so much that she could simulate her own disappearance, but...

2

So, "Ruby" it was to be. Miss Petticourt thought the name absurd, of course, but I don't pay her to think.

And how, you might ask, did I know I was dealing with a female of the species? That: How does one even know where to begin looking under such a seemingly undefined spillage of limbs? Well, the way to find out is not quite that conventional. But trust me, sexing an octopus isn't as hard as one might think. And if all else fails, trust the animal's disposition, as it will, more times than not, lead you to realizing its true gender.

In fact, that is how I came to discover that Miss Petticourt was, for all intents and purposes, female, as she once referred to Ruby as a "tentacled Houdini", prompting me to correct that common misunderstanding by explaining that only certain cuttlefish and squid have "tentacles", or "bothria", as I insist they be called here at the Institute, thereby inciting Miss Petticourt to counter with a contemptuous expression only the female of her species can effectively produce.

Not an air so much of disdain, I should amend, but of *jealousy*.

Besides gender, Ruby and Miss Petticourt share one other characteristic: both have blue blood. Well, Ruby actually has blue blood coursing through her veins, whereas Miss Petticourt only acts like she does, but I feel it's worth mentioning.

I strode over to the aquarium and tugged at the fastened lock for emphasis. "You see," I said, "her cage is locked, yet Ruby is gone." I shook my finger, careful to not yet point it in anyone's direction. "This can only mean that someone knew the whereabouts of the key's hiding place."

Although her expression remained firm, Miss Petticourt had begun a mild wringing of her hands; slowly, carefully, as if reallocating the sediment of an earlier applied balm or lotion.

An act of simple contemplation, I wondered, or of manifest guilt?

Then her eyes narrowed ever so slightly; her tone low but threatening. "Careful where you're heading, professor."

I met her scowl likewise. "There's only two people who know the whereabouts of that key, and I'm looking at the other. So, you can come clean, confess your sins, and I might take some pity on you. Employment is a hard thing to find these days," I reminded her, "as would be a letter recommending your talents, glowing or otherwise."

Indignant, chin up, Miss Petticourt became even more erect. "Very well then. She made me do it. Ruby, that ... that *sorceress*."

"Made you do ... what?"

"She imitated me. Behind the glass. At first, I thought it was my own distorted reflection, but then I saw those eight arms balled up beneath her and ... and it changed, my expression. *Her* expression, one of stark befuddlement, then onward to freeze in gaping horror! Sir, she mimicked my own death mask!"

I didn't tell the poor dear that Ruby didn't likely have to go to any extra lengths to achieve such a countenance.

"That sounds a bit preposterous," I said, though it didn't really. We were, after all, referring to Ruby's skills.

Miss Petticourt had begun trembling by then, an affliction that seemed embarrassingly incongruous to her otherwise bold persona. "A death mask, sir!" she repeated. "My own face behind the glass, staring back, appearing ... drowned!" She drew an arm to her mouth and gasped. "It was a warning! What, what else could it have been?"

"A warning?" I asked suspiciously. "Warning you from what?"

There was more of that hand-wringing as her eyes darted to random points on the floor. "My emotions, of course," she said finally. "Ruby knew I'd taken a ... a fancy to you, sir."

This I had not seen coming. But I hid my surprise, and finally

4

asked, "Where is she now, Miss Petticourt? Where is Ruby?"

Staring down at her feet now, Miss Petticourt said, "Gone, sir, I'm afraid. I took her down to the beach and eased her gently into a nice tidal pool."

"Eased her into a tidal pool," I asked, "or onto a salad fork?"

Miss Petticourt quickly looked up, aghast. "Granted, we weren't the best of friends, but I wouldn't have steamed her up!"

"Alright, for argument's sake, let's say I believe you. My other question would be then: How did you manage to get such a large, slippery and most evasive creature out of her enclosure?"

"Why, it was no chore at all, sir," explained Miss Petticourt. "After I unlocked the lid, she shimmied right up the glass and into my arms."

"Now I know you're lying."

Her upper-class accent had splintered now, becoming more a Cockney one. "On me mum's grave, sir, I swear it. Just plopped right into me arms, pleased as peas, and off we went, down to the beach!"

It was a feeble attempt, but I had to smile in spite of myself. Knowing now that Miss Petticourt was nurturing feelings for me had softened the blow of Ruby's abduction. But I was still determined to find the truth.

"Miss Petticourt, I should remind you that I've dealt with cephalopods for a very long while and – despite them having three hearts and you operating with a singular but most dysfunctional one – I'm confident that no such affections were on display!"

"Oh, very well then," she sighed, shoulders sagging, the weight of it all having finally become too much. "I muscled her into a pillow case, then tossed her into the shark tank."

It took three volunteers and nearly half a day to rescue Ruby from the sharks. But she'd managed quite well to keep them at bay, and I imagine it had something to do with her impersonation of a certain assistant of mine.

But I let her go, in the end. Ruby, that is. With Miss Petticourt's help, I had finally realized that Ruby the octopus had become, to me anyway, more than just another exhibit at the Institute.

Miss Petticourt, on the other hand, is still with me and has become well-known to the staff for her sober avoidance of all areas where cephalopods are kept.

She's quicker with the tea, as well.

Jon Michael Kelley has been writing speculative fiction for many years. He lives in a gold mining town in the mountains of Colorado where he often finds his inspiration. His recent credits include stories in the multiple award-winning anthologies *Chiral Mad, Chiral Mad 2,* and *Qualia Nous* (2014 Bram Stoker Award Finalist for Best Anthology) by Written Backwards Press; Firbolg Publishing's ambitious anthology *Dark Muses, Spoken Silences*; and *Sensorama* by Eibonvale Press.

*Ruby* was first published in *Strangely Funny* by *Mystery and Horror*, LLC, July 2013

# Incident On A Hillside

by Erik Bergstrom


"Someone's at the door."

The son looked through the curtains at the top of a short man's head. A large-brimmed hat hid his face, though the son could see his wrinkled chin, colored yellow by the porch light.

"Don't answer it. He'll go away," said the father from his chair. He was looking down through his bifocals at the family's latest property tax statement. The mother was on the couch drinking her blush wine, watching the TV turned down low.

The visitor knocked again, the same three raps spaced equally apart.

"Should I turn off the lights?" asked the son.

"Just get away from the door," said the father.

"Get away from the door!" yelled the mother. Two actors mumbled to one another on her TV, followed by a laugh track.

The son turned off the porch light. The visitor's silhouette didn't move. He stood at the door, unassailable, blacking out the twilight.

"He's not leaving."

One knock. Then another. Then another.

"He's not going away!"

The father muttered "Christ!" and pulled his glasses off his face. "Could you move away from the goddamn door?"

"Move from the goddamn door!" the mother parroted, though half of what she said went into her glass.

The father turned towards the mother. "Didn't you put up some 'No Soliciting' signage?"

The mother shrugged one shoulder. A Nutrisystem spokesperson reflected in her bloodshot eyes.

The father stood noisily and left the room. He pushed his son aside, pulled the curtain open, and looked out. "What the hell–" he said. He turned the light back on and opened the door.

From behind his father, the son studied the visitor: wrinkled chin, a bent nose, sagging cheeks. He smiled, but only a little, revealing thin, crooked teeth and pale gray gums.

"Do you have any idea what time it is?"

The visitor turned his shadowed eyes down to the son for a moment, then back up to the father.

"Pity poor Godfrey family upon being bothered. He doesn't mean to intrude. May he come in?"

"Come in? Hell–"

"He has something of interest..."

The visitor lifted a worn briefcase to shoulder height and shook it. Something light and plastic rattled inside.

"You want to bring that into my home?"

"If the Godfrey family should be so hospitable."

"Well the Godfrey family is not so hospitable. Now get off the Godfrey family's property before Mr. Godfrey calls the goddamn police!"

The visitor's grin stretched wider. The son thought his teeth looked like keys on a broken piano. "It is courtesy of the Godfrey daughter."

"What's that now?" said the father.

"He begs the Godfrey family not turn him away. The Godfrey

9

daughter would like not to see him again until he's made his delivery."

The father's eyes grew wary. "I'll have to call her and find out more about this. Come back tomorrow. During normal hours, for Christ's sake."

"Oh, just let him in." It was the mother's voice, all nicotine rasp and slurred speech. She slipped between the father and the son and looked down at the visitor.

The visitor entered. He was the same height as the son, though he walked as if his legs troubled him, stepping down with a pained limp on each foot.

"So what is it you have in there again?" the father said, sounding neutered.

"Patience first." The visitor led the group down the hallway and into the kitchen. He hoisted his briefcase onto the table and turned to guard it. Then, at last, he removed his hat.

He appeared to each of them something very close to a person, though off by a few important degrees. To the father, the wrinkles on his face were deep and shadowed, like an intruder's. To the son, he was a strange and unique curiosity, like from one of his stories. To the mother, he was simply not the father.

"He has for the Godfreys very precise and careful instructions he must first carry out."

"Yeah? What are these instructions?" the mother said, smiling. It was as if she was in her favorite TV parlor game.

The visitor put his fingers on the clasps of his briefcase and held them there. "Once opened," he said, "the truth cannot be put back. To this, do the Godfreys all agree?"

The mother cocked her eyebrow at the father. She wore her wine glass near her bottom lip like an accessory.

"Just open the goddamn thing already," the father said.

"As the Godfreys wish." The visitor pinched the clasps between his fat fingers and the top to his briefcase sprang open. What had likely been expected – a beam of light, or a winged creature from hell – did not appear. Instead, all the family saw was an unlabeled video cassette.

"A movie?" said the mother, dismayed.

"It is only the truth."

"What truth?" the father said. "Quit wasting our time." He reached for the cassette, perhaps to feel it was there, but the visitor yanked it away from his reach.

"The Godfreys know exactly what truth it is!" the visitor spat. He had an accusatory look about him, as if betrayed, cornered like a wild animal.

"What's on it?" asked the son.

At this, the visitor's old face softened again. "What's on it is not as important as what's always on the Godfrey family's conscience. Pity, pity, poor Godfrey family."

"The hillside," said the father, guessing at the answer. The visitor softly grunted, affirming his suspicion. "So that's what this is about. As if we had anything else to say about that day. Well, nice try. Who are you, anyway? Some kid she's babysitting?"

The father grabbed at the visitor's face as if it were a mask. In a stunning display of reflex, the visitor wrapped his fat hand around the father's wrist and twisted it around. The father barked a short, agonizing note.

"Pity poor Godfrey should he not keep his hands to himself!"

"He's heard that before," the mother said, lazily.

"Let go of me!" shouted the father. The visitor obeyed, though it was clear where the lines had been drawn.

11

"So what's on the tape?" the mother asked. "A confession?"

The visitor shook his head, slow and deliberate. "A confession and a truth are not one and the same."

"What's this got to do with what happened then?" said the father.

"He thinks the Godfrey family only sees a truth they've created to cover years of lies."

"So what is it? A recording of what happened?" snorted the mother.

The visitor nodded.

"All right. What do you want? A ransom?" the father said. "The case is closed. Justice was served."

"He thinks there is another kind of justice."

"Christ—"

"Another kind," said the visitor, gravely.

The mother splashed more wine into her glass. The father shook his head and rubbed at his eyes. The son snuck his cell phone out from his pocket and typed a message to his sister.

*Who did u send over here? What is the hillside?*

"He thinks the Godfrey boy should pay attention, lest he miss out on his reward."

The son looked up. "I'm sorry, I was—"

"He thinks the Godfrey boy knows not what sorry is. Not yet."

"What do you want from us? Money? Christ knows I send enough for her laundry every goddamn week."

"He only wants the truth."

"We don't even know the truth anymore," said the mother. "Hell, I could've admitted that earlier."

"He thinks there ought to be one last chance for the Godfreys to discover it. Generous as he is."

"Last chance? Is that a threat?" said the father.

"No threats. Only opportunities. Pity poor Godfrey."

"I'll tell him what happened," the mother said. She fell onto a stool near the kitchen. "Just let me take a goddamn seat first."

The son's phone buzzed. He slid it out of his pocket and read the newly-received texts from his sister.

*Sent who over? What r u talking about?*

*And who mentioned the hillside?*

\*

"It was just the three of us that day," the mother began, meaning herself, the father, and the daughter. "She liked to look at the bluffs," she said.

"And I wanted a babbling brook," the father cut in.

"You're the babbling type, all right."

"Now what the hell's that supposed to mean?"

The mother flitted her hand and continued. "It was the perfect place to stop. They had those bluffs down across the way, with his river there winding through them." She explained how they'd set out their blanket for the food and sat beneath a gray sky, burdened only by a small bit of wind. "I hadn't even taken a bite of the potato salad before the shrieking began."

The visitor watched, gleeful, as she told her version. Not once did he blink. Not once did his fiendish grin droop. "Please, do go on. He wants you to."

"We didn't know what it was at first. We sat and tried to eat through it. But it was so–"

"Incessant," the father jumped in when she paused.

13

"Oh, well it wasn't in*cess*ant. Do you even know what 'incessant' means?"

"I might have an idea."

"That'd be a first."

"Please, Godfreys. This is not how one tells a story!" said the visitor. "Now, go on. The shrieking."

"Yes. The shrieking," the mother continued. "There was a girl down at the bottom of the hill, standing next to the river. Next to her was a man. We figured it to be her boyfriend."

The mother went on to explain how, down along the shadows of the hill, a young girl was screaming at a man and beating on his shoulder with her fist.

"I remember her saying 'stop', over and over again. But what he was doing had him so preoccupied that he couldn't hear her. Either that, or he didn't want to hear her."

"How did the girl appear?"

"Oh, I don't know. Some pretty, little thing. A natural beauty. Everything from her hair to her skin. It was all so fair. I'd have to go back to maybe thirteen to feel that pure again."

"Try younger," said the father.

"Nobody asked you."

"Please. Do go on. Did it appear what she'd been shrieking about?"

"No, not really," said the mother, vaguely recollecting. "No, I suppose it didn't. Not at the time."

"And that is the truth?"

"To me, yes. It is," she said, returning from her haze. "He wasn't listening to her. And I think she felt threatened by it. That's why she did what she did."

"And what did she do?"

"She smacked him over the head with that rock. And who could blame her? What a woman wouldn't do if she knew nobody was looking."

"But you *were* looking."

The mother glared at the visitor drunkenly. "Yes. That's what we're talking about, isn't it?"

"And she saw you looking."

His words seized her and she suddenly couldn't speak. It was almost like he knew how often she saw the girl's face, burned like a flashbulb in her memory. Like he knew how often she called to her and asked for forgiveness. But what had the poor girl done?

"I sentenced her to death," said the mother, her voice mummified, her jaw trembling.

"Don't be so dramatic. She only got ten years," said the father. "She had more than that coming."

The visitor turned to the father and his smile fell away. "Pity, pity poor Godfrey. Must I make you wait so long to tell us your truth?"

"Oh, well, I don't – I don't know that it's so different."

"But it *is* different. Is it not?" He looked at the father as if casting a spell. Then he lifted the video cassette from his briefcase and tapped it with a long, cracked fingernail. "He has the truth right here, has he not?"

"Well I suppose – maybe there's a few parts she missed. I'd really just be filling in the gaps."

"Then fill them, Godfrey."

\*

During the mother's story, the son had been texting with his sister.

*How come u never told me about it?*

*Its not something I can just bring up*

*U heard a girl screaming?*

*Who did you say is there?*

*Idk some creepy old dude. He says u know him?*

*I know lots of creepy old dudes. Im in college remember?*

*He's really short. Wearing a hat*

*Not ringing a bell. U said he had video? Whats on it?*

*Idk... he keeps saying its what happened at the hillside*

*You havent watched it?*

*No. Says he'll only give it to us if we tell the truth*

*About what?*

*About what happened at the hillside*

*...*

*Whats up?*

*Can you do something for me?*

*...like what?*

*Can u tell my truth for me?*

At that moment, the son looked up from his phone and found the visitor watching him, his toothy grin etched on his face, and his eyes gleaming darkly.

*

"So we're sitting there, I'm trying to eat my salami sandwich – or was it turkey – and anyway, she gets up after saying she heard screaming down near the river. I follow her to where the hill starts to slope and we see these kids over by the thicket there. Looks like he's washing some clothes or something. Couldn't really see what he was up to."

"You know what he was up to," the mother said. She unscrewed the cap from her bottle of wine and poured the rest into her glass. "What else would make that girl so upset?"

"You're being too sentimental." The father turned to the visitor. "She's always been this way about what happened. Blames the guy. When she knows the girl likely orchestrated the whole thing!"

The visitor held the video cassette out in front of his chest like a warning. The father turned away from him, unnerved.

"Well, anyway. He was going about his business, this thing she put him up to, when she snuck up behind him and nailed him across the back of his head with that rock."

"What else was she s'posed to do?" shouted the mother.

"Well even if she got cold feet about it all, she still clocked the poor guy. Total sucker punch. Didn't even see it coming."

"That's all, then?" the visitor said.

The father nodded. "That's all I got."

"Two tales, yet only one truth. To which Godfrey goes the spoils?"

"Does it even matter? You give it to either one of us, we're going to destroy it," said the father. He turned to the mother. She wouldn't look at him. "Right?"

She shrugged.

"Right?" He said her name. She looked away.

"I'd maybe like to watch it first," she said.

"Once the truth is witnessed," the visitor said, "it cannot be

17

put back. Are both Godfreys comfortable with the truths they've told?"

They looked at one another, shrugged slowly, and nodded; an unsure compromise.

"Then no Godfrey gets the tape."

"The hell? You calling us liars?" shouted the father.

"Not even an honest man can tell a truth that doesn't involve himself," said the visitor. "Don't flog yourself, Godfrey." He laid the videotape back into his case and closed it, carefully, before replacing his hat on his head.

"He's bluffing. He's *bluffing*, right?" the father cried. "There's nothing on that tape!"

"Is Godfrey so sure of it?"

"What could honestly happen to us if we watch it, anyway? I know in the end justice was served!"

"What happens upon seeing the bare truth is that the Godfrey family will be compelled, finally, to correct its crimes."

"Wait!" The son emerged from the dark corner of the kitchen. "I have a truth."

The visitor smiled, eagerly. "Does he?"

The son nodded. The mother turned to the father, disbelief in her glassy eyes.

"Speak then, young Godfrey. Tell us your truth."

*

"They went down to the river to kill their babies," the son said.

"Now how in the hell would you know that?" said the father.

The mother waved him off. "Let him talk." She turned on her stool and leaned into the son. He smelled her, all her sourness and bitterness, and wondered if she'd ever smelled differently. "Go on. Tell your story."

He began again. "She said she wanted to kill them, but she hadn't meant it. She'd been sleepy, or..." He paused to look at his mother. "She didn't mean it. But the boy, he thought she was serious. So he took both of their babies, newborn twins, and he went to the river. She followed, I guess, and begged him the entire way not to do it."

The son's father stood with his bottom lip bubbled out, like he had something he was trying to swallow; a bitter pill, perhaps. He leaned back into the shadows of the kitchen and crossed his arms again.

"He held both of their faces below the surface of the water. He was strong, but he didn't need to be. They were just babies. She did all she could to stop him but she... she just couldn't."

"Oh Christ, I know where he got this," said the father. "He found one of those sensational stories on the web, or something!"

"Quiet, Godfrey!" The visitor held out his free hand as if he had the power to silence the father himself, gnarling his stubby fingers in a kind of detached chokehold. "One does not interrupt the truth when it is being spoken. Go on, young Godfrey."

"I don't know that there's much else. She tried everything to get him to stop. That's when she finally hit him with the rock. She tried to run when she saw my parents."

"Mm-hmm," said the visitor. He set his briefcase back on the table and opened it to retrieve the video cassette. He examined it, flipped the cover off the film, sniffed it. Then he ejected his fat, purplish tongue and tasted the plastic gears of the video cassette.

"What the hell is he doing now?" asked the mother.

The visitor pulled the tape away from his mouth and studied it a while. "Still tastes foul," he said.

19

"Foul?" repeated the son.

"Very foul." His voice sounded hoarse and old. "Show him to your cassette player at once. The truth shall at last set the Godfreys free."

For the first time that evening, the son saw how the visitor's shadow had grown behind him into the dining area. It gave him a new kind of height; allowed him to hold command over them in their own home, as if he'd performed this same task many, many times before.

*

They huddled together in the basement – the father, the mother, and the son. The visitor was only a hunched shadow again, leaned over in front of the idle blue TV screen, inserting the video cassette into the VCR.

"Been awhile since we used it," said the father.

"He knows how to work such things."

"TV keeps moving," said the mother, who then laughed at herself. The visitor stood at his full height and scowled.

"Many lies have been told this night."

"Hey buddy, speak for yourself," said the father.

The visitor glowered. "He does."

"Come again?" said the father.

"Even he has his vulnerabilities to the power of lies." The visitor's head drooped. "This delivery was not ordered by the Godfrey daughter."

A swell of panic filled the son, threatening to burst him like a grape. His sister's confusion made sense. Everything she'd said made sense at that moment, and it was almost too much for him to bear.

20

"The Godfrey family did not stop on the hillside for lunch, did they?" The visitor paused, but it seemed he wasn't waiting for an answer. "The Godfrey mother and father stopped because they saw something familiar at the hillside. Something they chose to investigate."

It was the car, the mother recalled. Their daughter's car, parked at the scenic overlook next to a few others, miles from where it should've been. They stopped there to spy on her. Though, like the room spinning before her, she couldn't be sure what – or who – she'd seen down along the hillside anymore; especially once the father started giving her new stories to memorize.

"And now she's come reckoning – the girl who was put away under the weight of the Godfrey family's lies. The girl who just happened to be at the hillside alone, reminiscing at an old rendezvous spot with her former beau. Of course, he couldn't tell the Godfreys it was her right away–"

"So your lies are justified and ours aren't?" the father shouted.

The visitor grinned. His teeth glowed blue. "A theoretical truth is black and white. But pragmatic truth is often buried by many colors."

Behind him the recording started, and the father and mother were transported back to the hillside. In their stories, the landscape had loomed monstrous beneath skies filled with storm and anger, sloping long into white-capped water. But there, on the tape, was only dying grass and a lazy-flowing river, and a white sun peeking now and again from behind some puffy clouds.

The father and the mother stood behind the sofa, unaware that their mouths were hanging, and clutched the leather cushioning. How had they not realized they were being recorded? Why would someone even think to record them in that moment, anyhow? Was the visitor so small, so unassuming, that they wouldn't have seen him there? Did he know they were about to bear witness to something so tragic that it would shape their futures, even the small bits, each remaining day of their lives?

The son, meanwhile, watched with a calm apprehension, knowing soon that he'd see the grisly event he'd only heard about in whispers here and there. He watched unblinking so long that his eyeballs dried in their sockets; like it was only some horror movie he was detached from, even as he followed the younger versions of his parents creeping towards the hill.

Like in the father's story, the boyfriend was hunched over the water's edge, arms moving with effort.

Like in the mother's story, the young girl was protesting and trying to stop the boy from whatever terrible mistake he was committing.

Like in the son's story, the man drew up for a moment to uncover the pale white blurs unmoving beneath the water.

Like in all their stories, the girl turned and found a rock near her feet, plucked it from the dirt and, in one sweeping motion, slammed it into the young man's head, killing him.

But then, in a moment from none of their truths, the girl looked up at the mother and the father, and they all recognized and at last accepted the girl as their daughter and sister, with her recognizable eyes rounded like dinner plates.

With her mother's trembling jaw.

And with her father's instinct to hide.

Erik Bergstrom lives in Minneapolis, Minnesota, where he spends most of his time star-gazing, feeding crows, and trying to attract pollinators to his yard. He enjoys writing about the magic of the natural world using the lens of horror, which results from too many scary movies growing up.

His other work can be found online in *Chantwood Magazine, Déraciné Magazine*, and *Horror Bites*. He was also a finalist in the STORGY: Exit Earth competition in 2017. Reach him online at http://www.erikbergstromwriting.com or on Twitter @erikbbergstrom to see pictures of the newest critters living in his backyard.

# Foggy

by Anthony Engebretson

The bloated yellow mouth protruded from the murky water. Its jagged purple teeth pointed to a mesh bottom throat, inviting some witless prey to hop in.

Or so the inner tube appeared to Alexandra. She eyed it from the bow of the boat, leaning back as if keeping her distance would somehow delay the ride.

Alexandra despised deep water and everything that lurked in it. She couldn't even close her eyes in the shower without being attacked by images of plesiosaurs, kelpies or giant tadpoles. But in the comfort of the boat, she was fine. It had barriers to keep the dark waters at bay, a motor and a steering wheel to get her to shore, and it had Dad.

Because the summer was a busy time for her mom, she often stayed with her dad, Owen, at his apartment. They frequently took trips to Fog Lake, a private mid-sized reservoir a few miles out of town. Owen's former boss and one of his only friends, Barry, had a membership and would let Owen take his little blue motorboat for a spin.

One morning, Owen surprised Alexandra by bringing home the inner tube in the bed of his pickup. It proceeded to spend most of its days losing air and collecting dust in the closet of Owen's bedroom. The idea of being exposed over those untamable waters in an oversized donut was too much for Alexandra. Sure, she'd seen other kids ride inner tubes, but she never shared her age group's idea of fun. Her idea of a good time was hanging out at home, watching a movie, helping mom or dad cook or playing with a pet.

However, today was the day of reckoning. She had finally

24

promised to ride in it.

"All right, good enough," Owen said as he finished tying the yellow rope of the inner tube to what they called the "metal thingy" on the back of the boat.

He lifted his cap to wipe sweat from his hairless head. It was a painfully humid day with only a slight breeze for relief. It was nearly cloudless, but in the western horizon a white mass of cream puff clouds was building toward an anvil-headed top. According to the Weather Channel app Alexandra obsessively checked, a nasty thunderstorm was on its way. Usually, Alexandra would have been zombified all day from dread about this, but right now the inner tube dominated her thoughts.

"Ya'll ready for this?" Owen hollered, turning to her.

Alexandra quietly nodded. It felt like any words would come up as vomit. She wished she could whip around in her seat and drive the boat back to shore. But even if she had the gall to do so, the keys were buried in Owen's cluttered pockets.

He sighed through his nose and kneeled before Alexandra, his bulky form nearly blocked the sun. "You all right, Al?"

Alexandra usually avoided eye contact but she couldn't help but peek. His blue eyes always glared wide with unflinching confidence, though lately they were sinking a bit. For most people, she would just nod in response, even if it wasn't the truth. But she was more open with her dad, so she attempted to mutter a sarcastic, "Whaddya think?"

Owen nodded understandingly. "Well, I'm really proud of you. You're overcoming your fear!"

Alexandra shrugged. There was only one reason she was doing this.

*

Her dad constantly searched for tactics and incentives to get her in that inner tube so she could have "fun." However, promised ice cream treats didn't do it, nor did the prospect of going to a movie; they always did that anyway. He once told her that if she rode, she'd get to pick where they ate for supper; if she didn't, he would. The flaw with this was that they both liked all the same restaurants, usually Chinese.

However, this time he finally hit the right mark. If Alexandra rode the inner tube, he'd buy her a new turtle. They used to have a turtle named Gamera, a little red-eared slider. He had been an obsession of Alexandra's; she would spend hours watching him bask on his log or scramble against the glass wall of the tank as if he could push through.

She also loved observing the black and green patterns of his shell. But the patterns gradually became discolored with white spots of shell rot. Alexandra religiously practiced the vet-recommended treatment of brushing him with an iodine solution and keeping him confined in the narrow kitchen sink for most of the day so he could dry. Owen continued the practice whenever Alexandra was at her mom's.

One day Owen found Gamera half retracted over the drain, stiff as a plastic toy. The turtle's death was the first heart-twisting loss Alexandra had ever suffered. Eventually the pain wore off, but she longed to again fill that empty tank in the corner of their living room.

The evening before this boat ride, Owen brilliantly promised Alexandra that if she rode in the inner tube, they would go to the city and buy a new turtle. He pulled out the big guns because it was his last chance to give his daughter this experience. Soon Barry was going to end his membership and sell off the boat.

Out of utter excitement at the prospect of a new pet, Alexandra had agreed. Now, sitting in the boat, with an entire butterfly pavilion in her stomach, she regretted her decision. But there was no backing out of her bargain.

"You ready?" Owen asked.

Alexandra scanned the lake around her. The chocolaty water was calm with only tiny waves to gently rock the boat. The lake was completely empty today. Though it was never bustling, there would usually be some activity here and there. Not even the elderly couple who often strolled along the sandbox-sized beach was there today.

"Okay," she mumbled.

*

Alexandra recalled something Barry once told her when he came along on a trip. She had been resting along the stern of the boat, watching the wake while the two men chatted.

"Say Al, you ever hear of Foggy?" Barry shouted to her above the roar of the engine.

Alexandra shook her head without turning around. She felt irritated, as only her dad could call her Al.

"Barry," Owen said, forcing a laugh, "don't tell my daughter one of your creepy patron stories!"

Barry downed his third can of beer, some of it dribbling onto his massive gut. After a refreshed sigh, he grinned, "Nah, Nah, it's what they call the monster that lives in this lake."

Alexandra's heart dropped into her stomach. *Monster?*

"B.S., Barry," Owen boomed, cracking open his second can of Diet Coke.

"No, it's true. It don't come out much, they say it likes to stay around the bottom. But once in a while, it comes up to play. Y'know Vince? Mr. Bloody Mary? He came out here once, and it was the last time too because…"

As Barry spoke, Alexandra backed away from the water and leaned toward Owen. Sensing his daughter's distress, Owen quickly

27

diverted Barry's tangent, "Say, what's going on with Vince anyway? I haven't seen him at the bar for a while."

Barry chortled, "You haven't heard? Sandy gave him an ultimatum, quit the booze or I quit you…"

Barry went on about Vince's domestic life. But for the rest of that trip, Alexandra could only think of the creature that lay in Fog Lake. Ever since, the foamy wake always reminded her of a reptilian hump.

*

Alexandra no longer believed Barry's story. Still, her imagination got the best of her. Her heart pounded faster and her lungs turned to lead. Owen noticed her erratic breathing and gently placed his massive hands on her shoulders. In the most soothing tone his bombastic voice could muster, he said, "Hey, hey, Al. It's okay. Listen, it'll only be for one minute, one lousy minute. Then I'll stop the boat and bring you in? All right? If you're having fun and want to keep going, that's great. But I won't go for more than a minute. Trust me."

Alexandra calmed down; nobody but her father could do this for her. He was too big for bad guys to mess with, too calm to be intimidated by forces of nature. Even in the worst situations, he always had a quip.

She wasn't the only person who liked him; he had been a favorite bartender down at Barry's bar. He was loved for friendliness, humor and his desire to please everyone. One night, he pleased a few college kids by giving them alcohol without carding them. They turned out to be high schoolers. It was the only mistake he'd made in all his years there. But he lost his job, his license and the respect of many people. Even his friendship with Barry was no longer what it used to be.

He lost his job and couldn't find another; his situation was tight and he feared for his custody. Yet he still carried himself like it was all just part of a plan. He convinced Alexandra everything was okay.

She took a deep breath. *Just one minute*, she thought to herself. *Just one minute, then it's over.* Then came the elating notion: *and I get a new turtle*!

She climbed over the edge of the boat and sat cross-legged on the squishy floor of the inner tube. She gripped the black handles on both sides as tightly as her sweaty hands would allow.

"All right, Guinness World Record for shortest inner tube ride, here we come!" Owen beamed at her with a wink as he gently nudged the inner tube outward.

Alexandra's heartbeat began to pick up again as she drifted out into the lake, the little blue boat and the large man on it growing smaller and smaller. She took a deep breath and kept clenching the handles for dear life.

"One minute. One minute," she repeated to herself out loud.

Out of the corner of her eye, she caught a brief flash of a shadow moving along the surface of the water. She jolted and looked in its direction: nothing. She sighed, frustrated with her brain for playing tricks on her.

Owen shouted to Alexandra, his voice echoing across the entire lake: "You ready?"

In lieu of trying to shout back, Alexandra just gave a big Roman thumbs up. Owen returned the gesture and plopped into the driver's seat.

"Let's go already," she softly sing-songed to herself. It seemed like her dad was taking forever to start the boat. Gently bouncing along the water and trying to keep the inner tube from slowly spinning around, she was a sitting duck. The shadow slid by out of the corner of her eye. She turned her head again but saw nothing.

"Damn it," she hissed, quoting her father.

Finally, the motor's noisy hum began and the boat moved forward. At first it seemed like it was leaving her behind, but the rope finally caught up and the tube was jerked along.

Owen drove in a large clockwise circle. The tube and Alexandra bounced up and own along the choppy waves left by the boat. She could hardly think clearly with her brain rattling around, the noise of the motor and splashing water ringing through her ears and her curly hair whipping into her face. The sensory overload had already made the short experience utterly draining.

Out of the corner of her wind- and mist-squinted eye she caught a glimpse of the shadow again. Alexandra turned her head. It was still there. One could have mistaken it for a cloud's shadow. But it was beneath the water, perpetually moving alongside the inner tube.

Alexandra went cold and her stomach sank. She turned ahead, screaming for her dad. Unfortunately her soft voice, even at the loudest and shrillest level it could achieve, couldn't get through to him.

After several moments, the boat mercifully slowed and halted. The motor's roar died, leaving Alexandra's hoarse cry the only noise. Owen, noticing his daughter's panic, scrambled to the stern to pull the tube in.

"Hey, it's all right! You did it, baby! It's okay," he shouted to her.

The shadow moved toward the space between the boat and the tube. Alexandra pointed a trembling hand to it.

"Look!" she shrieked.

Seeing the shadow, Owen leapt back. It was directly beneath the floating tussle of rope. The black water swallowed the rope, yanking it down. After a second, the rope resurfaced in two shredded ends.

Alexandra and Owen stared dumbfounded at the broken rope. Suddenly, a lurch threw Owen forward onto the seat of the bow. He carefully got back to his feet, sweating and trembling.

All Alexandra could do was watch. Her blood felt like lead.

The boat rocked again, so violently this time that its bottom swung up, facing the grey sky. Owen grabbed onto the driver's windshield. His legs dangled over the edge of the boat as it completely flipped over.

"Dad!" Alexandra tried to shout, but it came out as more of a broken gasp. She could hardly breathe. The boat was belly up like a flipped turtle, the water around it completely still.

Numb tears streamed from Alexandra's eyes. He was gone. She was alone.

Suddenly, Owen's glistening head emerged from the water between the boat and the tube. He sputtered and gasped. Alexandra felt the air flood her lungs again. However, her relief was short lived. Beyond the floating keel, the shadow was circling them.

"Dad!" she shrieked, beating her hands against the tube like a bongo drum.

Owen started doggy paddling toward her. Despite his athletic appearance, he had never been the best swimmer. The shadow kept its distance, as if allowing Owen to safely swim across.

He reached the inner tube and clambered on board, nearly sinking and flipping the tube in the process. He managed to awkwardly squeeze himself in, covering up so much space that Alexandra was essentially sitting in his soaked lap.

Alexandra trembled like a tiny dog. Owen wrapped his massive arms around her.

"It'll be okay," he said to her between heavy breaths. Alexandra could feel his pulse, pounding as intensely as hers.

Owen cocked his head about, observing the land around them. The white rocky dam in the north, the tiny slither of beach in the east, and the woods all around were about the same distance from them, too far. They were smack dab in the middle of the lake.

"Okay, okay," Owen murmured.

He stuck his massive hands into the water, gave a great heave and pushed the tube forward. The storm clouds in the west were pushing closer and a breeze was picking up with them. Owen paddled with the wind, toward the beach.

Alexandra remained squashed against her dad, too petrified to put her hands in the water and help. She glanced back at the upturned keel of the boat. She couldn't see the shadow, but knew it was there.

Owen paddled for what felt like an hour. His breaths turned into exasperated grunts, and every now and then he had to pause to shake his aching arms. Progress was being made; with every tenth push the white sliver of beach and the green cottonwoods behind it grew a little larger.

His eyes bulged in concentration. Sweat drenched his face and mixed with the filthy dried lake water in his clothes. Alexandra, whose hands were almost permanently attached to the handles, rapidly surveyed the water around them. She couldn't see the shadow.

The grunting and rowing continued for another lifetime. The shore was closer and closer. Safety was ever near.

Owen and Alexandra's cloudy minds didn't notice the slight tug. It wasn't until they started moving backwards when they realized something was wrong. Despite Owen's continued efforts, he couldn't keep them going forward.

"What? What?" He howled in a near manic rage.

The tube whipped around. A grey anvil cloud loomed above

them, dominating the western sky. The tube's yellow rope was straight and tight, leading to an underwater end-point where the shadow lay. It was dragging them back to the center of the lake.

"God *damn* it! No!" Owen hollered with the hoarse rage of a madman but the desperation of a child. Alexandra clenched her eyes and teeth. She hardly recognized the man she was clinging against. "No! No!" He yelled over and over. His screams pounded into his daughter's ears. She wanted to tell him to stop, but her throat was shut tight.

They reached the center. The shadow ceased its pulling and left them to float again. Owen's screams faded into hyperventilating gasps. His heaving chest pushed against Alexandra's head. She felt like he had to be joking. How could this sobbing and heaving man be the same man who had once simply chuckled when he scorched his hand on a monkey bread pan?

Within his heaves, there was a faint wheeze, like air escaping a balloon. This was somehow familiar to Alexandra. On the night Owen lost his job, she had heard this wheeze coming from behind the closed doors of his bedroom, a wheeze so chilling she never dared to investigate. She had simply watched a movie and waited for it to disappear. Sure enough, the noise vanished, and Owen came out with his face stretched in a grin. He then tickled her feet until she was in hysterics.

Owen clenched his eyes and puckered his lips, sucking air in and out. He put his fingers around a curly fry-shaped strand of Alexandra's hair and started kneading it almost ritualistically. At first he did it so hard it stung her. But gradually his grip relaxed and the heaves started to vanish.

With the episode finished, his hand gently tussled Alexandra's hair.

"I'm sorry," he whispered through heavy breathing.

The words passed over Alexandra; she felt outside of her body.

The one person in her life who she thought could protect her through anything had now just proven that to be false. All he had done before was pretend everything was okay, but now he couldn't hide behind his mask.

It was all because of this *thing*. Why did Foggy feel the need to destroy them? They never hurt anybody and wanted nothing more than to live their lives.

Alexandra released her grip from the handles and let her aching hands drop into her lap. There didn't feel like much of a point in holding on anymore.

*

An hour or two passed slowly. The massive anvil head gradually blotted out the hot sun.

The capsized boat was drifting away, but the inner tube remained captive in the desolate lake's center. Owen had attempted multiple other times to paddle off again, only to be pulled back by the shadow. It was toying with them. With each attempt, Owen's rowing grew more sluggish. By the last attempt, the thing barely even let him go a few feet before jerking them back.

Alexandra's stomach panged with hunger and her parched throat and lips stung. In her exhaustion she heard faint voices, like one does when falling asleep. One voice she recognized was her mom's. She wanted her now, badly. Even though Mom always made her go to bed at 10 and never let her watch movies above a PG rating and made her eat boring food – Alexandra wanted to be snuggled safely in her embrace.

Another hour – maybe less – passed and the anvil head now dominated the sky. Everything darkened: the lake changed from brown to dark grey and the waters grew choppy with the strong winds. The shadow's form could still be made out, making its patrol around the inner tube. There were approaching grumbles of thunder.

Owen watched the drifting hull of the boat, now nearly to

34

shore. He weakly chuckled, "She was always a fixer upper. Maybe Barry can flip her for a nice profit."

This was Owen's final attempt of heroism; if he couldn't do anything to save them, he could at least make her smile. And while Alexandra didn't, she felt relaxed for a brief moment. Her dad wasn't a shield, but he could at least be a warm blanket.

*

The rumbling thunder drew closer. The harsh whispers of cicadas could be heard along the shore. Rain sprinkled down and lightning bolts streaked in the west. Alexandra watched the shadow. It appeared to be erratically moving back and forth, as if anxiously pacing. Suddenly, an angry thunder crack shook the earth, sky and lake. When she looked again, the shadow was gone. It had retreated beneath the grey murk.

A chilly wind rose up over the surface of the lake, growing stronger until it began pushing the inner tube. This time, nothing was pulling it back.

"I think it's gone," Alexandra murmured weakly.

The shadow may have had power over them, but it, too, was small and helpless in the face of nature. It had to retreat into its domain and hope for the best.

Owen immediately seized the opportunity. He grunted as he pushed through the choppy waters. The intensity of the wind and the weakness of his arms ensured very little progress.

Alexandra knew she had to do something. She hunched over and, with as much strength as she could muster, stuck her arms in the water and paddled.

At first they seemed to be moving. But it was impossible to know. The rain pounded against their faces, obscuring their sight, and the wind whipped them back and forth. They couldn't keep control, no matter how hard they tried.

Alexandra kept paddling with all her might. But Owen stopped. He tightly wrapped his arms around her until she could barely move. She turned and pressed her head against his chest, which rose and fell with quiet sobs. All they could do was ride with the storm.

*

The next afternoon, an elderly couple ambled along the muddy beach holding hands, like they had done nearly every day. The man pointed his bony finger at something strange floating near the shore.

It was an empty inner tube, yellow with jagged purple patterns. It was nearly out of air, and its wide center opened and closed like a gasping mouth.

As a child, Anthony Engebretson always loved telling stories. Whether scribbling in a notebook or making little movies with his Godzilla figurines, his imagination was his favorite toy. That love has only grown.

He currently lives in Lincoln, Nebraska where he spends much of his days writing, playing with his cats and getting mad politically. His stories are included in several publications, including a short story published in the 2018 anthology, *Spring Into SciFi*. You can read more from Anthony at https://raccoonalleyblog.wordpress.com/

*Foggy* was originally published in *The Fable Online*, Sept 2017

# My Living Head

by Jenny Terpsichore Abeles

"I need to get out of my head a little." Henri is smirking in that way he knows I dislike, but I simply roll my eyes at him. I try not to – I don't want to show any response to his gambits – but I can't help it. "Do you know what I miss the most?" he continues.

"No, Henri. What?"

"Sneezing. I have a nose, so why can't I sneeze?"

"You have a mouth, but you can't seem to shut up, either."

"Aww, chérie is so grumpy today."

"Grumpy doesn't begin to cover it." I stare at him, hoping I look more furious than helpless. He stares back, and I watch as the mischief leaves his dark, wet eyes. Neither of us says anything for a long time, but I stand, finally, to adjust his neck stump from where it had begun to slip off the coffee table. I'd put him there rather carelessly. It's not easy taking care of a living head. Such a task is not conveniently accommodated in the day-to-day. The experience has tolled on me in ways I can't explain or even understand, although I also wonder sometimes if I'm just using it as an excuse.

"Are there any interesting jobs?" The teasing has left Henri's voice, and I can tell he's trying to be supportive. I still feel annoyed at him, but I'm also annoyed at myself for crushing his silly mood with my grumpiness. Henri has reminded me many times that a foul humor runs in my family.

"Not really." I don't lift my eyes from the computer screen to look at him.

"What is it you *want* to do, Katie? You'd be good at so many things."

38

"Yeah, like what?" I feel a flush of anger. "How about deli cook? Counterperson? School bus driver? Dental assistant? CPA? What is a CPA, anyway... ?"

"Certified Personal Accountant..."

"Front office manager? Medical biller? Property supervisor? Oh, wait a minute. This is it! Experienced door installer. Of course, all I've ever really wanted to do with my life is install doors! My *raison d'être...*"

"Sarcasm doesn't flatter you, Katie, and neither does despair. Let's go have fun."

"How can I have fun? I have to find a job and I *hate* job hunting. Door installer! I *hate* doors. What could be more useless?"

"*All is not lost...*"

"All *is* lost."

"*What though the field be lost?*" Henri insists. "*ALL IS NOT LOST; the unconquerable will, and study of revenge, immortal hate, and courage never to submit or yield...*"

I am jealous of Henri's ability to quote at length. He loves to read, but not having fingers, he stares at the same pages, sometimes for hours, until I come along and turn them for him. He sits in front of six or seven open books – if you can call it *sitting* when you don't have an ass – in the peacock blue library, day after day. I envy his life. There's never any question of his having to earn money.

"What would you know about it, Henri? All you ever were was a crook and a murderer." I seriously doubt that Henri was actually guilty of that murder, but the accusation shuts him up.

We are together in the library – the continuously repeating library – for about an hour, enfolded in its peacock-colored walls. I feel capable of peacock-shrill shrieks, but with a silence contrapuntal to my mood, I update my résumé. Finally, I close my laptop, very gently.

39

"Do you know what I really miss the most?" Henri almost whispers.

"What?" I sniffle.

"Scratching. Scratching my whole body in the morning, when the light comes through the window, and I know I will walk out into the sunshine and live one whole, beautiful day of my life. I have always been an Epicurean although I didn't know what that was until your grandfather taught me."

I get up from my desk and take him in my arms, one hand stroking his eternally silky, black hair. I cry into his neck stump, and occasionally sob.

"There, there, chérie, *Nothing is good or bad but thinking makes it so* .Get out of your head for a little while."

He loves that phrase. He thinks it's hilarious.

\*

Henri and I move often; we can't settle. I don't earn enough money; late rents pile up. One of my talents is the ability to pack up a moving truck silently and in the dark. Another is house painting. Everywhere we go, the first thing I do is paint the biggest room in our new apartment peacock blue and set up the library. I can paint a room in three hours flat. That includes the trim. The last time I did it, Henri suggested I add water to the paint, a technique called "color-washing" that he read about in a decorating magazine. It was a little messier, but we both like the effect: vaguely post-apocalyptic. "It could be the end of the world," I tell Henri.

"It could be." He smiles back at me.

With every change, every new job or apartment, I wonder, what kind of world is it now?

With the comforting perfume of paint in the air, I unfurl the heavy Turkish carpet, folding the edges under when the room's too small for it. The room is always arranged the same, but sometimes

40

the furniture crowds closer and there's not as much space to move. This isn't a problem for Henri. I wrestle his gigantic mahogany desk into the far corner and place on top of it the porcelain owl from Germany that he loves so much. The orange chaise lounge goes to the right of it. On the other side is where my smaller, oak desk belongs, and behind it, the English secretary filing cabinet where I stow our bills and other important papers. Kitty-corner to my desk is the tiger-print sofa. I sleep there much more often than in my bed, which feels too large for me. Henri doesn't sleep. He says that he dreams, though.

It's only the library that needs to be continuously repeating, like a very old story. Like a tradition or something you can't forget. The other rooms don't matter.

The bookshelves with our hundreds of books get tucked behind the furniture catch-all-as-catch-can, and there are a few little tables to scatter about for Henri. His favorite is a round marble-top held aloft by the reaching hands of gilded children. I always thought they were cupids, but Henri pointed out that they lacked wings, and I had to admit he was right. This is Henri's favorite perch. He thinks it makes him look regal. It's actually very strange to see the hands of those golden children reaching up toward his neck stump, which is covered in a moldering piece of leather that smells a little like the tobacco of Grandfather's pipe. Henri sometimes likes to smoke, but I have to hold the pipe for him after stuffing it with tobacco from the silver-scrollwork Burne-Jones tobacco canister.

Most of this stuff I inherited from Grandfather. I inherited Henri from my grandfather, too, and when he first came to live with me, we each searched our memories to recreate Grandfather's library just as it was when he was alive. I agreed to that mostly to make Henri happy, who I was a little intimidated by then, or maybe I was just eager to please him. Since then, I've gotten rid of some of Grandfather's brittle, old books and replaced them with the clean-smelling, edgy novels I like to read. Sometimes his books fetch some money, but I don't want to sell too much of Grandfather's stuff even though it's all old and heavy and a pain in the ass to move. Money would've been a better inheritance all around. Once I threatened to hawk the Tiffany, but I ended up selling my car instead.

I don't think Henri can die, but if I ever wanted to test that theory, I could sell our 1866 edition of *Paradise Lost* illustrated by Gustave Doré. That's the one he most often asks me to place in front of him, staring at the picture of Satan sailing past the stars of each of the seven heavens. I think Satan is his favorite literary character. I've never been able to get past Book V of *Paradise Lost*.

"Why didn't you die?" I asked Henri once. "How do you keep living?"

"*Cogito ergo sum,*" Henri replies, one eyebrow aloft. When I say nothing, he asks, "Didn't you ever read René Descartes?"

I did try one semester in college, and the attempt made me feel stupid. No matter how many times I read one of those paragraphs, I had no idea what the hell Descartes was talking about, but I don't divulge any of this to Henri, who is still looking at me. "I think; therefore, I am," he translates finally.

Henri didn't know Latin when he first met Grandfather. He couldn't even read French, his native language. Grandfather taught him. They met right after Henri's execution by guillotine. "Henri! Henri Languille! Look at me!" Grandfather had commanded, and Henri had opened his eyes and looked.

*

"I think I'm going to grow a moustache."

I heard him but wasn't listening, if you know what I mean. I was sitting on the orange chaise reading an email I didn't think would ever come. "Henri, I got a job." It was just in time. I had no money left.

"How marvelous, ma chère. Doing what?"

42

"Front office manager. In a law firm."

Henri looked uncomfortable, not having had any great success with lawyers in the past.

"It's an immigration law firm," I said quickly. "They help people, foreigners like you. People who need help."

"Just because I'm not a naturalized citizen doesn't mean I'm a foreigner."

"I know, Henri, I didn't mean..."

"I've lived in this country for almost 100 years, over three times as long as you have."

"Well, do you have an American passport?"

"I don't have any passport."

"We'll have to get you one, then. All we need is a headshot." After a second, we both started to laugh.

Living with Henri isn't always easy, but it might be easier than living with any other man I've ever met. He doesn't eat, which is perfect because I don't cook. He drinks wine, but only the cheap stuff and very moderately. Once or twice he's had a sip or two too much and fallen off his desk, badly bruising the lunar pallor of his forehead. He hardly smokes, and he's actually very funny and amiable most of the time. On the negative side, we can't go out to dinner together, or take walks, or go horseback riding. I bring him to the movies and occasionally to a concert, but he has to stay in my bag, peering out and at times laughing inappropriately. Laughter is always inappropriate when it's loud and male and emerging from your shoulder bag. It tends to draw stares. Telling your bag to "shhh" doesn't help the situation. And he's heavier than you'd think.

The worst thing about it, though, the thing that keeps me up at night staring at the darkened peacock blue walls, is that I fear that because of Henri I will never have a normal life. Whoever marries me also marries my living head. It doesn't seem feasible, somehow.

Sometimes Henri and I have picnics in the park, and he tells me about life as a thug in Belle Époque France. These stories rarely make Henri happy, but I think he has to get it out, all this baggage from his past life. He says he killed a woman in her bed. He didn't mean to, but she woke up while he was robbing her, and he cut her throat, just like that, without thinking. I can't picture Henri doing that – murdering, not thinking – but he reminds me (for the thousandth time) that he is an intellect with teeth. In such a quick, tense moment, he says, you forget how long life is, and that you live with your every action all that time, like it or not. Henri cannot cry. On one of these picnics, he got fleas, and we had a hell of a time combing them all out of his thick hair with the tiniest comb either of us had ever seen.

I'm happy about my new job. "I think you'd look nice with a moustache."

"I had one before, you know."

"I know. I saw the pictures." I'd seen pictures of Henri's body, too, before the incident with the guillotine. He looked strange with a body.

\*

At my new job, I got headaches from the fluorescent lights, the questions people asked me, the tightness of my ponytail, and the incessantly ringing phones. But that is where I met Estéban. He was twenty-nine, a little older than me, here on a student visa. I hardly noticed him at first amongst the throngs of other barely comprehensible clients asking me urgent questions about forms I had never heard of, but over time, I recognized that he was much nicer to me than anyone else. One of the senior legal aids, Kristen or Kirsten – I alternated calling her these names because I couldn't remember which one it was supposed to be – mentioned to me, "Estéban has a total crush on you."

44

"How do you know?"

"He told me. He doesn't even care if you have a boyfriend."

"I don't have a boyfriend."

"He'll be happy to know that!"

A couple days later, Estéban asked me out to dinner. I hesitated, but then he said he'd pay. That's not why I was hesitating, but it was a convenient excuse to hesitate. After all, a normal girl would go on a date with Estéban. He was handsome enough, though too skinny, and he spoke with that kind of enthusiasm that is supposed to be winsome and charming. Furthermore, he was an artist.

Later that night, I told Henri that I was going out on a date. He was poring over a book of Apollinaire's poems, *Gulliver's Travels*, a map of the Ottoman Empire, the *Oxford English Dictionary* A-O, a biography of Joan of Arc, an old issue of *House Beautiful*, and a book of Grandfather's about hunting and hawking. "Can you turn the page for me, please?"

I turned the page in each book. One of Apollinaire's lines jumped out at me. *It's raining, my soul, it's raining, but it's raining dead eyes.*

"Who are you going out on a date with?"

"Someone I met at work."

"A lawyer?"

"No, a client."

"Be careful with people you meet in a lawyer's office."

That seemed like good advice, and I said so. I tried to catch Henri's eye, but he was studying the pages of his books, his chin bowed seriously into his truncated neck. His moustache needed trimming. "Henri," I said, but he did not look up. "Henri!" After another minute, Henri turned to look at me. He did not have dead

45

eyes. They were bright and vaguely sad. But the next morning when I woke up for work, it was raining, and I thought about the line again.

*

Estéban wore all black on our date. He looked tall. He picked me up in front of my apartment and, as I was buckling my seatbelt, told me I was beautiful. Over dinner it always seemed as though there wasn't going to be enough conversation to get us through it, but somehow there was always more. I don't know if that was because of me or because of Estéban. When he dropped me off, he asked me to sit in the car and listen to a song with him before leaving. It was a Spanish song, and I asked him what it meant. Estéban just smiled at me, and when the song was over, he kissed me. His mouth was warm and wet.

There were more dates after that. Because Estéban was an artist and a student and alone in the world, after our first dinner together, I paid for everything, for dinner and movie tickets and new clothes for both of us to wear on our dates. It was nice to take care of him in these ways and nice to spend time with someone who ate dinner and wore clothes. Estéban started talking excitedly about how we were falling in love. I didn't think I was falling in love, but I didn't want to say so and ruin Estéban's happiness. Later there would be a time for telling him, I thought.

When he came into the law office, he would walk right around the counter to my desk, and I would stand up smiling, and he would put his hand on my waist and kiss me. The lawyers and legal aides frowned at this, but I didn't care. For me, a little bit of romance was like a shot of rum for someone who doesn't drink. It went straight to my head. I found it hard to care about anything else except the romance of me and Estéban. After a while, even Kristen or Kirsten stopped smiling at the mention of his name. Then one night I realized that I *was* falling in love with him. We were on the sofa in his apartment. We heard his roommate's key in the lock, and I sat

46

upright, pushing Estéban away with one hand and pulling my skirt down with the other. His roommate came in and walked through to the kitchen. A second later, he yelled, "Estéban, did you eat all my banana chips?" Estéban and I looked at each other and laughed, and that was when I knew he was right. We were falling in love.

Henri had taken up smoking cigarettes. He didn't say anything, but I knew what he was thinking. Shut up! I said silently, shut up, shut up! And then, Estéban, Estéban, Estéban. As I lay in the peacock blue room at night, I repeated his name to myself just to feel that fist of happiness wrenching my guts.

*

"*If I had a heart, I would tear open my breast and show it to you, so you could see from your image therein how beautiful you are.*"

"Who wrote that?"

"I did. I am composing poetry now."

"You're so *French*! And you're a bad poet."

"I know." Henri looked miserable, wincing at the smoke curling from the cigarette clenched between his lips.

The night after that, Estéban broke down crying very unexpectedly. He told me how his parents had hated him, hit him, accused him of being ugly and bad. Then they had abandoned him. All I could think of was Henri's poem, and I repeated it to Estéban. "*If I had a heart, I would tear open my breast and show it to you, so you could see from your image therein how beautiful you are.*"

"You are so nice to me," Estéban said, "No one has ever been this nice to me."

"No one has ever loved you as I do."

"Yes, that is probably true."

If Estéban liked Henri's poetry, he might like Henri, too. I wanted for Estéban to have Henri the way I did, because even though I did not have any parents, either, I had had Grandfather, and then Henri. I wanted to share everything I had with Estéban, to strengthen him.

At the law office, I became aware that something was not working with Estéban's visa, and then he told me that he was despairing, likely to be deported back to his country, a place that held nothing but memories of people who hated him. All he wanted was to be able to do his art, and live in America, and love me forever.

"I've got it!" Estéban said. "We should get married! Then I can stay in America, and when I am a famous artist, you will be the muse by my side, and everyone will know that all my wonderful work is because of you, only you."

Later I told Henri, "I am getting married." Henri did nothing, but what did I expect? Was he going to jump up and down? Was he going to hug me and spin me around? "What do you think about that?" I demanded.

"Nothing," Henri said. There were dark circles under his eyes and some tobacco stuck in his curling mustache. "Nothing, nothing, nothing."

"If you have something to say, say it, Henri."

"I cannot say it. I should, but you are so happy. I like to see you this way." He couldn't have looked more wretched. "I am an Epicurean at heart. Happiness is the only purpose of life."

*

That was something Grandfather had always said: "Happiness is the only purpose of life." He also said, "I am an Epicurean at heart." I didn't really know what that meant, but Henri did. As a little girl, I'd sit in the peacock blue library, listening to them talk for hours and hours.

48

Grandfather would leap around the room, which was larger than any of the continuously repeating libraries we've been able to reproduce since, pulling books off the shelves and holding them open before Henri, perched magisterially upon the marble-top table. Sometimes they'd glare at the words together, and then mumble half-thoughts as they reflected, staring in different directions. Sometimes they'd laugh uproariously or yell at each other. "I am an intellect with sinew," Grandfather used to yell. "And I am an intellect with teeth," Henri would yell back. That usually made them laugh. Grandfather would light his pipe, and I'd inhale deeply smoke that smelled of burning bark and clove. I learned to light Henri's pipe and hold it to his lips. Henri was always very courteous and thanked me, and Grandfather would stroke my hair as he searched his shelves for a book I might like to read. If I left the room for the world outside the peacock blue library, neither of them was likely to notice, and no matter where I went in the house, I could always hear their voices, not their words, but their voices.

Sometimes, in the continuously-repeating library, I close my eyes and hear him. Or almost hear him.

He never told me that my parents were in Heaven and that I would see them again. He didn't believe in Heaven; he beloved in atoms. I knew how they died, plane crash, and I knew their names, Julie and Robert. I saw pictures of my mother as a little girl, standing with Grandfather and Henri in the peacock blue library, and I wondered what she had thought of Henri. Henri had always been part of her life, as he had mine. Grandfather had met him in Orleans, France in 1905, long before my mother was born. I know this because I've read brittle newspaper clippings about it. The newspaper mentions Henri by name and shows a picture of him standing almost proudly next to the guillotine. People were surprised, after the decapitation, when Henri heard Grandfather calling his name and opened his eyes. Think of how much more surprised they would be to hear him reciting his own English translation of *De Rerum Natura* to Grandfather seventy years later.

49

Grandfather was a very successful doctor in St. Louis, Missouri, where I was born. I used most of his money, though, trying to keep him alive for another year, and then another month. He didn't want me to, but I couldn't bear the thought of life without him. After Grandfather died, it felt like the world had ended. I looked around and wondered, What kind of world is it now?

Henri and I could not stay in St. Lou. I did not have Grandfather's knack for being stable or earning money. We have moved out of apartments in the middle of the night, leaving town just as dawn was breaking on highways that I couldn't see the end of. Henri always rolls with the punches, easier than I do.

Henri says young people do not understand how to be happy, but that he can teach me. "Boethius had Lady Philosophy," he says, "and you have me." I'm not sure how this is supposed to be reassuring when everyone knows that Lady Philosophy didn't help Boethius from being bludgeoned to death. I often get annoyed by Henri, but when he smiles, it's hard to stay angry. He's all I have left of Grandfather – Henri and the continuously repeating library. And sometimes when Henri says, "I am an Epicurean at heart," I remember Grandfather's voice, and what it was like to feel his hand on my hair.

*

Estéban tore my clothes off every time I'd come to his apartment. My skirts and sweaters flew across the room, and he'd sigh in my ear how eager he was to be married. It was flattering and exciting. We hastily made plans. Even though neither of us really knew anyone, I wanted to have a real wedding. It seemed implausible, but I dimly pictured Kristen or Kirsten dancing with Henri. The fact of my imminent marriage made anything seem possible. I kept Estéban apprised of all my plans as he unzipped, unbuttoned, and untied my personal effects.

On the morning I was supposed to go to New York where a cousin was going to get me a discount on my gown, she called to tell me that her record deal had been signed and she'd quit Saks Fifth Avenue. "Oh, shit!" I said, but then added, "Congratulations."

I thought about calling Estéban to tell him my trip was cancelled, but decided to walk through the stores downtown to see if there might be a pretty dress there I could buy. Henri asked if he could come along, and although I didn't feel like bearing his weight, he looked so wretched I felt guilty saying no.

As we were crossing Main Street, I spotted Estéban on the corner, all in black. "Look, Henri!" I pulled down the edge of my shoulder bag. "There he is! Isn't he handsome?" And then, as we watched, a girl in dark tights skipped out of the record store and threw herself into Estéban's waiting arms.

"Apparently she thinks so."

We looked, our faces twisting with discretely rampaging emotions, as Estéban tangled his fingers in the girl's dark hair, pulled her face close to his and kissed her passionately. I almost screamed, I think, but my voice came out as a strangled whimper, and I began to cross the street.

"Don't go over there, Katie! Chérie, believe me, you don't..."

"Shut up, Henri!" This time my voice shrieked across the blacktop, causing several heads to turn our way, including Estéban's, and on his face was a look I had never seen there before. It was indifference, or indifference mixed with loathing, but the look only lasted an instant, and he shoved the girl away.

"Are you following me?" he asked.

"How could you, Estéban? Estéban?"

"Are you following me? What kind of creep are you?"

Henri was sputtering with rage from within my bag. "You dare to speak to her that way? You, you!" and Estéban just stared at us.

"Who is speaking now?" He was confused.

51

"You are a liar and a scoundrel! Liar, liar!" Henri would not stop yelling, and when I opened my bag to silence him, I saw that his face, usually so pallid, was dark with rage. One of his cheeks twitched with the effort of freeing himself. "I could kill you!" he screamed. I had never seen this side of Henri before.

It was clear from the expression on Estéban's face that he had also seen Henri, and he had the look of someone immobilized just when he most wanted to run. "The devil," he whispered, but barely, "you're the devil!"

"Ha! Ha!" Henri shrieked. I almost dropped my bag from the fury of his thrashing, and there was a nauseating moment when I imagined Henri rolling down the sidewalk in front of the record store, but instead, fumbling and tripping, I lost my hold on him and he sailed in a ferocious arc, landing on Estéban's shoulder, propelled by a bloodless rage. In the moment it was a horrifying sight – Estéban convulsing in an effort to loosen Henri from his black sweater. Henri did not get hurt, however, and I smile to think of it now. A few days later, when I went by the law office to pick up my severance, Kirsten or Kristen told me that Estéban had needed seven stitches before being deported. I will never doubt it again; Henri truly is an intellect with teeth.

\*

He is staring at the picture of Satan falling, falling from Paradise into Hell. *Better to reign in Hell than to serve in Heaven*, he mumbled. Imagine dropping out of Heaven, a perfect place, looking around and wondering to yourself, What kind of world is it now?

*Farewell happy fields where joy forever dwells! Profoundest hell, receive thy new possessor, one who brings a mind not to be changed by place or time. The mind is its own place, and in itself can make a heaven of hell, a hell of heaven*, I thought, having heard Henri recite it a thousand times.

I'd finished painting the library about an hour before, but

52

hadn't yet changed out of my peacock blue-spattered clothes. This, of all outfits, was the one that best illustrated what my life was like. Before moving from the last place, I'd taken every outfit Estéban had seen me in – the tweed skirts and wool sweaters I'd worn to the law office and the short dresses I'd worn on our dates – and put them in a white trash bag which I'd left on the curb as we pulled away. The most romantic love I'd ever felt, and yet it had been a mistake. I couldn't understand it, and even Henri couldn't explain it to me. Henri, who knew everything. Also before we moved, Henri asked me to shave off his moustache which he deemed not worth the bother, and neither was smoking cigarettes.

"Aw, what the hell, Henri. It's not like they're going to kill you. Live a little! I thought you were an Epicurean."

"I'm an Epicurean *at heart*," Henri corrected me. It wouldn't have been nice to point out that, literally speaking, he didn't have a heart.

After Henri gave up smoking, his color improved and the bags under his eyes receded. He smiled from time to time, reciting random lines of poetry as I painted the library. If he'd quoted, *Better to have loved and lost than never to have loved at all*, I would have choked him, but he avoided the topics of love and marriage. I had a feeling we'd avoid these topics for a long time. The windows were open to let the paint fumes out, and we both shivered a little in the early spring air; there were goosebumps on Henri's neck stump, and on my neck, too. It was spring but nature didn't seem to know it yet, remaining brown and flat and ugly. The sun knew it, golden and warm, and the sky knew it, but earth had not caught on. What if the world just stopped, this moment, and never became anything different from this? I asked Henri.

"Repeat this magic charm with me: *Double, double toil and trouble; fire burn, and cauldron bubble*." Henri had been re-reading Shakespeare.

"You really are the devil."

"Ha! Ha!"

"You take that as a compliment, don't you?"

"I always take it as a compliment when despicable people disdain me."

"So, now I'm despicable?"

"Chérie, I didn't mean you..."

"I know who you meant." It was done. I was grumpy again. I banged around the peacock blue library, continuously repeating, maybe, but not the same as when Grandfather was alive. It would never be that way again. I couldn't hope for that. Maybe that meant it was not continuously repeating after all, but just a bad copy.

I picked up Henri and roughly placed him on the coffee table to make room for his desk, so heavy, sliding over the Turkish carpet, the chaise, the secretary, the sofa, the bookshelves, the boxes, the tables. He watched, tipping precariously, with anxious eyes. The porcelain owl rocked a little as I slammed it into place, and I thought Henri was going to say something. The owl didn't fall, and neither did Henri, and he remained mute as I banged everything else, continuously repeating, into its accustomed spot. This library was on the smaller side, but everything fit, crammed and touching. I bumped my hip hard against the edge of my desk as I plugged in my laptop and sat down.

"Damn!" I yelled, flipping open my computer and punching the keys. "What new shitty job awaits?"

"What kind of job would you like to do, Katie? What would make you happy?"

"What does that matter? I'll never get a job I actually like, and if I did..."

Henri looked at me, waiting, waiting to fall off the table, which he surely would in a moment, and waiting for my answer.

54

"If I did, I'd lose that job, too. Who could hold down a job with a living head to take care of? It's pointless, pointless! I'll never have a normal life."

"Is that so bad, Chérie? Who's to say whether a normal life would make you happy? Your grandfather knew what he was doing bequeathing me to you. It might seem like a trial..."

"Damn straight it's a trial!"

"But I can help you, too. We can be happy together."

I did not answer him. I would not. I stared at the jobs on the computer screen. The stupid, stupid jobs.

"We are thinking about things too much. Life is to be lived! Let's go do something diverting. I am an Epicurean at heart, you know."

I knew. I'd heard all about it. Still I refused to look at him, hoping he would not crack the joke about needing to get out of his head. I waited, instead, for the thud that would signal he'd finally fallen off the table. I thought about Satan, falling, the stars lighting his descent. Somehow Satan had made the most out of hell, and Henri admired him for this. *What kind of world is it now?* A world with a heaven, a hell, a host of paradises and just as many paradises lost. Wasn't that what every life was? Mine, certainly. Yet amidst all this loss, there had been built principalities, kingdoms, empires, and somehow people found ways to subjugate their demons, to reign supreme in their own private hell. For a moment, my anger subsided, replaced by wonder, and I looked out the window at the ugly spring day, feeling irrationally that this day had been made for me, this day of mud and dead leaves – I was its new possessor. I could do whatever I wanted today, and suddenly I didn't even mind that it was ugly. I thought about Henri, long ago, scratching himself in the sunlight.

And then, as expected, he said it, smirking, his dumb joke, but this time, for some reason, I actually found it funny.

55

Jenny Terpsichore Abeles is a writer and educator living in Western Mass with three cats she smuggled out of Armenia. She teaches English in community college, writing in jail, and yoga wherever she can. Her work has also been published in *Lady Churchill's Rosebud Wristlet, Lackington's Quarterly, The Queen's Head, Fickle Muses*, and other magazines.

*My Living Head* was originally published in the online magazine *New Dead Families*.

# I Should've Known Better

by Art Lasky

I should have known that something was wrong the moment I saw the listing; 1400 square feet on Central Park West, a doorman, a high floor and a breathtaking park view for $1000 a month was just too cheap. If not then, I should have known something wasn't quite right when I found out that this choice apartment had been vacant for over a year. If not then, I should have known when I saw the sign in the living room *"Please stay within the pentagram when nexus is active."*

Though, in my defense, I just thought the sign was some kind of Pop Art. If not then, I should have known that something was wrong when Armando, the friendly rental agent, kissed me on both cheeks and burst into joyous song when I signed the lease.

I found out exactly what was wrong on my first night in the new apartment. There I was, watching TV; alarms started sounding in the nothingness above my head. A glowing pentagram appeared on the floor surrounding my recliner. I was trying to decide whether to run screaming out of the apartment before or after I put my pants on when one of the walls began to shimmer. It disappeared, and a troupe (Herd? Gaggle?) of centaurs came trotting into the apartment from the dark forest that was where my wall used to be. They paid me no mind as they paced across the room toward the beautiful sandy beach that had replaced the opposite wall. The earthy smell of pine mingled with the fresh ocean scent. It would've been a delightful moment if I weren't shrieking my terrified lungs out.

That morning Armando, the unfriendly rental agent, sneeringly tossed me a pamphlet: 'So Your Apartment's a Trans-Dimensional Nexus.' Here's an excerpt: ...*portals can be opened wherever there is a weakness in the fabric of reality along multiple axes. Nexuses*

57

*occur where a confluence of ley lines allow multiple interdimensional portals in proximity…*

And that was the most understandable part of the gibberish in the pamphlet. What it boils down to is this: eldritch beings on distant worlds and in different dimensions can travel from one world to another thru my living room. Basically, I'm screwed.

I've learned several things in the last few months while trying to get out of my lease:

First of all, some of those nubile centaur babes are H-O-T – hot, hot, hot. I've thought about crossing the pentagram to try some inter-species biological research (Dear Penthouse Forum, You will never believe…). Though, I am not quite ready to leave the safety of the pentagram. Those centaur stallions look like they would tear me in half with their blacksmith-like arms and then stomp what was left into a quivering pile of failing organs.

Flying Demon Things (that's my name for them, I don't know what they call themselves) cannot get thru the pentagram. Though I still pee myself each time one of those eight-foot-tall, bat-winged, long-clawed, many-fanged, nasty-tempered mountains of fury tries.

The building maintenance man charges one hundred bucks to haul away the wrecked furniture and dented armor left after two robotic gladiators fight to the death in my living room. My insurance does not cover damage caused by rampaging robots.

Then there are the Stink Lizards. While they can't get thru the pentagram, Stink Lizard spit has no problem getting thru the pentagram. Oh, and the smell of stink lizard spit (think condensed essence of skunk with notes of putrefying cabbage and a truly rancid finish) takes two weeks to wear off.

I got nowhere in landlord/tenant court. The judge refused to believe any of my testimony. He accused me of wasting the court's time and threatened to have me placed in a state mental health facility for evaluation. I was tempted to take him up on it just for a few nights of peace and quiet. But the trial was on a Monday, and Monday is usually centaur babe night.

So it looks like I'm stuck in this lease. Unless you know anybody who might like to sublet 1400 square feet with a park view, cheap – no questions asked?

Art is a retired computer programmer. After forty years of writing in COBOL and Assembler he decided to try writing in English; it's much harder than it looks. He lives in New York City with his wife/muse and regularly visiting grandkids.

You can contact him at: ALASKY9679@YAHOO.COM.

*I Should've Known Better* was originally published in *Keystone Chronicles* from *Third Flatiron Publishing*, Sept. 2016

# Staircase

## by Tom Wolosz

The small outboard motor coughed once, twice, a third time, gasped out a sputtering gurgle and fell silent.

Whipping the throttle to the off position the Old Man swung the motor up, the propeller clearing the water, and locked it in place. His breath caught as he glanced at the child, fearing the boy would understand.

Slumped forward in the front of the boat, elbows on knees, arms wrapped around his thin chest, the boy, looking chilled, hugged himself. Attention riveted on the surrounding water, his scrunched eyes darted from side to side, scanning the murky green water, body recoiling with each turn as if in anticipation of a blow.

The man exhaled his anxiety then forced a rich, false joy into his voice. "Almost there. We'll glide in."

The island, a singularity on the vacant horizon, waited sullenly as the small boat slid across the water. Dead trees framing an old Victorian house swayed in the breeze – frail, skeletal arms beckoning them forward.

The island had changed. Like a piece of cheese suffering the ongoing visitations of a mouse, the rising sea level had gnawed away a bit more each day, diminishing it, steadily shrinking it. Reduced to a small patch of barren rock and poisoned dirt jutting from the hungry sea, its greatest elevation was marked by the house and two attending trees – killed by salt water intruding into the soil.

The water's gentle drag slowed the boat until the muddy bottom reached up, grabbing it with a sudden jolt. Run aground, it rested a few yards shy of the shore.

"Well, we're here. All ashore what's goin' ashore!"

Lips quivering, eyes fixed on the Old Man and welling with tears, the boy pointed at the water.

"Now, now. It's only water and barely a few inches deep," the Old Man said through the lie of a warm grin as he stepped over the gunwale.

The soft bottom mud gave way, his leg sinking up to the knee. As cool water filled his boot, soaked his sock and ran down between his toes, a clownish, chagrined grimace blossomed across his coarsely stubbled face, quickly metamorphosing into an embarrassed smile choreographed with a hapless shrug. "Oops!"

The boy's face relaxed into a tiny smile quickly accompanied by a giggle.

Shaking his head and chuckling at his own foolishness the man finished getting out of the boat, repeating his original pantomime when his other boot filled with water.

The boy rewarded him with another giggle.

"Well, no sense in us both getting wet!" Leaning over he snatched up the child and carried him to shore.

Dragging the boat ashore, he gazed at it, thinking, considering their limited options – there were no oars.

*End of the line.*

Despite the soothing warm sunlight and gentle breeze, weariness reached out for him, strove to engulf him, freeze him into a statue of submission. Aware the child was watching, the Old Man took a deep breath, shook off his growing depression and forced himself to move. Taking the heavy duffle bag and backpack from the boat he placed them next to the boy then studied the island. Fists on hips, lips pursed, he made a show of surveying the land and building, all the while fighting to mask his growing despair. Finally, with a shake of his head, and a shrug, he said, "Not quite as magnificent as I remember it."

The child frowned at the old building, his sad-eyed look returning. "Not very big."

"No, for a lad from the Big City, I'd imagine not," the Old Man said with a grin, but his grim eyes methodically swept the ground, searching for any sign. "But for a country boy this was a wonderful place. An old sea captain lived here long ago." Shifting his gaze to the front of the house and seeing nothing unusual, he squeezed the boy's shoulder. "Come, let's look inside."

A once grand, now verdigris-crusted, bronze plaque stood sentinel by the door proclaiming the building a historic site. Sharing the wall was an equally distressed listing of visiting hours obscured by grime and the tattered remnant of a hastily pasted-on sign declaring the building closed until further notice.

The door was locked.

Taking the child by the hand, the Old Man led as they cautiously explored the outside of the house as if gently probing a wound. With each step the child's hesitance was a constant tension on his arm. Each shuttered and locked window, each dangling, peeled paint strip, undisturbed despite its precarious hold on the siding, was a zephyr blowing through the Old Man's soul, calming him. Convinced the first floor windows were all sealed he leaned against the wall, taking long, slow breaths, preparing himself for the next step.

On the east side of the building a shutter displayed a long patch of bare wood gone gray, which yielded to the light touch of his finger – sponge soft. His old army knife sank easily into the rotted wood, exposing the sinuous tunnels of an abandoned carpenter ant nest. He continued to explore with the knife until impenetrable resistance told him he had found the securing bolt on the inside. With a bit more effort, the Old Man pulled the shutter open, exposing the multi-paned window. Covering the small glass square by the window latch with his jacket, he shattered it.

The window opened on darkness.

Climbing in, the Old Man gingerly deposited the duffle and backpack on the floor, lifted the boy in and stood, waiting, listening.

Blessed silence danced in the darkness.

Fishing a flashlight from the backpack, he clicked it on. Only a ghostly memory of the flash's former intensity, the beam of light was just sufficient to reveal an undisturbed room, the furniture covered by sheets placed with loving care by the departing custodian.

Stepping forward, the cavernous stillness of the house magnified the high-pitched squishing of his wet boots on the hardwood floor into the trumpeting of royal heralds announcing his arrival.

*Damn fool!* Mentally cursing his carelessness, he hid his anger from the boy with a conspiratorial wink while whispering, "Guess I'm not sneaking up on anyone today."

The boy giggled.

Nearing the basement door, the Old Man grabbed the boy's arm, signaling him to stay still and quiet. Wetting his lips, he searched the floor with the dying flash's ghostly circle of light, finding only virgin dust. Despite the evidence, uncertainty nagged him like a gambler holding tight to his last dollar as the bet is called. Motioning for the boy to step back while handing him the flashlight, he lowered the duffle and backpack to the floor as gently as if they contained spun glass. Eyes never leaving the door, his hand sifted through the backpack until it found the cold metal of the 9 mm Beretta. Glancing at the child, he hesitated, running his tongue along his lips.

Taking a deep breath, he whispered, "Give me the flashlight. Open the door when I say to."

In a crouch, the Beretta hidden from the child, he slipped off the safety while aiming the dim circle of light at the door. Tensing, he nodded to the child.

The boy opened the door.

The musty smell of saltwater and rotting wood gushed out at him. The dim light, reflecting off still water, illuminated a Rorschach pattern of mold-covered ceiling hovering over submerged stairs.

Eyes closed, a huge sigh escaped him as his upper body deflated. "Well, boy, nothing to see here," he mumbled. "Let's go look upstairs."

The child's eyes widened and a smile of eager anticipation bloomed. "The staircase to Heaven? Is it finished? Can I see Mama now?"

The Old Man shook his head. "No. It's not finished yet. I told you, the angels only work at night. We just need to find the way to the top floor so we can wait there."

The boy's face sagged into a sad frown. "But I want to see Mama."

"Soon boy, soon," the man said, picking up the duffle and backpack and heading off in search of the stairs.

The second floor was a repetition of the first: rooms with neatly covered furniture, all undisturbed, patiently awaiting tourists who would never return.

They moved on.

The cupola was empty of furniture. The windows opened upon a grand panorama of cerulean ocean under a brilliant golden sun and sapphire sky.

The backpack hit the floor with a loud thump, followed by a sympathetic rattle as the duffle bag landed next to it. "This is our bedroom for tonight. Should have a beautiful view of the sky."

Rushing to the window the child gripped the sill and peered out at the cloudless sky. Eyes straining upwards, voice high-pitched and anxious, he asked, "Will we see the angels tonight?"

"Now, you know better than that." The man's voice rumbled in mock disapproval, but his eyes held the sad twinkle of dying stars. "I told you they like to work at night so the starlight can guide them, but also so we can't see them. Remember child, that's not allowed."

Frowning, the boy turned to him, eyes ringed with concern. "But we'll hear them? Won't we? We'll hear them working on the staircase. They're still building it – aren't they?"

Feigning interest in the view, the man turned away, gazing east over the open ocean toward the bitter horizon. The dark, blue-green waters met the luminous blue of the sky in a perfect line – an empty, straight line devoid of any irregularity, of anything that might despoil its desolate perfection or offer any hope. "Yeah," his voice was soft. "More 'n likely."

"Are they almost finished? I want to see Mama."

Refusing to look at the boy, he tried to sooth him with his voice. "Soon, child... Soon."

Leaning forward, placing his hands on the glass, he gazed wistfully to the east, wishing for the impossible, denying the west. Startled, he stared hard into the distance – had something moved on the distant horizon? His breath caught, an ember of hope flickered. But it was only a distortion caused by the moisture in his eyes. Breathing out slowly and rubbing his face dry, he said, "Well, we're gonna spend the night up here, so let's make it comfortable."

The second floor rooms offered a warehouse of luxury. They soon returned with a wooden chair and a pile of cushions, pillows, and sheets fit for a sultan. The man set the chair to stand guard at the west window then made a bed for the child in the center of the

66

floor.

Returning to the east window the Old Man noticed a small patch of sandy shore below.

Gentle, rolling wavelets caressed the warm white sand, awaking distant, happy memories of glorious sunshine, deliciously cool water, and beloved faces laughing and smiling. Closing his eyes, he drifted away as those intoxicating memories flooded over him, soothing him, dispelling the weary ache in his bones. Turning his gaze to the child, he knew an urgent need, a hunger to grant the boy this small joy. Pointing, he asked, "Why not enjoy this beautiful day down on the beach?"

The boy looked out at the sand then ran back to the west window, face creased with worry.

The Old Man refused to surrender to the impending inevitability of the west. Buoyed by warm memories, a longing to share the delight of one last day on the beach seized him, erupting in genuine, heartfelt laughter. "Come on, no sense in wasting it."

Sweeping up the backpack with one hand, he took the boy's hand in the other and led him down the stairs, out of the house, and onto the beach.

Plunking himself down on the sand, the contrast of hot sunshine and the cool, gentle sea breeze on his skin brought a huge grin to his grizzled face. "First thing I'm gonna do is get out of these wet boots." Following a brief tussle with his soggy shoes, he was enjoying the delicious warmth of the sand on his liberated feet when another idea struck him. "Well, we might as well get undressed and go in the water. We could both use a bath."

The child stared at the ocean, hollow eyes wet with tears, lips a quivering frown. Wrapping his arms around his knees he buried his head between them, rapidly shaking it from side to side.

The man understood he needed to slow down, let the boy ease into the moment, find a way...

"Hey, I know! Let's sing some songs."

The boy's head snapped up, his wide-eyed look of surprise slowly morphing into a hesitant smile.

"Come on!" the Old Man urged, waving his hands. "I'll start with one I know." Clapping his hands to supply a beat he began to sing in a loud, gravely and off-key voice. "A, bee, gee, ee, que, arrh, zee..."

All hesitation forgotten, the boy protested in his high-pitched voice, "That's not how it goes!"

Lips pursed, squinting and scratching his head, the man replied, "No? I coulda sworn that's right."

'No, it's not!" laughed the now bright-eyed boy.

"Then show me," the Old Man replied with a soft smile.

Jumping up, the boy started singing and waving his arms from side to side. Soon both were merrily singing, clapping their hands, and swaying back and forth.

The child taught him "Peter Cottontail" and "Hey, Diddle, Diddle." The Old Man offered some songs, but always mangled the words. When he started to sing, "Baa, baa, Black Jeep have you got a seat…," the child roared with laughter, holding his stomach as if it would burst, and shouted corrections.

Carried away by the joy of the moment the Old Man sang out, "Be kind to our web-footed friends..."

Wild-eyed horror erupted on the child's face.

Realizing his mistake the man switched to "Old McDonald." But neither his new song, nor his hopeful, pleading smile helped.

Enthusiasm vanished, eyes downcast, the child glumly sang along.

Struggling to think of a way to restore the mood, the Old Man's face suddenly lit with inspiration as he jumped up yelling,

"Let's play tag! You're it!" and scampered off along the shore.

Startled, the child took a second to react. Leaping to his feet, face contorted into a deep frown of juvenile outrage, he ran after the man shouting every child's eternal war cry of injustice: "No fair!"

The game was fixed in the delightful way that only occurs when adults play with children. The boy managed to run down and tag his nemesis in just a few seconds, but the Old Man's every attempt to tag the boy was pre-destined for utter failure. He tripped, slipped, fell and slid, always as he was just within reach of the child. The boy greeted each hairbreadth escape with a gleeful scream, running off wide-eyed and laughing, having again avoided the ignominious fate of being *it*.

Finally, huffing and puffing, the old man gave up. Bent over with hands on knees, trying to catch his breath, the sight of the child's joy was a sinful narcotic routing his pain and sending his anxieties fleeing. He proclaimed the boy the winner, and bowing low in submission offered his services for a piggyback ride. They were soon dancing around the island, the boy's face beaming, urging his steed on to greater effort amid loud squeals of joy and peals of laughter.

And so they passed the day. By late afternoon the man judged the time right and managed to gently coax the boy into the water. No longer needing to fake his laughter or joy, he held tight to the small child as he let him splash, or skim across the surface, or spin around in the water. Through it all, the boy's laughter and squeals of delight filled the air.

A cold breeze trumpeted the onset of evening. The Old Man noted the long shadows of the house and trees announcing the coming sunset as an annual flower might heed the first chill winds of fall.

The boy, lips blue, was starting to shiver. Unable to stop time, the man sighed, lifted the child up and carried him to the beach. Using his old, worn t-shirt as a towel, he dried the boy then helped him dress. Barefoot, they climbed back into the house, secured the shutter and window as best they could with an electric cord, and ascended to the cupola.

"Dinner time!" the man announced, producing a battered tin of sausage from the backpack. "With a special treat!" And with an elaborate flourish he revealed a can of soda-pop and offered it to the boy.

The child ate ravenously, each sip of pop eliciting a broad, toothy smile. The Old Man, ignoring the aching of his empty stomach, ate only a small piece of sausage and took only a few short sips of the drink, savoring the taste, but saving most for the boy.

Their feast was soon complete. The man stood, stretched, and looked to the west. The darkness was growing, as it was in his soul.

"Time for bed," he said in a soft, flat voice.

"But I'm not tired," protested the child, eyelids drooping, chin resting on his chest, sleep not far off.

"Okay, we'll sing some more songs then. How does that sound?"

Ignoring the question, hopeful longing grew in the child's suddenly wide-open eyes. "Will the angels finish the staircase tonight? Will I see Mama tonight?"

Looking to the west the man closed his eyes, keeping his back to the child to hide the weary pain in his face. "Possibly," he replied, voice pensive. Turning back to the boy, he forced a smile. "But first let's get you ready for bed and sing a song."

Wrapping sheets around the boy's legs, the man took off his jacket, draped it over the child's shoulders and zipped it closed. "Warm enough?"

The boy nodded, a bright but sleepy smile on his face.

"Good. So now let's sing!" Striving to make his rough voice soft and soothing the Old Man began:

"All night, all day,

Angels watching over me, my Lord.

All night, all day,

Angels watching over me."


The exhausted child was asleep in minutes.

The man sagged, a weary frown on his face. The warmth of the afternoon's joy surrendered to the icy determination of the night. After waiting a few minutes to be sure the child was sleeping, he unzipped the duffle bag, pulled out a high powered rifle with a night scope, an assault rifle, and spare magazines. Checking each carefully he placed them on the floor beneath the west window. From the darkness of the backpack he removed two packs of stale cigarettes and two handguns: the Beretta and an old snub-nosed .38. Then he pulled up the chair and sat, looking west.

Lighting a cigarette he inhaled deeply, feeling the acrid smoke pass down his throat, filling his lungs. He held the rich smoke for a few seconds, savoring it. *Filthy habit*, he thought, exhaling. *I was so happy when I gave it up thirty years ago, but not much point in worrying about cancer anymore.* Tendrils of fatigue crept through his body as he took another deep drag on the cigarette. It helped to keep him awake, alert. Opening the window, the cold evening air was sharp on his skin, jolting the haze from his mind. Face hard, resigned, he looked out across the bay. The sun had sunk beneath the horizon, the twilight glow illuminating the ruined city in jagged silhouette – smoke billowing, angry red flames cavorting across the skeletal skyline. *Abandon all hope, ye who enter here*, he mused as he watched the city burn. But the total silence struck him most.

*That's bad*, he thought, a chill running down his spine. *Very bad.*

Waiting by the window, rifle resting across his legs, he sat, a door warden with no exit, watching, praying. Twilight retreated, yielding to darkness, the tranquil bay lit only by a thin sliver of moon, and the hellish, dancing reflection of the distant city. The Old Man began to survey the waters below with the rifle's night scope – a methodical, slow scanning from side to side. The world grew colder, darker. Cigarette butts grew to a small throng of the fallen at his feet.

Starting awake, his head jerked up from the window sill.

*Must have dozed. Time?*

Fumbling, he tried to read the face of his watch, could not see it in the weak moonlight. Pressing the small button on the crown, the face lit; black digits on a weak blue-light background appeared, but the numbers faded out, followed rapidly by the blue light.

*Old battery's running out of time.*

Scowling at his poor joke, he glanced at the sleeping child. *As are we all.*

Fighting sleep he shoved a cigarette into his mouth, lit it, and again took up his vigil.

Three hours later he knew his prayers had gone unanswered. The distant v-shapes, bow waves in the water, heralded the approach of small, man-sized swimmers.

They were coming.

Stepping over to the sleeping child, he knelt, listened to the music of his soft breathing, kissed his forehead. Taking a deep, ragged breath, he bit his lip to stop its quivering, closed his eyes tight and felt a tear run down his cheek. With another deep breath he calmed himself, checked the .38 and tucked it under his belt. There was one bullet left in it. He would save it for the boy.

Back at the window he knelt, lit another cigarette, picked up the rifle, scanned the water below. Sweat ran down his forehead despite the night chill. With an angry swipe he brushed at it to keep it from his eyes.

It was time. Crushing the cigarette with his boot, he said a quick prayer for the child, then focused on the view through the night scope. His entire existence, his world, now consisted of a pale green reality. He was the wall separating the child from that reality.

*They'll be in the shallows soon. Stupid creatures, they'll come right at us. Just need to wait. Once they rise up from the water I'll have a clear shot.*

His entire being concentrated on that small green universe.

The first rose up, a totem of anger from a debased world.

*Head shot. Head shot.* He squeezed the trigger.

A loud bang startled the boy awake. Forcing his face down into the pillow, he squeezed his eyes shut tight, knowing if he looked, if he saw the angels, they would stop working on the staircase and leave. The sound of the loud hammer blows comforted him. They were coming fast, and so very close. Almost next to him! Tingling joy flooded him. *The angels must be almost finished with the staircase to Heaven. I'll see Mama soon!* Anxious anticipation throbbing through his body, the child curled into a tight ball under the blankets and waited for blessed sleep to take him.

Tom 'DocTom' Wolosz is a paleoecologist, hiker, writer and semi-pro photographer. Born in Brooklyn, New York, he learned to love the outdoors early in life, which might explain how he ended up as a Professor of Geology at Plattsburgh State College in upstate New York.

DocTom's first novel, *Agony of the Gods, Softly Falls the Snow*, was published in 2014. You can visit him at his webpage: Tom Wolosz.com.

# Do Reapers Grin?

by Stephen A. Fox

Death took me on June twelfth at one fifteen in the afternoon.

It was the first time in a month the three of us had the same day off, so Cora, Sharletha and I decided to have a Girl's Day Out and we headed for the City. Yeah, Atlanta, the Gateway to the South. I hadn't been to the aquarium since I was a little girl so we made sure that would be on the list, right after shoe shopping at the big mall.

We got to the Aquarium about one o'clock and I spotted Him hanging around as we left the elevator from the parking deck. I had found this adorable pair of red pumps and I had to try them out. Blue sky, a gentle breeze and new shoes. A perfect day, until He showed up.

Sharletha dropped her cell phone and bent down to pick it up when Cora giggled. "Look out, girl. Bent over in that skirt, you're showing me your China. Oh my God, now I think I see Australia."

Anyway, I spotted this guy in what I thought was a black hoodie. Then I realized it wasn't a hoodie, it was too long, like a dark, heavy dress. "A little early for Halloween, don't you think?" I said.

"Huh?" Cora said. "What'cha mean?"

"That guy," I said, pointing. "I wonder if he's paying off a bet or shooting a commercial?"

Cora stared that way, then looked back at me. "Who?"

I pointed again. "Him."

Sharletha looked confused. "What him, girl?"

The guy in the black dress thing – what's it called? A cowl? –

was in the middle of a crowd, but as I watched, he passed right through two ladies. Yeah, that's right, passed right through them, and raised his right arm to point at me. In his other arm he held a long, pointy thing. A scythe. That's when I knew who he was. Death, with a capital D. The Grim Reaper. I grabbed both girls by the arm and ducked around the corner.

"Hey, whatcha doing, girl?" Sharletha growled as I pulled them along.

"Did you see him?"

"Who?" She scowled and looked over her shoulder. "Did that no-good Levon follow us again?"

"You didn't see him?"

"See who?" Cora asked, scanning the crowd.

I left it there. I wasn't about to tell even my best friends I just saw Death. Especially when said girlfriends hadn't seen anything.

I started toward the entrance. *Wait a minute. That's where he was.* I moved in the opposite direction. *How will it happen? Will an elevator fail and send us plummeting? If I use the stairs, will I trip and break my neck? And my lifeless body bounce down a hundred flights?*

I thought of an old story my grandpa told me about a farmer who met Death in a market and fled back home. Answering a knock on the door that afternoon, there stood Death. The farmer complained, "Why did you beckon to me in the city?" Death's answer: "I was surprised to see you there. My appointment book said I would find you here at the farm."

No, you can't run away from Death when He comes calling. I was going to die, here and now, and there was nothing I could do about it. With a heavy sigh I turned back.

The Reaper was waiting at the entrance. Just like in all the pictures, I couldn't see a face inside the shadow of the hoodie, but the bony hands stuck out of the sleeves.

I faced Him and shrugged. "Okay, I'm here." I couldn't help adding, in my little girl voice, "Is this going to hurt?"

"No," he said. "In fact it's already happened."

I heard screams and people started scurrying around the corner where I had been. The ones going that way looked excited. The ones coming our way looked scared. "What happened?" I asked.

"Oh, nothing too traumatic," he said. "A tiny piece broke off an airplane that just took off. It severed an artery in your neck when it fell on you. There's a lot of blood but don't worry. I'm sure it'll be an open casket."

*Thanks a bunch for that picture.* "And my friends?"

"Cora got a little blood on her, and Sharletha broke a nail, but they're fine. Nobody else was even touched."

*Praise the Lord.* Aloud I said, "Okay, so I'm dead. What happens now?"

"Usually your soul goes one way or the other." With that, he paused.

I glared at him. "That's a 'but' face if I ever saw one."

He reared up. "A butt face?"

I studied the hood. Was there a face at all under there, or a skull? "That means there's always a word like 'but' coming along behind it."

Death's shoulders relaxed and he nodded. "But we have a choice to offer you. A job."

"You kill me and then offer me a job? No offense, but isn't it usually the other way around?"

Two paramedics got off the elevator with a gurney, and passed right through me. I glared at them, then turned back to Death as he said, "It's an unusual job."

It was an intriguing prospect. I was a checkout girl at Walmart with barely a high school diploma. Not exactly the fast track to a management position. Besides, I was already dead so it's not like I had many choices here. According to my music teacher, I wouldn't last a day with the heavenly choir. "What's the job?" I asked.

"As you probably know, when you die, there are three choices. If you have been really, really good, you go up to heaven. If you've been really, really bad, you go directly to hell. But the majority of people are neither saints nor super villains. Almost everybody sins many times a day in thought or deed. Because of this, most mortals are sent to the outskirts of hell, called purgatory. Depending on how often they sinned, and how bad the sins, they are tormented there."

"I'm with you so far," I said, trying to peek up the cowl. It made me feel like a pervert, but I was dying to know if he had a face. "I learned that in Sunday school."

"When souls are sent to purgatory, they're given a sentence, sort of like prison. They know they're going to suffer, but eventually the torment will end and they'll ascend to heaven."

"And so my job will be…?"

"You will be responsible for recovering the souls and sending them on their way to heaven. Most spend so long in purgatory that they lose track of time. They'll be thankful that you've come to release them."

I folded my arms. "That doesn't sound so bad, but I'm guessing you haven't told me the whole story. What's the bad news?"

The cowl drooped. How a faceless cloak could look embarrassed I don't know, but the Reaper managed it. "Well... um... The thing is, you see, the demons assigned to torment the souls have been known to be upset when their fun is interrupted. Sometimes they get physical." The cowl raised slightly, and I tried one more peek as he continued. "But we have designed you some protection." From somewhere in the cloak he pulled out an object that resembled a remote. No, not a remote, a...

"A stun gun? You expect me to take on demons with a stun gun?" This was definitely not one of my best days ever.

The paramedics were back, with a body bag on the gurney. Cora, wailing like only she can, was being escorted by a policeman. Sharletha, tears dripping down her cheeks, followed them silently. I stepped to the side this time. It had to be bad luck to have your body pass through your body. You know what I mean.

"It's not just any stun gun." Death sounded proud. Somebody in his family must have made it. "Most guns will shoot fifty thousand volts into the victim. This one fires a million. Guaranteed to drop even a demon. You fry a couple of them and the rest will give you some distance, if you know what I mean. And it never needs charging. It keeps firing like a Gene Autry six-shooter."

Something still bothered me. "Is this one of those equal opportunity things?"

Death spluttered. "What?"

"You know, if you hire a woman and she happens to be black you get credit for hiring two minorities? 'Cause I don't need no pity job."

"No, no." He sounded just like that fool from the employment bureau. "We need someone like you. Race and sex don't matter, but we need someone who can deal with demons. Believe me, it's hard to find people who *believe* in demons, let alone have the moxie to deal with them. The last three people who took the job didn't last a century. The rate of turnover has been slowing us down." The cowl stared at me. "Do you have the right stuff for the job?"

"Stuff? I got stuff! Moxie, attitude – you name it. But I got conditions."

"What? I don't think–"

"First, I want one of those hip hugger cowls. You know, the girly kind that shows off my full figure. Let them know I'm a woman; you hear what I'm saying?"

"I'm not sure that I can–"

"And I want a different color. Blue, maybe red. Something to make me look hot."

"Well, I'll see what I–"

"That way they won't get us confused. I mean black may be beautiful, but really! No, let's go with cream. That way we can do the whole ebony and ivory thing. And I want a cool name. Like yours, but cooler." I thought for a second while he made gurgling noises like he was having a stroke or something. "I got it. You can call me the Grin Reaper."

"The Grin–"

"'Cause they see me and they'll be grinning from ear to ear because they'll be heading to Heaven. Except for them demons. They won't be grinning. I got plans for them suckers."

"Anything else?"

"If I think of something, I'll let you know, tall, dark and bony." I tried to give him a hip bump, but he moved away from me. Shy, I guess.

"Done."

Death vanished and an instant later I was dressed in a cream-colored hoodie. Nice and snug in all the right places. I pulled up the sleeves. Sure enough, nothing but bone, as far up the cowl as I could see. Well, at least I didn't have to worry about sunburn anymore.

I pulled the sleeves back down and checked the robe. I pulled an electronic day planner out of a pocket on the right and opened it.

Two names flashed from the page. My first assignments, no doubt.

The left pocket yielded the stun gun. I studied it for a second and pulled the trigger. A bright arc of electricity shot out the end. Cool!

Now a third name flashed on the screen. I decided I'd better get busy. Nothing worse than getting behind on the first day of a new job. I put my finger on the first name and pushed.

I looked around. No more Atlanta skyline. Instead I found myself in a narrow tunnel, hotter than... well, hot. A line of humans as far as I could see down the shaft were chained together, pulling on a rope, while demons hovered over them, whips in hand. *A little clichéd.* I sashayed forward. "Ezekiel Cohen?"

One man raised his head a smidgen, a glimmer of hope in his eyes. Before he could speak, the biggest, baddest-looking guard stepped in front of him. The man dropped his head as the guard growled, "Who wants to know, girlie?"

*Girlie? Did that fat slob really say that?* I crossed my arms and glared at the eight foot tall behemoth. *Six inch fangs or not, he's not gonna talk to me that way.* "I'm here to get him released. He's going to heaven."

Laughter erupted all around us. The head demon didn't join in, but he let it continue for a minute, then raised a hand. Everyone went quiet. "Listen, little lady, this poor buttwipe ain't goin' anywhere. I've got plans for him."

Well, he did call me a lady, so I decided to give him one more chance. "I'm sorry, but I'm under orders to take him."

This time the big oaf snorted as his minions hooted and cackled around us. "And how do you think you're gonna do that, princess?"

I pulled the stun gun out. *Princess? I'll princess him.* I pulled the trigger.

No wires. Instead some sort of beam shot out the end, like a Buck Rogers ray gun. The demon started vibrating, and smoke curled out his ears. The next thing I knew there was a ten foot tower of flame where he'd been standing. A few seconds later, all that was left was a pile of ashes.

I turned to the minions. "Who's next?"

They clamored over each other to be the one to release their prisoner. Once he was free, I noticed his name on the list began to blink, so I pressed the spot once more. Cohen started to shimmer and sparkle. I thought about Spock in a Star Trek transporter. His body blurred, I heard a whispered "God bless you," and he was gone.

I stood there for a minute and stared at the weapon, while the minions groveled.

*A new job, a chance to really help people*, and *I get to fry some bad guys. Screw you, Walmart!* I pulled the trigger again, and grinned at the spark, while the minions squealed and jumped back.

*This is gonna be fun!*

After 32 years teaching middle school, I finally retired. The first thing I did was build an office in my backyard to spend more time writing and furnished it with two bookcases full of my favorite authors, a small desk to hold my laptop, and a hammock. Pay no attention to the man behind the snoring. I get my best ideas while horizontal. I live near Augusta, Georgia with my wife and a small herd of dachschunds.

# Days Of Our Lives

by John Bukowski

I've always loved bar mix. For the youngsters among you who have never heard of this almost forgotten ambrosia, it is a blend of peanuts, pretzels, oddly puffed cheezoids, and sharp spices – kind of like Chex mix with kick. It goes great with beer, wine, or cocktails; unlike pretzels, which for my money are strictly a beer snack. Years ago, bowls of this heavenly mélange, refilled from industrial-sized bags kept under the counter with the olives and cherries, would be found on the bars of most better establishments. Alas, fear of peanuts and communal eating have combined with corporate greed to almost completely remove this freebie that excites the palate and stimulates alcohol consumption. Almost, but not quite. Hence, my second love: the bar at The Wilmington Grille and Tavern.

On this particular Saturday evening, I was a happy guy. I had my center seat at the bar, near enough to the TV to make out the closed caption. I had a Tigers game on the tube, which is a rarity in Cincinnati; Detroit was even leading, five to one. I had a cold (not iced – God forbid) imperial pint of Fuller's ESB, the perfect beer. Unlike newfangled IPAs that almost raped your taste buds, the hops in Fullers seduced them with dinner and dancing. Mate that to the tangy munch of the bar snacks and it was almost a wedding dance.

The only fly in my otherwise contented ointment was the bar mix positioned too far to the left for easy reach. So, I was forced to query a fellow barfly, a dicey proposition that could lead to anything from a new friend to an hour fending off Cliff Clavin.

"Excuse me. Could you pass the bar mix?"

The guy didn't seem to hear me, or if he did was tuning me out. He was middle-aged and I didn't see any telltale ear lump and plastic tube, suggesting he wasn't in the hearing-impaired fraternity (of which I am a member in good standing).

"Excuse, me, pal? Would you mind passing me the bar mix?"

This time, bleary eyes turned to me. I guess the guy was in his forties, although it was hard to tell. He hadn't shaved and there were streaks of grey in his nine o'clock shadow. Some silver also sprinkled those hairs still swimming against the current of male pattern baldness. He was dressed in frumpy sweats, both shirt and pants; white socks, the kind bought in bags of ten pairs at Walmart; and beat-to-hell sneakers that were once red but now faded to a color found in gay bars. His overall appearance was more in keeping with a cheaper tavern, one where a shot of Seagram's and a Bud ran you $6.85. The stack of tens and twenties next to him suggested that money wasn't a problem.

Pointing to the bowl, I repeated, "Would you mind passing the bar mix?"

My fellow fly looked from me to the dish, then back again. "You want that?"

"If you don't mind?"

Mr. Smith or Doe or whatever shrugged and laconically slid the mix in my direction.

"Thanks."

I got a wave of the hand as he finished his shot.

"You like bar snacks, huh?"

Here we go, I thought. Just when I was getting comfortable, I opened the drunk spigot. Soon I would be hip deep in stories about kids today, how the government is experimenting with zombie viruses, and why his wife left him after fifteen years (duh!). My only hope was to keep contact short and pray for inertia to kick back in.

"Yep," I said.

He seemed satisfied with that, nodding too vigorously as the inebriated tend to do. "You like Knob Creek?" he asked matter-of-factly.

"Sure."

"Sam! Get us a couple of shots of Creek down here."

Although I am a beer drinker by nature, I will not turn down good bourbon when offered. But here was my dilemma. If I accepted his hospitality, we two would become linked in barfly brotherhood, and the chapter meetings were always the same. I'd be expected to chat with him amiably, agreeing that yes indeed the government is spying on him. I'd be expected to buy him a drink in return, prolonging the interaction as intoxication led to ever more bizarre topics ("Of course Superman could beat the Terminator – he's Superman!"). The baseball game would be forgotten. I'd be too drunk to drive home, although I would probably think I was doing just fine because I knew my 'cacapity.' I was just about to decline, when the problem solved itself.

"Just one more shot and then I gotta run. Big day tomorrow," said my benefactor with a shit-eating grin.

Sam brought the whiskey, straight up, the only way to mix with beer.

"Thanks," I said, toasting my newfound if short-term friend.

Good whiskey is like drinking smoke. It kind of whispers its way down the throat. You never feel liquid hit the stomach, just a spreading warmth like the passage of a tropical breeze.

"What's happening tomorrow," I inquired amiably.

My stool-mate began to chuckle. At first it was a snigger, like you get when you see some guy in new shoes step ankle-deep into a pothole that looked to be a half-inch puddle. But then it grew like the memory of a favorite joke. Finally, he was chuckling so hard, he had difficulty saying, "Same as today." The dam broke and he was laughing, tears streaming down his cheeks in manic release. It was contagious and I started laughing, even though I had no idea why.

I slugged down some beer and shook my head to clear away the giggles. "What do you mean?"

Mr. Smith became serious, the sudden change taking me by surprise. This could only mean that I'd hit a sensitive nerve and that he was about to either cry or scream at me. He did neither. Waving me over conspiratorially, he leaned to the right. I leaned left, hoping I wouldn't have to catch him.

"You seem like a nice guy," he whispered, nice sounding like nishe. "Can I ashk you a queshion?" He looked both ways, as if he was afraid Sam or someone was eavesdropping. "You know, kinda personal?"

Here we go, I thought.

"What day is it?"

I was expecting lewd or nutty, like 'do you dig feet?' or 'do helicopters shoot atomic rays at you.' Instead, I got mundane, which sounded even crazier than your typical barroom crazy.

"It's Saturday, June 16."

"And what day was yesterday?"

I wasn't sure where this was going, but thought it safest to play along.

"Friday, June 15."

"And what day will tomorrow be?"

I answered quickly. "Sunday the 17th." Now unless the guy started into next week, that should be the end of it. But my host shook his head vigorously, bits of drool spitting off his lip onto the bar.

"Isn't that right?" I asked.

He grabbed my arm and pulled closer, whiskey breath popping my chin like a Mike Tyson jab. Please don't throw up on me, I prayed.

"Yesterday was Shatturday the sixseenth and tomorrow will be Shatturday the sixseenth," he whispered, holding a finger to his lips in a shush.

I nodded and thought, sweet Jesus, why me?

I could have said a number of things here, but we were at a critical juncture, like deciding which direction to take in a minefield. I could humor him, but I better be damn good. Drunks can sniff out patronization like McGruff can sniff out a joint. I could disagree, but that might set off a tidal wave of excrement against the proverbial fan. So, I just said, "Okay."

He ignored my reply like my bar mix request. Leaning in again, he said, "It's like that Groundhog movie. You know, the one with Bill Pullman."

"Murray," I said.

"Right, right, the one with Murray Pullman. Everyday is Saturday. Now, don't get me wrong, I like Saturday, alwaysh have, but it gets old after while. Ya know?"

He expected an answer, so I nodded thoughtfully. "Sure, I can see how that would be."

I guess my acting wasn't very good, because McGruff nosed out the Mary Jane in my pocket.

"You don't believe me, huh?"

Shaking my head, I said, "No, No, it's not that…"

Pointing to the flat screen over the bar, he said, "What is it, bottom of the 6th, Detroit up five to two?"

I was about to say 5:1, when I saw a Cleveland runner cross the plate as another walked to first. Seems that he'd been keeping up with the game better than I.

I shrugged. "So?"

"They're gonna yank Baker, and that Cleveland shortstop, what's his name, Consuelo ..."

"Cargona," I corrected.

"Whatever. He's gonna slam a two-out fast ball down the left-field line, giving the Tribe a six five lead."

The manager and catcher were at the mound for a confab, so a reliever seemed likely. But Cargona had maybe two homers all last year. Still, given the ticklish nature of the conversation, I nodded politely and took a sip of whiskey, pondering my next move. I could wait until Cargona struck out or popped up, then try a logic confrontation. But I have learned that barroom drunks are like pop bottles – shake them up, and they blow up on you. Besides, his idea, delusion, psychosis (pick one) was an interesting one, as beery nutjobs go.

"So," I said, "if you *are* living the same day over and over, why don't you do like Murray in that movie. You know, use the time – learn the piano or read French poetry or something?"

"Why don't I do that now instead of sitting here? I tell ya why, it's boring! Everyshing is boring. Even getting' drunk ish boring, which I never sought possible. And I won't even have a hangover in the morning!"

"How long has this been going on?" I asked, the lubrication of the whiskey sliding me deeper into barroom crazy.

Mr. Smith waved me off. "I stopped counting at 200. After that, it musta been ..." Another chuckle interrupted his train of thought. "I almost said 'years,' like they mean somethin' when it's always June 16."

The guy was a tad agitated, but seemed otherwise tame enough. Still, thinking that playing along was the safest and most bar-neighborly path, I chose a new tack.

"Well, at least it's not a work day. And it's not February 2 in BumFart Pennsylvania. It's a nice June Saturday in Cinci; 78 degrees today, girls in shorts and halters." I shrugged. "Why not enjoy it if you can't change it?"

My companion (we'd moved past strangers, even though I still didn't know his name) snorted in derision and gave me an exaggerated 'go on' wave that threatened to unseat him from his bar-stool perch. "I can change it like that!" he said, twice bringing together fingers that wouldn't snap.

I was not expecting this turn of affairs. I also wasn't expecting the impact of the bourbon, which sneaks up on you when cannon-balled with beer. I found myself buying into the premise, and I found myself intrigued.

"So what's the problem? Change it. Move on!"

The guy looked at me like *I* was insane. "Are you freakin' kiddin' me? I'm immortal! If I change that, if I snap my fingers and tomorrow becomes Sunday June 17, I'm gonna die. I don't wanna die!"

The poor guy was almost in tears, the alcoholic blear in those eyes replaced by stark raving terror. I really felt for him. He scared me a little, but I felt for him just the same.

Sam walked over and asked, "You okay, Mr. Smith?" What were the chances?

Fear has a way of sobering you, and Smith was suddenly clear headed, his drunken lisp and exaggerated movements gone. He nodded twice, both head bobs properly proportioned.

"Why don't you let me call you a cab, Jon," Sam said.

Smith shook his head. "Just some black coffee, Sam." He smiled at the bartender. "I'll get home alright, I always do."

Suddenly I felt uncomfortable. I wanted to leave, but in an odd way felt responsible for this guy. Bars are funny like that. You sit down with strangers that become a family of the moment. Next morning they're replaced by a headache, but at the time there is kinship – a sense of community and communal obligation, if only for that microcosm of time in which you share varnished oak planking and the pleasures of alcohol. I remember once in my twenties getting hit on by a fiftyish woman at a bar near UC. She wasn't unattractive in a matronly way, but she was drunk and seemed sad and tired, used by life. We spent at most an hour chatting before she made her move, and I can't even remember her name (if I ever knew it), but I was more concerned with letting her down easy than I ever was with the half-dozen girlfriends I had before I got married.

"Listen," I said. "I don't know a lot about immortality, but it seems to me this isn't doing you any good. I know you don't wanna die. Hell, nobody wants to die. But isn't life about more than not dying? Sitting in a bar, living the same day over and over, well it seems to me that isn't living. That sounds more like dying in slow motion, like some Twilight Zone idea of hell."

He nodded in relief, as if he'd been thinking the same but needed reassurance from another human soul. I realized that no matter how many times he thought he'd done this, this was the first time he'd ever actually talked about this obsession of his. I smiled encouragement. "Why don't you give life a chance for a change? You might like it. And maybe it wouldn't hurt to go talk to someone. You know, like you're talking to me. Someone who knows more about, ah, things like immortality than I do."

I tossed down the rest of the bourbon, and uncreaking my sixty-four-year-old bones from the stool, reached for my wallet. His hand grabbed mine and he shook his head. He said only, "That's okay, I've got this," but his eyes said thank you. I drove home carefully, feeling good.

I began my Sunday, June 17 with a walk down the drive to get the paper. I'd follow the same routine I had every Sunday since Meg passed: read the paper over a breakfast of coffee, juice, two eggs over medium, and potatoes, the kind that come frozen and look like mashed-down tater tots. I put on the Mr. Coffee and fired the oven to 425 before looking at the headlines.

Man dies in fiery crash

The story indicated that Mr. Jonathon Smith, 47, of Milford Ohio ran into an abutment while driving home on I-275 at 9:45 PM last night. Alcohol was definitely involved.

I have to admit that the coincidence threw me, but then I sloughed it off. Smith is a common name, and Jon Smith perhaps the most common, even in our modern world of Brandens, Carters, and Jamals. Then I flipped to the sports page.

Tribe beats Detroit 6 to 5 on Cargona grand slam.

I lost my appetite.

John Bukowski is a recently retired veterinarian, epidemiologist, public-health scientist, and medical writer (his wife made him stop after four college degrees). He's seen a lot of North America during his career and experienced wildly different work cultures ranging from mom and pop vet clinics to US and Canadian governments. His many publications as a technical writer cover everything from journal articles, to op-eds, consumer handbooks, radio scripts, advertorials, and more. Since his fiction muse spoke up, he's written several novels in the thriller/crime-fiction genre, still seeking that special literary agent who appreciates his gift for humor and tale spinning. When asked if he's related to the famous Bukowski, he never answers, preferring to make it on his own merit. Favorite authors include Stephen King, Elmore Leonard, Stephen Hunter, Robert Parker, EA Poe, and Ernest Hemingway. Hobbies include old movies, singing, acting, military history, and Facebooking. John and his wife Susan split their time between Dayton, Ohio and Townsend, TN, sharing their lives with two dysfunctional dogs, Alfie and Moxie.

# The Scroll and the Silver Kazoo

by Paul Stansbury

I was there.

Along with my fellow writers that is, for WACKY day – the annual reading day sponsored by the Writers Alliance of Central KY. We hold it every April in a field in front of a little country store, located at the end of a dusty gravel road deep in the rolling hills of our namesake state. The sun was shining somewhere up above the clouds of the overcast sky. A lady from a little place with a compound name whose claim to fame was that it was near some other place, had been reading for twenty minutes. The temperature was typical – somewhere between heatstroke and frostbite – which meant you started with a winter coat in the morning and ended up in a tee shirt by four in the afternoon. She was about a third of the way through a fistful of loose manuscript – something about the crops grown in Kentucky during the War of 1812 and their impact on 20th Century geopolitics. Upon finishing a page, she would pause, scanning it to make sure she had left nothing out, then carefully move it to the bottom of the stack. She was in that process, when one of those mild spring zephyrs we had grown so accustomed to rolled over the grass toward the podium. It ripped the manuscript from her hand, sending the loose pages flying down the gravel road. The reading tent, meant to shelter the readers from the intense shade of the clouds overhead, rose up from its foundations, looking much like Dorothy's house in the tornado. It tumbled almost all the way over to the creek before landing in the thick vegetation along the banks.

The dogs and some of us from the audience chased the wily sheets of paper as they danced along the ground. I don't know about anyone else, but I had in mind to stealthily stash as many in my pocket as I could in the event the lady decided to return to the mic. Meanwhile, Chad our emcee announced that while the papers were being retrieved, it might be a good time to open the mic up to anyone else who wanted to read.

But the last syllable of the invite was drowned out leaving his lips. High above us, the scrim of cloud brightened, and a sound – something between a whoosh and a roar, but not entirely unlike a howl – filled the sultry air. I turned, hands full of soon-to-be-stashed pages. The crowd gave a collective gasp as the clouds split open, and a blinding shaft of sunlight broke. Some sort of craft, its patchwork metallic skin reflecting a rainbow of colors, slid down the beaming light, wheezing and churning all the way. It came to rest on the dewy lawn, standing like some fantastic galactic rat rod, encrusted with antennae and dishes and protuberances of all manner.

Like a crowd of extras from a Steven Spielberg movie, we all stood motionless, mouths agape, as a figure, covered from head to toe in purple, emerged from the craft. It had one eye situated in the center of its forehead, directly below a white horn that curlicued like a corkscrew. Bright pink gills lined its stubby neck. While it glided just above the wet grass toward Chad and the podium, the spindly hands on each of its six arms gave us the Queen Elizabeth parade wave.

To Chad's credit, he held his ground – surely the sign of a great emcee. Those of us gathering the papers gave up the chase and made it back to our seats just as the alien reached the podium. Ever the trooper, Chad asked the alien if it had anything to share. It responded in a peculiar voice that sounded like Alvin the Chipmunk burping while throat-singing a Tibetan chant. Chad adjusted the mic and stepped back. The alien produced a scroll from a pocket and unfurled it with two of its six hands. By now the dogs, who had been steadily making their way toward the alien, were nosing our newfound friend's grey flipper feet, tails wagging. Apparently, one of the good things about having six arms is that you can pet three

95

dogs while holding a scroll and still have one hand with which to gesture in dramatic fashion.

Our purple reader began, voice now a deep baritone. We couldn't understand the language, but we were enthralled nonetheless. Its voice moved from a rumbling bass to a quivering tenor in a single phrase. Its free hand made sweeping gestures, while its eye looked into our souls. Then, to our utter astonishment, the alien reached into another pocket and brought out what looked like a silver kazoo, which it held to one of its gills. While continuing to read, the alien produced a sound so mellifluous it could have only been surpassed by the sweet warble of Gabriel's trumpet. It floated out over the fields and rolled up the hillsides. We basked in its beauty, swayed in its rhythm. It was so grand, so wondrous, the birds flew down from the treetops, alighting in silent reverence on the podium.

The Alien read and played on until it reached the end of the scroll and the last sweet note from the silver kazoo echoed across the fields. Then there was silence, utter silence. Silence from the birds, silence from the dogs, silence from the crickets, silence from us. A silence of wonder, a silence of respect. We let the moment linger in our collective consciousness as long as we could before erupting in applause and shouts and whistles. The birds flew off like doves released at the Olympics. The dogs barked in joy.

Our alien friend waved its Queen Elizabeth parade wave and floated back to the galactic rat rod. As soon as its door closed, the contraption whirred and hummed, rising back up through the hole in the clouds, then whooshed off, clouds snapping shut behind it. We rose to our feet, pumping our fists, slapping our thighs and "whoo hooing" at the top of our lungs. We hadn't comprehended a single word, but we celebrated all the same. Because we understood. We understood the courage it took to travel down unfamiliar roads and stand before strangers. The courage it took to speak our words and play our music. The courage it took to believe in ourselves. We understood.

Paul Stansbury is a life-long native of Kentucky. He is the author of *Inversion – Not Your Ordinary Stories* and *Down By the Creek – Ripples and Reflections* as well as a novelette: *Little Green Men?* His speculative fiction stories have appeared in a number of print anthologies as well as a variety of online publications. Now retired, he lives in Danville, Kentucky.

Email: paulsstansbury@gmail.com

Website: http://www.paulstansbury.com

Facebook: www.facebook.com/paulstansbury/

# The Woman in the Cave

by Geoff King

The wind blew so hard, Hugo could lean into it with his coat open without falling over. Some of the gusts threatened to lift him from the ground but he found it exhilarating; he imagined spiralling away across the ocean like a stringless kite, free from his troubles. He tried steeper and steeper angles until finally he plunged face first into the wet grass laughing with the abandon of a carefree child. The wild air thrummed, fully charged with oxygen, smelling of salt and seaweed, sheep and damp pasture. He felt so much more alive here.

In the last few days, he had grown to love wandering the hills and cliff tops around his late grandmother's home on this remote and rocky peninsula. It made a welcome respite from sorting through her endless paperwork and effects. With no siblings and both his parents long dead, he remained her only surviving relative. It fell to him to put her affairs in order after she passed away. Although he spent all his childhood holidays in her care, she didn't move here until she retired, by which time the only breaks he took from work involved jetting off to warmer, drier countries where he lay on the beach in the sun and read escapist fiction. Now he was happy to take this convenient excuse for a few weeks away from his stressful life in the city. The pace of everything in London was rapid and relentless. At home in his flat, a radio, a television, a computer and a hi-fi, all cried out for his attention like needy puppies. Even if he resisted their appeal, the noise of the outside world intruded into his consciousness. He loved the natural world and would have preferred to live in the country, but felt trapped in his job by the necessity of earning a living and, without a car, he was dependent on the urban environment.

As a naive teenager, he allowed his parents and teachers to steer him towards a treadmill of drudgery as a wage slave. He fared no better in his private life. His romantic experiences thus far were few, short and unsatisfactory. His grandmother's death gave him a temporary respite. Of course he would not have wished this fate upon her, nor anyone else for that matter, but he felt grateful for the opportunity to take a break, to have both the time and head space to contemplate how to lift himself out of his depressing situation and speculate on whether he could do anything to improve his life.

Here in this sleepy backwater of rural Wales, the village covetously cradled its precious grocery shop, seemingly rooted firmly in the nineteen-seventies, where sad looking old tins with faded labels huddled in reproachful groups at the back of dusty shelves like schoolboys not chosen for the football team. The inevitable pub, where Hugo would wander in to meditate over a daily pint or two, lacked any kind of atmosphere. A television, always tuned to news, sport or game shows, with the volume muted, flickered its images out to the indifferent clientele. A slightly sloping pool table sulked in a back room, neglected except on Saturday mornings when a small group of disgruntled adolescents used the facilities as an unofficial youth club.

Hugo soon discovered the only single women remaining in the village were at least twice his age. Despite this difference, several of them tried to chat him up, but he wasn't interested in anyone so much older than him. He talked to the locals; they were generally a friendly lot, happy to while away their seemingly unlimited hours in amiable discourse, but they remained rather provincial and remarkably superstitious, often embellishing their conversations with cautionary tales of unlucky miners, cursed fisher folk or foolhardy hill walkers. The one person never to speak to him, nor anyone else as far as he could tell, was old Joe Evans, universally regarded as the most elderly man in the village, who seemed to spend nearly all his time seated at the same table in the corner of the pub, slowly sipping his beer. Despite the smoking ban, his pipe was always alight. Hunkered in the shadows and immersed in a cloud of fumes, he resembled a diminutive, wizened dragon. It was remarkable the landlord let him get away with it. Hugo had never been anywhere else that would tolerate such behaviour and risk prosecution. He guessed it was a testament to the backwardness of this isolated and rustic community.

After the first week in his grandmother's house, Hugo shifted a huge pile of boxes full of magazines heaped up at one end of the study. Instead of trying to make sense of them all, he decided to recycle the lot. The backs of the last few boxes were damp from condensation. Behind them he found a safe set into the wall, its front rusty, scratched and dented with dark green paint flaking off like dead lichen. He felt a tingle of excitement; the prospect of discovering hidden treasure was a welcome change from hours of sorting. He leaned in closer and bent to inspect the door. It had a tarnished brass handle but no keyhole, just a dial edged with numbers. He made a few attempts at the combination, twisting the dial back and forth, his ear pressed to the cold metal, listening for tell-tale clicks like the fictional criminals in old movies. He soon realized the futility of this and gave up frustrated. There must be something important inside. He would ask in the pub if anyone knew a tradesman with the skills and equipment required to break into a safe.

Later that day he decided to get another dose of fresh air and exercise. He wanted to explore more of the windswept slopes high above the rugged cliffs, against whose feet Atlantic waves crashed relentlessly, day and night. As the afternoon wore on, the clouds thickened and darkened, threatening rain. Soon the first drops began to splat heavily onto the rocks protruding from the rough turf. On a steep, scrubby hillside he discovered a cave entrance, shaped like a single eye socket in a human skull, and took cover from the sudden squall. Inside he saw a dry, sheltered rock he could sit on and wait for an improvement in the weather. He edged forwards with his head bowed to avoid the low ceiling and, seeing footprints in the moist dirt, guessed that others had sought shelter here before him. Sniffing the dank air, he detected a hint of wood smoke. He ventured a little further in and saw a faint orange glow flickering from around a curve in the passage in the deepest recesses of the cave. He crept onward to investigate. Half crouched and squinting in the darkness, he kept his hands on the wall for balance. The rough, wet rock had patches of slimy growth, but the gravelly floor remained flat and dry. The noise of the storm grew more muffled the deeper he went. Rounding the corner, he saw a fire burning at the end of the tunnel. He entered a chamber, a round room with a raised ceiling, high enough for him to stand almost upright. Smoke escaped through a hole in the ceiling; the rain trickling through it found its way down the wall into a small, dark pool. Various personal belongings were arranged neatly around the edges of the cavern. This subterranean hollow was actually somebody's home. Peering beyond the central hearth, he made out a low shelf of rock. On it was the sleeping form of a woman.

Hugo froze and stopped breathing, entranced by the captivating figure. He could hear her soft breath, see her chest rise and fall. He inhaled and thought he could smell flowers, but could see none in the cave. Long tresses of wavy, auburn hair lay strewn across her pillow like rumpled silk, as bright as a robin's breast. Her face, as smooth and pale as marble, held a faint rosy sheen on one cheek where it reflected the firelight. Her mouth was slightly open and her lips, the colour of fuchsia blossoms, looked soft and moist. She wore a white gown finely embroidered with intricate patterns worked onto the delicate cloth in golden thread. The material was so thin he could make out her nakedness beneath it and felt even more of an intruder into a very private and personal domain, yet still he found it hard to resist the urge to reach out and touch her. She looked in every way like a sleeping princess in a fairy tale.

The woman stirred. He stood motionless, unsure what to do. He remained mute, as if this would somehow make him invisible. She yawned, stretched and then rose, her movements as fluid and

101

graceful as a cat's. Hugo couldn't help admiring her body beneath the flimsy garment. His pulse radiated out to his fingers and toes and he realized his hands had begun to shake. But fear did not grip him; it was more akin to the nervous excitement and awe one might feel on glimpsing a rare or mythical creature. Suddenly the woman looked up and stared straight at him. Her powder-blue eyes were so bright and intense they pierced the rising smoke. He was stunned into silence by her bewitching face. Without cosmetics, hairstyling or Photoshop to enhance her features, she was the most beautiful woman he had ever seen. He knew true love couldn't arise instantaneously but his fluttering heart told him otherwise.

Finally he found his voice. "I… I'm sorry," he stammered, "I didn't know there was anyone in here… I was just trying to shelter from the rain."

Her eyes sparkled as they reflected the flames and a slight smile brightened her face, crinkling the corners of her eyes. "You are welcome here."

Her voice was warm and rich and soft. "Please take a seat and I'll make some tea." She indicated a low stool and hung a blackened kettle on a tripod over the fire.

Watching her elegant movements Hugo sat transfixed, but still trembled with a mixture of uneasiness and elation. Even so, he took a deep breath and forced himself to make an attempt at some sort of conversation.

"How long have you lived here?" In his own head Hugo's voice sounded weak and pathetic.

He cringed inwardly.

For a few moments she looked up at the roof of the cave as if counting and then looked back at him with an ironic smile. "Longer than I can remember."

"You don't look that old."

She blushed slightly. "Thank you."

The noise of the wind outside intensified as the weather built towards a storm. The rainwater pouring down the smoke hole overflowed the pool through a narrow channel before disappearing into a crack in the floor of the cave.

"Do you live here alone?" Hugo asked. "How do you manage? Where do you get your food?"

The woman crumbled some dried leaves into an ancient teapot, poured on the steaming water and sat back on her bed. "Yes, I live here alone and I manage tolerably well. It's a simple life, but it suits my temperament. Nature provides me with most of my needs, and from time to time a villager leaves me a basket of food..." She paused, but Hugo could tell she had more to say. "I have to admit there are occasions when I *do* get lonely, especially at night." She looked at him strangely as she said this. Was she inviting him to stay? Or was that just his own wishful thinking?

"So why do you stay here, away from everyone else? Why not move into the village?"

She didn't answer straight away but stared into the fire thoughtfully. She moved to kneel by the hearth, poured the stewed tea into earthenware mugs and handed one to Hugo without meeting his gaze. She returned to her seat, took a sip of her drink and then finally looked up, her eyes tinged with sadness. "I used to live in the village, long ago, and I was happy...but things changed and I was no longer...appreciated. Then the locals drove me away."

"Whatever for? Why would anyone drive you away?" Hugo frowned. He couldn't imagine any reason why this beautiful woman would be unwelcome anywhere.

For a moment she looked troubled and slowly hung her head so her hair fell in front of her face like curtains drawn against the storm. She sighed. "Please don't make me talk about it." Looking up again her face brightened as she casually flicked her hair back from her forehead.

"Let's change the subject. Tell me about yourself."

So Hugo told her about his grandmother and how he came to be in the village. He spoke of his life in the city and his dissatisfaction with it. They talked about nature, the plants and animals found in this beautiful landscape and how the wilderness made them both feel so alive. They shared their passion and wonder for all living things and the time passed quickly by. Before he knew it, Hugo realized the storm had abated and it was beginning to get gloomy outside.

"I had better get back before it's too dark to find my way home."

"Don't go," she said. "Tomorrow evening brings the new moon, but tonight will be the darkest. Please stay and warm my bed."


In the morning Hugo woke with the smell of her hair and her skin, and felt the warmth of her body next to his. A beam of sunlight shone through the smoke hole and illuminated her face, giving it an otherworldly glow. She opened her eyes and looked into his. Their vibrancy swelled his heart. She moved closer and kissed him tenderly on the lips. He realized that for the first time in many years, he was happy. However, he had to go back to the house to continue sorting his grandmother's possessions or the task would never end.

"Come back with me," he urged. "I'd love to have your company. It will make the work so much more enjoyable."

She bit her lip and frowned. "I can't return to the village. I would not be welcome."

"I say sod the villagers. I don't care what they think. What could they do anyway? You'd be with me."

104

She sighed and looked away. "I can't explain... it's complicated."

He asked for her number, but she laughed. She had no use for a telephone. Holding his hands in hers, she made him promise to return that evening before sunset.

And so he did. It was a bright clear night, and they went out into the starlight to see the thin shim of moon as it sank towards the purple ocean.

"Take your shoes and socks off," she said.

She was already barefoot, so he did as she suggested. He hadn't realized his feet felt confined until they were free. He marvelled at the texture of the grass on his naked soles: soft and springy, damp and cool. It was invigorating.

"Have you read any Kahlil Gibran?" asked Hugo. "My grandmother used to quote him all the time. I stayed with her a lot when I was a boy. I remember one quote in particular. *Forget not that the earth delights to feel your bare feet and the winds long to play with your hair.*"

She giggled and said, "That is beautiful and so true. Tell me more."


He returned to see the woman in the cave every night for the next two weeks, forgetting about the pub and the locals and their insignificant banter. The relationship between them deepened to such an extent that he realized the love he'd felt when first laying eyes on her was now beyond any doubt. Anticipating a comfortable inheritance from his grandmother, he decided he need not go back to live in London. He had found love and happiness here. Regrettably, this required returning to the city in order to wind up his job and his tenancy and to collect his few possessions from his flat.

105

On their last night together before he left, everything was perfect. The moon was full and bright, creating a magical atmosphere and adding an extra intensity to their love. Endowed with a heightened awareness, it became a transcendent, almost mystical experience.

In the morning Hugo gave her his most cherished possession, the gold fob watch his great-grandfather had bequeathed to him as a boy. "This is to show how much I adore you and to prove I'll be back as soon as I can."

She took the watch and stroked it reverentially, her eyes wide with wonder. "Thank you. It is beautiful and I will treasure it always." Her voice was husky with emotion. She looked up at him, tears trickling slowly down her face. "And thank you for completing me."


When he returned, just over a week later, he rushed across the hillside to see the woman in the cave. Entering her home, he first noticed the fire was not alight, the hearth empty but for a few cold ashes. He looked around and saw the remains of her possessions scattered and broken, seemingly covered with the dust of abandoned years. He searched frantically for any sign she might have left for him, any indication of recent occupation, but he found none. He didn't understand. What could have happened to her? She wouldn't have left, knowing he was returning so soon. Was it possible she had been kidnapped? Why would her abductors do this to her home and her belongings? Confused and distraught, he ran back to the village and burst into the pub. The usual crew of half-a-dozen regulars turned their heads, surprised both by his dishevelled looks and at his sudden reappearance after three weeks absence.

"Where is she?" he blurted, looking rapidly from one bemused face to the next.

"Who?" said two or three people simultaneously.

"The woman in the cave!"

The others glanced at each other warily and then back to Hugo. There was an awkward silence as each person waited for another to speak. Then, someone in a dark corner cleared his throat.

"You'd better come here and sit down lad." Old Joe Evans indicated a seat next to him at the table. His voice was gravelly and hoarse but loud enough to carry across the room. "Davie! Bring the boy a pint. He's going to need it." It was the first time Hugo had heard the man speak. He sat opposite him and the landlord brought his beer.

Evans gazed into the distance with his grey, rheumy eyes. "I'll tell you a tale of long ago, when I was just a boy..." The haze of pipe smoke seemed to emulate the obscurity of distant years.

"I don't want to hear about that," said Hugo. "I want you to tell me where I can find the woman from the cave!"

"That's what I'm doing lad, that's what I'm doing." Old Joe's voice remained calm and kind. He gestured with his hands for every word he spoke as if to emphasise their importance. "It's just not as simple as you think. Now just sup your ale and listen to me."

"In those far off days there was a young and attractive herbalist living in the village. Her good looks got her a lot of attention from the menfolk – even the married ones used to turn their heads, she was that pretty. If it weren't for her remedies, she might've been spurned by the other women, jealous of her beauty. But her treatments were popular with most folk, and she was often consulted for help with minor ailments... until the new preacher came along." The old man shook his head sadly and sucked on his pipe again, but it had gone out. He picked up his box of matches and relit it. "He'd only been in the manse a few weeks before he began warning folk that her practices were evil and she relied on *the devil's magic*. See, the respect for the power of the church and its official earthly representatives was well and truly established in the community back then. Soon the bugger managed to generate fear in the hearts of enough villagers that they became convinced of the truth of his words and they rallied round to help him drive the herbalist from the village. She went to live in a cave up on the slopes above the cliffs..." Evans pointed over Hugo's head with his pipe stem in the direction of the hill, "...and for a while, those who still valued her services would go up and visit, giving her food or other necessaries in exchange. However, it soon became apparent that she was with child, and there was much speculation as to who the father might be. Some imagined it was the simple lad who used to help in her garden; others thought it could be the woodsman who was often seen to visit; the priest proclaimed that it must have been spawned by Satan... yet many folk believed it was the preacher himself, and this would explain why he felt compelled to drive her away, projecting upon her his own guilt and shame. No one ever discovered the truth though because the poor thing died soon after giving birth. The baby was sent off to the city to be adopted by strangers and was never heard of again." He looked down at the table, then knocked his pipe out in the pub's only ashtray and began packing it with fresh tobacco.

"But I don't see what that's got to do with what's happening now," Hugo said, throwing up his hands, "or the woman I've been seeing."

Old Joe Evans relit his pipe, sucked on the stem a few times and then sighed. He took a swig of his beer, turned to Hugo, and looked him straight in the eyes. "After the woman died there were... stories. Rumours that her spirit remained to haunt the cave. Some said that all she longed for was a man to fall properly in love with her before she could be at peace. The dread of the supernatural was so great at the time, no one would venture near the place for fear of becoming enchanted. However, although I was just a young whippersnapper, my mother had taught me not to believe in such things, so one day I decided to go up to the cave and have a look for myself. When I got up there I crept inside. I felt suddenly and unaccountably afraid. I tiptoed along the tunnel and in the chamber at the end... there she was! The herbalist woman looking just like she had in real life – but I knew she'd been dead for years. Well, I screamed and turned and ran as fast as my little legs would carry me and I never went back there again."

Hugo raised his eyebrows and shook his head, forcing himself to smile. "You're just winding me up! You don't seriously expect me to believe I've been having a relationship with a ghost? I mean... she was real... and solid... with sweet breath and soft flesh and warm skin..."

Old Joe Evans took another draw on his pipe. Clouds of smoke hung about his face as if he was an apparition emerging from the mist. "Did this woman have long wavy hair as bright as a robin's breast?"

"Well...yes," said Hugo.

"And did she have skin as smooth and as pale as marble?" asked Joe.

Hugo nodded, frowning.

"And were her lips the colour of fuchsia blossoms?"

"Yes but..."

"And was she was wearing a thin white gown finely embroidered with gold thread?"

Hugo wondered how Evans could have guessed all of these things. His rational mind could not accept the suggestion that ghosts existed, let alone that he'd had one as a lover. Perhaps the whole thing was some weird and cruel conspiracy against a resented incomer from the city, but he couldn't believe his sweetheart would have been party to that. He walked out of the pub and went home, his mind in turmoil and his heart aching with loss. That night he dreamt of the cold, empty cave echoing with her last words to him: *And thank you for completing me.* What could she have meant by that?

He returned to the cave every day for the next week in the forlorn hope that the woman would miraculously return in the same way she had disappeared. He tried to convince himself she must have been called away on some urgent matter and before long she would return. However, the presence of the disorderly jumble of broken, dusty remnants in her home made this almost impossible. He sunk into depression, with bouts of insomnia interspersed with vivid dreams. Sometimes it would be exactly like their happiest times together, but in others, halfway through making love, her flesh would crumble into powder and blow away, leaving her bone-white skeleton beneath him, the empty skull with cave-like eye sockets and a ghastly, lipless grin.

One day a letter arrived from his grandmother's solicitor informing him that her estate was finally settled and all her affairs were now in order. It seemed as if the old lady went on a bit of a spending spree in her final years because her bank account was inexplicably empty, but in addition to the usual bundle of necessary paperwork, the envelope also contained the combination to the safe in her study. Hugo had expected her financial legacy to see him through to his next period of employment. Now he had to hope the safe would contain a hoard of cash and jewellery, otherwise he might have to beg for his old job back, and that was a prospect he did not relish on top of everything else he was feeling. Heart-broken and emotionally fragile, he began to doubt his own sanity. Nonetheless he went into the study to try to open the safe. Consulting the note from the solicitor he turned the dial in the correct sequence to the numbers given. He pressed down on the handle. It was stiff and made a worrying, grinding noise, as if important components were disintegrating under the pressure, but he managed to push it all the way. The hinges gave a grating screech as he pulled open the door.

To his surprise, all he could see inside was a sealed envelope and a small, locked wooden box. He opened the envelope and found a tiny brass key with a letter that said:

*My dear Hugo,*

*You were never told, but when I was a baby I was adopted. Although I never knew who my parents were, I was informed that they came from this village and that is the reason why I decided to retire here. I only had one thing that belonged to my mother. Apparently just before she died, she said it had been given to her by my father and so, as my only descendant, I am now leaving it to you.*

*All my love Grandma x*

Hands shaking, Hugo took the small brass key and unlocked the box. He slowly lifted the lid and saw, nestled in the velvet lining, the golden fob watch he had given to the woman in the cave.

Geoff lives in the north of Scotland with his wife, cats and chickens on the organic woodland small-holding they have created over the last 23 years. He designs and makes hand carved wooden jewellery, which he sells on line and at craft fairs, trading as Woodland Treasures.

Geoff also loves to write whenever he can make time. His self-published first novel, *Echoes of the Ancestors*, was the Press and Journal's book of the week in 2014, and his second novel, a futuristic thriller, will be available sometime in 2019.

Connect with Geoff on Facebook:

https://www.facebook.com/Geoff.F.King/

# Rabbit Hole Poems

by Kelsey Dean


## What the Hare Said

The March Hare asked me

why a raven was like a writing desk.

"They both have puppy dog tails?" I answered.

"No, that's what little boys are made of!" he yelled,

"and you are no boy, you are bleeding!"

and I was – I could see it dripping down my legs but

it was all rainbow-colored and I laughed.

"Twinkle twinkle," said the dormouse

and I told him he was right, because the moon

was glowing orange in my teacup.

I fished it out and ate it like a wafer

and the March Hare leapt upon the table

and twinkled sparks from angry eyes – he yelled,

"Alice never ate the moon! She would never!"

so I told him, "I am not Alice."

"How I wonder who you are," said the dormouse.

"Me too," I laughed, as the moon slid down my throat

and the rainbows fell from between my legs.

## The Third Conversation

"Who are you?" asks the caterpillar, and I try to say my name. The A won't come out and it blocks up all the other letters and I choke. "Who are you?" he says, and he is angry and he has purple lips that shake. I forget, my name isn't Alice – Alice was a spiteful lady who liked to gossip with schoolgirls and hated foreigners. She had salty french fry fingers and she cared about what color the sequins on our swimsuits were and she grew icicles in her eyebrows when we were late. Then I remember that the rabbit wasn't white, it was black and it died when I was nine and all it left behind was a skeleton and a Hawaiian name. There was a funeral and we drank tea with lots of sugar that made my mouth feel dry; I think there are flowers growing out of its bones now, but my name doesn't start with A so they don't sing when I walk by them. I broke my watch when I dived into the ocean – I couldn't stand for my skin to be crawling with air for another second and the water all around me tasted like tears, maybe Alice's. The cat that lives under my bed disappears sometimes but it never smiles and it never cries like Alice or me over dead rabbits. There are bird feathers nesting in a disorderly pile because the cat only eats the fleshy bits, and the queen doesn't need those little songbirds for her games. But the caterpillar is spewing smoke at me and he will eat me up like the cat and I will become a pile of songbird feathers under the bed if I don't answer him.

"Not Alice," I tell the caterpillar.

## Tea Party

The sugar cubes cascaded down the tablecloth,

And "One lump or two?" asked the hatter –

but actually there were three

that lived and lumbered in the tissue.

"The doctors took them out with knives

and fixed her with needles" I said.

"And there were tubes and tests tangled in her breasts."

"How curious!" replied the hare.

I nodded and stacked the cubes neatly in my mouth

while the sparrows nested in my hair;

we sipped and slurped

and the violets twinkled at our toes.

"Another cup?" asked the hatter,

but it was quite the opposite, and I told him:

"No, a less cup actually, or two."

"Curiouser and curiouser!" sang the hare.

Kelsey Dean is a teacher, artist, writer, and ice cream aficionado. She often dreamed of Wonderland as a child and has been experimenting with words and colors ever since. Her artwork and poetry can be found in numerous journals and anthologies, including *Cicada*, *Liminal Stories, Arsenic Lobster*, and *Eclectically Heroic*, among others.

*The Third Conversation* and *Tea Party* were originally published in *The Rain, Party and Disaster Society* magazine.

# Quicksilver Falls

by Daniel Link

Day 1

"I think it's mercury," the gap-toothed man said, rolling the liquid around in his hand for the camera. "Look."

The reporter winced as the two balls of silver-blue metal flowed around the grease-stained palm. They came together in the middle to form one oblong blob, then split apart again as he moved, continuing their dance.

"Mercury is dangerous, you know." Even though he wore a hazmat suit, the reporter took an involuntary step back. The camera zoomed tighter on the hairy man in the sleeveless flannel shirt. "It's poisonous."

"It's not that bad." When he smiled, he revealed a second missing tooth. "Looked it up on the Net. It's the vapor you got to worry about."

The reporter shrugged and faced the camera. "I'm standing here with Mr. Wilfred Scupps, corn grower and owner of the farm you see behind me." He waited while the camera panned across the emerald field. "Today, on this farm, something amazing and unexplained has occurred. Could you tell our viewers what happened, Mr. Scupps?"

"You bet your ass I can. About two o'clock this afternoon, this mercury started falling from the sky. It came down like rain out of the clear blue. Lasted about twenty minutes, then it stopped."

"You say there were no clouds?"

The camera panned up to show a bright, clear day.

"That's what I'm telling you." Scupps put both hands up to the

117

heavens. "Looked just like this, then all the sudden it's raining mercury."

"The incident seems to have been isolated to a relatively small area," the reporter told the camera, "falling solely on a couple hundred acres belonging to Scupps. Samples of the strange liquid have been gathered and sent to a nearby military facility for research."

"Those Army boys tried taking it all, but there was way too much." He laughed, then snorted. "Hell, it's hard scooping this stuff up. It rolls all over and tries to get away from you. My wife, Laverne, she's a smart one, though. Put out buckets and Mason jars. We got lots left."

"Our meteorologist, Kurt Billings, has no explanation for the phenomenon. There is no record of a liquid metallic rain, and even acid rain has never, as far as he knows, fallen from a cloudless sky. Whatever happened here in the valley this afternoon seems to be a first." He turned back to Scupps with the microphone. "Mr. Scupps, what do you make of all this?"

"How the hell am I supposed to know?" He took off his baseball cap to scratch at his greasy brown hair. "All I can say is this is the most interesting thing happened round here in a dog's age." He giggled as he let the two fat drops of silver-blue run down his arm, then snatched them up again in his hand.


Day 9

"Mr. Scupps." It was a different reporter, the familiar CNN in red on his microphone. He wore khakis, dress shirt, and tie. "Could you take us on a tour of your farm, tell us what's transpired here in the last few days?"

"Sure." Scupps hooked a finger. "Come along, I'll show you."

The cornfield that had been seen all across the world for over a week came into view. The corn was taller, the stalks standing over eight feet off the ground. When the reporter reached the end of the path, he was dwarfed by a wall of green that spread over two hundred yards wide.

"Look at these babies." Scupps pulled on a stalk, bending it at the middle to lower the top toward the reporter. "You ever see an ear of corn like that?"

He held up an arm for comparison, the cob longer than his forearm.

"Frankly, it's amazing."

"And they ain't even full grown yet."

"How much bigger will they get?"

"Not too much, I reckon."

"Is it true, Mr. Scupps, that the government has come in and seized some corn for inspection?"

"They didn't need to seize it. I told them to take some. They wanted to go digging in the ground, too. I told them go ahead, as long as they don't disturb Laverne's rosebushes."

"What was the reason for taking the samples?"

He puffed up and put on a haughty air. "They was looking for biological contaminants, they called it. But that's just the official story. Me and Laverne ain't stupid."

"What's the real story, then?"

The camera moved in tight on Scupps, who was chewing a piece of straw. "They think it's aliens."

"What makes you say that?"

He laughed and slapped his belly. "Come on, man. You seen all them soldiers in them yellow suits. Why else would they be wearing them if they didn't think it's aliens?"

119

"The quicksilver could be toxic," the reporter tried.

"Toxic, my ass." He pulled out a Tic Tac container, showed it to the camera. Instead of the little candies, it was half full of the shiny bluish metal. He popped open the top and poured it into his hand. "I've had this stuff all over me, put my arms in buckets up to my elbow. Hell, it got in my eyes and ears when it was falling from the sky. I stood there and stared up at it as it came down, probably drank a drop or two. Laverne, too."

Scupps motioned for his wife to come. "Get over here, Laverne. Show 'em how healthy you are."

She moved in tiny steps, coming into the shot a few inches at a time. She was a big woman, wearing a drab tan muumuu and a green Fitbit wristband. When the camera zoomed, she seemed to sense it, turning her head down and to the side.

"Mrs. Scupps." The reporter tried to use the mic to pry her face away from her shoulder, the CNN logo actually touching her dress, lifting the ruffles around the neck. "How much contact have you had with the quicksilver that fell here at the farm?"

"I dunno." She turned to the camera, smiled, then tucked her chin back to her chest. "It's gotten into everything. I was in the garden with my roses when it happened."

"And how are you feeling?"

"Fine."

"Do you think it was aliens that sent the quicksilver, Mrs. Scupps?"

"I dunno."

The camera tightened in on the reporter. "Scientists' initial reports are vague, but it's clear that what fell from the sky nine days ago was not mercury. There's no sign that it's radioactive, and the tests have given no clues as to its origins. All the government's spokespeople are willing to say at this point is that it is a material

120

that is unknown here on Earth. Was it something sent from an alien intelligence, or an extraterrestrial element that just happened to collide with our planet? It's too soon to tell, but all eyes will be on Plunkett Indiana as we try to figure it out."


Day 33

"Are you saying you've eaten the corn?" the CNN reporter asked.

"Course I ate it," Scupps said, scratching at his nose with his index finger. "What do you think we grow it for?"

"But surely you've been warned of the health risks?"

"Yeah, yeah. Those scientists have been studying it for a month now. You know what they've figured out? Not a damn thing. Well I can tell them something. This here's the best tasting corn I've ever grown. Once people get a taste of this alien corn, they ain't ever going to want to go back."

"You can't possibly be thinking of feeding your corn to the public. Until the proper tests have been run–"

"The proper tests have been run. Just look at me." The camera moved in on Scupps, focusing on his missing tooth. He pointed to his wife. "Look at Laverne. There's not a damn thing wrong with us."

"It's only been a few weeks. It could be years before the true effects are known."

"Well, I'll tell you something. I feel like a million bucks." He flexed for the camera, his sleeveless flannel showing off the pale undersides of his chubby arms. "Matter of fact, I feel like I did when I was young. Strong as an ox, and…" He lowered his voice and raised his eyebrows. "Horny as a toad, if you get my drift. Ain't that right, Laverne?"

The camera panned to his wife, a hand over her mouth, her cheeks flushed. She nodded.

Day 44

"A man whose farm borders yours claims to have dug up an earthworm over three feet long. What do you make of that?"

Scupps gave a sly smile to the camera. "Probably a fisherman. They think everything's bigger than it really is."

Day 51

"Look at this," Scupps motioned for the camera to come closer. He took off his sweat-stained ball cap and pointed to his hairline. "Look here. Before the alien rains came, I was ready for the Hair Club for Men. Now look at these lovely locks." He raked his fingers through his matted brown curls, then held one out for display. "You can't get hair like this from no bottle."

"You attribute this to the quicksilver?" the reporter said.

"What else could it be? You know of anything that makes a forty year-old grow his hair back?"

"You called it the alien rain. Does that mean you're still of the belief that an intelligent species sent this to you?"

"What else could it be?" He grabbed one of his giant corn stalks and gave it a shake. "It's the only thing that makes sense. This ain't random."

"What do you mean by that?"

Scupps barked his now familiar laugh-snort. "What do you think makes more sense? That a batch of weird space shit hits my farm and makes the best corn a man ever ate on accident? That it

122

can grow hair and make you feel like a sexual dynamo by accident? No way, no how. This was part of some kind of cosmic plan."

The reporter's eyebrows knitted together. "You mean God?"

"Well, now that you mention it, maybe there is a divine hand at work here." He scratched the stubble on his chin. "I suppose if you want to say it was God's rain and not alien rain, that would make sense."

"Mr. Scupps, I wasn't proposing–"

"Matter of fact, the way my corn tastes, it would stand to reason that God himself had blessed it. And this power of regeneration, and the benefits to a man lying with his woman…You may have hit on something there. This could be a sign from God. My little corner of Indiana sure has been turned into a slice of Paradise."

The reporter looked flustered, his hand twisting the microphone as Scupps spoke.

"You know, the more people try this corn, the more they're going to see it for the miracle it is."

"You've been ordered to stop giving out the corn to your neighbors, Mr. Scupps. Are you saying you've defied that order?"

"What's mine is mine," Scupps said, then spit through the gap in his teeth. "To tell me I can't do what I want with my own crops is a violation of my rights. I haven't even started selling it yet. I've just given out a few ears to some people who are interested in the benefits."

"You run the risk of the military coming in here and seizing your entire farm."

"Not with you reporters around. That would be unconstitutional." He held up his Tic Tac container for the camera, shook its contents. "They've got their samples, and they can't find a scrap of evidence that says this magic liquid is harmful in any way."

"Is it true that a number of organizations, including major pharmaceutical companies, are interested in obtaining samples of your quicksilver?"

"Sure as shit. Can you blame them? Everybody's going to want in on this. It's too bad there's not enough to give out to the whole world."

"If this turns out to be the miracle you're assuming it is, you would be willing to share it with the world?"

"Willing?" Scupps shook his head. "I'd be obligated to share it. This miracle may have been sent to me but it could help a whole lot of people. It would be a sin to keep that to myself."

The reporter's voice lowered, becoming grave. "As you yourself have stated, there is a limited supply. How would you choose who would get some and who would be left out?"

"I'm glad you brought that up. You see, I've decided to do a little auction." A hard zoom on the Tic Tac container, held between thumb and forefinger. "Starting with this right here."

The reporter's mouth formed an O, his eyebrows shooting up. "You mean to sell it to the highest bidder?"

"This here ain't about money. What I'm holding here in my hand is going to change the world. The government's already got their piece. Now I want to give someone else a chance to see what they can do with it. If they've got what it takes to study it, reproduce it, and make the best use of it, I want to hear about it. I'll give you a month to come up with an offer, and I'll pick the best one."

"You do realize the government will–"

"I realize that this is my chance to do what I can for humanity," Scupps said, then held up the candy box for emphasis. "It's the least I can do."

"Well, I'm sure you'll be getting some proposals from all over the world." He turned to face the camera. "This has to be history's biggest writing contest, and this man is the judge. Wilfred Scupps is looking to share his miracle with you."

Scupps shoved his way back into the shot, craning his neck to put his face next to the reporter's. "Oh, and keep it short. No more than a page. Laverne's little cousin Delia loves to read to us over dinner, but her folks want her in bed by nine, so don't go writing a damn novel."

The reporter shook his head. "One month, one page, one vial of quicksilver. You'd better get started."

Day 83

The little girl cleared her throat as she approached the mic. She was tall and birdlike, all arms and legs. The frilly dress she wore was dotted with strawberries, and a red bow was tied across her middle.

"What I Would Do With Your Magic Rain," she read in a timid voice. "By Anthony Boudreaux from Lubbock, Texas."

The sound guy rushed over and adjusted the microphone, trying to hide behind the podium as he worked. He dropped to his belly and army-crawled out of the shot. Delia tapped the black felt with a finger and started over.

*What I Would Do With Your Magic Rain*, by Anthony Boudreaux from Lubbock, Texas.

*Dear Mr. Scupps, I am writing this in the most sincere hopes that you will let me have some of your magic rain. It is a gift from God, and you said you want to share it with the most deserving person. I don't think I'm the most deserving, and I don't even think it should go to a person. If I had some of your magic rain, I would give it to my dog Judge, who is an eleven-year-old Lab. He's been*

125

*with me since I was three, and he's my best friend. He has a lump on his skin near his front leg and the doctor says it's cancer. He sometimes poops blood, too. They want me to put Judge down. I don't want him to die. I think your magic rain could save Judge, and I hope you can give me some so I don't have to lose my best friend. Please consider this and say yes, you'll give me the magic rain. Thank you.*

*Sincerely,*

*Anthony Boudreaux*


Delia stepped back from the podium and smiled. She set the papers down and folded her hands in front of her. There were no sounds from the audience of reporters gathered in front of her. Wilfred Scupps nudged her aside and pulled the mic up closer to his mouth. He was dressed for the occasion, a tweed sport coat over his flannel shirt, and no hat. His hair was unruly and much thicker than it had been two months before.

"Now I can't tell you how much this poor boy's story touched me. When Delia read that to me, Laverne and I started to cry. Can you imagine that little boy and his dog, and him willing to do anything to save him? We read over some of the others, but that one really stuck with me. How could I say no to that?"

Another long moment of silence before a female reporter found her voice. "Mr. Scupps, are you aware of how many entries came in response to your call?"

"There were a lot, I'll tell you what."

"According to our sources," she said, "there were close to fifty million."

"Wow." Scupps scratched his ear. "That many?"

"How many of the letters did you read, Mr. Scupps?"

126

"Well, we're very proud of Delia. She's reading ahead of her grade level. But there was no way she was going to get through them all."

"Are you saying your niece was the only one who read any of the letters?" A man from CNBC asked.

"She's my wife's cousin, actually, twice removed. She lives with my sister ever since her daddy had a little accident and had to go away for a spell, but we all love her like she's our own."

The reporter let out a sigh. "What I'm asking you is how many of these letters did you get through, and are you really considering giving this quicksilver to a Labrador?"

"I'd appreciate it if you'd ask your questions one at a time. But in answer to the first, we got through a lot of letters, but you heard it yourself. After little Anthony's letter, there was no need to read any further." He reached into his pocket for the world's most famous Tic Tac container. "And for your second question, hell yes I'm going to give Judge my little gift. In fact, I called up Anthony a couple weeks ago and told him and Judge to be here today."

A low murmur started among the reporters, and it soon turned into a rumble as the nervous chatter increased in pitch and intensity. Cameras panned in a shaky search for the boy and his dog. They entered from stage left, Anthony pulling the dog by a yellow nylon rope. He was a chubby kid wearing corduroys and a brown-and-green striped t-shirt. He wore braces, which reflected the flashing lights as he waved to the crowd of reporters like a Miss America contestant.

Judge looked every bit of his eleven years, his once-brown face gone mostly white, his step the slow shuffle of an older dog. Aside from that, he seemed fine. His tail wagged in time with his steps.

The CNN reporter that had first been given the story took the stage beside the boy. He couldn't suppress a bemused grin as he spoke. "You're about to witness history. Here we have perhaps the strangest and most unorthodox clinical trial in human history. I don't know how many animal testing laws this is violating, but here we go."

Without fanfare, Scupps emptied his container into a metal bowl. An overhead camera caught the bluish silver drops flowing around the stainless steel and converging on a ball of ground beef at the bottom. Scupps held a fork at the ready, but set it aside when the quicksilver went into the wad of meat and disappeared.

"Here you go, Anthony," Scupps said, handing the bowl to the boy. "Why don't you give it to him?"

The kid milked the moment, keeping the dish out of the dog's reach and staring open-mouthed into the cameras and flashbulbs. When he put it down in front of Judge, the dog ate it in two large bites. Anthony's shoulder slumped and he stopped smiling, and the room was so quiet the dog's breathing was picked up by the boom mics.

The silence went on for two minutes, until Judge lay down and flopped over on his side. A collective gasp came over the watchers. Then Judge wagged his tail.

"Well," the CNN correspondent said, "it looks like he liked it. And now the eyes of the world are going to be on this lucky Labrador Retriever."

Day 161

"It's been seventy-eight days since Wilfred Scupps gave his quicksilver to Judge, and from all reports, this miracle rain – as many have dubbed it – is living up to the billing."

The camera panned back to take in a throng of people, thousands crammed into a tiny dirt patch. Cars were parked on one side of the road from horizon to horizon. On the other side were hundreds of jeeps, Humvees and transport trucks. A line of National

Guardsmen stood in the middle of the road, armed with rifles and wearing riot gear.

"As you can see, people have gotten miracle fever. Folks from all across the world have come to Indiana in hopes to get a glimpse of what's happening here."

Most of them were waving to the camera, and many were holding signs. *Scupps for President, Share the Miracle, Let it Rain.* A quick pan across the street showed another group, another kind of sign. *It's Not Right, Rain of Terror, Scupps Must Die.*

"People obviously have different views of what's going on in this cornfield, but one thing is impossible to deny, and that's what has happened to the world's favorite Labrador." A small box appeared in the corner showing a video of a dog running in circles in a patchy yard festooned with crabgrass. He bounced and played with the energy of a puppy, and the white hair on his face was gone. His chocolate coat was shiny and thick. "He's been watched every day, and from the look of things, he's as healthy now at eleven as he was at two."

Anthony got a close-up, his metallic smile on full blast. "He don't poop blood anymore."

"But this raises the question," the reporter said. "What is Scupps going to do next? The world is lining up for a sample of this miracle elixir, and the government claims they've made no progress in reproducing it. And as it stands now, they refuse to let Scupps give any more of his quicksilver or his corn to the people who have gathered here. While there are skeptics out there who believe high-ups in government are keeping the secret for themselves, everyone is in agreement that Wilfred Scupps may hold the keys to the future of humanity."


Day 222

"Reports of giant locusts, and of rats that are impervious to

129

poison keep coming out of this small county in Indiana. Some say it's a rumor spread by miracle rain naysayers, others believe they are the beginning of a plague that could end the world."

Day 383

"Despite the fact that it's been over a year since the miracle rain fell, the latest crop of corn from the Scupps farm is just as big and plentiful as the first. Scupps has given buckets of the soil to other local farmers, ranchers, and to Weeks Roses, Laverne Scupps favorite supplier of fine roses. He continues to give the corn to his neighbors, despite warnings by the government to cease and desist. Not one of his neighbors who admit to trying the corn have taken ill since. And just look for yourself at Wilfred Scupps." They showed a before-and-after photo comparison of Scupps: the first showed patchy, lank hair flecked with gray, wan skin, and a missing front tooth; the second showed a full head of shiny brown hair, an unlined face with a healthy glow, and the beginnings of a tooth starting to grow in.

Day 515

"I'm not waiting any longer," Scupps said. He pointed an accusing finger at the camera. "It is not right to try and stop me from sharing what's mine. This stuff is harmless. Sure, maybe we got some nasty crows flying around that you can't kill, and some raccoons may have figured out how to steal a tractor, but I'm not sweating the small stuff. It's a miracle, and I'm not going to let Uncle Sam tell me what's right."

"So what do you propose, Mr. Scupps?" the reporter asked.

"All of these people didn't come out here for nothing. So we're going to give them something to remember."

"Any hints?"

"You're just going to have to wait." Scupps smiled, his tongue flitting over the new incisor. "But you won't have to wait long. At five o'clock tomorrow afternoon, we're going to make history."


Day 516

"The National Guard is on high alert. An additional three thousand troops were brought in overnight in anticipation of today's events. The whole world is on tenterhooks as we wait to see what Wilfred Scupps has planned."

A countdown clock was placed behind the reporter, the eight-foot red digital numbers ticking down toward zero. When they reached five minutes, the once-raucous throng calmed and stood silent in nervous anticipation. Large Jumbotron monitors had been placed along the line that marked the first row of miracle corn, broadcasting the countdown and the empty podium at center stage.

When the one-minute mark arrived, people counted along, the chant louder than any New Year at Times Square. When their voices faded away, a commotion could be heard in the cornfield.

"Here they come," someone shouted.

First the corn parted, then the crowd, as Scupps trotted from his field to the stage. He took to the podium like a politician at a rally, waving to everyone and smiling. The reporter from CNN was waiting for him.

"Well, Mr. Scupps, everyone here is dying to see what you've got in store for us."

"My friends, my countrymen, my fellow Americans," Scupps held his hands out to the gathered crowd. "It has been almost a year and a half since God sent this gift to me. I know the U.S. government doesn't want me to, but today, I'm going to share that gift with all of you."

A cheer erupted from the onlookers, followed by a thunderous

131

applause. Shouts started to spring up among those in the front with the best view.

"What is that?"

"Look. Over there."

"Holy shit. It's a balloon."

Fifty feet behind the massive wall of corn, the top of a hot air balloon began growing, the globe rounding out as the liquid propane burned. The reporter had to position himself in front of it to get into the shot.

"Behind me you can see what has to be one of the biggest hot air balloons ever made. It's enormous. It looks patched together like a quilt, no rhyme or reason to the design. Now Scupps is going to the balloon. Look," the reporter's face lit up and he ran along with thousands of others, jockeying to get as close to Scupps as possible. "It's Judge. He's taking Judge onto the balloon. And there's Laverne and Delia in the basket. They're all getting on board the balloon. It's like a scene straight out of the Wizard of Oz."

Indeed, Scupps, his wife, cousin, and Anthony Boudreaux's dog all boarded the balloon. A man with a megaphone could be heard yelling warnings, but Scupps threw sandbags over the side and men on the ground untied ropes fastened to stakes. The balloon started to rise.

"This is my gift to you," Scupps shouted, then threw an ear of corn over the side. "My farm, and everything on it, I leave it to everyone gathered here. It is no longer the Scupps farm. From this day on, this land is Quicksilver Falls, Tennessee."

"Mr. Scupps, this is the National Guard. We will shoot down your balloon if you do not land immediately."

Scupps ignored the man with the megaphone, and hoisted a large potato gun on his shoulder. He began launching giant ears of corn into the crowd, which either hit the ground or smacked into onlookers with a wet thud. People wrestled for the corn and dove after those which were still falling. Delia and Laverne started tossing ears, as well.

When all the ears were gone, Scupps turned to his last gift. From two large metal buckets, he scooped dried corn kernels a handful at a time and sprinkled them out over the clearing. People scrambled on hands and knees, either stuffing the kernels in their pockets or swallowing them on the spot. The man with the megaphone continued to yell, but when the thousands of people entered the cornfield and started tearing the ears from the stalks, he threw up his hands in defeat.

"This is amazing," the reporter said, inhaling the few kernels he'd managed to pick up off the ground. "Wilfred Scupps really did it. He's defied the government and shared his miracle with all of us. As he promised we've become a part of history here today."

The camera panned up to a cloudless sky to show Scupps, now just a silhouette, still pouring corn out over the field. Delia and Laverne waved, and Judge stood with his forepaws on the edge of the basket, looking down at the ground below. Behind them in the sky, hundreds of giant crows swirled and dipped en masse, moving toward what had been the Scupps farm.

Daniel L Link lives in Northern California where he writes short stories, novels, and flash fiction. He's an assistant editor of the *Gold Man Review*. His work has been featured in *New Reader Magazine*, the *HCE Review*, the *Lowestoft Chronicle*, the *Eastern Iowa Review*, the *Penmen Review*, the *Tulane Review*, the *Soliloquies Anthology*, and others. His website is daniellinkauthor.com, and his Twitter is @DanielLLink

*Quicksilver Falls* was originally published in the first issue of *New Reader Magazine* in February 2018.

# Satori from a Consulting Gig

## by Barry Rosen

Management consultant Frank Dow showed no surprise at the new client's evident desire for a genuine consultation rather than a canned endorsement of plans already made. Though unusual, the client's sincerity was still less surprising than the client's identity. The client was God. Dow listened intently as God began to describe His problem:

"Forget any twaddle you may have heard about omnipotence and omniscience. The universe is too immense and diverse to be micromanaged, even by Me. Roughly speaking, I built a big machine and let it run. But it's not boringly deterministic. The universe is all about probabilities."

As God continued, the proud-parent joy in his voice was clear:

"The probability that a randomly chosen planet will be suitable for life to appear at all is tiny. The probability that creatures with any ability to understand and appreciate the universe will evolve is tinier still, but not exactly zero. On the other hand, there are a lot of planets in the universe. There's no need to crunch the numbers right now. The bottom line is that a few planets luck out. On your little blue planet, life thrived and your species evolved advanced abilities to observe and learn, to imagine and reason, to build bridges and write poems."

With joy replaced by sadness and frustration now, God explained what He hoped Dow could provide:

"While I mostly let things run, I am not absolutely hands-off when a planet has intelligent life that blunders into being cruel or stupid. I nudge them in good directions by inspiring a few of them. In your planet's case, I have had a little success and a lot of failure.

I keep it simple and age-appropriate, but they oversimplify half of what I tell them and obfuscate the rest. The Golden Rule gets through as something to proclaim but not as something to practice. Absurdly, much of what they think has been revealed to them is just their own bigotry and bullshit. The way they distort My message is so alien to the corporate culture here that nobody has a clue about how to handle it. As someone who is closer to the problem without being part of it, you may be able to help us."

Given a temporary office with read access to the case histories (and full access to a plentiful supply of coffee and nutritious snacks), Dow went to work. A recurrent pattern emerged:

Inspirations that did not fizzle attracted disciples, often with authoritarian personalities. Authoritarian disciples misinterpreted God's nudges and stridently claimed they could speak for God on all kinds of topics, now and forever. Many of those who were strident were also willing to coerce people they could not convince. Many of those who were willing to coerce were also willing to kill people they could not coerce.

Poring over the case histories was depressing, but Dow kept at it (with the able assistance of good coffee and good snacks). Eventually, he was ready to offer God a suggestion:

"I believe there is a personnel issue here. You have been inspiring people who mean well but score high on credulity and low on humor. Maybe it would help to go outside the box. For example, You could inspire a nerdy atheist who digs sacred music and pushes the envelope of haiku poetry."

God was skeptical: "Does anybody like that exist?"

Frank Dow smiled the enigmatic Mona Lisa smile that sometimes appeared when he was moonlighting as a Zen master. He leaned forward and spoke softly: "Does anybody like You exist?"

At that moment, God attained enlightenment.

136

Barry Rosen has been a computer scientist, a software engineer, and an Alzheimer's caregiver. He lives in the Hudson valley, tries to age gracefully, and blogs on a wide range of topics with images, poems, and prose. His posts on MellowCurmudgeon.com often try to reveal humor in serious things and serious undercurrents in funny things, without any fixed theme or schedule. Inspiration is capricious.

# The New Neighbors

by Victor Acquista

Stooped forward, he rushed to lace his shoe, straightened, then quickly picked up the pace. Not that he needed to rush; after all, he had all day and then some. But he did want to be the first to know. Hurriedly, he moved down Hickory Lane, quiet and peaceful in the early morning sunlight.

John Henry Roberson was an early riser, had been his whole life. So, it was likely that at this time of day, no one had noticed the car slowly moving down Hickory. John's property had the advantage of being at the front end of the lane. From this prime location, it took just a few minutes to make it to the bottom, to the cul-de-sac where the only remaining vacant land stood empty. He recognized the vehicle out in front as belonging to the developers. Two men spoke quietly between themselves in business-like fashion as they surveyed the land, took some measurements.

"Yup," he nodded to himself, "no doubt about it; we're finally going to get some new neighbors."

Hickory Lane was in an older section of a much, much larger development. John wasn't sure how many plots made up the development. *A few hundred at least, maybe even a few thousand*, he mused. The older streets and lanes were named after trees: Oak, Maple, Pine, Cedar, and so on. Most new residents moved to the newer sections. These had numbers, which made sense to John, since unlike names of trees, numbers never ran out.

Done with his study of the workmen and confident in his conclusion, John made his way back. He would have preferred a location on Hemlock Lane – made him think of Socrates, and, after all, he was a retired Professor of Philosophy. But Hickory suited him just fine; it was picturesque and tranquil. He figured the new

138

folks ought to like it here. Of course, the joke in the development was that all the nuts lived on Hickory. The professor agreed that they were a curious collection.

*It sure would be nice if whoever moved in knew a thing or two about philosophy. I could stand for some late-night conversation about the nature of life, death, metaphysics and epistemology. Ehh, wishful thinking!*

"Good morning, Mary!" A playful twinkle in his eye accompanied the salutation.

Mary Jones lived alone. Technically, with her six cats she had plenty of company. Most, including John, found her to be a bit eccentric. One of the first inhabitants of the lane, she no doubt contributed to its reputation.

"Goood daay, Professsor." She spoke with a cat nestled underneath each arm. A certain mewing quality made her voice distinctive.

"New neighbors coming, Mary."

Her eyes widened, "Oowh, I hope they don't have any dogs!" She drew the two felines close to her breasts. John couldn't be sure, but it looked as though the hair on her head stood up a bit as she abruptly turned around.

A familiar voice greeted him from across the lane. "Hey John, did you catch the game last night?"

"No Jim, I missed it."

"Angels and Devil Rays split a double-header. Those two teams are always battling it out."

"Jim, looks like we'll be getting some new neighbors soon."

"Really!"

"Yeah, I just saw the developer's men at the vacant lot. You'll let Sally know?"

"Oh, for sure. Finally – I thought no one would ever move in there. She'll be excited. Do you think they will know Tai Chi? Sally's wanted to practice here in the neighborhood with someone forever. I could care less, but I hope they like sports... and poker... and beer!" He laughed while rubbing his prominent beer belly.

"I don't know, Jim. I guess we'll find out soon enough. I'll be calling a meeting in a few days."

"Yes sir Mr. Mayor, Jim and Sally O'Shea will most certainly be there."

John, the unofficial Mayor of Hickory Lane rarely called a meeting. In fact, he couldn't recall the last time the residents gathered, but new neighbors seemed as good a reason as any.

"Good morning, brilliant Professor!"

John sighed; he recognized that voice. His curt yet polite response followed. "Good morning, Dolores!"

She oozed, "It would be so much better a morning if you would stop by for coffee." Brushing back her hair, she chided, "I'm sure Frank wouldn't mind."

He knew Dolores from way back when; they had even gone to school together ages ago. Frank, her divorced husband certainly would not mind. Margie, on the other hand, now that was a different story. While death separated John and his wife Margaret, he knew that eventually they would be reunited. He shuddered at the thought of Margie nagging him about Dolores for eternity.

"Thanks for the invite Dolores, but I'm right in the middle of something important."

"How about tonight then? We can talk phi-lo-so-phy..." she cooed.

"Thanks again, but I'll take a pass. We're getting new neighbors. I'm calling a meeting."

"What?" she exclaimed. "When? Are they married or single?"

"C'mon Dolores, how would I know? I'm sure we're all going to be anxious to meet them."

As the Professor moved toward the end of the lane, Billy Johnson sped by riding his bike. He was the sole child on Hickory Lane. Needless to say, after learning the news, Billy wheeled off, yelling, "New neighbors, finally someone to ride bikes with…. I hope… yippee!"

The Marley sisters stood outside, looking a bit befuddled as always.

"Good morning, ladies! I've got some exciting news to share… We're getting some new neighbors."

The Marley sisters, spinsters both, expressed their delight. "We'll be having a meeting; I'm sure all the neighbors will want to know." He waved goodbye.

He encountered no other residents, so the professor made it back to some peace and quiet without further interaction. He felt certain that in just a short bit of time everyone on Hickory Lane would be talking about this new bit of excitement.

*

Nearly every person that resided on Hickory attended the meeting. Even Shirley and Bill Hendricks, both quite hard of hearing and rather demented, were there. Janice Stevenson, the retired librarian, thoughtfully brought the elderly couple.

"First of all, let me thank everyone for being here." John Henry started the meeting.

"What did he say?" Shirley yelled loudly.

The professor raised his voice. "We don't know for sure anything about the new folks moving in, but we are like one big family here on the Lane and we want to make sure they are welcome. So, we need to figure out the particulars of a welcoming committee."

Mixed in with the hubbub, chatter and speculation about the new neighbors, the particulars regarding a welcoming event began to emerge. Professor Roberson, the de facto mayor, would lead the delegation. The Marley sisters started a gift basket. They had already wrapped their two offerings: a fancy deck of cards and the most recent book club selection. Inside, they included invitations to join their bridge group and to attend the book club. Janice offered to make some punch and pretty much everyone agreed to help in some small way. Time slipped by quickly as they made preparations.

*

On the day of arrival, they all gathered at John Roberson's place, at the beginning of Hickory. They had agreed that congregating at the end of the cul-de-sac might be a bit overwhelming. They would travel together as a group to greet the new arrivals.

"Everyone remember," the professor called out. "We need to show respect and be neighborly. We want to welcome our new neighbors and they will probably be a little intimidated at first. So, let's give them a chance to settle down a bit then introduce ourselves after I get things started." Heads nodded in agreement.

In mounting anticipation, they all stood silent, patient and impatient at the same time. Slowly, a long black hearse turned the corner onto Hickory Lane. They all gasped as a second hearse also rounded the corner, followed by a lengthy convoy of cars filled with friends and family. As a group, the residents trailed the last car and stood at a distance to watch the graveside ceremony. The minister tearfully spoke of the tragic accident that had claimed the lives of this family. Memories of their own burial ceremonies filled the thoughts and minds of those who were laid to rest here on Hickory Lane. After what seemed like an eternity, all the living had left, and the new neighbors stood alone looking as though they did not know what to do.

With respect, Professor John Henry Roberson approached and greeted them. "It's a bit disorienting in the beginning," he said, "but you get used to it pretty fast and we are all here to help."

Stanley and Wanda Krysminski, their two children, Stephanie and Stanley, Jr., and Wanda's older brother, Walter Sminkoski looked bewildered at first. Gradually, they began to look more comfortable.

"Hi, I'm Stanley. We're a little confused about what's going on."

"Welcome to your new home. Meet your new neighbors." The professor gestured to the ghostly crowd.

Billy broke the ice. He practically yelped in glee as he ran up to Stanley Jr., about his same age, all the while looking gratefully at younger sister Stephanie, a real cutie. It took but another moment for Dolores to acquaint herself with Walter, who as fortune had it, happened to be single.

The Marley sisters introduced themselves to Walter, inviting him over to play cards.

"No, I'm more of a poker player; don't play bridge, but my sister Wanda does."

As conversation warmed, John learned that Stanley was an engineer, who just so happened to have minored in philosophy in college. Stanley enjoyed sports, sharing with Jim that if something involved a ball, running, and a cold beer, it pretty much amounted to heaven. Sally was thrilled to learn that Wanda practiced Tai Chi. As an avid reader, Wanda readily accepted the Marley sisters' invitation to the book club.

"Just a bit curious," John put his arm around Stanley and pulled him aside. "You don't by any chance have a dog on the way?"

143

Stanley shook his head and sighed, "No, Archimedes didn't make the trip with us, but we'll somehow make do." He pulled out his wallet to show a picture of the family's beloved dog.

The Mayor of Hickory Lane stepped back and watched the residents mingle with the five new members of the neighborhood.

"Yup," he nodded in approval. "Looks like the new neighbors will fit in just fine…"

Victor Acquista, M.D. is an international author and speaker. He writes both nonfiction and fiction. He is author of several books, short stories, and multiple articles. Dr. Acquista has a longstanding interest in consciousness studies, is a student of Integral Theory, and strives to do his part to make our planet a wee bit better. Learn more at www.writingtoraiseconsciousness.com.

# Birds

## by Dana Hammer

It was a lovely spring morning in Huntington Beach, but Ruth was completely unaware of it. She was doing her third set of crunches on her bedroom floor, sweating unattractively onto an old yoga mat, her curtains drawn, her lights dim. The breeze outside was salty and fresh and lightly warm, but Ruth's windows remained closed. There were surfers out catching the early a.m. waves, but Ruth would never speak to any of them. She was afraid of surfers, and the thin layer of toxic sludge that no doubt covered them at all times. She was also afraid of swimmers, and children, and garbage collectors, for the same reason.

She finished her final set of crunches, and, her first workout of the day completed, she rose to check her phone. She had sent out an invitation last night to several of her neighbors and a few work acquaintances, inviting them over for an afternoon party. It was her therapist's idea. He seemed to feel that her "social isolation" was exacerbating her obsessive compulsive disorder, and that she needed to make an attempt to reach out to people, to make friends with them. Thus the invitation.

No responses. Not one. Ruth's heart raced, and she felt sick inside. Was she really so terrible, that no one wanted to come to her party? That no one could even be bothered to hit a "yes" or "no" button on an invitation? The effort required to RSVP was so minimal, that refusing to do it was tantamount to a direct insult. In Ruth's mind, every one of her neighbors and coworkers had just shouted a big "FUCK YOU" right in her face.

Hot and flustered, Ruth set down her phone and headed to the shower. She had to be at work at 9:00 am, and so she needed to start her cleaning rituals now if she had any hope of getting out the door in time. Checking her phone, and standing around feeling bad about the results had used up four precious minutes. She stood under the fast hot water and worked methodically, scrubbing every inch of her skin from top to bottom, switching washcloths every time she encountered a particularly unclean part of her body, except for her feet, which were the last thing she washed.

After her shower, she had several other cleaning rituals to perform; flossing, pouring hydrogen peroxide in her ears, dipping her hands in bleach water, and taping up any bits of broken skin, to avoid contracting AIDS, hepatitis, or any other blood-borne pathogens. Once, a coworker suggested that she just use bandaids, but Ruth shook her head. People could be so ignorant about these things. Everyone knows that bandaids are porous and breathable; two qualities that Ruth was NOT looking for when it came to disease prevention.

Ruth double checked her bag to make sure she had everything she needed for the day. Then she checked it again. Then she checked it again. Then she realized that she had only checked the bag with her left hand, instead of using both hands, and so she had to do it again. Then she realized she hadn't really been thinking about what she was seeing the last time she checked her bag, so she had to check it again. Then she realized that she'd checked it six times, which was a bad number, so she had to check it again.

"DAMMIT!" She shouted at herself, near tears, so frustrated she wanted to throw the bag in the trash.

No. No. She couldn't even think such a thing. That kind of thinking was dangerous. That kind of thinking would get her bag stolen from her, by some thug in a dark alley, and it would be all her fault, because she was ungrateful, and had let ungrateful thoughts sneak into her head.

She loved her bag. "I love you, bag," she said aloud, feeling ridiculous. And she *was* ridiculous, she *knew* she was ridiculous, but it didn't matter. This is what she had to do. This was her life.

After her breakfast, she did her morning "leaving the house" chants, checked all the light switches and outlets, and of course, the stove, and opened her front door.

And froze.

Her little green car was covered in bird shit.

Not just one splotch of shit, as often happened, especially since she'd moved to this beachfront condo. But many, many splotches of shit, almost as if the gulls had planned some kind of shit-bomb attack, to fuck with her.

Ruth's hands clenched into fists at her sides, and her eyes filled with tears. What was she going to do? Normally, she would drive to the drive-through car wash and get it cleaned off, nice and easy, no touching required. But that wasn't going to work. She wouldn't be able to see through the window, and even if she had been able to, she wouldn't have been able to get the car door open, because the doors were covered in shit too. How did that even happen? Did the freaking gulls shit sideways?

She started to see spots in front of her eyes and she felt lightheaded. She realized she was hyperventilating, and so she went back inside and sat down on her spotless beige couch. She listened to her blood rushing around in her ears, and began to count her breaths (a technique her therapist suggested she try the next time she had an "episode"). When she felt able to get up again, she went to the kitchen and violently scrubbed her hands, and changed her tape, to make sure none of the bird shit had contaminated her.

She picked up the phone.

"Hello? Yeah, this is Ruth. I'm not going to be able to make it in to work today. Yeah, I've come down with some kind of flu. Yeah. Alright, thank you."

Relieved that she'd solved one problem at least, she sat back down and thought about what to do. Was there some kind of car-wash service she could call, that would send someone to her house?

Was that even a thing? She wished desperately that she had some family close by who might come rescue her. She thought about calling a neighbor, but immediately discarded that idea. These were the same assholes who couldn't even be bothered to RSVP to her very nice invitation. If they were too lazy to click "yes" or "no" on their phones, then they couldn't be counted on to save her from a mountain of bird shit.

She opened her living room curtains and glared outside at the gulls soaring overhead. There were a lot of them; way more than usual. The sounds of their cawing didn't normally bother her much, but today each cry was deeply unsettling. She wished she had a crossbow.

Just then, there was a knock at the door. Alarmed, she sprang up from the couch. She wasn't expecting any company, and door-ringers always made her nervous. Was it a police officer? A salesman? A murderer? A rapist?

She peeked through the eyehole and saw a young man's face. He looked clean cut and friendly. His dark blond hair was cut short and parted on the side, and his face was smooth. He was medium height and unremarkable looking. He couldn't have been more than twenty.

*Ah, a salesman*, she thought. *Some kid just out of high school selling magazines or knives.* She did not want to open the door. She hated salespeople. She hated the forced, awkward, manipulative interactions and the phony smiles. She hated that they shook hands with any number of infectious people, and then dragged their wares from house to house, like the bubonic plague spreaders of yore. Most of all, she hated how they came by unannounced when you were in the middle of something, like a chant, or a cleaning routine, and it made you lose track of where you were, and you had to start all over again.

But she wasn't allowed to not answer the door. Because what if that young man was trying to escape from a serial killer, and she didn't answer the door, and the killer caught him and killed him? It would be all Ruth's fault. His blood would be on her hands. She would be a murderer.

She answered the door.

"Hello Ma'am, we're with the Church of Jesus Christ of Latter Day Saints, and we were wondering if we could have a moment of your time?"

Ruth then noticed that there was a second young man, who she hadn't been able to see through her peephole. He was standing off to the side, dark haired and short, lurking like a troll. It made her feel extremely anxious. Who knows how many people she hadn't been able to see before this? There could have been an abandoned baby left on her doorstep, and she never would have known. Maybe the baby had sat out there, cold and hungry until it died. She tried to remember if she had ever smelled baby powder or diapers when exiting her home. Icy fear washed over her.

Ruth felt faint. "I'm not sure..." She swayed.

The first young man stepped forward and put an arm out for her to grab. "Ma'am... are you alright? Should we call someone?"

The second young man looked equally concerned.

"I'm fine," said Ruth. "I'm ok. I'm just... having a bit of a rough morning," she said, with a strained, slightly hysterical chuckle.

"I can see that," said the first young man, looking pointedly at the second young man. "Well, is there anything we can do to help?"

There was a pause, while Ruth stared at the Mormons. They were young and healthy, and smelled vaguely of the clean sweat that comes from outdoor exercise. She gave a weak smile. "Actually, there is. I know it's not your job, and please feel free to say no. But... do you, by any chance, like to wash cars?"

*

150

The Mormons got to work with bizarre cheerfulness, while Ruth sat on the couch, frantically googling "baby left on doorstep" and "odds of someone leaving a baby on your doorstep" and "statute of limitations for infant neglect".

Just as she started to feel a bit calmer, and had almost convinced herself that she was in the clear, and was not likely to be charged with neglecting the baby that might have been left on her doorstep without her knowledge, the missionaries knocked on her door.

"We're all done, Ma'am," said the first Mormon.

"Oh, thank you! Thank you so much! I know this was really weird, but I'm so grateful!" Ruth gushed. "In fact, here," she said, rushing for her checkbook. "I'd like to pay you for your trouble. Who should I make it out to?" Ruth would have liked to pay them in cash, but she never touched cash, for obvious reasons.

"We don't need your money, Ma'am," said the first Mormon, seriously. The second, lurking-troll Mormon looked unsure, and a little unhappy, like he might have wanted the money, but he stayed silent.

Ruth looked troubled. "Are you sure? I would really feel better if–"

"No money, Ma'am," said the first Mormon again. "We were happy to help."

"Well, there must be something you want," she said. "Do you want some coffee? Oh wait, no. How stupid of me. Um... do you want a glass of milk?"

"Really, it was no trouble, Ma'am," the Mormon repeated. "But maybe we could come in for a moment and talk? We have some information here we'd love to share with you."

Ruth froze. Of course, she knew, morally speaking, that these gentlemen had just scraped a festival of bird shit off her car, for

151

free, and that the least she could do was let them come in and give her their sales pitch for Jesus. She knew that. And she wanted to.

But... the thing was... now they were contaminated. With bird shit. If she let them into her house, her whole house would be contaminated. She would have to take the entire week off from work to disinfect every inch of the place with bleach. It was either that, or she'd have to move.

She looked at the bird-shit Mormons, feeling helpless and exhausted. And, hating herself, she said, "Do you have any materials for me to read? Or, like, a Book of Mormon? See the thing is, I'm very late for work, and I have to go. But I'd love to read anything you have for me."

She could see the second Mormon grit his teeth. The first Mormon kept a neutral face. "Of course." He reached into his satchel and pulled out some pamphlets and handed them to Ruth. Ruth took them gingerly in her left hand, keeping the arm extended out straight.

"Oh, thank you, thank you!" Ruth grabbed her keys and pushed past the young men and raced to her sparkling clean car. She opened the door, right-handed, and hopped in. She rolled down the window with her right hand, keeping the pamphlets in her left hand, making sure the papers didn't touch anything. "Thank you! Goodbye!" She shouted to the Mormons, as she backed out of her driveway.

The Mormons stood on her doorstep, looking at each other, aghast.

Ruth drove down the street and turned down an alley, where she quickly parked near a dumpster. She pulled out her wipes from the glove compartment and used them to open the dumpster lid, and threw the bird-shit pamphlets into it, closing the lid carefully, making sure it didn't touch any of her skin. She tucked the wipes into the space between the lid and the dumpster and got back into her car. She quickly sanitized the door handle and steering wheel,

152

and any other surfaces the pamphlets might have touched. Then she got out her hand sanitizer and applied it liberally to her hands, arms, face and neck.

Then she went back home.

It was 10:30, and she was completely worn out.

*

The next morning, she woke up and knew something was off. It was something about the sound. It reminded her of waking up in the middle of winter, back east, when she was a child. It was that muted, muffled feeling, like everything outside was cushioned by the snow. Except that was impossible. There was no snow in Huntington Beach.

She got up and opened her window. And shrieked.

Gulls. Gigantic, smelly, filthy California gulls as far as her eyes could see. She couldn't see anything but white and gray feathers and assorted beaks and taloned feet. She raced to the living room and looked out that window. Still more gulls. She checked every window in the house, growing progressively more frantic with each new bird discovery.

What were they doing? Why were they here? Most importantly, how could she get them to leave?

She banged on the window closest to her, to see if she could scare them away. A few were sufficiently alarmed so as to move away from her banging, but their places were immediately taken by new, braver birds. Ruth screamed and banged some more, but the birds weren't going anywhere.

Ruth pulled up her phone, looking for news about strangely behaving birds. She found nothing. A few minutes into her search though, and she got an email from her brother, Stanley.

"Isn't this your house?" His message said. Attached, there was a photo, that was indeed of her condo. Or it had been her condo.

Now it was just some bizarre mountain of gulls. Some lovely neighbor had taken a picture and posted it to the internet, where it had become something of a viral sensation. The picture was taken a mere half hour ago.

Ruth messaged her brother back. "Yes! It's my condo, and I'm freaking out! What am I supposed to do?"

Stanley messaged back, "I don't know. Scare them away, I guess? What did you do? How did you get all those birds on your house?"

"I didn't do anything! They just showed up sometime in the night!"

"Let me see what I can do," replied Stanley.

Ruth put her phone down. Stanley lived in San Diego. Not too far away, but far enough away that there wasn't much he could do, unless he planned to take the day off work to go hunting for gulls.

She decided to call the police. She figured that was her best bet. Should she call 911? No, that was only for emergencies. And while this did sort of feel like an emergency, she wasn't sure the authorities would see it that way, and she shuddered to think that someone might get stabbed to death while Ruth took up the 911 operator's time with her seagull problem.

"Huntington Beach Police Department, how may I assist you?" Said the professional sounding voice, after Ruth spent the required seven minutes navigating the phone web.

"Um, yes. I'm having a bit of a problem at my house. With seagulls." Ruth looked down and saw that she had picked the skin away from her left thumb, and it was bleeding. When had she done that?

"I'm sorry. Seagulls, Ma'am?"

"Yes. My house is entirely covered in seagulls. Like, so many I can't see outside."

154

There was a pause. "I see. How many seagulls are we talking about?"

Ruth sighed. "I... I don't know, exactly. But a lot of them. Like, way more than is normal."

"I see. And are you on any medications at this time, ma'am?"

"Well, yes. But not anything hallucinogenic. It's just regular, prescription medication. Nothing that would make me see birds that aren't there."

"And what medications are those, ma'am?"

"Look, I'm not seeing things that aren't there," Ruth spat, knowing that if she told the operator that she was taking anti-depressants at the insistence of her psychiatrist, she would never be taken seriously. "There are a shit ton of birds surrounding my house, and I want something done about it. If you want, you can look on the internet. Search for... I don't know... house covered in birds, and you'll see it."

"Alright, ma'am. I'm going to file a report here, and we'll see what we can do. Is there anything else I can help you with today?"

Ruth slumped over, deflated. "No. That'll be all."

"Alright, ma'am, you have a nice day."

Ruth realized that the woman on the phone hadn't even asked for her address. She would have liked to think it's because they knew her address, because they traced her line, but she knew better. The lady on the phone thought she was batshit insane, and wasn't going to do anything to help her. She probably thought Ruth was one of those crazy old ladies who called the police because the neighbor kids were playing baseball too loudly, or because a car drove through the neighborhood playing rap music.

As Ruth sat on the couch, wringing her hands in a panic, her phone pinged. She picked it up. "I'm sending help. They should be there soon. Hold tight, Sis. Love, Stanley."

155

Help? What kind of help was Stanley sending? Animal control? This didn't seem like the sort of thing they handled. They just found lost dogs and whatnot, didn't they?

Ruth decided to eat some breakfast. It was Saturday, so she didn't need to go to work, which was good. So she figured she might as well follow her usual Saturday morning routine, as well as she could, to try to keep herself calm.

But as she was rooting around for food in her cupboard, all she could hear was the rustling and cawing of the terrible, terrible birds that surrounded her house. She could only imagine how much bird dander and disease was floating into her house, through every nook and cranny that wasn't sealed airtight. It hit her then, that her food was all contaminated. Every bit of it. She would have to throw it out and completely replace everything. There was nothing else that could be done with it. She glanced around her spotless blue kitchen and began examining the counters and cupboards, looking for feathers and stray bits of dander.

She brushed at her clothes, which were also contaminated, obviously. Everything in her beautiful, super-clean condo was now infected with bird diseases, and she didn't think she could take much more stress.

She went to the medicine cabinet, where she kept her emergency stash of panic attack meds. She intended to swallow down double the prescribed dose, knowing that she wouldn't be able to make it through the day if she didn't have some help.

But when she opened the cap, her hands were shaking so badly that she dropped the vial, and her pills spilled down the drain.

"NO!" She shrieked. Not only was she upset because she lost her pills, but she now had to deal with the guilt of having contaminated the public water supply. Weren't they always saying you should never dispose of medication down the drain, because it got into drinking water? Now she was responsible for tranquilizing her neighbors. Now one of them, or possibly several of them, would

156

innocently drink a glass of water and then drive to the grocery store, only to have the tranquilizers kick in at the worst possible time, and they'd plow into a farmer's market and kill dozens of innocent shoppers. And it would be all her fault.

She got on her phone and searched "where does your sink water go?" and "if you spill medication down the sink, can it poison others?" and "who to call if you suspect drinking water contamination." She was about to call her local water department, when she heard the greatest sound she had heard in ages.

A dog barking.

Yes! A dog would scare away the birds! Dogs loved to chase birds, and birds were afraid of dogs. It was a perfect solution. She knew it was common for people to bring their dogs to the beach of course, but she couldn't help but wonder if the dog had somehow been psychically summoned by her distress. They said dogs could do that, didn't they? They could sense when someone was in trouble, and come to the rescue. Dogs were so good. They were such good, wonderful animals.

"Rusty! Get away from there!" A voice shouted. The dog continued to bark.

"RUSTY! I SAID GET YOUR ASS AWAY FROM THERE, YOU NO-GOOD PIECE OF SHIT!"

Ruth dared to peek out her curtains. The birds were all lodged firmly in place. It was as if they didn't see or hear the dog, and she wondered again what the hell was wrong with these gulls. Why were they behaving like this? What were they doing?

She needed to do something constructive. She needed to try to get her mind off things. She filled her bathtub with the hottest possible tap water, and added a thick layer of bubbles, reasoning that the hot water and foam would insulate her from the worst of the contamination. Probably. Maybe.

She put on some music. Soft, classical string quartets were

157

what she needed, and she needed them loud and she needed them now.

She got in, ignoring the stinging burn of the heat on her skin. It felt good to her. It felt like cleanliness. At the last minute, she leaned out of the tub, reached under the sink and retrieved one of her bottles of bleach and poured a little into the bath water, for extra protection. She sank back in and tried to think about anything but birds. She thought about the calming scent of the bleach. She thought about Vivaldi. She added more bleach, just to be on the safe side.

After adding bleach a few more times, her skin started to itch and burn, so she got out of the tub. But then, she was faced with the problem of what to wear. Her clothes were contaminated. Her towels were contaminated. Then it hit her: her winter clothes! They were sealed up in a bit plastic bin, and she was sure she had some things that were still in dry cleaning bags. Perfect!

She hunted down the plastic storage bin in the back of her closet and quickly found what she was looking for.

It was a floor length maroon ball gown with sequins on the bodice, and a velvet skirt. She had purchased it for a fancy Christmas event a few years ago. It was not an ideal outfit for a hot spring day, but it was the cleanest thing she had. And while she knew that it was going to be contaminated as soon as she took it out of the plastic, it would be less contaminated than the clothes that had been sitting out in the open this whole time.

She slipped into the ballgown, hating how hot it was and how sticky it made her skin feel. The saltiness of her sweat irritated her burned, bleached skin, but she ignored it. She had bigger problems to deal with right now. Namely, how to sanitize this house.

She knew that she was fighting a losing battle. No amount of cleaning would make her condo truly clean, until the birds dispersed. But she also knew that that was the thinking of a lazy person, and everyone knew that lazy people got what was coming to

158

them. She had to work as hard as she could to keep things clean, even if it was a Sisyphean task at this point.

So she filled a bucket, and got to work.

*

The sound that shocked Ruth out of her scrubbing spell was like nothing she'd ever heard before. It was like a bird's squawking, but amplified a thousand times, and stretching into eternity. Raised voices could be heard somewhere in the distance, but they were muffled and indistinguishable.

Still feeling slightly drugged, coming out of her cleaning trance, Ruth rose from the white-tiled kitchen floor and stumbled to the window and looked outside, cringing a little in fear.

Her fear was justified. Outside was the bloodiest battle she had ever seen, carnage sprayed this way and that, bits of bird bodies decorating the fence and the sidewalk, white and gray feathers strewn all over her porch and the sand falling through the air. It was like looking at a pillow fight gone terribly, terribly wrong.

But the sound was the worst part. Terrible cries of agony as the gulls were ripped to pieces, snatched out of the air by new, larger, dangerous birds. Ruth tried to get a good look at these newcomers, but had trouble seeing them. They were so fast, and they were all busy with the gulls, sinking their talons in and ripping them apart.

Then, there was a *splat* as a gull was slammed against her window, and Ruth had a chance to identify the gull's assailant.

It was a falcon.

Now that she'd seen one up close, it seemed obvious that the predators were falcons, and she wondered how she hadn't identified them at once. Her brother was into falconry, and had been for several years. For obvious reasons, Ruth had never taken an interest in his hobby, preferring not to think of her dear brother subjecting himself to such unnecessary danger. But she had absorbed the odd tidbit here and there, and she had seen pictures of her brother, arm proudly outstretched, a sinister looking bird sitting on it, looking hungry and beady-eyed.

Ruth's phone rang. It was Stanley. She answered it.

"Ruth! Are you alright? I've been calling and calling, but you never answered."

"Sorry... I was... asleep."

"You managed to sleep while your house was covered in birds? That doesn't sound like you." Stanley sounded skeptical, and Ruth understood why. It was no secret to Stanley that Ruth was, as he put it, "a bit of a stress case." But she didn't want him to know about the bleaching and going into cleaning-zombie mode; she'd promised him that she would try to clean with gentler, less harsh products, and that she would ease up on her cleaning routines. It was a promise she'd had no intention of keeping.

"I'm making progress," she said. "I'm better at managing my stress now."

"Oh," Stanley sounded taken aback, "Well that's great, Ruth. Anyway, my guys say they showed up and took care of it. You should be able to leave your house soon."

"Your guys? Do you mean the falcons?"

Stanley laughs. "Well, the guys in my falconry club, yeah. I sent out a message to everybody and most of these guys couldn't wait to get out there and help you. Kinda sick, when you think about how happy they are to watch their birds murder a bunch of other birds. But still. Problem solved, right?"

Ruth looked out the window again. The terrible sounds were dying down, but the mess was beyond appalling. It looked like a hell designed especially for her.

But her house was no longer covered in birds.

"Yeah," she said, weakly. "Stanley, I think the birds are all gone now. It's just... quite a mess out here."

Stanley chuckled. "Yeah, you never did like messes," he said. "Neat and tidy Ruth."

Ruth laughed mechanically. "Yeah... look... thank you for your help. And for sending your friends out here. It means a lot to me." And she meant it. She was grateful.

"Aw, no big deal, Ruth. Happy to help. But hey... what happened to make all those birds swarm on your house like that? That's not normal behavior for gulls, is it?"

"No. No I should say not," she said. "And I don't have the slightest idea why they came to my house. I mean, it's not like I put out a bunch of birdseed or anything. I wasn't practicing bird calls in the house."

"No, no, of course not," said Stanley, sensing that his questions had upset his sister. "I just wondered, that's all. You know, you might want to talk to someone up there. Maybe an ornithologist or something. I bet there's somebody at UC Irvine or somewhere you could talk to. Figure out what's going on out there."

"Yeah. Yeah, I'll do that," said Ruth. "Look, I've gotta go. But thank you Stanley. Really."

"You're welcome, Sis."

*

When the last of the gulls was gone, either ripped to shreds by ravenous falcons, or flown off to safer skies, Ruth finally emerged from her condo.

She looked around, trying to find the falconers _Stanley's friends_ but had no luck. After the attack, most of them had packed up and left, and there was such a large crowd of people by this time, that she wouldn't have been able to find them easily anyway, especially since Ruth did not enter or go near large crowds, for any reason, ever.

Not only were her neighbors all standing outside, gaping at the carnage, there were numerous surfers and tourists there too, many of them taking pictures with their phones. There was even a news van, with a well-groomed, pants-suited woman talking into a microphone, gesturing at the pile of dead birds behind her.

As Ruth stepped into the sun, two of her neighbors rushed over to her. "Ruth, are you alright? What happened? We saw your house with all those birds on it this morning. And then those falcons! What happened?" The woman who was speaking was named Tonya, and Ruth recalled that she was one of the people who never responded to her party invitation. Her boyfriend, Uri, stood behind her, looking concerned and ridiculous in his bright red track suit.

Ruth was dazed as she answered, "I don't know what happened. I don't know how to explain it. It was all just... a freak happening."

Tonya shook her head, a gesture that was meant to be sympathetic. Ruth thought she looked judgmental.

"You know, it's extremely easy to RSVP to an event nowadays," said Ruth, forcing her tone to be light and breezy. "With everything online, it's so convenient, isn't it? I mean, you just push a button. One little button. Am I right?" Ruth said to Uri, who looked startled at being pulled into the conversation.

"Um... are you alright? Is there... anyone we should call, or anything?" Tonya asked, looking uncertain.

Ruth swallowed. "You know what? I'm sorry. I don't know what I'm saying. I've had a really rough day. In fact, I think I'll go in and lie down." She spun on her heel and marched back into her house, where she closed the curtains against all the bloody damage that had been done on her property. She didn't know what to do next. How would she go about cleaning all of those bird guts up? Was there some kind of cleaning service she could hire? She

162

couldn't just wait for nature to clean up, could she? Wouldn't the smell be unimaginable after a few days in the hot California sun? And the ocean breezes would blow that scent right into her house, all day and all night, until it drove her to drink.

Ruth nervously flapped her hands. She picked up her phone and checked her party invitation.

Four people had RSVPd. Two yes, two no.

Ruth took a deep breath. She filled a bucket with bleach, grabbed some cleaning rags, and got to work. Now it was time to get her place clean for real.

A few moments later, she heard a barking sound. Again.

She opened the front door and looked outside. There was a cinnamon brown pitbull standing on her porch, tongue lolling out of his head, looking up at Ruth with big, blank, brown eyes. His stumpy little tail was wagging.

Ruth stood there biting her lip for a moment. Should she call animal control? Should she shoo him away? Should she feed him some water? Yes. Yes, that was the best thing to do.

She went into her kitchen and found a plastic container she never used and filled it with water from the Brita in the fridge, knowing that the tap water was still contaminated from her pill spill. She put on some yellow rubber gloves from under the kitchen sink. She brought the water to the dog and knelt down in front of him. He had a collar.

"Ok, boy. Let's see if there's someone we can call for you." She gently reached a hand forward and slowly grasped the tag on his collar, looking for a number to call, or an address.

RUSTY

If found call

714-333-4445

"Rusty," Ruth said softly. She remembered the yelling from before. "You're not a piece of shit, are you? No. You're a good boy. A good boy who tried to help me, huh?" She patted him on his head. "And where's your family? Did they just up and leave you here, all by yourself? You must be so scared, and lonely."

Rusty ignored Ruth, and continued to lap up his water. As he did, Ruth looked around, scanning the beach for anyone who might be looking for the dog. She stood to her full height, making her decision.

"Come in here, boy," she said, opening the door for Rusty. She didn't want to touch him, she wasn't there yet, but she liked him. She imagined a bright new future where she and Rusty went to dog parks and beaches. He would accompany her on walks and keep her safe. He would add a burst of merriment and silly dogginess to her life.

There was a moment of shiny optimism in Ruth's heart. And then there was a screech. Both she and Rusty started. The light in the condo changed. It dimmed, as if there was an eclipse blocking the sunshine.

The screech sounded again, louder. It was a low, deep throttling noise, a horrible moan from something unimaginable. She cracked open the front door but didn't dare look up at the sky. Before she could stop him, the dog squeezed though her legs and burst outside in a frenzy of barking.

"Rusty! Rusty, come back! Oh, my God! Rusty…"

A few seconds later, her ray of optimism was nothing more than a dwindling speck in the sky.

Dana Hammer is the author of *The Taxidermist* and *Rosemary's Baby Daddy*. Her short stories have been featured in *It's All in the Story: California, Murder Park After Dark, Cliterature Journal, The Moon Magazine,* and *Jakob's Horror Box.* She loves birds.

# The Shadow Of The Great Nebula Of Orion

## by Boris Glikman

One day, the nebula in the constellation of Orion, already the brightest nebula in the night sky, started to shine more intensely, emitting a piercing blue-green light. Its luminosity became so brilliant that it cast shadows during the daylight hours too, something that had always been the sole prerogative of the Sun.

Naturally, this generated great excitement, for never before had such an extremely bright celestial body been seen in the day sky. Everybody rushed outside to look at this heavenly wonder and to gawk at their double shadows, the old familiar one and the new one created by the Orion Nebula.

It was then that the world was hit by a very unpleasant surprise, for there was something quite peculiar about the shadows caused by the nebula. Instead of being mute, inert outlines of a person's physical form, they revealed the shadow of a person's character. Everyone's inner anxieties, delusions and insecurities were now exposed for all to see.

No one could be found who did not possess a nebula shadow. Even newborns had a shadow accompanying them; thus, coincidentally, vindicating some psychological theories and theological dogmas, while demolishing others.

Naturally, the consequences of this new phenomenon were immense in their scope. Billions of lives were wrecked, relationships destroyed and careers ruined as a person's innermost complexes and most tightly guarded secrets were revealed to their spouses, family, friends, work colleagues and complete strangers. The very structure of society was threatened, for its smooth running depended so much upon one's true feelings and nature being suppressed and hidden, even from oneself. Consequently, these

166

revelations came as a heavy shock to the many who didn't know what apprehensions, doubts and self-deceptions they had been concealing from themselves in the remotest reaches of their psyches or in the deepest substrata of their unconscious minds.

Humanity was in a dilemma over how to cope with this situation. It certainly couldn't dim or extinguish the nebula's brightness. It could have tried to adapt to a nocturnal existence, when the shadows would be less distinct, but surely that would have been too radical and onerous a solution. Yet who could risk or put up with the shame, the disgrace and the burden of walking around with all of their flaws and aberrations showing?

Inevitably, cults arose that chose to embrace with enthusiasm this new state of affairs. For them the Orion Nebula was The Bearer of Truth, The Great Enlightener of Mankind. Just as the Sun brought outer illumination, so the Orion Nebula was deemed to bring inner illumination to the world. The adherents of these sects took pride in letting others see their most intimate neuroses, and experienced catharsis in coming face-to-face with their fears, self-delusions and insecurities for the very first time. Having accepted their shadows, they felt more fulfilled and whole than they ever did before.

And then, just as suddenly as it flared up, the Orion Nebula dimmed to its usual luminosity. It didn't take long for people to readjust to having only one shadow again. Lives, relationships and careers wrecked by the nebula were quickly rebuilt and almost everyone resumed living their old lives, maintaining total silence about that awkward period when their failings were revealed. It was as if the exposure of their inner selves was nothing more than a minor faux pas that is ignored in polite company.

Boris Glikman is a writer, poet and philosopher from Melbourne, Australia. The biggest influences on his writing are dreams, Kafka and Borges. His stories, poems and non-fiction articles have been published in various online and print publications, as well as being featured on national radio and other radio programs.

Boris says: "Writing for me is a spiritual activity of the highest degree. Writing gives me the conduit to a world that is unreachable by any other means, a world that is populated by Eternal Truths, Ineffable Questions and Infinite Beauty. It is my hope that these stories of mine will allow the reader to also catch a glimpse of this universe."

Blog: https://bozlich.wordpress.com/

# Worker in Stone

## by Tina Kirchner

Its eyes followed me. At first, the slight movement of the hardened irises was almost impossible to detect, but an odd-shaped black mark gave it away. The mark jumped around like a gnat on its gray eye. On closer inspection, the dark fleck in the granite shouldn't have moved. I twirled my keychain around my finger, jingling the gold heart inscribed with "Follow your heart" while I stared at the tiny black speck.

With my face inches from the statue's eye, the mark moved again. After I realized the statue was watching me, the smartest thing to do would've been to clear out of Zeke's Fountain and Statue Yard as fast as possible, but I didn't. That poor choice made me dumber than the stone the lion was sculpted from. "Here lies Mason. He was dumber than granite" would have been an accurate epitaph to carve on my gravestone, however, not a great way to go for someone whose name means "worker in stone."

I took a step away from the three-foot lion. Its wide-open mouth displayed a full set of sharp fangs. I glanced around, but nobody was remotely close by. "I saw you move," I whispered. The statue didn't answer. I really hoped it wouldn't. "If you think I'm taking you home, you're crazy. I didn't come for a fountain." The lion's eyes didn't shift. I shook my head and mumbled. "Low blood sugar. Just buy the frog planter and go already."

After a long day of fixing cars at the garage, the thought of dinner sounded good. I strode away from the statue, twirling my keychain and thinking about spicy fries. I stopped short when something pelted me square in the back. On the sandy path was a piece of granite about the size of a quarter. I looked over at the lion. Its mouth was closed, and its eyes faced away from me.

169

"Nope. You didn't do that." I swallowed hard.

The lion eyes shifted to look my way, and his mouth curved into a smile.

I gasped. "Are you kidding me?" A lesser man – or a smarter man – would've ran for sure, but some strange feeling told me not to.

The lion shook his head slowly, which sounded like rubbing chalk against a pavement.

Zeke's two-acre yard boasted the largest selection of statues in town, but it was my misfortune to wander to the back corner where a moving granite lion sat on a crumbling fountain. "I can't buy you. I don't think the fountain will fit in my Dart." Cobwebs and dust covered everything on the bottom half. I winced. "It looks broken anyway."

He squinted, and his smile turned into a frown.

The lion had the saddest expression I'd ever seen, and I was a sucker for cats. "All right. Let me get someone who works here to load you up."

When I showed the sales guy the lion fountain, his sideways glance confirmed I'd lost my mind. "We have other fountains. Nicer ones." He ran his hand over a large crack. "Not that I don't want to make a sale, but I'm pretty sure this one doesn't hold water. It's been crumbling in the same spot the ten years I've worked here."

"That's fine. Then it'll be really cheap, right?" If I was going to die from a possessed statue, I certainly didn't want to pay for it, too.

The sales guy shrugged. "I'll talk to my manager. He'll probably want to give that hunk of junk away. It's just taking up space."

His manager gave me a similar sideways glance and sales

pitch. Apparently, the statue had been there since day one. So I wouldn't seem as crazy, I lied to them that the fountain was going to be a Halloween prop. It was February.

My free fountain split into three pieces while the workers loaded it in my Dart's trunk; however, the lion statue stayed intact. As I drove home, I looked many times in my rear-view mirror, expecting the lion to leap out like a Chuckie doll and shred me into tiny pieces.

I made it home alive but dreaded opening the trunk. Panic set in. Sweat dripped from my forehead, and my mouth was bone dry. I considered leaving my keys in the car, hoping someone would steal it. My apartment was located in a pretty seedy area of town – two nights tops before the Dart was taken. Besides, the thief could deal with the lion. I walked around to the back of the car. When a knocking sound came from inside the trunk, my car keys slipped through my fingers.

The knocking grew louder until I was afraid the lion would break out on his own. I ran to the driver's side and pushed the trunk release button. I swallowed hard and gazed into the rear-view. The trunk lid blocked the back window. A loud thunk came from the back, and the vehicle rocked. I grabbed a plastic fork off the floormat and slid it in my jacket pocket. Plastic fork versus granite – my odds weren't good. Each step closer to the trunk made more sweat beads roll down my forehead.

"Ya need help?" someone shouted. I almost wet myself. When my first-floor neighbor waved from his patio, I gathered a little composure.

I wiped my forehead on my sleeve. "Thanks, but I think I can carry it." My voice cracked. I took a deep breath and peered around the car. The fully intact and pristine fountain sat on the ground next to the Dart. The lion smiled at me. I waved to my neighbor and shouted, "On second thought, Iggy, I'll take you up on that offer."

Iggy hopped the railing and jogged over. A handful of chains jangled from the back pocket of his ripped blue jeans. He scratched his chest while he gazed at the statue. More hairs poked through his white tank's neck hole. "That's sweet. Are you going to make it a beer fountain?" He reached under the back of it to get a grip.

The lion poked out his tongue, and his eyes shifted toward Iggy. I almost choked. "What? No! Water…just water." I lifted the front end of the fountain, and the lion grinned.

"Too bad." Iggy gazed up at my second-floor apartment door. "Must've cost you a pretty penny. I seen cheaper lookin' things for like five hundred at the hardware store."

The lion stared at me and rolled his eyes. I regripped and looked up the stairs. "Really? Well, this one was a deal. Pump's broken, et cetera." We carried the statue through my apartment to my patio, sitting it down next to the only electrical outlet. I really didn't believe I'd ever plug it in.

Iggy wiped his forehead with the bottom of his grimy tank. "Whew! That was a workout. Makes ya thirsty, don't it?" His smile displayed several gold teeth.

I headed into my apartment with Iggy at my heels and closed the sliding glass door. "Thanks for the help…you know, I'm out of beer at the moment, but as soon as I restock, I'll bring you a six-pack."

He cupped his hand around his ear and grinned. "Twelve pack?"

I nodded and guided Iggy to the front door. "I meant twelve pack." I pushed him outside and closed the door, leaning up against it. I took a deep breath and gazed across the room. The granite lion sat on the carpet ten feet away. I retrieved the plastic fork from my pocket, but all the tines had snapped off. I tossed it aside. "What do you want?" My heart pounded.

The lion puckered his lips and closed his eyes.

He had to be kidding. I rubbed the back of my neck and walked over to the lion. The sliding door was closed. I'd never get away now. "You want me to kiss you?"

The puckered lion nodded.

I kneeled beside him. My first thought – I was an idiot. Unsure what to do with my hands, I clasped them behind my back and leaned into the lion's face slower than a drip of honey slides down a jar. One quick kiss. That was my plan. I puckered, closed my eyes, and pressed my lips to the lion's. The stone was smooth and cold. I couldn't pull back – my lips were stuck like a tongue to a frozen pole. My eyes wouldn't open either. My body shook so much, my key ring jangled out of my pocket. The statue's lips warmed and softened in a few seconds, and I stopped shaking. I thought I was done for.

My eyes opened. The lion was gone. In his place was a beautiful woman with wild hair and hazel eyes. She smiled at me. "Thanks for setting me free." She held up my keychain, the gold heart dangled in front of my face.

A lot of things didn't make sense. The lion turned into a woman, and now, I couldn't move. I caught my reflection in the gold heart. I was the lion statue.

She stared at me for a moment and sighed. "The witch wasn't picky. She put me into the closest object around, which happened to be the lion. I hated to do this to you, but I was tired of being a statue." She patted my head and gazed into my eyes. "I'm sorry. You seem like a really nice guy."

She took my keys and headed for the door. I tried to yell for help, but nothing. She opened the door and gasped. "Hey, Iggy."

"Hey yourself. Who are you?" Iggy stepped through the open door, eyeing her up.

"Listen Iggy. Mason said you can have the fountain. It doesn't fit with his décor."

I cringed. I was going to spew beer from my mouth for eternity.

Iggy raised his arms, displaying his ape-like armpits. "Awesome! Party at my place…do you want to join?"

She smiled. "As tempting as that sounds, I've got somewhere to be." She stepped outside. "By the way, make sure to kiss the lion, it's guaranteed good luck."

Although writing is T.W. Kirchner's passion, her first loves are her husband, two children, and furry menagerie known as the Kirchner Zoo, which includes five dogs and three cats. Besides writing, she likes to paint, draw, play tennis, hike, and do yoga. If she could, she'd spend all her time outdoors. Anything wolf, pirate, or zombie-related will grab her attention.

Along with writing short stories for adults, Kirchner recently published the first book in her novella vampire series *Reno Red* and the last book in her YA supernatural horror series *Dagger & Brimstone*. She also has two children's book series published, *Pirates Off* and *The Troubled Souls of Goldie Rich*.

Website: www.twkirchner.com

Blog: https://aceinlv.wordpress.com/

# The Adventures of Conqueror Cat

by Leigh Ward-Smith

I smelt its breath parting the air before I felt the bristles along my jaw. It carried the odor of a gym locker mixed with the pungent musk of a Kong smeared in pork peanut butter and wet-dog slobber.

And then it disappeared again – at least two of the three sensations at once, leaving only the reeking – while my eyes reeled to focus. Normally, my vision is at least way beyond your measly 20/10. But today, the New Year's Eve after I'd successfully made the jump through the mouse-hole at the Happy Tails Ever After Shelter... today was a different narrative entirely.

I batted at the sleep gunk in my eyes, more aware of my age than back home where it was calm and comfortable. And predictable. My servants cared for me, but I longed for something more. A tinge of adventure. Wanderlust had already overtaken me when I had stepped onto the peak of the cat tree and wiggled up into the top hidey-hole and said the magic words.

*Now, I was here in this foul-smelling place. But where am I, really? And who's ever heard of a Cheshire stink?* I remembered a book Gramma-ka had read to me when I was but a kit, one of my favorites: *The Cheshire Cat's Adventures in Wonderland, with a girl called Alice.*

Seconds later, the smell strengthened, but I was properly on guard this time. Claws fully extended and in my best Muhammad Ali boxing stance, I waited for the apparition to re-appear as its revolting miasma took hold.

A silhouette materialized around the stench but farther away, if my whiskers were any astute judge. (And they were, of course.)

"Hewoh and wewcome, fwend!" The vision stretched out fur-

strung arms, backlit by which light I could not determine, and looked like it wanted… perhaps an embrace? Wasn't it humiliating enough to have been kissed by this thing already!

I gasped, biting down a soul-crushing hiss of utter revulsion.

Instead, it bounded closer and repeated itself dumbly. "Hewoh and wewcome. I luff ooo. Do woo luff me?" I thought I caught a mimic of movement behind it and to the right; something like a paddle slicing through the light streaming from around its figure.

There was a nimbus around the being – or so said my subconscious mind.

*What is going on with this tricky light? I mean, it was only my third substantive experience with traveling through the mouse-hole of time, but my senses simply could not be this faulty.*

As it drew closer, I kept my paws up but retracted the blades. It was a mere simpering, slavering canid I saw before me. A standard four-legger, and typically smelly.

For some reason, its shaggy face crinkled as it moved closer still to scrutinize me, if that was what it did. I doubted it had the capability and sentience.

"The Chief, she luff doggies. Woo not dat kind. Hmm. Cats... she towerate." It lowered its arms that were most recently elevated in greeting.

"Me be Willoughby. Who you be, fewine?"

"Why, myself, I am Herr Trinket the Stupendous of the 7-Lives Clan, and I have come exploring." It was no use kow-towing to this dog-beast, so I did not.

"But that is entirely beside the point. I want to know who is this Chief, and who in the Nine Levels of Litterboxes does she think she is? I must be taken to meet her. At once."

"How woo get hewah?" Clearly I was dealing with a moron.

"How I arrived here is never mind to you and your kind. In fact, you probably would not even understand the process." I stifled a harrumph, as the creature was slightly larger, maybe one of those wheaten terrier types, like that dog Dodo in the famous movie *The Chivalrous Lion and Some People in the Land of Oz, including Dorothy and a wizard.* (It pays to know your enemy.)

"I demand to meet with your leader. The chief as you call her, of this place, whatever it is."

"Dis be Woof Ha-wwoh."

"Woof Hollow?"

"No, no. Woof Ha-wwoh."

"I said Woof Hollow."

"No. No Woof Hollow. Wepeat wiff I. Wuuuf Ha-wwoh."

"Woof Hollow."

"Newermind."

The lupine simpleton did not even know the name of its dimension. I was suddenly sad, a sensation that shocked me. And then that second passed.

Its body began to fade again and appeared at some distance away, about 8 feet and 5 inches by my reckoning. It was just as well, as my nose was feeling the toll of the animal's presence. The figure calling itself Willoughby (who chooses such a pompous-sounding name?) motioned its arm like it wanted me to follow.

*Ah, must be a retriever then. Obviously a mix.*

Weighing my options and realizing I would always land on my feet, figuratively and literally, I decided to creep forward as it gesticulated.

"Come, come. Woo come, fuww-face." I let that one go.

On the way, we passed a sign with an arrow that glimmered

178

"Wolf Harrow."

"Faster, kitty-kat, faster!"

"Only sycophantic dogs come when called, you twit!" I called ahead to the romping canine and its air-slicing tail.

He tossed a glance back at me. "If woo say so, cuz."

"To be sure, I am no relative of yours!"

I imagined it looked crestfallen, but it had morphed out again, appearing many strides ahead in a landscape that revealed itself to me only as I padded cautiously along.

It was not a yellow-brick road, of course, nor was it exactly a path. It was simply where we walked as all else remained in shroud. No matter how, when I swiveled my head left or right, back or forward or up, my pupils would not focus on any clear surroundings. It was as if we were in a void and this ribbon of green carpet unfurled within that space. Had I the time, it might have elicited a momentary thrill to discover the texture of the path, determining if it could be moved, scratched, thrown, sprayed-on or rearranged in any fundamental way. In the main, was it a real ribbon and could it be chewed?

But there wasn't time for that as the fool coaxed me on.

"Woo meet Chief soon. Her is gweat. Also wemember you mayw not get what woo are wooking for."

"What right have you to lecture me, simpering knave? I am clearly your superior in every way, *Felix exemplarius* to your *Canis commonplaceus*. I understand full well what is occurring, and don't you try any filthy tricks whatsoever, like laser-light tag or grab-the-feather, on me. And I can smell cat-nip from hundreds of clicks away. In short, I shan't allow any dog deception to pass without proper retribution!"

For the first time in our odd experience, I sensed that the creature in front of me... well, it seemed as if he pitied *me*. I, Herr

Trinket the Stupendous, official String-Reader of the 7-Lives Clan, designated so by Queen Zenna Amethystine, her highest highness of the Catniverse.

Still, he remained quiet as the way spilled into a vaster expanse of field. It was quite possibly the most, well, fetching thing I had ever laid my jade eyes on in five Siamese life-spans, but I certainly was not going to mention that to my guide. A swath of flowers as pearlescent as the sun on my world swayed with the breeze and tugged with them the pleasant scent of catnip. That did not make sense, but I did not care, as my eyes were drawn, thanks also Willoughby's hasty retreat, to several circling figures at the other end of the field. These moving dots were flanked by a massive residence as large as the pyramids of Giza back on my world. Instead of a standard castle, however, with many turrets and keeps and a drawbridge, it appeared to be a single structure of brilliant white with a sign hanging under its gabled roof.

The sign said, in maroon capitals as large as several stacked lions, *Sheena*.

Drawing near, I heard Willoughby call. "She see woo nowh. She come. Bow. Bow."

"Don't you mean bow-wow, you chestnut-hued coot?"

This time, he demonstrated an awkward curtsy, speaking the words again, as if they were a mantra. "Bow." Then "Booooowwww," enunciating as if *I* were the simpleton.

Knowing I would never do anything of the sort, I stood agape, in dismay, as the figure lumbered out of a gargantuan doorway, making all of us below look like Lilliputians.

The life I almost lost with the shocking New Year's Eve kiss from the interdimensional dog Willoughby came full-circle upon witnessing this spectacle shambling toward me, the ground cracking a little under my paws with its every step.

I no longer doubted my senses. Before me, her name was

180

Sheena and she was the giantest Yorkshire terrier I had ever seen, thousands of litterboxes wide and perhaps a million cat-trees tall, with a flotilla of hair streaming about her, longer than some rivers I had seen.

Clearly, I had arrived in hell, and it was only the beginning of 2078, the year of the Cat (as is every year).

Aiming her voice down at me, Sheena spoke. "Hewoh, woo wan to play bawll?" At the word *ball*, an automaton rolled out an equally big-as-big-gets yellow-and-white-striped orb as if it were a boulder for a catapult.

Right then, I knew. I really knew, and it delighted me from the tips of my ears to the end of my tail. In less than 6 earth-months, *this* kingdom would be in my able paws. And then I could start squeezing.

Leigh Ward-Smith writes, edits, and parents – weirdly and otherwise – from the center of the U.S.A. She has an affinity for nature and animals, sometimes including *Homo sapiens*. Access a growing list of her publication credits at Leigh's Wordsmithery:

https://leighswordsmithery.wordpress.com/awards-and-publications/

# Palindrome

## by Marc Sorondo

To be effective, the word has to be said backwards, then forwards. That is the key. It doesn't matter that it sounds exactly the same in reverse; what does matter is the intention.

Backwards, then forwards, again and again. There's no telling how many times it will take. That will vary. Once it will only take a handful of repetitions; the next time it could take several thousand, spread across days and weeks and months. It can seem to take forever, but it never fails.

If it is said correctly, backwards then forwards, again and again, always with proper intention, the person of my choosing will die.

I've been saying it again for weeks now, over and over, backwards and then forwards, and I've had you in mind.

Marc Sorondo lives with his wife and children in New York. He loves to read, and his interests range from fiction to comic books, physics to history, oceanography to cryptozoology, and just about everything in between. He's a perpetual student and occasional teacher.

Website: https://marcsorondo.com

Facebook:

https://www.facebook.com/Marc-Sorondo-470345476415859/

# The Fate of the White Wolf

## by CB Droege

Klaxons sounded. Crewmen dashed about in an organized panic. The White Wolf, the flagship of the Confederacy's fleet was under attack by United Protectorate forces. An ambush. Three dark ships had appeared, seemingly from nowhere, and had begun launching attack boats without even a warning hail. Crewman Rose had been knocked from his feet at his station during the first volley and was watching dazed as his comrades bustled around him. Specialist Harris grabbed Rose by one arm and hauled him to his feet.

"You okay, Sweets?" Specialist Harris's face was very close, and Rose could see blood spattered across his left cheek and eye. It didn't look like it was his own.

"I–" Rose gasped, struggling to find his breath after the impact, "I think I'm alright." Harris nodded hurriedly and moved away, disappearing immediately into the mad rush.

Crewman Rose tried to concentrate. The klaxon pattern was indicating general quarters. He turned back to his action post, but the starboard communications monitoring station was fried; the portholes were blackened and the equipment was smoking. He didn't have a secondary action post, so what next? He tried to think. His thoughts were stuck in deep mud, and if he pulled much harder, he would only lose a boot. He was likely concussed. There was nothing for it but to try to find a medic – or his CO. Luckily the med-bay and his CO's quarters were in the same direction. He took off down the passage, becoming one more among the frantically moving crew.

The ship shuddered. The hull of the ship peeled back to reveal open space beyond. The transverse bulkheads fore and aft sealed

185

instantly. His emergency helmet activated, washing his face in a rush of oxygen, as he grasped for something, anything, to hold on to...

*

The timer buzzed softly and broke Rose out of his reverie. He was in the galley of the White Wolf, staring down at a brown-green nutrient patty blackening on the hotplate. It was burned again. He frowned and pulled at his greying beard. The timer buzzed again and he slapped it to shut it off. He scraped the blackened patty off the hotplate into his bowl and stared at it. The rations didn't need to be cooked of course, but it introduced a bit of variety into his life to have a warm one occasionally. The spices had run out in only five years, leaving him with an endless supply of nearly flavorless rations, all identical. He daydreamed of spiced food often, whenever he wasn't reliving the day of the attack.

The timer buzzed again, and Rose slapped it off without thinking and walked over to the nutrient recycler with his bowl, dumping the mess. He looked up at the bulkhead where he marked time. Forty-six years, as well as he could reckon, since the White Wolf was ambushed and destroyed, leaving him the only survivor, trapped inside the sealed and shielded galley compartment, tumbling aimlessly through space. The galley had food to support a forty-man crew for three years, a water purifier, a waste recycler, a hydroponic garden to keep him in oxygen, and solar panels to keep it all running.

The timer buzzed again, somehow more insistently than before, and he glanced at it, annoyed. Except it wasn't the timer. The timer had been broken for over a year. It sat inert in the console next to the hot plate. Rose's eyes widened as he looked around. If it wasn't the timer...

He spun to stare at a panel on the bulkhead next to the aft porthole where the kitchen radio was suddenly all blinking lights, in time with the buzzer. He sprang across the deck – knocking over his carefully set table in his rush – and switched on the speaker.

"-lie Farmer of the C.F.S Wildflower calling the occupant of the unidentified wreckage. Please come in. Is anyone there?"

Rose pressed the transmit button with a trembling finger. His voice cracked and stuttered as he spoke, "W-Wildflower, this is Crewman Dexter Rose of the C.F.S. White Wolf. I'm h-here. I'm here!"

"Sweet name!" said the voice. She sounded young, and pleasantly disposed. He'd heard the joke before, of course, but never had it sounded so good, "Nice to hear you made it, Crewman Rose. I'm not familiar with the White Wolf. How long have you been out here?"

Rose glanced at his tracking wall again, "forty-six years, one-hundred and thirty-nine days... I think."

"Hold the Launch!" She exclaimed. "That's amazing! I've never heard of anyone surviving inside a wreck for more than a few days. You've been in there since right before the end of the rebellion."

Rose grinned. It was heartening to hear that the war had not lasted much longer. "I was lucky," he said. "I b-brought the kitchen with me."

"I want to hear all about it," Farmer said, "but let's get you out of there first. You have an evac suit in there with you?"

Rose glanced around, as if he did not already know every square centimeter of the inside of this galley. "No, just my pop helmet," he said, taking it off the hook on the wall and fitting it around his neck. It would activate the instant it detected vacuum.

"Space me! You guys already had pop helmets way back in The Rebellion?" She sounded even younger then. "Okay, let me just send for operational clearance." Silence for a few moments, then: "My CO wants to know The White Wolf's regnums. She can't find them in the database."

"Erm alright, charlie - foxtrot - sierra - tango - whiskey - two - seven - one - ate - dash - tree" he recited.

"And your Crewman I.D.?" she asked.

"fower - two - eight - fife - seven - tree - zero - ate - ate - bravo." He didn't even have to think about that one.

"Okay, I'll send that info up." Rose waited, surprised at his impatience after over four decades of waiting to be rescued. "It'll be a mo' for that to get sent up the chain, Sweets, sorry."

"It's all right," he said, but he didn't feel all right, Something about what she said just then, or the way she said it, bothered him. He felt nauseous and his head was swimming.

"So," Farmer said conversationally, "What happened to the White Wolf forty-six years, one-hundred and thirty-nine days ago?"

Rose forced himself to focus. "We were ambushed by Protectorate forces; unknown objective. They came out of nowhere."

"How did they get through the shielding of a Tower-class flagship?"

"I don't know," Rose said, "I was just a comm tech. I didn't even see what happened before... before..." What had happened after he left his post? He couldn't remember. How had he even gotten to the galley?

"Where was the White Wolf headed?" Farmer asked.

"Covert mission," Rose said, "We'd discovered the location of the Protectorate shipyards in the atmosphere of Jupiter. We were on our way to take it out. We were decelerating toward Vesta Station for a refueling when we were attacked."

Silence dragged for a few moments, then: "Okay, Crewman Rose, We've got clearance to get you out of there."

188

"What should I do?"

"Just grab anything you want to take with you, shut down the seals, and leap from the transverse bulkhead. I'll catch you." There was a smile in her voice at the last sentence.

Rose looked around the compartment that he'd been trapped in for two-thirds of his life. Was there anything in here that was important to him after all this time? There wasn't, and it surprised him. Why didn't he keep a journal, sculpt or paint something? Why didn't he create anything or decorate the bulkheads? "I wasted so much time here," he said.

"Let's not waste another minute, then, Sweets," she said, and the headache and nausea returned instantly. He felt like he was floating down through the deck, and it was all he could do not to vomit. *Sweets*? How did she –?

"Crewman Rose?"

"I'm here," he said, "but I can't shut the seals down. The shielding controls are behind this bulkhead, and I can't get to them while the seals are up."

"Hmm..." she said. "Hang a tick."

There was a minute of silence. Something had concerned him greatly just a few moments ago, but now he couldn't remember what it was. Something about Farmer...

"Okay," She said. "I've tapped into the shield controls for that compartment from my boat's computer. I'll take them down from here. I just need the ship's remote shield control code. You were comms, you should know it, right?"

"Yeah," Rose said, but hesitated. The shield command code was top, top secret. It was treason to share it, even with other crew members.

"C'mon, Crewman," Farmer said. She sounded just a bit impatient. "I can't get you out of there without that code."

Rose closed his eyes, and recalled the code, "six - seven - niner - foxtrot - victor - fife - one - six - niner - papa - fower - six - foxtrot"

"Thank you, Crewman Rose," she said, but her voice sounded different, closer.

He tried to open his eyes, but could not. Everything was darkness, and his head was feeling light again. He was frantic, frightened, but pain kept his words slow. "What's going on? Did you get the seals down?"

"I will have soon," Farmer said, her voice close now, right beside him and clear as a bell. "Thanks to you."

"Wait!" he shouted. He struggled, trying to push himself to sitting, but he could not. He was reclined, strapped to a bed, his arms and legs held in restraints. He still could not open his eyes.

"Stay calm, Sweets," she said. A soft hand brushed over his smooth, young cheek. "Our surgeon tells me you have a fresh concussion."

CB Droege is an author and voice actor from the Queen City living in the Millionendorf. His latest book is *Peacemaker and Other Stories*. Other recent publications include work in *Daily Science Fiction* and *Nature Magazine*.

*The Fate of the White Wolf* was previously published in *Balloons Lit. Journal*. Issue 4. 2016

Learn more at cbdroege.com

# Eggs On End

## by Atthys J Gage


*(Beep)*

*"Hi, Claws. I don't wanna get your heart all fluttery but me and Meem talked to the guy with that gallery with all the plywood in the windows out on Cecil B. They'll let us use the whole space while they're remodeling. I told Meem you'll definitely do something. I mean, you do wanna do something, right? Call me, Claw Claw. Bye."*

*(Beep. Hmmm.)*

Claudia wanted. Glendin and Mimi had been angling for months to get a show together, something just before the end of winter term so the Riley students would still be around. How they ever talked the owners of that old gallery into allowing the use of their space was more than Claudia could understand. But that was Glendin.

Something. She would do something.

\*

*Riley School of Art and Design* had not been Claudia's first choice. Riley probably wasn't anyone's first choice, but it had two things going for it: it was in Philadelphia, a whole country's length away from her hometown and family; and it had very casual admission standards, particularly regarding the applicant's portfolio.

*"Riley assumes a dedicated young artist willing to work hard in a creative atmosphere to realize his or her full potential. Our staff of qualified professionals will be there to assist and guide the individual."*

The two-year program had been all her parents had been willing to spring for. Claudia could see their point. Two extra years at Riley wasn't really going to improve her prospects all that much.

"What kind of a job can you get out of this?" her father had asked.

She rattled off a list of possibilities: publishing, commercial design, computer drafting, book illustration, costume design. In fact, none of those things interested her. She wanted to be an artist expressing her own vision, not mechanically producing someone else's. With deadlines no less.

She pondered the people she knew, former fellow Riley students. It amazed her how many of them found ways of being artists in the so-called real world. Glendin did layout for a magazine. Mimi was a cake decorator, for crying out loud! Claudia had the same qualifications they did. But they were good at presenting themselves.

More than that, they were good at *packaging* themselves. That had been the case right from the start. The first time she had seen Glendin, he had been wearing a feathered fedora and a tatty silk dinner-jacket, a touch of black eyeliner around one eye. Sure, it looked effete and affected, but Glendin embraced effete and affected. The clothes went with the voice and the walk and the curlicue hand-mannerisms. It all may have been like a Truman Capote knockoff, but it brayed out the word *artist*. Who else but an artist would dare be so cavalier?

None of that worked for Claudia. She hadn't even had the nerve to introduce herself as "Petra" first year. "Call me Petra." It would've been so simple. Instead, fearing discovery of the affectation, she had been honest. Only later did she find out that affectation was part of the game, a recognized and respected strategy. By then she was already stuck being Claudia.

"Claudia" proved to be a tough trap. She looked in the mirror and wondered how she could make her skin be paler, her hair

193

straighter. She bought austere clothes from second hand stores: a severe grey jacket; a long black skirt that didn't reflect light. She pulled her bushy hair back and caked her skin with the whitest foundation she thought she could get away with. But Claudia still showed through the white. Her cloddish Claudia-self.

First year, second semester, she'd fallen for a slim, serious boy with a German name who wore a suit and a tie and talked about "shattering the matrix that was personality." This sounded good to Claudia. She loitered in his presence whenever she could, hoping for pointers on how to find this personality-shattering device. But no hammer ever materialized. Dietrich or Joachim turned out to be all talk and glower, and her passing fling with existentialism or nihilism or whatever it was left her matrix infuriatingly intact.

She looked at the problem in terms of marketing. If she could just focus on the part of herself that she wanted people to see, she could crop out all the rest: Claudia, but reframed. She winced to hear her own name sometimes, just as she did to look in the mirror. She'd blown her chance to be someone else. Maybe she needed to move somewhere new, start fresh as smooth and stony Petra, bury Claudia and forget her.

"Anything can be great," Glendin said one night over coffee at Temple Grounds. "I don't care. Bricklaying can be great, if a guy knows." Glendin was fond of quoting old movies. Claudia didn't know who he was imitating and she found the sentiment unconvincing.

"You think I should get an office job, discover how filling filing can be?" Claudia sipped the decaf concoction she always ordered. She had no tolerance for stimulants. Other artists took amphetamines and stayed up for days on end, immersed in their work. She couldn't even handle regular coffee.

Glendin folded his paper napkin into four neat squares. "You never know until you try, Claws. There's actually something kind of relaxing about mindless work."

Mindless work. As if her real work – art – was an all-consuming passion she needed relief from. If only. She longed for something, someday, that would set her imagination aflame. Feverish imagination. She loved that phrase. Her imagination, alas, wandered vaguely from idea to idea like some grandma walking the mall and never once broke ninety-eight point six.

*

Claudia sat at her kitchen table staring at a tiny portable TV set. Everything in the kitchen was made on the same small scale: a double burner hot-plate, a toaster oven, 2.5 cubic feet of refrigeration. The TV droned, and she stared with perfect detachment at the screen. It was one of those shows where ordinary people submerge their bodies in tanks full of nematodes or eat live crickets. A smeary half-empty glass of bourbon sat on the table in front of her. She was having a hard time finishing it.

What was she going to do for the show? She needed to tell Glendin something soon. They had room for twelve. If she didn't want the space, someone else would.

"Just do something, Claws. Some kind of installation or some performance thing. I'm sure you've got ideas."

Ideas. When Claudia essentially washed out of all the more conventional visual arts, performance had seemed the ideal refuge. High-concept was all about the ideas. Every new performance piece was itself a redefinition. No one could criticize your technique when you were its inventor.

She picked up the bourbon glass and gave it a swirl, then she put it down again. This guy, a third-year she'd met a party, once told her that solid glass was not actually solid; it was a liquid at room temperature. "When glass cools down from its molten state, it doesn't form a crystal lattice. It simply becomes more and more viscous. All liquids have viscosity. Syrup is stiffer than water. Glass is even stiffer."

195

She had thought the whole thing was bullshit. The guy was trying to impress her, and she was pretty loaded at the time. It was odd how the words had stayed with her, though. She remembered clearly "crystal lattice" and "stiffer than water." She opened her notebook and jotted the words "stiff drink" across the top of a clean page. She stared at the words, waiting for them to generate ideas, associations, images. Nothing. She took a meagre swig of Old Crow and held it, burning, in her mouth.

Of course it *was* bullshit. Glass was not a liquid, not really. Bottles from ancient Rome had not slumped into little glass puddles. Glass was solid. Just a very disorganized solid.

The masochistic reality show cut to commercials. She watched each one, admiring their concise perfection. She wished her art could be like that. Simple, direct, memorable. Slogan art. Does she or doesn't she? The quicker picker-upper. Betcha can't eat just one! The incredible, edible egg.

She stood up. This was getting her nowhere. She would come up with something solid, something doable, without leaving this kitchen. And it would not involve buying new software or supplies or anything. She would make something entirely from materials available to her here and now.

She threw open her pantry cupboard. Dried pasta. Rice-a-roni. Two cans of tomato sauce. She could fill a colander with tomato sauce and suspend it over her head. Her *shaved* head. Let herself be slowly covered in sticky, red rain.

Right.

She opened the junk drawer: batteries, string, rubber-bands, a cupboard knob that had fallen off. Birthday candles she couldn't remember buying. A magic-marker. If you wrote on yourself with a magic marker, it would wear off eventually, right? She could draw tattoos all over herself with a sharpie. Wait! People could *watch* her draw on herself. Not tattoos but a complete coat. Every inch of her body inked. Pale white Petra becoming Claudia the Black.

196

Interesting, in the context of race and all. Identity versus appearance. But what would all of that magic-marker ink do to her skin? It always smelled so volatile.

She tossed the marker back into the drawer and crossed to the fridge. Enough. She'd make herself a late supper, finish her drink, then call Glendin and tell him to give her space away. She checked the egg carton for an expiration date but found it curiously absent. Well, how old could they be? She took one out and examined it. She sniffed it. It smelled like the refrigerator. It looked and felt like a perfectly good egg. She put it on the countertop and gave it a spin. You couldn't really tell for sure about eggs. Until you cracked them open. She kept the egg spinning. Maybe that could be her act. See if she could keep a dozen eggs spinning like a plate spinner. Play manic circus music in the background. Funny. But pointless. Maybe she could balance them on end instead.

Claudia felt a jolt. Her eyes snapped open. The TV was silent and the refrigerator was silent and the spinning egg wobbled to its silent rest. From some far off invisible world, a winged creature crossed a thousand crowded rooms, drifted over oceans and through foggy moors and planted a lingering kiss on her brow. She felt her forehead. It was hot and moist.

She looked down at the egg.

There was, of course, a prevailing urban myth that at midnight on the vernal equinox, you could balance an egg on end and it wouldn't fall over. In truth, you could do it anytime. All it took was steady hands. Appearances to the contrary, an egg is not perfectly smooth after all. Tiny imperfections in the shell and the table made it possible for the egg to stand. Her dad had shown her this trick when she was twelve. She'd balanced eggs lots of times.

She pictured a table covered with eggs, all standing on end like a little oval army. How many? Eggs, ovulation, menstruation, moons. Eggs as moons. Thirteen? The witches' number! Thirteen eggs. She could balance thirteen eggs on end. No! A matrix!

197

Thirteen by thirteen! A hundred and sixty-nine eggs? No, she couldn't do that. Thirteen was good. All in a line diagonally across a table. And red! Dye them – no, paint them – pale menstrual blood red!

She picked up the tumbler of Old Crow and knocked back the contents in a throat-searing gulp. When she put the glass down, she realized she was sweating.

*

Glendin had loved her idea. Or perhaps he had merely been relieved to see that she had one. In truth, it was Claudia's own uncharacteristic confidence and enthusiasm that had impressed the others.

"Vibrations are going to be a problem," someone warned.

Thomas helped her build a low platform of two-by-fours and plywood, and they covered it with a carpet remnant. Claudia found a heavy display table in the basement of the gallery and borrowed a white linen spread from Glendin's mom in Allentown. She practiced balancing, choosing eggs that seemed to work best and painted them a dusty rose.

She wrote:

"The balancing of eggs is an age old practice of women in pagan Europe. Tonight, I shall attempt to stand thirteen eggs on end in a straight line between the magnetic north and south poles. This I do in honor of all women everywhere. Silence would be appreciated."

She printed the statement out in a cool Lucida Grande font, and made a tag-board placard.

The evening of the show was the usual mix: jugs of white wine; small plastic cups; toothpick-skewered cubes of yellow and orange cheese arranged on platters. Glendin hovered everywhere, flitting from room to room like a plump, lavender butterfly. Mimi was rehanging everything for the third time. Lakota was profoundly, prophylactically, stoned. Only Claudia seemed truly immune to the opening night jitters. Her normally crippling insecurity was nowhere to be seen. She felt poised and alert, relaxed and ready. It was about the oddest she'd ever felt. She passed on the bargain chardonnay. She didn't need it, didn't want it. She collected the two cartons of hand-painted, hand-selected, grade A extra-large eggs from the cooler and took her place in the folding chair at the clean white table. "Like a fresh sheet of paper," she thought. She folded her hands across the blankness.

She would begin at eight. The whole process might take a while. Egg balancing was no sure thing. She might not finish at all, but even that, she knew, was okay. Succeed or fail, it was a performance either way. People would wander through, watch her for a while, then move on to something else. She closed her eyes, waiting for time to pass.

At 7:59 she opened the carton and selected her first egg and set it on the tablecloth. It looked lovely in the insufficient light, pale red against crisp, creamy white. She lifted it again and cradled it in her palm. Leaning low, she set it in the middle of the table and began nudging it one way and then back the other, subtly turning and sliding and tilting, making imperceptible, incremental adjustments. When she finally eased her hand away, the egg was standing, sitting improbably on its fat, rounded end.

A voice said: "One down."

She looked up. A man, plain-looking and fortyish, stood watching through wire-rim glasses. Claudia nodded, and the man walked away. She opened the carton and took out another egg.

Egg balancing is not, for the most part, a skill you can perfect. Given equal amounts of patience and steady hands, one person will be about as good at it as another. Finding that spot where imperfection of shell meshes with irregularity of tabletop varies uniquely from egg to egg. In such a task, luck and skill begin to

199

look very much the same, and there's little to be learned from either success or failure. Either way, you proceed to the next egg.

And so did Claudia. Eggs two and three went as easily as the first, and she began to think it would be too easy after all. But egg number four was an agony that seemed to be without end. She rejected the first number four, and the second, substituting other eggs from her initial two dozen. None of them seemed to want to sit. She examined the spot, scratching carefully at the linen, trying to roughen up the fibers without knocking over the other three eggs. Even when the fourth egg finally agreed to remain in place, it did so only grudgingly, and she wasn't happy with it at all. She frowned at the reluctant egg without satisfaction and moved on to the next one.

She worked her way out from the center, alternating one side then the other. When she needed to, she got up and circled the table, changing her reach and her angle like a pool player choosing his shot. Egg number five, number six, number seven. She hummed as she worked, almost inaudibly, a tune she couldn't have named for the life of her, moving methodically, egg by egg. Egg eight stood up. Then number nine. Claudia heard an appreciative murmur. She looked up. She had an audience. Claudia, who had spent her entire young life seeking the attention of an audience, scarcely even noticed.

She stood and stretched her kinked back. It was 10:26. She took a deep breath and looked at her creation, her nine ruddy ovoids stretched across the field of white. She hunkered down and sighted along the line. Not bad. Number four still bothered her, but it had held up so far. She selected her egg and took her position.

Number ten was the worst. Stubborn beyond all reasonable expectations of gravity and physics, the damn thing would not stand up. She tried a different egg. She shifted to a crouch, eye level with the table. She worried the linen cloth gently with a fingernail. Nothing worked. She sat up and stretched again, uncrimping her bunched shoulders. Leaning back on her heels, she stared at the recalcitrant egg in her palm. What does it want from me?

And then she forced herself to answer: it doesn't *want* at all. It is an egg.

She tried again. With the passionate delicacy of a nesting bird sitting its brood, she poised and steadied, held, withdrew, touched, retouched, eased off. Then, like a parent creeping away from the crib of a child who has finally fallen asleep, her hand drifted in slow silence, pulling away from the standing egg.

The audience, all of six people, breathed a collective breath. And tragedy struck. Number-ten egg toppled. And in its fall it wobbled perilously close to its neighbor, number eight. Claudia's hand shot out and plucked the stricken soldier from the field of battle before it could cause the fall of others. The crowd sighed and moaned in sympathy. That had been close.

Claudia felt surprisingly calm. It surprised *her* how calm she felt. Maybe the egg just needed more shaking. She had shaken all the eggs thoroughly beforehand. It helped with the balancing, something about settling the yolk at the bottom of the shell. She shook it vigorously, sincerely, passionately. After a half a minute, she stopped, and set the egg back into its position. No one in the room uttered a sound as she withdrew her untrembling hand. The egg stayed. Someone in the audience whooped quietly and was simultaneously shushed by everyone. Someone else said, "Don't egg her on," and there was nervous giggling.

Claudia had passed the tipping point. Nothing could stop her now. Eleven was easy, and after twelve she was one away from completion. She didn't care about the audience, didn't care that it was nearly midnight and she had been squatting and kneeling beside this table for the better part of four hours. She wasn't even thinking about what she would do when she was finished. She had nothing planned. Walk away? Or sit in her chair and stare silently at her creation? It didn't matter. All that mattered was egg number thirteen. Finishing what she had started.

The last egg did not go quietly. Again, on the verge of triumph, she almost foundered. She laid the uncooperative egg on its side and rubbed her eyes, pressing the heels of her palms between cheeks and brows. One more. One more egg and nothing else would matter. She just wanted one precious moment when she could look at all thirteen, her true creation, standing serenely in a perfect line. It could all fall down after that.

She opened her eyes again and picked up the egg. Rolling it between her palms, she visualized the end, pictured the little near-sphere sitting like a Buddha. All right. Once again, she brought the egg into position, eased back until only two fingers touched it. Then gently, until only the barest pressure remained, her hand rose into the air. She leaned back until she was sitting on her heels again. The crowd murmured. Several clapped, almost silently, and Claudia allowed herself a smile. Number thirteen was standing. They were all standing. She had done it.

And then?

*Then* she simply wasn't there any more.

*

Where was she? That would be a matter of conjecture. Doubtless her body was still in that dusty gallery. People saw her crumple over, collapse beside her masterpiece. But Claudia had gone somewhere else.

Her transportation had been sudden and, except for the slight woozy rush that she had mistaken for euphoria, quite unannounced. She looked around.

Where on earth...?

It would be impossible to describe the strangeness of Claudia's surroundings without mentioning the smell. Musty and familiar, like an old closet – an unsettling mix of coffee and mothballs – but also incongruously sweet, like someone had burnt the cinnamon toast. It seemed to be coming at her from very far away through layers of gossamer.

She was lying flat on her back. Her head refused to move, so she stared up at a high, vaulted ceiling. It was like a monumental warehouse. Sunbeams crossed from high-windows, and a shimmering dust was perpetually settling. Also worth mentioning would be the sound: a tapping sound descending from the endless brightness. Every now and then a tiny bell would ring, followed by the sound of a ratchet and a clunk.

"Where...?" she began.

Through leagues of tepid tap water, a voice rippled against her: *"Say... what you... will."*

"Who is that?"

*"Speak what... you... will?"*

There was the creak of a metal folding chair, the whistle and chirp of an oscillating frequency. Someone invisible hummed quietly as adjustments were made.

"Better?" the voice asked, perfectly clear now.

"Uh, yeah?"

"Good, good. Just a minute now, while I review your application." More quiet humming. "Eggs, I see. Hmmm, thirteen." Claudia waited in languorous paralysis. "All right," he said finally. "Everything seems in order. Have you reviewed your options?"

"Options?"

"Yes, yes. Normally with this sort of thing, there's an ascension to a higher plane, but this being your first attempt, we recommend reconnection with the earthly sphere. Spread the wisdom. Bestow boons."

Claudia felt her scowl muscles try to twitch, but even they seemed paralyzed. She said – or maybe only thought – "I have wisdom?"

Mr. Invisible chuckled. "Well, not as such. But really, your mere presence will convey volumes."

"Is it hard?"

"No effort on your part will be required. No sermon on the mound for you. We specialize in the ineffable. Arcane knowledge, mystical connections, strange coincidences, urban legends." There was another squeak of a chair leg. "Myths, puns, things like that. Of course, there is compensation. You will have powers."

"Powers?"

"Well, *a* power, let's say. I need to caution you though, super-strength has been discontinued. Really, it never works out."

"What do you mean? Like... making objects float, or turning water into wine?"

"Wellll..."

"What do *you* suggest?" Claudia asked.

"In your case?" She distinctly heard papers being shuffled and saw the light that streamed in from above shift from white to periwinkle, periwinkle to pink, pink to canary, canary to goldenrod. He muttered something indistinct, and then said, apparently to himself, "Yes, that would be appropriate." Then out-loud: "Standard twenty-eight day contract. Good, good, good."

"Wait," Claudia mentally stammered, "I don't understand."

"Well, like I said, that's one of the first components. Go in peace, think of your fallow man. Lather, rinse, repeat..."

"What?"

"Done and done. The goldenrod copy is yours."

\*

When Claudia woke up, Glendin was crouching beside her. A crowd of faces obscured the light. Her opening eyes prompted a wave of relieved murmurs.

"Are you all right?" Glendin asked.

She gave a vague nod, and Glendin helped her sit up. "Boy, you really threw yourself into *that* performance!"

There was a smattering of nervous laughter. Claudia didn't smile. "Why is everybody still here?"

Everyone went silent, staring at her with confusion on their faces. Glendin asked, "Why shouldn't we be here?"

In that instant, a moment of sudden clarity struck – as if a scrim had been lifted, and beneath that skirt of fog and uncertainty, the naked ankles of truth glimpsed. Claudia sat up straighter. "We need to get everyone out of this building! As fast as possible!"

Of course, inevitably, disbelief was the leading response to this. But her conviction had a chilling effect on the skepticism of many, and as Glendin and Thomas helped her down the stairs to the front door, a crowd gathered, and even the most stalwart couldn't help but feel the prickle of apprehension. It was then that someone smelled smoke.

Doubtless, the wiring in the old gallery was faulty. Probably it should've been condemned. But by the time the fire engines had left Cecil B. Moore Avenue, Claudia was lying on an emergency room examination table with a handsome and disheveled young resident shining a penlight in her eyes.

"Did you hit your head?"

"Soft landing," she answered.

He clicked off his light. "Your eyes look normal."

"Yours are bloodshot."

He smiled. "Blame it on the thirty-six hour shifts."

"I'm sure your girlfriend does," Claudia said. "Congratulations, by the way."

"For what?"

"Johns Hopkins. Your fellowship."

But that hadn't happened yet. It would be another day before he would find out about that. They admitted her for observation, mostly because of the vertigo. It was quite impossible for her to walk without assistance, due to her constant mistaking of floor for ceiling. This cleared up in a day or two, but by then, they had other reasons to be interested in her. She had become a genuine hospital celebrity.

The disheveled resident was only the first. Blame it on the ineffable, but Claudia was picking up information faster than she could dispense it: Nurse Bryant's pregnancy (twins); the MA with the marriage proposal; even a car accident she was unable to prevent because she thought the name *Doctor Bonebrake* was some kind of glitch in her reception. But Lester Bonebrake, alas, was a real doctor who, fortunately, recovered. After that, she learned to trust her intuition even if it seemed loopy. She detected a case of polycystic kidney disease when a patient walked down the hallway, and atrial fibrillation when she heard another one yelling at the charge nurse. Soon the doctors were dropping by for regular, though surreptitious, consults.

When she left after three days, her fame followed her. Hers was the sort of story people were likely to talk about, and soon everyone wanted to ask her about everything. When she told the local newspaper about the *E. coli* break out two days before it happened, her reputation went national overnight.

Every trade magazine and website with an interest in paranormal phenomenon wanted to interview her, and the mainstream press quickly got on board. A professor at U. Penn wanted to set up clinical trials on remote viewing. She did a spectacular turn on Oprah. She was even offered a column at the *National Enquirer*. When she accurately predicted the engagement of a notable pop-singer to a notorious movie star, she became a star

206

in her own right. She bore the frenzy with a surprising and impressive calm. To her credit, she told no one who was going to win the Superbowl.

And then, of course, it ended. She woke up one morning, feeling calm and well-rested and with her psychic antenna picking up absolutely nothing. She checked the calendar: twenty-eight days exactly. She turned on the TV to watch herself on a morning news show they'd taped the day before and made breakfast – two over-easy on toast.

That night, she had a dream. She was walking the hallways of a dim office building holding a sheet of yellow paper. In a cramped office, a balding and bespectacled man asked her a series of questions, none of which she could remember upon waking. When she left, he thanked her with a pleasant smile. She rode the elevator down, and when the door opened, it was morning.

Needless to say, there were a lot of disappointed people. Guest appearances had to be cancelled, and the professor from Penn tore up his grant application. Glendin kicked himself for not having asked her for lottery numbers.

"I'm not sure that would've worked."

"Why not?"

Claudia shrugged. "Misuse of power, maybe. Probably there would've been some kind of karmic payback."

Glendin wasn't convinced. "There has to be some way to capitalize on this."

In the end, his fertile imagination came through, and *Eggs by Claudia* was born. They were quite the fad for a while: polished wooden eggs in nests of excelsior, with a hand-lettered fortune inside each one. Well, perhaps not an actual fortune – but something cryptic and mystical sounding. Claudia, it turned out, had a gift for generating these:

"Collect the day in handfuls, but scatter them again before night."

"Seek the blooms of fortune among the boughs of conscience."

"Dream from the middle and let the ripples spread outward."

They had a zen-like quality that people seemed to enjoy. Their lack of any specific meaning let consumers interpret them as they wished. A website even sprung up where aficionados sparred online about what they meant. Rumors quickly spread that Claudia spoke her dark pearls from sleep-like trances, or channeled an ancient prophet. In fact, she usually wrote them sitting at her laptop, associating freely with her own whimsy. Sometimes she would even assemble them at random, trusting in people's ability to find meaning and poignancy in almost anything.

It wasn't, she knew, anything anyone would call art.

"People don't want art, Claw Claw," Glendin told her. "They want mirrors. Shiny, reflective baubles they can see themselves in."

Maybe. And that was all right. She knew this wouldn't last either. She'd keep writing her little slogans, producing her little eggs until people weren't interested anymore. And then, she'd do something else. And that would be all right too, probably.

Something had changed since that fateful day when everything had balanced. Through a series of purely random steps, her life had ascended to a more ordered plane, and it pleased her in a completely new way. She did not dread each new day. Each had its own odd sort of perfection, and even if one spoiled on her, there was always another one coming tomorrow. If she had to give a name to the way she felt, she might have called it *being happy*. It wasn't like anything she'd ever felt before.

And it was nothing she ever could've predicted.

Atthys Gage is a writer with a lifelong love for myth, magic, and books. His second real job was in a bookstore. As was his third, fourth, fifth and sixth. Eventually, he stopped trying to sell books and started writing them. He has always had a fascination for that cloudy borderline between the normal and the paranormal and spends a lot of his time thinking about flying carpets and sentient flecks of alien consciousness and other stuff like that. In the so-called normal world, he lives on the coast of Northern California with his long-suffering wife, strong-willed children, and several indifferent chickens. He can be found occasionally blogging at atthysgage.com, and all of his books are available at Amazon.

# Earth, Sky, Ocean

by Melinda Giordano

## Bump In The Night

I live near a park flooded with tar. It is bound with thick lakes linked together in a chain the color of onyx, dark and bruised. Its currents are hidden and dense, circulating like a mole beneath the city – the slow, knotted arms digging below streets, houses, lamps, cars.

Once, animals in their primordial stage stumbled into the sticky murk to suffocate, to have their essence dissolve into the depths. Now the tar is rich with their marrow, vertebrae, ribs and teeth. It bubbles and winks – its surface is awash with petroleum rainbows; its depths are restless with the stifled lives of prehistory. Their cartography maps the destruction of the Pleistocene – the smiling skulls, the hooked fangs, the rippling spines.

The vents of asphalt and oil travel for miles, clogging pipes and roots, a torment to the plumbing of the city. They are under my home, where 25,000 years ago there was rain and fog, where forests grew high to disappear into the maw of vapor and cloud. I live where the mists dried into savannahs covered with pale grass, choking in the heat of a vindictive climate change.

I walk over the concealed pools – stagnant and viscous – that lurk under my floorboards; the assorted square feet of plywood and nails. The slow tides of melted wood and earth twist around the buried foundations of my house. The composition is stained with the animals' DNA – the fabric of extinction.

Sometimes the floors will creak with the protests of myriad interred lives; when I walk, a chorus of voices follows me. And when I sleep, I dream of the monsters, prehistoric and whole, striding towards their demise. I see the march that would only end when their flesh had curdled and melted into the ancient earth.

Awake or asleep, the sounds of detached bones invade my thoughts, an unfocused bumping like the spars of a wrecked ship caught in aimless waters. I sense the invisible grazing herds, the feral, bloody hunts. I live with these phantoms that have relinquished their earthly lives and are trapped within a ghostly jurisdiction. I live with the things that go bump in the night

### The Bruise

The coil of wind curled around the fallen blossom, taking it in its fist and hurling it into the helix of airstreams knotting the sky. It climbed, high and hypnotic: a scarlet crumb of fabric torn from a hem, a rose from a petticoat, its color as bloody as a scraped knee. It was such a dainty scrap of shrapnel wheeling over my head: a compelling design that traced a gory path through the air, shedding cherry-colored drops that stained my hair.

It rose as confused as a butterfly, twisting and captivating, yet for all its folly acting as if it was taking the most careful aim. I stood, a willing target, in the path of its willful temper. It circled closer and closer, until – as if it was overcome by a burst of shyness – it dropped back to the ground. Like a modest shuttering of eyes, or a suddenly bashful child seeking solace behind his mother's skirts, it lay there still and muffled.

I waited a moment longer, watching the dying wings struggle in a ruby pool at my feet. It drowned very prettily. And when all breath was gone, its blood became thick and clotted: a decorative bruise to join the others that mottled the sidewalk.

### My Wedding

I found the shell by the rim of the ocean, a ring of bone

balanced on the wreckage of kelp and wood verdant with the opaque scents of brinish decay. Its center was round and musical: like a bell, it must have rung repeatedly as it spun through its submerged world, dappled with prisms of light and scales. But before me now, a stationary instrument, it was quite silent.

It was the color of froth and ivory; drenched in gentle sepia and pale like the ships' sails that billowed with the ocean's nautical edicts. Cut by the whim of the sea and the fist of the tide, its outline was a crooked landscape. Its maritime alchemy was made of brine, of riggings as tangled as discarded corsets, of drowned fogs and the breath of fishes. Its core was a rosette, curling like the architectural heart of a flower. Polished by currents of sand, molded by the curving, relentless acres, it came to an end on the rocks: broken and finished.

And that is where I found it – my accidental gift refined by the jeweler whose horizon extended into a silver oblivion. I placed it on my finger and I sensed the approval: in the salty breeze heavy with the voices of whales and seabirds; in the sounds of the pearls and scallops that tumbled through shrimp-pink grottos. I sensed their misty chorus: their pelagic blessing on my marriage to the sea.

Melinda Giordano is a native of Los Angeles, California. Her written pieces have appeared in the *Lake Effect Magazine, Scheherazade's Bequest, Whisperings, Circa Magazine* and *Vine Leaves Literary Journal* among others. She was also a regular poetry contributor to CalamitiesPress.com with her own column, *I Wandered and Listened,* and a Pushcart Prize nominee. She writes flash fiction and poetry that speculates on the possibility of remarkable things – the secret lives of the natural world.

*The Bruise* was originally published in *The Vine Leaves Literary Journal.*

# Tiberian Minnows

## by Stephen McQuiggan

The two dogs approached Livia as she ambled up the sprawling drive to Whinstone House but they were too salty around the muzzle to be a threat to her, and even if they had been young she would have beaten them to death with her cane before a growl warmed their throats. She had done such things before, bringing down a cow once; though that had been exhausting, and if the damn thing hadn't been so docile she would never have managed it. She stopped to admire the large pond in the garden, kneeling to peer through the murk at the strange creatures on its bed.

'What do you think you're doing?' The raspy, querulous voice buzzed waspishly round her head. Livia bit back the urge to spin round and smash the source in with her cane. She plastered on her trademark professional smile instead.

'Mr. Loney? My name's Livia Preston. Your Health Visitor.' She offered her hand. 'Didn't they tell you I was coming?'

The old man regarded her with eyes as misty as his mutts'. 'I never answer the telephone,' he said. 'If I wanted to speak to disembodied voices I'd hold a séance.' He stared at Livia's hand until she was forced to drop it. 'And it's *Doctor* Loney,' he pouted, turning his back on her as he began struggling up the steps to his door.

*Silly old sod*, thought Livia, *he's been retired longer than I've been alive. It will be a pleasure to turn him over, rob him blind.*

'What *are* these delightful creatures you have in your pond, *Doctor*?'

He paused but didn't turn. 'They're Tiberian minnows,' he said, a hint of mocking laughter in his wheezy old voice. *Pretty big*

214

*for minnows*, Livia thought, *more like salamanders with those little legs. Old fool's probably doting.* 'Hurry up,' the old man said; a sandblast hiss. Oh yes, she was going to enjoy this one.

The interior of Whinstone House was every bit as impressive as its setting suggested; the hallway alone contained enough knick-knacks (that would fit oh so discreetly in her voluminous pockets) to make the trip worthwhile. Livia paused on the threshold, drinking in the heady scent of antique furniture and the pleasing undercurrent of hardwood. So much more dignified than the stench of boiled cabbage and full nappies that pervaded the council house she had been reared in.

Her mother had always called her a little magpie, and there were enough baubles and trinkets here to feather her nest to her own eclectic, expensive tastes. A cruel smile twisted Livia's mouth as she followed the wheezy old Doctor (*Physician, heal thyself!*) down the heavily carpeted hall, musing all the while – *This could be the one, no more need of grubby pawnshops and greasy banknotes with such big game finally in sight.*

The old man was muttering to himself, his grumbling muted by the rich, lush wallpaper. 'Excuse me?' said Livia, slipping into her obsequious professional routine without even thinking.

'I said "Keep up", I haven't all day. The children need feeding.'

*Children?* Livia felt her heart sink as she entered a large room filled with leather bound books. Then she saw the dogs and breathed a sigh of relief.

There were six of them; six ugly, shitty arsed little pugs. She had been worried for a moment, expecting a stern-faced son or a cold-eyed daughter to appear, intent on protecting their inheritance. Her relief presented as snorting laughter. Loney paused, gazing at her over his shoulder as the pugs yapped at his feet.

'When you said "children",' she began, but he cut her off with a wave of his wrinkled, delicate hand.

'I've no time for the kind of family you mean,' he said, pulling stale treats from his musty old pockets and scattering them onto the floor. 'I never could abide babies.' He rubbed his hands together; dust, that may or may not have come from the dog biscuits, falling from them in a misty cloud. 'Perhaps that's why I killed so many.'

'I beg your pardon?' Still on a high that the old fool had no progeny to interfere, Livia was certain she had misheard.

'Abortion, Miss Preston,' he enunciated with relish. 'It was one of my specialties. I must have terminated thousands of the little blighters, and took pride in it too. World's overrun as it is. Our species needs to evolve, find another way. Do I shock you?' His tone was hopeful.

'Not at all,' she said, 'if I'd my way they would all be aborted up to the age of ten.' If the old goat thought he could shock her he was in for a very rude awakening.

Dr Loney studied her as he chewed on his bulbous lower lip. 'What's this all about?' he demanded, a hefty dollop of colour in his dewlaps.

'It's just standard procedure,' said Livia, touring the room, rubbing her fingers along the ornaments as she mentally positioned them in her own flat. 'You were hospitalised recently, a breakdown of some sort I believe, and this is really just a follow up to make sure you're not heading for a relapse.' She turned to look at him, to watch her words strike home. 'At your age, you can't be too –'

'I didn't have a breakdown!' His voice rebounded off the polished floor with a shotgun crack, and Livia was hard put to suppress a grin. 'Those fools, they don't understand... ' he trailed off, his rant strangled by a sudden shortness of breath.

'Don't worry, Dr Loney,' she beamed, 'you know how these things are. A few questions, a quick look round, then I'll leave you to your adoring children.'

216

'Ask what you will, but you'll be poking your nose nowhere,' Loney said. 'I don't care what laminated cards or artistically tasteful letterheads you have in your bag, I won't have you rummaging around my house.'

'I assure you, it's merely a matter of –'

'Tea?' He cut her off as he headed off toward the door; 'I always find tea beneficial for a headache, and talking to you I feel a migraine is imminent.' *Oh, you have no fucking idea of the headache I'll cause you*, she thought as he left the room.

She inspected the sideboard up close – not a single mote of dust. He must have a maid who does for him, she reasoned and made a mental note to quiz him on her arrival and departure times. Her eye fell on a door by the corner, half concealed by a heavy curtain. She grasped its ornate handle and gave it a sturdy rattle. Locked.

'You have no business down there,' Loney said; for an old man he was light on his feet.

She turned, unruffled, a woman used to working on the wing. 'I have to view the entire house, Doctor, if I am to assess it for my report.'

'Are you aware of the Emperor Tiberius and his penchant for what he liked to call his minnows?'

'So what's in there?' she said, ignoring him; she could afford to be brazen, it was clear he was already paddling in the pool of senility. 'It must be dangerous, or valuable, if you have to keep it locked up.'

'It's where I work... where I perfect my projects.'

'Work?' Livia sneered. 'You do realise you're retired, don't you? You shouldn't be exerting yourself at your age, you'll have another *incident*.'

'You don't retire from a vocation,' he said, setting down the tea tray; 'Sugar?'

'One, please. Is your "work" so volatile you must keep it behind a bolted door, Mr. Loney?' she asked, taking the proffered cup.

'I wouldn't want my children to stray,' he said, stirring his own reflectively; 'At least, not yet.'

Livia looked at the foolish little dogs with barely concealed contempt. 'I'll have to put those in my report I'm afraid. They simply can't be hygienic... unless you have a cleaner, of course? Six little mutts defecating everywhere,' she wrinkled her nose, 'well, it's an accident waiting to happen.'

'My dear,' the Doctor smiled, 'when you have studied the workings of the inner body as I have, you find that shit is a thing of rare beauty. Tell me, Miss Preston, do you have any children of your own?'

Livia snorted in reply; the very idea of spending money and time on such things.

'I see you share my feelings somewhat,' smiled Loney. 'I don't *hate* them, per se, it's just I find them badly designed.' He sipped eagerly at his tea, glad of an audience. 'They're ridiculously vulnerable and take years to shed that fragility. Then, when they reach maturity, they are so indoctrinated by modern mores, brainwashed by our shallow society, they are virtually useless. We are breeding a species of duds, Miss Preston, filling the world with creatures Nature would cull in a heartbeat if we let her.'

'You sound quite the little Mengele, Doctor,' Livia smirked.

'Don't act so coy and virginal, my dear. You're a cruel one – I could tell the moment I laid eyes on you. That hawkish nose, those thin callous lips... your physiognomy is a very revealing book.'

Livia set her cup down hard enough to rattle the saucer. She was genuinely insulted. She was a natural beauty, everyone said so

218

– if there was a hint of cruelty in her face then surely that only added to her allure; her nose was a tad sharp, but undoubtedly noble.

Loney produced a key from his pocket and waggled it like a dog treat in front of her. 'Would you like to steer that big rudder of yours into my Lab? Have a little snuffle around, eh?'

'I'm required to assess the entire house,' she said. 'If you wish to start in your little playroom, I'm more than happy to oblige.'

She watched as he waddled over to the door, fidgeting the key into the lock. He was infirm, his bald patch and his hands mottled with liver spots. He was exactly the kind of old duffer who fell downstairs or tripped on a rug and broke his neck, and she would relish helping him on his way. Maybe she'd drown the sarcastic old bastard in his pond – *hawk nose indeed!* – and let his Tiberian minnows chew the saggy old jowls from his brittle skull.

'Why, thank you,' she simpered as held the door wide for her, beckoning her through with old fashioned gusto. A strange mix of saline and soap assaulted her nostrils before Loney flicked on the fizzling lights to reveal a large room filled floor to ceiling with aquariums, vivariums, and cages. She wandered over to one of the tanks, her spirits soaring.

'Oh dear,' she said, 'I'm going to have to put this in the report, I'm afraid.' She rapped the glass with the edge of her ring; the snake behind the glass flicked out a malicious tongue. 'Is it poisonous?'

Loney smiled. 'Nothing here is as venomous as you, Miss Preston.'

She ambled down the aisle between the tanks, staring at the hideous prehistoric looking fish; their jaws filled with a tumble of barbarous teeth, their eyes darker than any ocean depth. She paused by some salamanders. 'Are these the same ugly brutes you stock your pond with?' She could afford to be chatty; she had the old

219

bastard over a barrel now.

'Distant relatives,' he said; he seemed to be enjoying some private joke. Then Livia saw what she was after – there on the shelf by the back wall, pickled in jars: *Leverage.*

And in the jars, twisted and squashed, their faces elongated and blanched but still recognisable: 'Babies,' Livia breathed. She spun to face Loney. 'You... ' He was folding a small handkerchief, humming to himself. 'What have you done?'

He came at her with surprising speed, pressing the cloth over her mouth, her nose. 'I've no jars big enough for you, my little adder,' he said, as her knees buckled and the room swam in a chemical kaleidoscope, 'but I'm sure you won't mind sharing one of the tanks.' He laughed, and all the colour drained from the world.

*

Drawn to the pond, Tara stood awhile admiring the sweep of Whinstone House and breathing in the sharp pine scented air. Normally her work brought her to rundown estates or crumbling tower blocks but, thanks to a colleague's sticky fingers, finally she had been sent out to the fresh climes of the countryside.

She felt a momentary pang of shameful guilt – nothing had been proved regarding Livia Preston's incipient kleptomania but, really, why else would she disappear? Her Area Manager had let it slip that when the police searched Livia's flat it was a veritable Aladdin's cave of stolen goods. The guilt slid away easily. Tara had never liked her, hated her, if she was honest; there was something about her angular face, something she couldn't quite put her finger on.

'Can I help you?'

Tara turned at the unexpected voice to find a little red cheeked man scowling up at her. 'Oh, hello,' she said, 'you must be Doctor Loney. My name's Tara McCormack, your new Health Visitor, I believe you're expecting me? Can I just say, you have an absolutely

220

beautiful home.'

Loney continued scowling as if searching for a hidden barb, but Tara smiled so sweetly he visibly softened beneath her gaze. 'Yes,' he said, his voice mellower now, softer, 'I am rather fond of it.'

'I was just admiring your pond too, Doctor. I hope you don't mind.'

'Not at all, I made it to be enjoyed.' The old man seemed boyishly pleased by her interest. 'Take a closer look,' he urged, 'you may see some of my specimens down there.'

'Your specimens?'

'My children, I call them. A lonely old man's fancy, no doubt. I breed new strains of amphibian in my lab, release them out here.'

Tara hunkered down, peering beneath the glassy surface of the water. 'Yes!' she said, 'I see them – why, they're magnificent Doctor, and so huge! I've never seen their like.'

'You're too kind,' Loney said, kneeling beside her. 'Perhaps, when you've finished your little inspection, I can show you where I create them, so to speak.'

Tara burst out laughing, a high joyous cascade that tingled on the water and caused the old man to frown. 'Sorry,' she said, blushing, 'it's just... well, that big one at the very bottom that seems to be watching us,' she pointed at the cause of her sudden mirth, at the cold eyes and sharp features that made her realise what it was exactly she despised about Livia Preston, 'it reminds me of somebody I used to know.'

Smiling, taking her by the hand, Dr Loney led her toward the house.

221

Stephen McQuiggan was the original author of the bible; he vowed never to write again after the publishers removed the dinosaurs and the spectacular alien abduction ending from the final edit. His other, lesser known, novels are *A Pig's View Of Heaven* and *Trip A Dwarf.*

# Sweet And Bitter

## by Deborah Whittam

Full, bright red lips tilted to form an impertinent smile, her heels beating a rhythmic staccato as she crossed the floor with a languid stride. She was unperturbed by their scrutiny, her chin raised proudly as she nodded towards the dowager, who eyed her with open condemnation. Some might blush beneath their judgmental gazes or be mortified by their obvious scrutiny but she had no intention of acknowledging it. With natural grace she raised her hand, luxuriating in the attention as she pushed her amber curls back so they cascaded over her shoulders.

Their hatred was a tangible force; their attendance at her afternoon tea was prompted by the bitter brew of hatred and jealousy. They sought scandal and she was determined not to disappoint; as she reached the sideboard she pivoted towards the French window, allowing the sun to kiss her ample bosom displayed in a low cut décolletage. Her garb might be deemed unsuitable for the occasion but it was more than appropriate for him, and as she dutifully turned fulfilling her role of hostess by pouring tea into the delicate white china cups, she raised a hand to her neck in a deliberately provocative gesture. They believed that she was tethered by a need for their approval but in truth she held them captive by their desire to know, they were embarrassed to watch but more afraid to miss the anticipated spectacle and at the first pluck of guitar strings she swung towards the balcony.

As the sound feathered down her spine, causing a tingle within, she saw it – a bright green eye peering through the peephole in the silken screen. For an instant she was disconcerted, a slight frown marring the smooth perfection of her brow. Then her lips curved to form an enticing smile: how delightful, a spy.

Her laugh was a trickle of water within a babbling brook and while it served to satisfy those in attendance, there was no denying that this routine was proving tedious, for there was no more fractious child than boredom and with a toss of her head she cast a droll aside to the ladies, a half-smile her silent acknowledgement of their predicament. They were so intent, so desperate, that they barely dared breathe and she threw a glance towards the source of their curiosity, meeting eyes that were dark pools casting no reflection.

Here was the perfect choice to relieve the tedium of her daily existence, the perfect foil to her ivory beauty, the perfect contrast to her luxurious life; but most importantly, here was the perfect accomplice for disrupting propriety. With a gold ring hanging from his earlobe, garbed all in black except for a brightly coloured handkerchief at his neck, he was a renegade of another time, a shadow cast by disrepute and dishonour and she felt her lips tingle as she recalled the harshness of his formidable passion.

As he rose to his feet, the dowager cleared her throat in displeasure, pursing her lips and tightening her grip on the handle of the porcelain cup. The dowager's reaction was of no consequence when she was so attuned to his every movement. She knew the moment he decided to act, to discard the guitar, which had been his convenient excuse to gain entrance. She knew when he slipped with a catlike grace from the balcony. She knew what prompted the cascade of murmurs from the old dears and, unnerved, she turned, meeting her spy's gaze, even as she tensed at the telltale flex of the floorboards.

Her lips parted in a soundless gasp as an arm crept around her waist, pulling her close and clasping her lithe form to hard contours, as a chorus of outraged murmurs erupted. Delighted at their shock, she allowed her body to relax into his embrace, felt her nipples tighten, felt his breathing grow harsh and labored, and she flushed with desire. It was a delicious sensation, this perverse delight their astonishment, and she lifted her chin, determined to wear her shame proudly.

Amused, she arched her brow as he jerked the handkerchief from his neck to hold it in front of her waist – then frowned as he pulled it tight and began to twist. As the ladies' murmurs grew, the first inklings of doubt beset her; discomforted, she endeavored to break his hold, but his arms locked her in. Even before the shriek vibrated through the room, instinct compelled her to reach out towards the handkerchief, but his movements were swift and the cord was at her throat in an instant. Her audience rose to their feet as one, dismissing her as they seized the opportunity to flee, and in that moment she sought the eyes of the only one who remained, the only one who hadn't abandoned her, the one who continued to watch through eyes which were so familiar. As she caught sight of the horror reflected in his eyes, recognition dawned.

"Damon..."

Her voice broke on the word as the cord was applied to her throat and in desperation she fought as her son watched on, even as her lover thrust his knee into the small of her back, causing her spine to arch.

She struggled but he didn't relent, he only leant closer, his breath warm against her earlobe as he murmured in a cold, mocking voice, "Damon? You call for your husband now? But he is the one paying me." She thrashed in desperation as he whispered his message through the gathering darkness, "Your husband bids you farewell ma petite chérie. He requests that you remember him in your final sleep."

Deb Whittam is a graduate from Macquarie University Bachelor of Arts and she is currently traversing the great continent of Australia in a caravan. She seeks to explore the many forms of reality in her writing and examine how perspectives can alter when life is viewed through an alternate lens.

Twitter: http://twitter.com/@DebbieWhittam

Blog: http://debbiewhittam.wordpress.com

# Hell In A Handbasket

by Mimi Speike

Ever wonder where the phrase came from? (1)

I say it originated – one memorable evening at an inn in Saxony – with John Dee.

German inns were the worst in Europe. A nice hayloft was preferable, at least in the summer months. The aristocracy glided from estate to estate, intertwined lineage affording them lavish private accommodation nearly anywhere. A Freifrau (an insignificant title, third lowest rank of nobility) like Annette von Droste-Deckenbrock patronized inns. She, along with her daughter Drusilla and her daughter's tutor, a Herr Heinz-Helmut Wakenroder, are making their way from Bremen to Hameln.

Having covered that stretch many times, she has her favorite stops, where she is often awarded the owner's own bed (he not in it, of course) with the cleanest sheets and fewest bedbugs in the joint.

On this journey, she is joined by the redoubtable John Dee, celebrated scientist, mathematician, and advisor to Her Majesty Queen Elizabeth, and by Sly, Sylvester Boots, his cat. Sly is my all-sass-all-swagger reincarnation of Puss-in-Boots.

This material is an excerpt from my novella *Paying The Piper*. John Dee and Sly have fled London, where they'd been fixtures at the English court until they'd managed to offend the Queen. Dee, broke – he was always broke, his position as Royal Astrologer paid mostly in prestige – has answered an ad for a rodent-eradication expert in a North German town. His trusted assistant – they had just foiled an assassination attempt on the Queen – is pleased to tag along.

Dee is determined to win the advertised reward. The town, overrun by rats, is frantic for relief. Dee, with his solid scientific reputation – he is no fly-by-night – has been hired by a skittish town council. There had been previous disastrous experiences with fast-talking exterminators, most notably when, two centuries before, the town's children had been lured away over a disputed payment.

Dee has an off-the-wall scheme that he believes in whole-heartedly. (In his later years he'd become fairly unglued.) Sly will eventually devise a plan of his own. Heinz-Helmut has an iron in the fire, he's after that dough himself. Who will prevail? Read the novella to find out. It will be available shortly on: MyGuySly.com

‡‡‡‡‡
‡‡‡‡‡

At Zum Wilden Eber (The Wild Boar) mother and daughter are immediately shown to Frau Diefenbach's apartment, the common room, full of exhausted travelers arguing, pushing, and scuffling, no fit place for a fine lady. Dee and Heinz, left to fend for themselves, take seats at a long table and are served a meat broth with bread, the meat tough, and tasteless. There is salted fish, but it disappears before the platter reaches them. Wine of the most inferior sort flows freely.

All guests in a German inn are expected to turn in at the same time. (So says a period account by Desiderius Erasmus, a Dutch Renaissance humanist.) Dog-tired or not, Dee and Heinz must bide in place until all diners have eaten, or, more correctly, drunk their fill. Sooner or later the patrons take wing *en masse* and are up the stairs to a nasty bed. No wonder they tarry. Bottomless vino verses a bed full of bedbugs, no contest, right?

German innkeepers pride themselves on their ability to remain indifferent to their customers' comfort. How does the Freifrau rate? She is eating the owner's own dinner, a lovely rabbit stew, and drinking his excellent beer. Simple. She flatters a tradesman by cultivating him as a friend, and also tips magnificently. Her traveling companions eat the you-get-what-you-get menu in the

228

dining hall. But they are not unhappy to sit and talk while they down all the grape they can hold.

Let's see now, where's that cat? *Ah!* He's tucked under the table, at Dee's feet, housed in his hamper for safety's sake. The lid ajar, he's being handed down the more inedible bits of the meal. Drusilla had thrown a tantrum, demanding he remain with *her*. He's relieved to have been denied the pleasure of being wound tight in her arms, she whispering her undying devotion into his ear half the night.

"A toast, my friend!" Heinz lifts his goblet.

"Hear, hear," John Dee reciprocates.

"To *Herself.*"

"*Huh!*"

"Queen Bee."

"Absolutely."

"The pipsqueak takes right after her."

"Sure seems to."

"Better days a-coming, Doctor."

"Let's hope so."

"Skol!"

"Salut!"

"Bottoms up!"

"You're not a bad guy, you know." (If you've lost track of who's speaking, don't fret. The thought is in both heads.)

"I appreciate that."

"How'd you latch onto her?"

"A weak moment."

229

"Do tell."

Heinz sighs. "I intended to earn my degree and teach."

"A commendable goal."

The corner of Heinzie's mouth clenches. "The daughter of my professor made eyes at me. He got wind of it. He expected better for her than – *one of no extraordinary expectations* is how he put it. He went for the throat. He questioned the quality of my scholarship, accused me of plagiarism, destroyed me."

"Did you plagiarize?"

"Please. Water under the bridge."

"We all have skeletons. Beg, borrow and steal is *my* motto."

"I landed at a lesser university, nowhere near the prestige. There I chanced upon the Freifrau, hunting for a tutor to instruct a precocious child with great potential. Precocious! I can think of better words. Pestilential, for one. Worn down from barely getting by, pea soup in a frigid garret – you may know the routine – I jumped on it."

"I lived high during my student days, but I feel your pain."

"You might's well–" Heinz is beginning to slur his speech "– hear it all. To seduce a fine fortune, I felt it not beyond me. Annette worships scholarship, and I am a pretty fellow, why deny it? I set to work at being the *prochain ami*, the best friend, attentive to a fault, as solicitous as the closest kin. My previous dalliance influencing my choice, I fixed my sight on" – he paused to refill his glass – "Sir! To the darling Drusilla."

"Drusilla? Lord Above! I guessed *Annette. Drusilla!* How do you cope with the brat? She's driving my poor cat wild."

"*Ha!* You can say that again!" hoots Sly. Dee kicks his box.

Heinz, not attuned to the small, odd voice, misses it. "From the first, she despised me. That's not saying much, she despises

230

.

everyone. I quickly understood that avenue to be a dead end. The mama is another story. I'd made considerable hay on that parcel, until recently. Quite a situation, eh, Doctor?"

"Damn right!" says Dee, reminded of his own unhappy entanglements. (2)

"I am in a bind," confides Heinz. "Things have gone downhill for me with the Freifrau. I may find it necessary to leave Hameln. I need money. A *lot* of money."

"Don't we all!"

"That reward will do for us both," says Heinz. "I don't care what you have, or think you have up your sleeve, you ought to hear my idea."

"Proceed."

"I'll be frank. I dismiss the reputation that sold you to those village idiots, our town council. It may be a money-maker for you, but it's all spark and no catch, and we both know it. The problem will be solved by a mechanical solution, not a mystical one. At the same time, there must be a magical aspect to it, the dolts expect it. We would make a good team, you on the hocus-pocus, me, the grunt work."

"A two-pronged approach. Couldn't hurt."

Heinz continues. "I have a familiarity with calmatives, my father a medical man. I have devised a formula that renders a true terror relatively docile. I do not administer it at present. Her mother, forced to deal with the girl in her natural state during our recent sojourn, is reminded of the miracle I have wrought." He taps his forehead. "Having achieved a good outcome with my disorderly pupil, I wondered what effect it might have on rats. When I heard you were on your way to us, I said – *aha!* – *the final piece to the puzzle.* Your reputation, the town has gone for it hook, line, and sinker. Someone is going to connive these imbeciles out of their savings. Why not us?"

"I see where you're going. We taint granaries, monitor nightly, discover rats sedated, smash their skulls, and, I presume, disappear them to a ditch on the outskirts, in other words, into thin air. A bit dodgy but, who knows? We have two good brains here…"

"*Three!*" corrects a party below, unmistakably aggrieved.

Dee distracts from the interjection with an equally explosive, "*Sir!* Why not a common poison, easier and cheaper to obtain?"

Heinz is delighted to instruct a celebrated scholar. "Poison, kept clear of the grain, is easy for an intelligent critter – and they are highly intelligent – to avoid. My formula mixes *into* the grain. The right dosage will affect a small animal powerfully, though such as you or I would feel a pleasant relaxation, nothing more. But it will take a *vat* of the stuff to treat even one storehouse, as a proof of competence. That's been my roadblock. That takes money I don't have."

"If you would forego your *per diem*, I may manage."

"For thirty percent of the reward I am willing to throw in, our previous agreement voided. (3) I am more and more optimistic that, between the two of us, we'll crack this nut."

"To you, sir." Dee hoists his goblet.

"Your turn," prods Heinz. "You've got *my* thinking. Let's have yours."

Dee rubs his chin. He doesn't care to mention Uriel. (4) He feels his way: "My cat, he's a *very* special creature."

"You can say that again, brudder!" howls the irritated animal.

This shout-out Heinz hears clearly. "Dear God in Heaven," he cries. "What in Satan's name was *that*?"

The complaint continues. "If I'm so damn special, you bastard, why am I treated so abominably? Earlier, fine. I'm *in*, past the gatekeeper. Let me stretch my legs at least."

232

Dee bends down to address the container at close range. "It's for your own good, old pal, you and your smart mouth. I don't trust you out and about just now." He latches the lid against the cat making a dash for freedom. "This crowd, look at them wrong, you'll be kicked to Kingdom Come."

The animal erupts. "I'm not a pug dog to be carted around in a handbasket. I'm a free-roaming rascal. Live free or die, *my* motto. Have a heart, eh? I'm falling apart in here. These walls are closing in on me!" He kicks at the side of his cage in a fit of rage, wears himself out, and falls silent.

"Thank you merciful Lord," whispers Dee. But it is the calm before the storm.

A frenzied voice, raised to full force, embarks upon a stirring speech. "I am lion, hear me roar!" (5)

The old man tugs at his beard. "Dear God in heaven! I might have known. Here we go. Here we go. Here it comes. The noble savage. Shut your yap, critter!" he demands. "Not here! Not now! Have you lost your mind?"

A screech to end all screeches is the cat's jubilant rejoinder.

"No!" cries Dee. "No! *No*! God, no!" He lifts the hamper to the tabletop and holds it down – it is vibrating. The cat is pounding at the lid, trying to dislodge it. Bam! Thump! Bam! Thump! Dee pulls a ladle out of the bowl of beef barley soup and bangs on the box in sync with the cat's agitations. Adjacent conversation has ceased. All eyes are turned his way.

The pummeling pauses. The recitation resumes: "Magnificent on plains of yore…"

Dee has heard it many, many times. He shrieks in unison, to mask the cat's anguished *cri de coeur*. "A sneaky slurp, heart-stopping-fleet, I owned the earth beneath my feet."

The cat soldiers on: "As fierce… " A series of theatrical roars

233

and snarls interrupts the flow, as usually executed, of the piece.

Dee is on tenterhooks, waiting to jump back in. He lashes out at his dumbfounded companion. "*Sing*, damn you," he spits at Heinz. "Help me out here."

"Don't know the words," whimpers Heinz.

"Make some up, creep."

Heinz mounts the tabletop and sings, inserting between Dee's dramatically paced phrases, an upbeat lyric delivered in a high-pitched whine.

D: "As fierce as ever I was then...  I walk my *sod-you* walk again... "

H: "I'm walking, you can see... " (At the end of each line Heinzie mimes an action; here, he's high-stepping.)

D: "dismaying with my fine rampage... "

H: "as swizzled as I can be."

D: "a meaner world, this surly stage."

H: "Won't someone please rescue me... " (He's on one knee, hands clasped.)

"from this loon, name of John Dee." (He gives a sweep of the arm in Dee's direction.)

The wails (from the cat) continue. "Dee, you dog! I'm dying in here! I can't breathe! I'm having a heart attack! *Mama*! Your bad boy is coming, Mama! Forgive me, Mama! I had to see the world, Mama. *Had* to, though it broke your poor heart."

He's suddenly inspired to address the diners at large. "Live free, you peons!" he proclaims. "Live free or die! *No* masters! *No* rules! We are born with brave hearts. Find your brave heart – it's in you, beaten down. This head dips for no one! *No* one!" This was dangerous talk. Rulers kept a chokehold on their subjects, and society colluded to keep you in your place.

*He's gonna get us thrown into the deepest darkest dungeon they got*, thought Dee. *Fomenting rebellion, a nasty business.* (6) *Up*, he motions to Heinzie, who has reseated himself.

Dee blasts: "Waa-waa-waa-waa-walking!" Heinz repeats it, adding ambulation. Every time the cat tries to emote, they fire a volley of "Waa-waa-waa-waa-walking!"

Heinz seizes the basket and hurls it to the floor, putting an end to the cat's exhortations to resist tyranny. He bends down and applies an ear to the wicker weave, trying to assess the animal's state of being.

"You crud," hisses Sly, stunned, but thankfully (for us) still able to speak. "You better pray I never bust outta here, cause when I do, I'll rake your pretty face, pretty boy, but good. I knew a pretty boy once, another full-of-himself. *Pretty Boy, Pretty Boy, Pretty Boy*," he taunts his abuser.

He'd teased a parrot once, thusly. He mimics the bird's invariable come back: "*Go-to-hell-to-whore-son-hell-you-half-wit-horse-face-whore-son.*" That line had always gotten a big hand at the Cock and Bull in his long-ago hometown. A parrot, the big attraction in the local (and only) hotspot in Borrowdale parish, Cumbria, would chirp *kissy-kissy* from his perch behind the bar. When an enchanted newcomer leaned in for a sweet peck, Pretty Boy would grab onto the nose and refuse to let go. (But I digress. Back to *this* watering hole.)

‡‡‡‡‡

The packed room stands, mesmerized.

"Down, please, gentlemen," Dee implores. "Show's over. Beer for all," he barks at a serving girl.

"No, sir. Wine only with the bed and board."

"Pitchers of beer on every table!" he thunders. "And keep it coming! On the well-established generosity of my patroness,

Freifrau Annette von Droste-Deckenbrock, at the direction of her advisor, Doctor John Dee, Royal Astrologer to Her Majesty Queen Elizabeth of England."

The onlookers break into a sustained cheer. Heinz grabs up the hamper and makes for the stair.

Dee raises his arms, a signal for silence. "My friends! My apologies. I've had a bit to drink. Thank you for putting up with me." His face falls. He clutches his middle and spews wine – he hasn't much of the dinner in his belly – across his trestle-board, onto the table beyond. "Woman! Your best brandy for those I've insulted with my unfortunate emission," he screams as he flees, mortified.

‡‡‡‡‡<br>‡‡‡‡‡

Every locale has its visiting salesmen, itinerant teeth-pullers, and the like. The room is full of such flotsam.

"C'n you beat it!" marvels a tinker. "Here's a laugh! Some big shot, as much a booby as you n' me."

"Royal Astrologer?" A peddler dealing in notions – ribbons, laces, buttons, thread – is unimpressed. "Dresses worse n' me."

"A big noise? I guess so. A word from him, out comes the sweet stuff. I get a snort or two of Diefenbach's top swill off it, John Dee, up-chuck on me *any* time."

The notions vendor takes an appreciative slurp. "Dee, never heered the name in m' life. T'other fool, I swear I know the face, from *somewhere*."


Chapter Notes

1. There are several theories of origin for the phrase. One is that it derives from the guillotining method of execution, heads caught in a basket. The first version of *in a handbasket* in print is

found in one Samuel Sewall's Diary in 1714, although the English preacher Thomas Adams referred to *going to heaven in a wheelbarrow* in *God's Bounty on Proverbs* in 1618. The notion of being wheeled to hell in a cart is very old. The medieval stained glass windows of Fairford Church in Gloucestershire, England contain an image of a woman being carried off to purgatory in a wheelbarrow pushed by a blue devil. Going to hell *in a handbasket, in a handcart, in a handbag,* etc. describes a situation inescapably headed for disaster.

2. A demanding wife, and a manipulative partner pushing for a perfect union of minds through wife-swapping. (All true. I couldn't make up a better story than the historical fact.)

3. Dee had previously agreed to hire the tutor as a translator at a daily rate.

4. Dee believes he is advised by an angel named Uriel. (Again, absolutely true.)

5. *I am lion* was written years earlier as Sly attempted to launch a career on the stage:

I am lion, hear me roar.

*– Insert roars here –*

Magnificent on plains of yore, a sneaky slurp, heart-stopping fleet, I owned the earth beneath my feet.

As fierce as ever I was then, I walk my *sod-you* walk again, dismaying with my fine rampage...

a meaner world – this surly stage.

6. Dee, having heard this spiel many times also, knows what's coming. Unfortunately, Sly's German, ragged as it is, is excellently intelligible.

Mimi Speike, after a spotty career of arts-related endeavors (various crafts, freelance graphic design), works a graphic production job and puts her creativity into her writing. Nothing she's produced is without at least one wise-cracking animal, most often, a cat.

Find out more about Mimi's astonishing 16th Century cat at: myguysly.com

# A Study in Scarlet

## by Kim Michelle Ross

I sense the soft tip of the creator's paintbrush, and with each new stroke I feel more alive. Gazing longingly up at the godlike being, somewhere in my inner depths I've formed a strong connection to him. And simply watching the Adonis-like artist as he works his magic upon me, I'm aware of being a female, and his gorgeous blue eyes are causing my insides to go all gooey.

My two-dimensional body tingles in anticipation as he fills in parts that are blank. I wonder about my appearance and the kind of persona he'll imprint upon me: shy and sweet, or perhaps a femme fatale? If truth be told, I'm hoping it'll be the latter. Could I somehow influence his ready hand as it flows from inkwell and glides with little effort across the paper? *Oh, please make me a bombshell-goddess.*

I noticed his colour palette: he's using a deep, dark red and its bloodlike richness tempers my emerging soul – come to think of it, I wonder if actually have one of those? Perhaps my awareness is a simple extension of the creator's imagination. It doesn't matter – I'm alive, and that's miraculous enough. Though I do think he's overdoing the red – lashings of it cover my entire torso. Is he painting me in a cerise dress? Yay me! Bring on the femme fatale.

However, I realise, so far, he has only used shades of red colour. Does it mean my hair and lipstick will match my clothes? *Please don't make me too hippy.* I really don't want to be worrying if my bum looks too big in my dress. Hang on, he's started on my head – I'm getting long, burnishing locks. Now my face – *what, are you kidding me* – RED! Wee-war-wee-war, alarm bells fill my head. *Steady on, I know I wanted a dramatic effect* – but this is like, total overkill – *enough with the red!*

He changes his brush; I'm holding my breath as he dips its fine pointed bristles into the black. He adds light touches to my eyes, ears, and down to my toes – ooh, that tickles! He sits back studying me. Sighs. Smiles. "Scarlet, my pretty, you're done."

Done – but what am I? I don't know if I'm sexy, frumpy, or just a burgundy blob…?

He made a call. "Sara, ask the head copy editor to come down. Scarlet's finished."

Within minutes another man enters the room. He scrutinizes me, smiles and nods. "Oh, yes, I like her. A beauty, Brad. You were right – chestnut rather than straight out black. Much better."

"Yeah, she can't be black. We've already got the hero, Bill."

*Whoa, that's interesting! I must be a superhero's sidekick or something.*

"For a guy like The Onyx Blade, a red and chestnut mare is just right."

And there it is, the corollary of my existence – I'm not a heroine bombshell, not even a sidekick, but an equine cherry bomb accessory that now understands what it is to be a horse's arse. Bummer.

Kim Michelle Ross is a Speculative-Fiction author and has several short stories and flash fiction pieces published in eleven anthologies in Australia, UK and US under the names of: K.M. Ross, Kim Ross, and Kim Michelle Ross. But mostly she answers to Mum. Her career has been as varied as her name, from biology research assistant to pathology & blood bank lab technician, a short stint as a landscape gardener, mail officer and medieval re-enactor player with the Society for Creative Anachronism (SCA).

She lives in Newcastle, NSW, Australia, with her husband, three (sorta) grown-up boys, and Benny, the family's golden retriever. She's also a belly dancer and performs professionally with Silk Caravan Belly Dance Troupe. During a tour of Egypt in 2010, Kim and her fellow Silk Caravan troupe members danced on the Nile River – not actually on the water – but a cruise ship sailing from Aswan to Luxor.

*A Study in Scarlet* was performed at a live reading event *Tales After Dark – Storytelling for Adults* (Canberra Writers' Festival, 2017)

https://www.facebook.com/KimMichelleGroette25/

https://twitter.com/KimMichelleRos1?lang=en

Kim also has recently published her debut novel, *Netherrealm Book 1 Heed the Darkness*, the first book of her Historical/ Fantasy trilogy.

https://www.amazon.com/dp/B07GXMKYCX/ref=cm_sw_r_f a_dp_U_Zm1HBbBSTN9GB

# Mission Blue

by Debra Liu


Murky orange had invaded the horizon. Not a good sign. Menacing grey, thickening by the second, covered the rest of the sky. Alia pushed her through the dense air-sludge, legs aching from the pressure of near solid haze. She cut a path through the atmosphere using the PM2 knife she carried everywhere. *Guaranteed to cut the thickest haze and open a clear path in front of you"* went the advertising copy. She smirked as she pressed the knife icon on the air quality app on her Smidgie. *Wonder if this is going to work?* The line wavered, mercury red indicating the toxic components in the air were lessening. Marginally.

The winds picked up, a crazy, chaotic swirl of air that pushed and pulled her in all directions. The Smidgie monitored their force, computing the complex, erratic air currents and showing her the best path forward. So she wouldn't trip as gale force winds battered her. So she wouldn't waste time fighting the winds pushing in her face only to get knocked over by a sudden sou'wester coming from behind . So she wouldn't push past the line of least resistance only to find a pocket of haze so thick it hijacked the filter she wore and deadened her vision. So she'd survive. Step by step she ducked and danced her way through air so thick it hurt her hyper-padded shins as she strode forward. The wind-howl was so strong the ear monitors she wore were threatening to blow. Before they could, the wind pushed her forward, and the earmuffs fell.


A terrifying silence. The haze had gone, in its place, nothing. No trees, no vegetation, no roads. The violent swirl that was there a second ago she could deal with, but not this emptiness. No sights, no sound -

"Oh shit."

The air was no longer gray but silver-spotty, with sudden fluorescent sparks that jabbed at her eyeballs. She knew what it was, this void followed by flashing silver: a command to jump. The random portal was opening before her eyes – it would take her out of here, but to where?

Alia stepped backwards in a hurry, not even checking the Smidgie. How the portal had suddenly appeared or who had sent it, she didn't know. She kept moving, not looking, trusting the solidity of the ground she had just trod on. Her eyes were intent on the flash of silver, the oscillating waves of light that flushed out of what was now a tight ball of fluorescent air, calculating how long it would last in the haze. Not long. The air was too thick.

As abruptly as it had appeared, it was gone. In the wake of the portal, Alia could now see the earth in front of her: a stretch of pavement veering off towards what must be a city in the distance, a road hobbled by slow-moving traffic, a road-side café and a group of men sitting outside, drinking. A garble of Senegalese accents grew louder as she walked past the café. *Great, a group of crypto-revolutionaries, that's all I need.* She'd already taken off her face-protector and ear-muffs – no one around here wore them. Perhaps they'd mutated and the polluting air no longer bothered them. Alia was already coughing and spluttering, chocking on the very air.

"Come over here and have a drink with us," shouted one of gang in the common language, English.

Casually she pulled the Smidgie of her wrist and shoved it in her pocket.

"Come on girlie," another one shouted, standing up and beckoning her. The Crypto-Revolutionaries were noted for their odd mix of interests – they'd hack code one moment, breaking in to government information, and be brawling in the streets the next. She fingered the Smidgie, deciding between creating a jump-portal or fighting this bunch for fun. The second guy had sat down, but five of them were staring at her.

"You got a long way to go outa here. Hey, we can give you a lift."

No thanks. She pressed in a few lines of code into the Smidgie without looking, landed five kilometres away from where she'd been, shook herself, and kept walking. Towards the city. It would be dark when she got there. No point destroying the Smidgie's battery just to arrive early. She'd have to do her work in the dark anyhow.


"Hop in. You shouldn't be walking – It's lethal out there." A car had stopped beside her. She caught a glimpse of a woman with an orange scarf wrapped around her head before the window wound up. The back door of the car opened. "Quick, get in." Two women in the front, one in the back with a kid. "Hurry up, the air's toxic, don't want him to breathe it. The woman pointed to the kid.

Risk assessment, minimal, she determined. They were harmless, and she'd be in the city just as night fell. Out of danger. She jumped in the back of the car and slammed the door shut. The woman took her hands of the kid's eyes and ears. "It's okay, you can breathe again now."

"Who are you?" He stared at her, the mask over her face that supported her oxygen intake, her thickly padded clothing. "Jonston, don't be rude."

Alia took of her face-protector– even inside the car the air was toxic but she needed to fit in. No-one in these parts was wearing any kind of mask.

"You won't need those in here," said the driver. "We've got purifiers. From New York."

"The best kind." Alia let a tinge of relief enter her voice, even though she knew the purifiers that were used here dissolved only a fraction of contaminated air. She pushed down the cough that was building in her throat, and resisted the urge to put her face protector back on. It was instinct: where she was from, if she breathed natural air for more than ten minutes she be disabled for weeks, more than half an hour, she'd be dead within a day.

"Where are you headed? We're going to the Rockside."

"Rockside will be fine."

The driver threw a glance at her in the rear-view mirror. Alia decided she'd have to be friendly if she was going to keep out of trouble. Everyone knew not to hang around the streets in Rockside at night – even in her world.

"You got an address?"

"Up near Portside. You can just drop me off on Main Avenue."

The passenger in the front looked around at her sharply.

"But it's not safe at night," screeched the boy.

"My cousin lives just near the borderlands." She was not going to say she was headed for Barry's Bar. Only trouble was to be found there.

"We'll drive you to your cousins." The driver was speaking again. "It really isn't safe at night."

"I can't remember the street name though. I only know how to walk it. It's near the gas station just before you get to the borderlands."

"No worries. We'll take you there. You just give us directions."

"Really don't want to trouble you…"

"No trouble."

Alia made up directions, looking for a house with a longish driveway and a light in the house that suggested someone was home. "Turn left... right into that avenue... oh, just here will do. It's this one." She'd seen a lowset house backed up off the street. "Thanks, appreciate the lift," she said. She walked slowly up the driveway till she heard the car disappear into the distance, replaced her face protector and back tracked, heading towards the main avenue. Barry's Bar should be at the next intersection.

Dimly lit, smoky, and jam-packed with people who'd sell their Aunt Maisy for tuppence, Barry's Bar was a haven for misfits, criminals, and anyone with a vengeance. Alia ordered a drink and headed to a quieter corner at the back. There were the usual fist-fights, loud arguments, and threatening postures, but nothing fatal was happening near the table she'd sat by. Unlike the rest of the bar. She watched with nonchalance as a tired looking sweeper came in, picked up the latest bleeding corpse with an oversized pair of tongs and dropped it into the dumpster behind him. The dumpster driver did a tight turn and exited. Before she could blink, he was back inside for his next cargo.

Alia sipped her beer, scanning the action at the bar. It was a place of thuggery where no one asked names, where life was marginal, and where you'd go to find the kind of contact you'd need. She' d seen pictures of Reece Weatherby – *an odd name to chose as his cover* – and had one eye trailing around the bar looking for him. She'd need to find him – he had no idea she was scouting him.

An hour passed. She fiddled with her drink, ordered another one. Not to do so could be a death sentence in a place like this. Half way through the second drink, she saw him. A thin, weedy character, odd silver-framed glasses, and an eclectic taste in clothes. Long black coat, with tailor-cut raggedy edges, thrown over patched shorts and a teeshirt. By the look of him, he was a walking target – neither his shorts nor his coat contained pockets – none that were visible anyhow. To her trained eye, there was nowhere to conceal a

247

weapon. The drinkers saw him, and moved out of his way. Some walked quickly, almost running. *Lives up to his reputation.* She tossed her drink down and went to order another one. He was reaching for a glass of gaudy lime liquid, but before he could pay she tossed notes onto the bar. "For mine and his." She returned to her spot and waited. He took his time.

Four drinks later, each consumed at a different table, with a separate group, he ambled over to her. She kicked the chair opposite her, giving him a place to sit. He wasn't about to.

"Reece Weatherby," she said.

"Whose asking?"

Slowly, with eyes locked on his, she took out the phone from her pocket. She'd transferred significant data from her Smidgie to this out-dated, 21$^{st}$ Century technology. She watched as he swiped. Photos, faces, documents, code – he looked at them all. Alia rescued a gold coin from her pocket and slid it over to him. An eagle was engraved in the coin, wings outstretched, and the date. 2152.

He looked up at her. "Whose asking?" he repeated.

"You worked with Jimmy Watson."

His eyebrows raised a fraction, a movement so quick she would have missed it if she wasn't staring at him.

"Two years ago. Botched mission."

His lower lip twitched and curled, then his face was blank again.

"I've come to complete the mission."

Weatherby pushed his chair back and left. She waited. Then waited some. He'd tossed back five more glasses of the lurid lime green drink (a corkscrewer, strongest liquor in the bar) before he swaggered over and sat opposite her.

"Same method of payment."

Alia nodded.

"Double the fee."

She nodded again. She'd expected as much and had come prepared.

"When?"

"Night after tomorrow. Should be fine. How do I contact you?"

She gave him the number of the phone. "It's a secure line."

He nodded, then turned around and clicked his fingers in the air. Five people jumped up and hurried to the bar, more looked like they were about to stand up before realising they'd been beaten to it. Out of the five who went to the bar, a thick-set guy, elegantly dressed in pressed trousers and a Cardin shirt ordered first. He delivered the drink to Weatherby, then left. A light-framed woman, no more than five feet tall, with two corkscrewers in her hand, sauntered over and casually left on one their table. She walked off, taking a large gulp from the other drink. Two of the others who had rushed to Weatherby's orders left the bar now, returning to their deals and brawls. A third drink arrived. Weatherby looked up this time and raised his hand to slap the palm of the guy who'd brought it. Pock-faced, balding at the forehead. The back of his head covered with thick, black hair. Alia noted his defining features as he returned to the bar. The guy bought a beer and instead of returning to the group he'd been sitting with, took up a seat on a bar-stool not far from their table.

"Watson had tools. Did you bring them?"

She nodded. She wasn't about to place the 22$^{nd}$ Century cryptohacking tools on the table in front of him. Instead, she scrolled through her phone, then passed it to him. He looked for longer than it took to recognise the splicer and deflector.

249

*He wants some.* She'd brought extra tools with her, and would give one to him as part payment. She'd engineered it to connect with her Smidgie. She could monitor what he was using the tools for, and stop him, in necessary. Or make it much easier.

"I'll call you at 8, day after tomorrow to confirm. Meet me at the same place as Watson did." He sculled his last two drinks.

Alia casually placed her right leg over her left, foot pointing towards the last guy to give Weatherby a drink. Her hand went over her knee and she pressed it slightly with her third finger, not letting the smirk she felt appear on her face. An old trick from a 20th Century television show she'd watched. Shoe-cam, technologically updated.

She waited ten minutes after he'd left, then sauntered out of the bar. Her right hand was poised on the Smidgie in her pocket, just in case she needed to get out of there quick. – though it would not be good to draw attention to herself by dematerializing inside the bar. By this hour everyone would be too busy with their own concerns to notice her, but she'd been drinking with Reece Weatherby. There'd be many eyes watching her every movement. Just as she was leaving, the sweepers were coming in to clean up two more bodies. Outside, the night air was almost as toxic as daytime, but she could breathe. Just.

*How do these people live here without masks?* . Even at night Main Avenue was packed with traffic. When she was sure she was not being followed, she took a side-street, and pressed the Smidgie.

Maximum jump allowed in a different time-zone: 5 kilometres. She landed on her feet and kept walking till she arrived at the dive she'd chosen to stay the night in. Cheap, no ID needed, no questions asked. She was scratching at her arms and legs before too long. Lice. Alia was tempted to use the Smidgie to create a portal, and jump through to the time-zone she'd be meeting Reece Weatherby. Instead, she got out of bed, opened the reader on her Smidgie and began scrolling. She'd use the two days to go over the files. The cryptohackers back home were pretty sure where Watson had gone wrong – he was meant to stop the plant, instead, it began emitting a foul haze. She'd poor through the algorithms again anyhow. A lot was riding on this mission.

She'd landed in a timezone two months after Watson's trip. She checked the readings on the Smidgie. Nitrates, sulphites, black carbon. All at hazardous levels. Particulate matters at dangerous levels. The plant would blow and cause a massive nuclear leak that would affect the air for centuries. A century later, back in her time-zone, everyone was living with the after effects of that leak.

Watson had come to blow the plant, to disengage it permanently. Change the timelines. His mission was to abort the plant so the future would use renewable energies. The air would be breathable again. Maybe the sky would even be blue. But when Watson had returned home, the timelines had changed in ways they hadn't expected. Mutants were everywhere. Her own grandmother had some kind of wasting disease that she was born with, when in the previous timeline she'd been healthy. Alia had inherited the genes, but kept the illness at bay with a mix of medicines her mother had been feeding her since she was a kid. The Great Wars had come – a cycle of global catastrophes which had decimated the population. Thousands of people she had known before simply hadn't been born. She wanted her friends back.

Watson too. He'd been so remorseful at the sheer cost of his mistake, he'd suicided. It was probably not even his fault. The algorithms were correct. Some guy had fiddled with his work – the night guard, of all things. Who could have known he was a crypto-hacker, working at the Plant, waiting for an opportunity to run it down. When the plant started steaming, he broke into the control room to try and stop the damage. To this guy, it looked like a leak of hazardous material: how was he to know a time-jumper from the 22nd Century had come to shut the plant down? In the new timezone, his mistakes had become legend in crypto-hacking circles. The code the night guard had used to correct the steam was now a classic lesson in what could go wrong in shutting down plants. Everyone knew his story, minus the time-jumping. The mistake was written in the text-books as the Night Guard's code – entry-level hackers were taught to study the sequence, and never to use it. Alia shuddered, glad that despite all the time-glitches she'd retained her memory. Most don't. The elite group in her crypto-hacking circles who worked in time-jumping could, like her, retain their memories across timeline changes. None, not one, of her time-jumping colleagues vanished after the great nuclear debacle. She could never work out why.

She activated the program on her Smidgie that projected the files she was looking at to a hologram. She could read them clearer this way, and no one was likely to break into the dingy hotel room. Better she stay up late going over the files, than risk looking at them in daylight. Using $22^{nd}$ Century technology in public during time-jumps was definitely in the prohibitions – printed in huge dark print in the front of the Time Jumper's Guidebook!

After two nights of solid appraisal of all codes, logarithms, algorithms and protocols – along with estimated time needed to complete each step – she was certain Watson's codes were not to blame. As she suspected – and had discussed with her colleagues – it was the unexpected intervention of the night-guard that had caused the timelines to alter so negatively. Her team had added a new code to be punched in at the end sequence. She hoped it would stop tell-tale signs of smoke, and deactivate the plant rapidly. She'd have to get out of their quick. What if she succeeded? Would ensuring the nuclear blast didn't happen even bring her friend back? Would other time-co-ordinates be activated? Would other negative futures they had not foreseen unfold? Who was to say? There was always the unknown element, the rogue factor that could change the future. She would be stuck back in her timeline as a stranger, without an identity. They weren't strange thoughts. Her group had discussed these issues constantly. The answer was always the same: if they did nothing, the human race would be wiped out, or mutate beyond comprehension. Nothing would grow in the toxic world she had come from. Children grew up never seeing sunshine. Alia smiled, recalling the first time she had time-jumped, and seen a marvel – a bright orange ball in a blueish sky. The stuff of fairy tales. Its warmth was comforting. Breathing was like a dream. She'd been amazed at the physical capacity of her body – the fresh air gave her strength and vigour. "Have you been to an oxygen spa?" people had asked her when she got back.

She looked at the time. Almost daylight. She should get some sleep. She took a mild sleeping pill and set her alarm for midday. She planned to have a solid meal when she woke up and check out the area while she was waiting for Weatherby.

Alia had intended to walk to the plant in the afternoon. Although her Smidgie contained extensive maps, drawings and a time-sensitive guide which would tell her the best path forward at any given moment, seeing the building with human eyes was always a bonus. She paid for one more night at the dive and went out for food. She hadn't counted on the air being so thick with haze, and wished she'd put on her facial protector. She'd left it at the hotel – it wasn't a good move to openly display future technology. No point tempting fate – she'd have to make do with the Smidgie. Alia wasn't planning on staying at the dive for any longer than she had too, but after lunch she went back. It gave her a place for the afternoon. By nightfall she'd gone over the algorithms so many times they were spinning around in front of her eyeballs like a malfunctioning hologram.

Weatherby's phone call came in at 8. Brief, and to the point. "Meet you there at 11. Same place that Watson met me." The phone clicked, and he was gone. She did a run through of her tools, packed them discretely in an inside thigh pocket, and walked out into the hazy night. Despite the smog, the sky was clear enough to see a handful of stars. Three flickering stars in a row: Orion's Belt. Alia stared at the constellation – apart from the first time she'd time-jumped, she'd only seen them in photographs and computer simulations. She paused, wondering if it wasn't a sky projector in a large dome – but the stars here had a clarity like no dome simulator she'd ever seen. Turning off the main road, she found a back street with no street-lights, activated the Smidgie, and jumped in the direction of the plant. Settling down amidst a clump of bushes, she watched the guard's movements while she waited for Weatherby.

He arrived two minutes before 11, sauntering up to the gate and waiting there in plain sight. She stood, so he could see her, but kept her distance. The garbage truck arrived on the dot of 11. She saw Weatherby pass the driver something, then beckon her. They ran behind the truck as the gates opened. Weatherby lasered the solitary guard, stole his access card, and they were in. That simple. She activated the Smidgie and placed it in hologram mode. A map opened in front of them. Alia looked at it briefly – she'd been studying the layout of the plant for months now, and knew it by heart. Red dots on the hologram showed them where to expect guards. Weatherby lasered them, then stole their access cards. They'd need them on the way back. It took fifteen minutes and ten guards deactivated ill they had reached the final set of doors. Five guards here. Weatherby handed Alia a laser – they both fired at once.

Only one of the guards had an access card. Weatherby grabbed it and pressed it against the screen. As the panel opened, Alia keyed in a series of code in tight sequence. The doors opened. She ran to the control panels and brought the algorithms up to the hologram. With access granted, she implanted the disabler and let it run the code.

The Protector next. She reached into her pocket and brought out a shiny piece of metal. Punched the numbers, and a 360 virtual display opened in front of them. Weatherby almost smiled. The whole plant was spread in digital array before them, complete with electronic circuits, security systems, and pop-up windows that displayed the algorithms needed to bring each section down.

She directed the Smidgie's hologram to settle in front of the virtual display. It would be easy enough to set the Smidgie to deactivate the plant – but nothing would be left to chance. Not this time. Alia brought out the splicer next. It was a simple tool designed to fit into machines from any timezone – she plugged it into the USB port and within seconds the plant's mainframe had given her access. As easy as a hairpin in an old-fashioned lock. Following the algorithms lit up in front of her, her fingers flew over the keyboard. The circuits at 12.00 turned green, she moved onto 1.00. Sorted. Two, then three o'clock. She swiveled in her chair. Four o'clock, five –

"Security alert at 6. Looks like some guard has noticed anomalies in the system."

Alia brought up the visuals from the security cameras, zooming in on the guard's keyboards. "He's good," she said. "He nearly has it reset."

Swivelling her chair back to 12.00 she smirked as she typed leisurely. The screen in front of her turned red. "There. Helped him out a bit. You know what to do."

Weatherby kicked back his chair and ran to the door. She placed the 6.00 security camera screen to the left of where she was working on the 5. This one controlled the effluent flow. She punched in the upgrade. When the system came down, the refuse systems all needed to be working at capacity and beyond. Her team had targeted a waste-land to redirect the effluents too – the poison couldn't be allowed to flow into the city.

The guard had his feet on the table, drinking coffee. Weatherby had changed – he was now wearing a guard's uniform. Most have stolen it from one of the lasered dudes. His hat was pulled down covering his eyes. He looked directly into the security camera, lifted his hat and smirked at her. *Just as well he shaved his beard. Now he fits right in.* She set about changing the discharge flow. The guard must have heard Weatherby – he sat up, taking his feet off the table.

Before the guard could spin around, Weatherby had dislocated his shoulder. The guard moved his knee – Weatherby intercepted his action.

"No, no alarms needed." He pulled the guys chair back so he couldn't activate the button, placed discretely under this desk. The guy was a fighter. His gun was now in his left hand, pointing straight at Weatherby. Weatherby was waving something in his hand – Alia recognized the Deflection Tool. 22$^{nd}$ Century technology.

"Go ahead, shoot." He sounded amused.

*He must have got that from Watson.*

The security camera's video seemed to go in slow motion. The guard triggered the gun, a bullet flew out, it slowed down, hit something invisible, pulsated, then returned. Its pace quickened as it flew back to the guard. He must have set his gun to automatic. Bullets from his own weapon were hitting the deflection shield and reverberating back to his body in rapid fire. Alia fingered in the last section of code, directly the effluent to wasteland. 5.00 went green.

The guard was down. Weatherby was heading back. Her fingers flew across the keyboards, 6.00 turned green. She was working on 7.00, when Weatherby returned. Followed by two heavily armed guards. Alia grabbed her gun, leant to the side and triggered, kneeling on the floor to avoid their fire. Weatherby had been hit. She activated her Deflection shield and dressed his wounds quickly as the guards went down, killed by their own reflected ammunition.

"They'll have radioed base. We'll have to be quick. I'm gonna set his thing to deactivate in five minutes. We'll have to be out of here fast."

Weatherby nodded, scanning the security cameras.

"Lock down at the front."

"We'll jump out."

"What?"

"Space jump. Five kilometers at a time."

8.00 clear. Her fingers rushed over the keyboard, eyes flickering to the hologram , checking the code as she entered it. 9.00 green.

"Two coming up the central channel."

"I've sealed them in. they won't get through the channel door."

"More coming up from the basement. Fifteen in all. I'll take them all down."

"No need. We knew about this. They won't get out of the basement." Alia flicked a switch and the frightened faces of the guards enlarged on the screen. A torrent of effluent was flowing towards them. They turned and ran.

"10 – nearly got it…. 10 green."

"The lift's opening."

"Only one of them. Protect this door from the outside. Stay there till I finish in case more come."

She was working on 11.00. She slowed down – couldn't afford to get this one wrong. The 11.00 gate controlled the energy centres around all the major cities – one small error and a city's whole power stations could explode. Off. Off. Off. Off. She watched as all plants, high- grade nuclear reactors combined with old-fashioned coal emissions went offline. 11 cities in total. Then she keyed in the last code, the new end sequence, to seal it and prevent others from tampering with the process. No more Watsons.

She heard a shot from outside. Then another one. *Hope Watson gave him a Deflector with a long battery life.* 12.00. The final 12.00 sequence was to check and confirm all of the other codes – nothing much for her to do, but sit and watch. 1.00 2.00 …. More shots. Weatherby was back inside, bleeding heavily.

"Damned Deflector."

9.00, 10.00

"Malfunction?"

"Once you've got it, get us outa here. There's at least 12 of them outside and more coming."

She switched the visual.

"All security. None of them have online access."

"Who's to say? That guard who deactivated Watson's programming…."

"Won't happen again. Can't happen."

He tore at off the sleeves of his coat and wrapped the material around his arm wounds.

"If anyone tries my Smidgie will be alerted. Across timezones. I'll deactivate any attempts. Besides, this things gonna blow in 5. We gotta get outa here quick."

12.00 turned green.

"Ya ready?"

Alia typed in code on her Smidgie. *Deactivating.* Large red letters across the screen. She paused to look at it, and smiled.

Kicking her chair back, she grabbed Weatherby's arm.

"Outa here. Hold on."

She pressed the Smidgie. Nothing.

Shots fired outside.

"Damn! It doesn't work so well in different time-zones. Should be outside to activate it. We'll have to get out a different way.'

She pressed the Smidgie's red button. *Three minutes left.* Grey smoke appeared in front of the console.

"It's gonna blow! Get us outa here!" Weatherby seized his Deflector as shots fired through the door,

"It won't work. Try this one." Alia grabbed a Deflector from her tool snatch and tossed it to him.

Silver edges to the grey. Luminescent bubbling.

"It's gonna blow."

"No." Alia grabbed Weatherby's arm. The portal opened just as the guards burst in.

"Don't let go. Just don't let go of me!" She pulled him towards the portal.

Rapid fire caused a stream of blood to pour from Weatherby's leg. Or was that hers? That close to the portal her senses were confused. A tingling sensation rushed through her body. She grasped Weatherby's hand tighter.

"What's this fog?"

"Sssh. Don't waste energy talking. Just hold my hand tight."

*

When she woke, her vision was clear. *Wait – the very air was clear!* She jumped out of bed and looked at the open window. *Blue skies.*

Alia smiled. *It worked! The plant shut down! The global chain reaction must have followed and the cycle of toxic emissions stopped.* She'd changed the timelines. Back in the 22nd Century, the sky was intoxicatingly blue. She stared out the window, drinking in the sights. A group of people in matching jackets were kicking a ball around a large, green field. She put on her boots and raced downstairs to join them.

A huddle of people were watching the game. "Are you in town for the millennial party?" someone asked her.

"We drove in from Texas," someone else said.

"We're just up from Jersey."

The game was over. Music erupted over the loudspeakers. *Tonight I'm gonna party like its 1999.* The crowd before her started singing along.

Alia looked at her Smidgie and amplified the time code. December 31st, 1999. 11.43 am.

*Shit. I've gone backwards. What the fuck?*

~ ~ ~ ~

Debra Liu is a writer of fiction and non-fiction. Her early poetry was published in an Australian anthology, and her story *The Chang Gate* was included in a collection of short stories published by the Suzhou Bookworm.

# Life Changing

## by S.T. Ranscht

The first life-changing decision Lawrence made changed more than his life; it changed the very universe he'd spent the first thirty-seven years of that life in. Not that he noticed it right away. He was kind of busy.

"Mom, no." Without looking up from the paperwork, Lawrence put out his arm to block her path. "Stay here. We'll go for a walk after I finish this, okay?"

She scrunched her eyebrows together and pushed his arm down. Inspecting his profile, she extended a finger to stroke his tawny mustache. He glanced at her. Her eyes seemed to glimmer pixie dust blue as they focused somewhere beyond him, but she smiled, smoothing the furrows on her forehead and deepening the lines that asterisked her eyes and parenthesized her mouth. Lawrence sometimes suspected each wrinkle had deleted a year's worth of memories from her mind. He turned back to the admission form. Tugging at her sparkly gold sweater, his mother moved from his side toward the big glass door in the huge glass wall.

"Is this Grandma's house?" she asked. "Are we buying it?" With gnarled hands splayed on the glass, she peered through the door at the lawns and gardens on both sides of the curved drive and murmured, "I don't remember this front yard. Mother won't let me climb the trees." She pushed on the bar, but the door wouldn't open. She shook it and a thudding rattle reverberated through the lobby. "It's stuck," she called over her shoulder. Her eyes widened and her voice screwed itself into the ceiling like it always did before she lost herself to panic. "I can't get out! I can't–"

Lawrence had already put the pen down and sucked two lungfuls of air through his nose. He went to retrieve her. "No, Mom, it's all right. The nice lady at the desk will open it when we're ready. She has a special button she has to push. Come on, sit down for just a minute, and she'll show you."

His mother didn't follow him. She twiddled a lock of her silver-threads-among-the-gold, champagne-shimmery hair, and squinted at the petite, dark haired young woman behind the counter. "No she won't. She's not going to let me out."

Lawrence closed his eyes and rubbed his forehead. "Sorry," he muttered, reading the receptionist's tag, "Thuy."

"No need," Thuy replied reading his mother's name upside down on the form.

"Catherine? Do you like to be called Catherine?"

"No," Catherine sulked. "My name's Cathy."

Thuy smiled. "It's nice to meet you, Cathy. Would you like a mint?" She pointed to the red and white peppermints in a bowl on the counter. "Sugar free," she whispered to Lawrence.

Hesitant steps brought Cathy to the candy. "Is this Grandma's house?" she asked, her eyes glittering as she crinkled the cellophane open with arthritic fingers.

Lawrence concentrated on the paperwork. A large, dark-skinned attendant wearing black Dickies and a palm-tree-themed Hawaiian print shirt arrived to fill the lobby with rehearsed energy. Cathy stiffened.

"Hi," he boomed. "I'm Bernard. I'll be helping you get settled today." He bent to pick up Cathy's bags.

"No!" Her cry echoed off the glass. "They're mine! Who are you?"

He looked at Lawrence who put his arm around his mother's shoulders. Wild-eyed, she flung herself away, screaming, "What are you doing? Where am I?" She settled on Lawrence. "Who *are* you

262

people?"

Clenching his jaw and swallowing hard, he tried to smile. "Mom," he said, reaching for her hand.

Yanking it away, she shrieked, "Don't touch me! I don't know you."

A woman in light blue scrubs took her place beside Bernard. Tucking an escaped strand of steel gray hair into her bun, she stood in front of Cathy with her meaty hands on ample hips. Her ebony face wore a frank, no-nonsense expression. Her name tag labeled her, "Shiela."

"Hey," Shiela said, "what's all the noise? Is there somethin' you need? Somethin' I can do for you?"

"Don't let them take my things," Cathy pleaded.

Considering, Shiela nodded. "That's easy. *We'll* take 'em – you and me. All right?" She picked up the larger bag. "You comin'?"

Cathy looked uncertain. "Aunt Becky?"

"Come on," Shiela said, "we haven't got all day."

Cathy picked up the smaller bag and followed Shiela down the hallway to the residents' apartments.

Thuy tilted her head to look up at Lawrence's face. Hers was an apology. "Why don't you come back tonight? Or maybe tomorrow." She buzzed the door. He left.

His mother, the only parent he'd ever had, was the strongest person he'd ever known. She'd been his rock, his refuge, his hero. The first time she hadn't recognized him, more than a year ago, it had stung. Every time since, it lasered off a little more of his hope. Caring for her as she slipped away had swallowed him, and he'd finally had to admit she needed more than he could possibly do for her.

263

Lawrence settled in behind the steering wheel and looked back at the sprawling complex. A short sigh sagged his shoulders. Leaving her here broke his heart, but it was also a wake-up call. He would do whatever it took to avoid his mother's fate.

Somewhere online he'd read an article about boosting brain health by changing even one lifelong habit. Like grocery shopping in the direction opposite your normal path. Or brushing your teeth with your non-dominant hand. *That's it*, he decided – but he'd do even more. He'd turn his right-handed brain upside down and become left-handed.

For the last time, he unlocked his phone with his right index finger. Someday he'd get a phone with facial recognition, but scanning in his left index print now offered even more opportunities to change his brain. Then he texted Stephanie using only his left thumb. He mistyped. He deleted. He began again. *"On my way home."*

She responded, *"How'd it go?"*

He paused to savor the challenge. *"Life changing. See you in an hour."*

*

Stephanie stood in the bedroom doorway, undoing her auburn ponytail, her dark eyes sparkling. Lawrence had just changed into lounge pants. "Hey," she said, "you need to get dressed. We're meeting Kachina and Chivonn for a movie in an hour."

"We are?"

She walked up behind him and wrapped her arms around his chest. "Yes, Lawrence. As much as I love your mom, it's our first night of freedom. You deserve – *we* deserve – some fun. When was the last time we went out?"

He couldn't remember. "Hey, I'm all for it," he said. He reached with his right hand to pull jeans out of the closet, caught himself and used his left hand instead. "I just didn't know you'd planned anything."

She smiled and kissed him on the cheek. "We planned it. You just forgot." She watched him struggle to zip up left-handed. "You need a little help with that, mister?"

He grinned. "How much time do we have?"

Pursing her lips, she looked at him sideways. "Enough."

*

Lawrence zipped up his hoodie left-handed, then reached with the same hand to hold the lobby door open. They stepped out of the theater into the mall, flowing along with the crowd.

"I love time travel stories," Stephanie said, "but I think this one got it wrong. Whatever happened, happened because it's always happening all the time. Like in LOST," she continued, "when they went back in time and caused the incident they were trying to prevent because they'd already been there and caused it."

Taking her hand, Lawrence said, "That theoretical physicist – uh–"

"Dr. Kaku?" Kachina asked.

"Yeah, that's him. He would agree in the sense that your past is fixed, but he also says you could go back and change the past – like, say, kill baby Hitler. Only then, you've forked off into a parallel universe because in *our* universe, Hitler lived, so you'd be saving a different universe's timeline from Nazis."

"And how did you arrange to get to *that* parallel universe?" Stephanie asked. "What if you showed up in a universe full of aliens?" She smirked. "You'd be really forked then, wouldn't you?"

Chivonn shook her head. "How would your body even *get* to a parallel universe? Wouldn't just your mind go?"

Lawrence searched the sky. "If there *are* parallel universes, their existence wouldn't depend on time travel, but what if you created – or landed in – a parallel universe and its timeline simply by showing up in the past of your own timeline? Like the appearance of a second you causes a split in the time stream."

Aggravation pricked Chivonn's voice. "What would happen to the 'you' in the timeline you left? Would you be a missing person? If your body stayed behind, would your mind be the same as always?"

"I don't know." He shrugged. "Seems like if you could go back to a point before you'd been born in your universe, you'd have to take your body with you. Or maybe you just couldn't go back that far. But it would still be history as you knew it till the moment you got there, right?"

"I guess it would have to," Stephanie agreed.

Kachina whipped her waist-length, straight black hair over her shoulder with a dancer's swing of her head. "That makes sense to me, too. And I think that either way, you wouldn't erase yourself if you killed your grandfather or kept your parents from meeting, because time-traveling you was already born, and you're time traveling in your personal present, even if you go to your own past. This one was more like Doc Brown's time travel."

Lawrence laughed, "Yeah, but without the DeLorean."

Wagging her head so her curls bounced, Chivonn grumped, "I would have liked it better if it'd had a DeLorean. But I still don't see how your physical body could survive the trip. Maybe your mind would just inhabit the 'you' in the new timeline." She rubbed her temples. "Time travel gives me a headache."

Kachina put her arm around Chivonn's waist, "But you loved Hermione's Time-Turner, didn't you, babe?"

"Well, yeah, but that was magic. This was… pseudoscience, and it gave me a headache."

The "Restrooms" sign pointed to their right. "Hold on. I need to use the facility." Kachina detoured down the side passage.

"Okay," Lawrence said, "Chiv gets to choose the next movie."

Her eyes lit up. "How about something with Zoe Saldana? You know I love me some Zoe S."

"Sure," he said. "How about tomorrow?"

Chivonn turned to Stephanie. "What's going on? We haven't seen you guys in forever, and now you're up for two nights in a row?"

Stephanie took Lawrence's arm. "Larry is set on changing our lives." She grinned and twitched one eyebrow up and down. "He's making new habits."

"Larry?" Lawrence asked.

Stephanie didn't respond. "So where are we going now?"

Raising her hand, Chivonn said, "I vote for food."

Kachina joined them. "Did I hear 'food'? Yes, please."

Lawrence, still puzzling over being called 'Larry,' looked at Stephanie as though he'd never seen her before. Something across the mall behind her caught his eye: a woman in a sparkly gold sweater, with hair that sparkled like champagne. "Mom?" The woman disappeared into the crowd.

Stephanie cocked her head. "Um, no, Lawrence. I'm Stephanie." She held his face and looked into his eyes. "Are you all right?"

"Yeah." He waved it off. "Yeah, I'm fine. I just thought I... I guess today was harder than I realized."

"We can go home, if you'd rather," she said.

"No. I'm good. Let's go get something to eat." He flexed the fingers of his left hand. "How about Chinese?"

After a week of concentrated practice, his effort was beginning to pay off. One of his most notable accomplishments involved chopsticks: he could now feed himself left-handed without embarrassing his dining companions. Another was developing acceptable skill shaving, although he'd had to give up his mustache following an unfortunate miscommunication between his eyes and his left hand as he attempted to negotiate a sharp turn of the razor using the information reflected in the mirror.

"Lawrence!" Stephanie had called as he emerged from the bathroom after the shaving incident. "What happened to your face?"

But the next day, as he wiped up the coffee he'd sloshed when he poured, she said, "What would you think about growing a mustache, Larry? I don't know why, but I keep imagining you with a Fu Manchu, and I think it'd be kind of sexy."

Laughing, he followed her into the living room. "If I'd known you felt that way while I had one, I would have been more careful."

She reacted as if he were speaking in tongues. "What are you talking about? I've never seen you with a mustache."

"What are *you* talking about? I had one until yesterday – not long after you started calling me 'Larry'."

Her eyebrows drew together as she studied him. "Honey, I'm beginning to think your brain training experiment is backfiring." Her genuine concern caught him off guard. "I have always called you 'Larry', and you haven't had a mustache in all the time I've known you."

"What?" he sputtered.

"I can show you photos." She picked up a framed 5 x 7 from the mantle and held it out to him.

It was from their trip to Hawaii with Chivonn and Kachina two years ago, but in this shot, there was some guy he'd never met standing there with his arm around Chivonn. Stephanie was right about his own lack of facial hair. The edges of his vision blurred. Words were hard to find.

"Huh," Lawrence said. "Who's the guy? Where's Kachina?"

"Who?" She tapped the guy. "That's Kevin." Lawrence just kept staring at the picture. "My brother?" she prompted. She returned the photo to the mantle and guided him to sit with her on the couch. She kissed his hand and searched his eyes. "Maybe you should think about making an appointment for a physical."

The blurry edges coalesced into a thin, rippling mist. His own voice sounded far away and took the mist with it. "Okay. I'll think about it."

The next day, he went to visit his mother. She had no idea who he was.

*

After a month, his new signature was no longer jagged and cramped. Compared to the signature on his mother's admission form, a handwriting expert might not have identified it as his, but Lawrence suspected if there were any truth to the idea that handwriting reveals the writer's personality, his brain must be evolving a new, improved version of his.

He certainly felt different – lighter, freer. His thoughts were less tethered than he remembered them being. He frequently found connections between seemingly unrelated ideas. His powers of observation had intensified; details he'd never noticed popped out as if they were brand new, like unfamiliar spices pricking his tongue and wafting into his nose. Life was no longer routine. He felt vital.

He seemed to have loosed his imagination as well. More and more often, he caught glimpses of women who might be his mother. They always vanished into a crowd as soon as he looked harder.

This afternoon, as he pushed his cart through the busy grocery store, he was sure he saw her with her aunt Becky. They were just about to leave the aisle. He raised a hand and called out, "Mom!"

The woman standing next to him whispered, "What are you doing?"

He turned to look at her as she took his arm. He had no idea who she was, and pulled away more forcefully than he'd intended. "Excuse me?" he asked.

"Lawrence, your mother's not here." On the verge of tears, her eyes pleaded with him.

She seemed enveloped in a mist. He tasted panic. His mouth was so full of it, there was no room for words. *If I don't get away right now, I'll be trapped forever…* Run! He ran out the door and kept running.

*

Stephanie drove up and down the streets surrounding the store. *He couldn't have gotten far*, she kept thinking, but she couldn't find him. She left him voice mails till his box was full. At dusk, she went home and called the police. They told her if Lawrence had no history of dementia, she would have to wait twenty-four hours before filing a missing person report. Her stomach was in knots.

She called Kachina. "Lawrence is missing."

"What?"

Her voice edging up the scale as she explained, Stephanie couldn't keep the tears back. "He just ran off. It was like he didn't recognize me and he panicked. I looked for hours, but he's nowhere!"

"I'll order pizza. We'll be right there."

*

They arrived before the pizza. Chivonn pulled out her laptop.

"Do you have a recent photo? I'll make a 'Have you seen me?' poster."

"I haven't taken any since he shaved off his mustache, but I have some from a couple months ago." She pulled one up on her phone and shared it to Chivonn's laptop. "We're not big on selfies," Stephanie apologized.

"That's okay," Chivonn said, "I can edit it out."

The other two spent the evening calling family, friends, people from work, and hospitals.

At midnight, Chivonn went to the all-night copy store to print a ream of posters. When she returned, she left a third of them with Stephanie. "We'll put some up on our way home and do the rest in the morning."

"Thank you," Stephanie said as she hugged them on their way out. "I don't know what I'd do without you guys."

Kachina took her hand. "You're an only child. We're your friends, and we're your family."

\*

Stephanie hadn't slept. By sunrise, she had stapled or taped posters on power poles, street lamps, and walls from home to the store. She'd posted them in parks, coffee shops, and on all the freeway ramps within a mile of the house. Twenty-four hours after Lawrence had vanished, she walked into the neighborhood police substation to file the report.

"This is your husband?" the duty officer reviewing the report asked.

"No. Does it matter?" Stephanie asked, drumming her fingers on the counter.

The officer shrugged and ticked an empty box on the form. "You left the answer blank."

271

"We live together. We're not married."

"Sounds like one of the elderly folks who wander off with no idea where they are or where they're going," he volunteered.

"He's only thirty-seven," Stephanie pointed to the number on the form. "I answered that one."

"It is unusual." He raised an eyebrow. "Did you have a fight before he left?"

Her patience was gone. "No."

"Well, we've got your contact information. I've issued a local alert, and we'll call you if we find him." He leaned forward over the counter. "Look, it helps that you have posters up. Somebody might find him and bring him home. He might even show up on his own."

She went home to wait and to sleep if she could.

*

Her unknown caller ringtone dragged her from a deep, dreamless nap as the room was growing dark. "H'lo?" she mumbled. Fearing immediately that whoever it was would assume she was drunk instead of groggy, she cleared her throat and tried again. "Hello?"

"Yes. Hi. Um, my name's Victor. I think I've found your friend Lawrence. Do you want to meet us someplace, or is it okay for me to bring him to your house?"

She was already pulling on her shoes. "I'll come to wherever you are." She grabbed her wallet and keys. "Where are you?"

"At the pot pie shop on Box Street."

"I know right where that is. I can be there in five minutes. Thanks," she said. "Don't let him leave, okay?"

*

They were waiting outside the restaurant when she parked the

272

car. Victor appeared to be homeless, and Lawrence looked almost as bedraggled and grimy as Victor. Lawrence stood apart, muttering something she couldn't understand and showing no signs of recognition as she approached.

"You're Victor?" she addressed the other, who nodded.

He pointed at a street light down the block. "I found him right over there, drawin' a mustache on this pitcher of him." He handed her the poster.

Tears welled in her eyes, and she laughed. "Thank you. Thank you so much. You don't know how relieved I am." She opened her wallet.

"Nah," Victor turned away. "I don't want your money."

"But I want to do something to thank you," she pressed. "What can I do?"

He paused. "They make real good pot pies here. Lawrence might like one, too. I don't think he's eaten in a while."

Nodding, Stephanie said, "Sounds perfect."

\*

While they waited for their food, Victor said, "Ya know, maybe I *can* imagine how relieved you are. Somethin' like this happened to my dad when I was a kid."

"Was he gone long?" she asked.

"You might say that," Victor traced the tabletop pattern with one finger. "He never came back."

Stephanie blinked. Twice. "I'm sorry."

Victor shrugged. "He wasn't right in his head. He got confused and couldn't remember stuff." He looked at Lawrence, who sat staring at the table, holding his fork in his left hand like it might be preparing to bite him. "Kinda like your friend here."

As soon as they finished eating, Stephanie drove Lawrence to the nearest emergency room.

The doctor's tidy brown braid curved around the nape of her neck. Her name tag read, "Dr. Brace". Everything about her was professional, but soft-edged, as she stood back and contemplated the silent Lawrence. "Has he said anything since you found him?"

"Nothing coherent," Stephanie acknowledged, "and he doesn't seem to recognize me or even know where he is. He ate, but other than that, he seems like he's someplace else."

"I'm afraid there isn't anything I can do for him right now," Dr. Brace said, writing something in her notes, "but if you're willing to admit him, we can keep him under observation tonight and run some tests in the morning."

Stephanie closed her eyes. "What kind of tests?"

The doctor watched Lawrence for a few seconds. He held up his left arm, apparently watching something they couldn't see, and almost smiled. She turned to Stephanie. "From what you've said about his changed behavior the last couple of months, I'd like to start with an MRI. The physical condition of the brain can explain many things. It can indicate or eliminate possible problems. Then we can discuss our options."

Lawrence smiled and came alive. He focused on a point beyond the doctor and said, "Steph and I had a great time in Greece."

Dr. Brace's head snapped back to Lawrence. "I enjoyed my time there, too. Where did you stay?"

Lawrence didn't respond.

Stephanie said, "We've never been to Greece."

In her office the following day, Dr. Brace bit her lips and tapped her pen on the monitor. "Here's the scan of a healthy brain, and here's Lawrence's. The dark areas are degraded tissue – pits, if you will."

"What does that mean?" Stephanie clenched her hands in her lap.

"Lawrence's brain shows levels of deterioration we would expect to see in a much older person with an advanced form of dementia."

Stephanie's desperation leaked out of her voice. "How can that be? He's too young. He hasn't shown any symptoms till recently."

"I understand your confusion," the doctor sympathized. "I've never seen anything this extreme in early onset cases. I can't explain it." She took a slow breath. "Unfortunately, I can tell you I've never seen improvement once it reaches this stage."

Standing, Stephanie shook the doctor's hand. "I'd like to see him."

*

In a sunny room containing two beds, two chairs, and an oppressive number of tubes, bags, and electronic devices, Lawrence lay in his bed, his eyes wide open and empty, apparently unaware of his guest. Relentless beeping perforated the antiseptic air. It might have been a trick of the sunlight, but Stephanie thought she saw something misty glittering through his pupils.

She held his right hand as tears dripped onto her shirt. "I don't know what to say, Lawrence. I know I've lost you, but I'm afraid you've lost yourself, too."

His other hand rose from the bed. Her breath caught, hoping he was reaching for her, but as his arm fell limp by his side, the light in his eyes vanished. The beeping continued.

Sobbing, Stephanie collapsed into a chair. "Where have you

gone, Lawrence?"

*

Lawrence stepped off the cruise ship's gangplank with Stephanie's hand in his. He pulled his phone out of his left back pocket and looked at it to unlock it. Kevin and Chivonn followed them, laughing, while he held it up to take a shot of the four of them.

Lawrence's mother had brought Great-Aunt Becky to meet them at the dock. "How were the islands?" Cathy asked, hugging them all before she took Stephanie's hand to inspect the engagement ring her future daughter-in-law had texted her a picture of.

Stephanie waggled her finger in the sun. Sparkles lit on all of them. "Larry has magnificent taste, doesn't he?"

"You only say that because I chose you, and I don't mind that you insist on calling me 'Larry'."

As Lawrence hugged Great-Aunt Becky, his golden tanned face broke into a smile. "Thanks for coming to pick us up. Kevin and Chiv will complain about all the ruins, but Steph and I had a great time in Greece!"

S.T. Ranscht answers to "Sue" in person, but prefers the dubious gender uncertainty of S.T. Ranscht as an author's name in the style of J.R.R. Tolkien or J.K. Rowling or P.G. Wodehouse or H.G. Wells. One can dream. If you enjoy her writing, she would be happy to hear from you. If you don't... well, everyone is entitled to an opinion, and she would welcome your constructive critique.

Although she has written a yet unpublished Young Adult SciFi novel titled *Enhanced* with Robert P. Beus, four of her own short stories have been published in international anthologies within the last two years. While she continues to pursue critical acclaim as an author, she lives, writes, and sews in San Diego, California.

Sue's website is *Space, Time, and Raspberries* at https://stranscht.com/

Twitter: @STRanscht at https://twitter.com/STRanscht

# Conrad Usry's Estate

by Tom Bont


Professor Clinton Dempsey
Miskatonic University
Department of Psychology

December 17, 1957

Dear Professor Dempsey,

It is with great sadness that I must report the death of my uncle, Conrad Usry. He lived a long life and entertained us for hours on end with tales of his exploits and travels around the world. The family adored him. It was only when I went through his papers after his lawyer revealed I'd been named executor of his will – which came as a great surprise to me for he had numerous brothers and sisters who could have just as easily fulfilled the role – that I came across letters he'd received from you while he served these United States during World War I. I skimmed them for any information in relation to his estate, and finding none, bound and included them in this package. As he did not specifically name you in the will, I felt you might appreciate having these reminders of your friendship. Should you desire to visit him, we buried him in our family plot next to my older sister, Cynthia.

In addition, I have included a photograph of three men standing in front of a burned-out German tank. The man on the right is obviously Uncle Conrad, but I am not familiar with the other two. I am assuming you know who they are, as I found the picture in the same folder as your correspondence.

I wish you and yours a Merry Christmas.

Sincerely,
Randy Usry, Esq.

Professor Clinton Dempsey
Miskatonic University
Department of Psychology

December 28, 1957

Dear Professor Dempsey,

I received your letter in this morning's post with much delight. Thank you for asking after my family. They are all hale and hardy and looking forward to our New Year's party. Should you find yourself in South Carolina, please accept my offer to reside at my home during your stay. Since my eldest son has elected to leave for Harvard early this year, we have a spare bedroom for you. I know you will enjoy the snowy mountains here at Caesar's Head, our crackling fires, and my wife's hot toddies.

Learning Uncle Conrad once held the Physics chair at MiskU took me entirely by surprise. He never once mentioned this during his many visits with the family. Still, I was pleased to discover it, for I possess a minor in physics. I seriously considered the teaching profession at one time. It is nice to know we had more in common than I originally thought.

In reference to the photograph, I had a hunch that one of them might have been you. As to the other gentleman, Eric Abernathy, I have found references to him in Uncle Conrad's belongings. You have my condolences on the injury that ended your military career. It is unfortunate you didn't keep in contact with Mr. Abernathy after the war.

However, not all is lost. I have found a series of diaries dating from that time. I intend to read them when I have finished my duties to Uncle Conrad's estate. Perhaps there is reference to Mr. Abernathy in them. If so, I will post a letter with my findings.

Sincerely,
Randy Usry, Esq.

Professor Clinton Dempsey
Miskatonic University
Department of Psychology

March 17, 1958

Dear Professor Dempsey,

Happy St. Patrick's Day from South Carolina!

I apologize for the tardiness of this letter, but my leave of absence from my law firm expired at the first of this month and working through Uncle Conrad's estate has taken longer than I first envisioned. Excuses aside, I have found time to read his diaries as promised.

After I finished the first two volumes, I decided to embark on my own adventure. Uncle Conrad published several papers before he took to his globetrotting. I am something of an amateur genealogist, and the thought of having a small library containing nothing but his writings excites me.

As he published most of these papers during his tenure at MiskU, and if it isn't too much of an imposition, would you do me the great favor by submitting the attached letter to the Office of Historical Publications? It is a request for copies of all papers authored by Professor Conrad P. Usry. In the meantime, I plan to continue my literary sojourn into his diaries.

Sincerely,
Randy Usry, Esq.

Professor Clinton Dempsey
Miskatonic University
Department of Psychology

June 2, 1958

Dear Professor Dempsey,

I hope life has treated you well these past few months. I received a package from MiskU's Office of Historical Publications yesterday containing copies of everything they could find concerning Uncle Conrad. You have my warmest regards for your help in delivering the letter. Regardless of your protestation that it did not put you out, having the letter delivered by one of their own, I am certain, went a long way towards them delivering the package with such celerity.

I have finished my uncle's diaries. It appears that he and Mr. Eric Abernathy continued their association after the war as research associates on a personal project. If we are to believe everything he's written, they experimented with paranormal physics, specifically in the arena of temporal and dimensional travel. These experiments seem to have ended quite abruptly. This final entry poses more questions than it answers:

*"Eric believes our failed attempts to pass lower lifeforms through the Incident is due to their inferior mental faculties; they're unable to comprehend their situation. He also feels the apparent rapid aging they experience is the result of this unadulterated fear and does not think humans would be as terrified as we possess rational minds. I asked him if we truly knew, and he reluctantly admitted that we did not. We both agreed to not attempt it ourselves until we had successfully passed and retrieved an animal, preferably a higher primate, unmolested by whatever forces we are dealing with.*

*"As I walked home, I realized I had forgotten my house keys and rushed back to retrieve them, just in time to witness my friend's left foot disappear through the Incident.*

*"The destination dials showed a planned jump of 10 minutes. I could only pace helplessly. When the allotted time had passed, he fell out of the Incident and onto the floor, hair white, fingernails pale and cracked, teeth grey, skin wrinkled and translucent, eyes wild, and like so many of our past experimental subjects, quite insane. That's when the screaming started, and it never stopped, his only coherent word being 'zot.' The last I saw of him, the doctors were taking him to the Arkham Sanitarium under heavy sedation. I still wake up in a cold sweat when the insanity I saw in his eyes intrudes on my nightmares.*

*"I spent months combing through our math, seeking the answer. I could not, and thus, have given up on my theories. I do not wish to subject another living creature, soulless or not, to the energies generated by my machine. I have established a trust to care for my friend as I cannot stand to visit him as often as I should, for he is nothing more than a sedated and tied-down decrepit skeleton with darting eyes deep within darkened sockets, misshapen hands carved into arthritic claws, and legs, weak and bowed, trying to run from something I cannot see. This is no longer the man I shared a trench with in France."*

Professor, I have read this passage numerous times, and each time I do, I get more excited. This topic appeals to my ego. If I could, I would use this technology to save my older sister's life. You see, during a particularly heavy rainfall, Cynthia dove into a flooded creek to save me from drowning. The effort drained her, and the roaring waters washed her away. I wish you could have known her, sir. She was sunlight with a smile. Hair as black as coal dust and eyes as blue as a warm summer day. She always cheered me up when I was down. Not a day goes by that I don't miss her.

If you have any further information on my uncle's experiments, I beg you to please send it to me without delay.

Sincerely,
Randy Usry, Esq.

282

Professor Clinton Dempsey
Miskatonic University
Department of Psychology

June 9, 1958

Dear Professor Dempsey,

I received your letter in this morning's post. It is disappointing you were not more familiar with Uncle Conrad's activities. This either means he left the diaries as his last practical joke, told from the grave, or he intended to keep his research a secret and never got around to destroying the evidence. I have, however, been reviewing his publications. There are bits and pieces scattered about them that reference experiments; information is vague, though, and I, unfortunately, am not familiar enough with the technical discourse. I'll have to find someone more educated in the field. Though Eric Abernathy, at last report, is insane, it appears he is my last hope. I shall start my search for him at the Sanitarium.

Sincerely,
Randy Usry, Esq.

Professor Clinton Dempsey
Miskatonic University
Department of Psychology

June 19, 1957

Dear Professor Dempsey,

I have news of mixed feelings to relay. First, I regret to inform you that your friend, Eric Abernathy, has passed. He died within one year after being admitted to the Arkham Sanitarium. I have enclosed a photograph of his headstone. Uncle Conrad's trust used its remaining funds for the glorious marker you see. The engraved encomium, *He Traveled Beyond Imagination*, indeed sums up his life.

On the opposite end of the spectrum, I found a nurse at the sanitarium, a stout woman with eyes which have seen too much in the 30 years she's worked there, who remembered him. We sat in her office, and she told me of a man, Stockard Wilmoth, who showed up one day claiming to be his nephew. He had an experimental drug which he believed would return his poor uncle to lucidity. As he had the proper credentials to prove he was indeed family, the doctors allowed it, as their attempts at curing him had all failed. The nurse recalled that the liquid in the syringe glowed a purplish-green when they dimmed the lights.

Mr. Wilmoth injected the fluid into his uncle and within minutes, his sanity returned. It is the nurse's belief that Mr. Abernathy traded what physical abilities remained in exchange for a mostly sound mind. He was still a broken man, though, and became confused at times, but he was able to carry on a conversation most days. In either case, Mr. Wilmoth spent the final two months with his uncle, recording everything they talked about into a journal. He had to tread lightly, though, for when he asked about the word 'zot,' his uncle would again fall into fits of delirium that lasted anywhere from hours to days. When at last he settled down, they would continue their discussions. On his passing, Mr. Wilmoth disappeared with the diary, leaving many unanswered questions about his miracle cure.

As I made my good-byes, the nurse abruptly pulled me into a broom closet – which I found quite forward as I am a married man – where the dim light hanging from the ceiling cast grotesque shadows onto our faces. Her motives, however, became clear when she gripped my wrist with surprising strength. "There's more," she whispered, shuddering with dread, and looking into the darkness as if to see if anyone was there hiding who might overhear our conversation. "What came out of his mouth wasn't human, Mr. Usry!" She clutched the silver crucifix hanging around her neck. "Only madness or satanic verse could truly describe it, because whatever happened to him was not natural. Not for man. Only the work of the devil could do that to someone." With that, she opened the door and walked swiftly back to her office.

I have engaged the services of the Hendershot Detective Agency out of Boston to track down Mr. Wilmoth. I must solve the black riddle my uncle could not.

Sincerely,
Randy Usry, Esq.

Professor Clinton Dempsey
Miskatonic University
Department of Psychology

February 2, 1959

Dear Professor Dempsey,

The last few months have been hectic. Mr. Hendershot located Mr. Wilmoth in near-record time. He had purchased a large warehouse on the waterfront outside of Arkham and was attempting to rebuild the machine from Mr. Abernathy's sketchy instructions. He had all but given up on his project due to a lack of finances and knowledge until I showed up with the box holding Uncle Conrad's papers. Knowing we were close to solving the mystery, I resigned my position at the law firm and mortgaged everything I owned to fund the project. My wife, bless her soul, never knew poor Cynthia, so she doesn't quite understand what the world lost. Still, she resolved to let me finish this project and has taken the family to live with her mother.

Mr. Wilmoth and I have spent the last four months putting the pieces of this puzzle together. Luckily, he is a physicist himself, trained in all the modern theories, or else we would be no further along than when we started. I am recording a layman's understanding of Professor Conrad Usry's Theory of Interspatial Transportation, mainly because most of the description would require volumes of mathematical formulae, most of which are beyond me.

As I understand it, there are an infinite number of dimensions, and each dimension represents a unique and infinitesimally short-duration Temporal Tick, an event that has happened, or could happen, no matter how improbable. There are two and only two dimensions next to each unique dimension, one before and one after. However, counterintuitively, there are an infinite number of dimensions between any two dimensions.

My uncle referred to the process of jumping between these

dimensions as Creating an Incident. As each dimension is theoretically right next to every other dimension, the Incidental Distance one must travel is a constant, regardless of the Temporal Tick differential. This means the energy required to jump one day or 100 years is identical, either into the past, the future, or sideways into another timeline.

The main problem we have encountered is that in order to specify the destination dimension, precision calculations must be performed. Mr. Wilmoth checks them dozens of times before we send anything through an Incident. He has dedicated a substantial amount of time teaching me the proper way to solve the functions, and I can now plot an Incident as accurately as he can.

The fantasy of saving Cynthia no longer drives me, though, for travelling into the past to rescue her is a non sequitur; she already lives in an untold multitude of different dimensions where the rushing waters never took her. I look forward to the day when I can Create an Incident that will take me to one of these dimensions where I can see her radiant smile once more.

Sincerely,
Randy Usry, Esq.

Professor Clinton Dempsey

Miskatonic University

Department of Psychology

February 24, 1959

Dear Professor Dempsey,

My name is Cynthia Wilmoth. You have my thanks for taking the time out of your busy schedule to read this letter. I feel I may be wasting your time, but my conscience will not allow me to ignore a dying man's wish.

That dying man showed up at my mother's estate a couple of weeks ago, hair white, fingernails pale and cracked, teeth grey, skin wrinkled and translucent, eyes wild. And quite insane. According to my mother, and despite his physical condition, he bore a striking family resemblance to my Uncle Conrad Usry. I had to take her word for it as I never knew him; he died years ago during World War I.

His identification said his name was Randall Usry. This may sound odd, but I had the strange feeling he could be my younger brother, Randy. Which is impossible, because Randy died when we were children. I don't know how, but I feel he has returned to me, a fully-grown, yet decrepit man.

My husband, Dr. Wilmoth, is a paranormal psychologist. Through his research, he has developed a serum that brings lucidity back to the insane under certain conditions, but at the expense of their physical well-being. He gave up that line of research years ago. However, in this case, he felt the risk worth it. Randy came to his senses, and when he saw me, cried for hours, hugging me, and telling me how glad he was that "it" had worked. When he calmed down, he would wander off into tangents for hours on end. Still, his ramblings formed a story, one so fantastic and sane that I doubt a madman could have conceived it.

If I am to believe what he told us, he jumped timelines to save my life.

I'm afraid, however, that his fortitude was not strong enough to survive more than a couple of weeks. We buried him in the family plot, next to the body of what I came to believe was his younger self.

One person in particular that he kept referring to in his stories was you, Professor. He kept talking about you as if you were a long-lost friend. His final wish was that I send you a letter describing the final piece of some puzzle he was working on, since he didn't have the faculties to do it. I agreed. Forgive me if my descriptions are less technical than required. Even though I possess a degree in physics, I am not as familiar with the mathematics behind this new science as my brother seemed to be.

*"As time flows from one Temporal Tick to the next, we naturally assumed there was nothing between them. This is not the case. There exists a non-space-time event between each Tick. Mr. Wilmoth* (I assume he is talking of my husband in this other timeline) *has coined this a Zot. Uncle Conrad and Mr. Abernathy would have discovered these Zots had they simply been more precise in their calculations. Unfortunately, Mr. Abernathy discovered them the hard way.*

*"Armed with this latest information, Mr. Wilmoth convinced me that he could solve the problem of Creating an Incident, which would allow us to traverse to another dimension. He was wrong, as it is either impossible (or highly improbable) that the calculations will ever be accurate enough to Create an Incident to such a precise degree; there are too many irrational actors in the formulae."*

There were more ramblings on this subject that my husband and I could not create coherent sentences out of, much less coherent thoughts. His descriptions about Zots, though, are quite horrifying.

*"A Zot is a subway tram traversing the entirety of creation and never reaching the next station. Forever. A location where*

*everything is... Not.*

*"René Descartes stated, 'Cogito ergo sum. I think; therefore, I am.'*

*"In a Zot, that becomes, 'Cogito, ergo non sum. I think; therefore, I am not,' as does the corollary, 'I do not think; therefore, I am.' And as Zots exist between Temporal Ticks, time does not exist either, only eternity.*

*"Professor, a Zot is a realm where everything in creation exists simultaneously, whether it's the mind of the our most psychotic sociopath or our greatest engineering marvels. Pure instinct. Pure hunger. Pure lust. It is the epitome of Chaos.*

*"Ancient cosmic intelligences, never sated, devoured my mind, over and over and over, until my own sense of self slowly dissolved, whereas I, too, sought out other intellects to consume."*

I fear the man I now believe to be my brother spent eternity being Not. The more I consider this topic, the more excited I become, as it appeals to my ego. If I could, I would perfect this technology to prevent his death as a child, to stop creation from removing him from my side.

You see, during a particularly heavy rainfall, I dove into a flooded creek and tried to save his life. I was not able to reach him. The effort to remain afloat drained his physical reserves, and the roaring waters washed him away. I wish you could have known him, Professor, before he became the skeletal man I buried. Hair as black as coal dust and eyes as blue as a warm summer day. He was sunlight with a smile. And he always cheered me up when I was down. Not a day goes by that I don't miss him.

Do you have any information that may assist me in recreating my brother's experiments?

Sincerely,
Cynthia Wilmoth

Tom Bont is the author of *Howlers: Lupus Rex* and *Transplanted Yankee: Lest All My Balderdash Be Forgotten*, as well as scores of short stories, essays, and articles in various magazines and other online portals. Tom is a United States Navy veteran, has a degree in computer science from Louisiana Tech University, and lives in north Texas with his family. Even after 25 years of marriage, he still spends as many hours as he can on the dance floor with his wife.

You can catch Tom at www.TomBont.com, on Twitter @TomBont, or the DFW Writers' Workshop.

# Flash Fictions

by Mitchell Grabois

## Doberman Empire

1.

The old man's cane fell from his table and, after a moment, he slowly bent to pick it up. The air was redolent with dinner prep. Chalked on the *Gate's* blackboard was: *Chicken Fried Steak*. The smell of mushy collard greens wafted from the kitchen. Sometimes all I'd order would be corn bread and a heaping plate of greens I'd sprinkle with pepper sauce.

2.

The black men stink of pesticide. They've been on a road gang. This is the Deep South, how deep you can never guess. The ghosts of the brutal past animate the present as the ghosts of our brutal present animate what-comes-next.

3.

Since I'd moved to the South something had happened to my body that made it crave vinegar.

4.

The black men have been chopping brush, spraying poison. The blacker they are, the more poison they absorb. The blackest must die first.

5.

I gained vitality from those infusions. Peppers in vinegar killed viruses and bacteria, protected me from Hepatitis B, always a danger when working in a psych ward.

6.

The roadway is not asphalt but the bodies of Doberman Pinschers laid side by side, their bodies recruited from junkyards from Mobile to Apalachicola, Galveston to Jax.

7.

I often dreamed that a patient filled with the deadliest diseases was biting me, and I woke with the sheets sweated out. Then I'd go to the kitchen and soak a piece of bread in white wine vinegar, bring it to my mouth, gasp at the fumes, but made myself eat it. I worshiped its prophylactic powers. I wanted to survive.

8.

The highway is Doberman and black men with blue muscles reeking of pesticide. Sometimes all the Dobermans come back to life. They spring at the black men's throats. They engage in pitched battles, as it was back in the Stone Age.

9.

My sister was stabbed forty-two times, and they still haven't caught the killer.

10.

Do you see why I have so much trouble traveling, with all this roiling around me? I tremble to get on a bus with the image of a stretched-out Doberman on its side.

11.

I saw her. I saw the "perp" leave my sister's house, a black woman wearing a purple bandanna, big gold hoop earrings sparkling in the street light, jangly bracelets, a big-boned woman as sinewy as a slave. A woman like this should be easy to find.

12.

I climb into the belly of the beast and comingle with blue toilet disinfectant and xombies travelling en masse to the next xombie jamboree

13.

But the murderess has disappeared into the roadway. The roadway inhaled her like cigarette smoke, then exhaled through an eighteen-wheeler's smokestack.

14.

I don't need to be in the Mental Hell System. I've served my time in Hell. I've been in levels One thru Nine. I've been in Seclusion at every level. Yet I am as pure as that black murderess's gold hoop earrings. That slave deserves her freedom until we put her to death.

15.

O, mister, please, mister, give me a ride in your white Cadillac with fins like an angel's wings. My race is nearly run and I prefer to fly in the clouds with your drunken hand between my legs and your clothes dirty and rough.


**Bad Omen**

1.

I'm sitting in my niece's crappy living room in a rundown house in a working-class neighborhood in Portland, but no one's working. I'm pissed at Tammi because she's a whore and an alcohol and drug abuser and won't listen to any of my advice. Give her three pieces of good advice, and she'll do the fourth, stupid, self-destructive thing, so I don't even try anymore. I recite the Al Anon prayer: *You can't help anyone. They've got to help themselves.*

2.

If I had my babies I would lay them in a crib. They would glitter like diamonds. My legs would splash through surf, sending droplets of pacific jism to sparkle in the sun.

3.

Tammi hands me the bottle of bourbon and I take a slug.

4.

When the jism droplets fall on me, I am pregnant again. I am whole. I am the essence of female-animalism. I am invulnerable to murderers and rapers. I am the Virgin Mary, protected by God.

5.

Tammi and her boyfriend Cleve never have any money. Sometimes they rent, most times they can't. Now they're crashing with George, a skinny guy in his sixties with faded tattoos of naked women on his arms, old school tattoos from the war.

6.

But the problem is: there are so many Virgin Marys, bloody Marys, cross-eyed Marys, Marys whose eyes are carbolic wedges of cheese, leprosy Marys, revolving door Marys, recidivist Marys...

7.

I walked in on a party. The house is filled with Cleve's co-workers, guys from the moving company, about half of them ex-cons. Their personalities are as exaggerated as TV wrestlers. They make crude jokes and chew with their mouths open. They're like the guys I grew up with, my co-workers when I worked in the sawmill before I got disabled and had to go to college. Tammi brings out her prize possession, an eight-year-old iguana named Guan. Her last one was named Iggy. Guan's a big mother. Tammi cradles it like a cat and feeds it pieces of Kraft processed cheese out of plastic wrappers. *Can they eat that shit*, I ask.

*Sure*, says Tammi, *It's bad for him, but he loves it.*

8.

...Marys who work at convenience stores, Marys whose lives are inconvenient, Marys whose life force shoots out like jism into

295

the milky way universe, Marys shot out of a canon, Marys laid off from *Buffalo Bill's Wild West Show*, Marys lynched and called *nigger*, Marys who died tens of thousands of years ago and whose voices are reaching us, only now...

9.

I watch Guan eat. His tongue is surprisingly big and human looking. He gives me the creeps. Tammi, feeding him, gives me the creeps. Without any warning, Guan spits at me, right in my eye. I remember the movie where lizard spit is acid and eats human flesh.

10.

...Marys on their backs in cheap motels, Marys putting quarters in vibrato-beds, Marys who were my roommates in the asylum

11.

I run into the kitchen and run water over my eye for at least ten minutes. I come out dripping. Everybody's drunk, high, laughing at me. *Fuck, Tammi*, I say, *I'm outta here. That lizard gave me an omen. I don't belong here anymore.*

12.

There are so many Marys, an incalculable number. I am hitchhiking to my babies. I will arrive soon.

13.

I move toward the door. An ex-con, whose muscular arms are covered with ugly prison tattoos, steps in my way. *We all gots omens, bitch*, he says, *and ain't none of us belong here.*


### Rust, Dust, Lust

I do not have blockages in my sinuses – I have Dustbowl allergies, allergies my parents brought from Oklahoma in the thirties. I don't sleep. I'm unpleasant. I just want you to know the truth.

Cheryl rusts from the inside. Her organs are pig iron, the connectors (intestinal, esophageal, eustachian) are lead, green corruption at their joints. She was made strong by Russian ancestors but not made to last. She's rusting on the inside and her female organs are doing something down there – she doesn't know what. She's only seventeen but already menopausal. Three years of sex was all she'd had before this odd disaster befell her, erasing her maternal fantasies. But boys still crawl in her bedroom window, the sex as mechanical as heavy metal drumming, but satisfying for us all the same.

The glass shards embedded in my side usually work their way out slowly but sometimes emerge quickly, as if my body is spitting them out. Once a Vietnamese woman woke up bleeding. My projectiles had pierced her as she slept. She screamed – she knew a bad omen when she saw one, a lover whose body was an unconscious weapon. I had to run – her father was the police chief. I never had time to explain. I crossed the border into Cambodia.

Mitchell Krockmalnik Grabois has had over fourteen hundred of his poems and fictions appear in literary magazines in the U.S. and abroad. He has been nominated for numerous prizes, and. was awarded the 2017 Booranga Writers' Centre (Australia) Prize for Fiction. His novel, *Two-Headed Dog*, based on his work as a clinical psychologist in a state hospital, is available for Kindle and Nook, or as a print edition. To read more of his work, Google Mitchell Krockmalnik Grabois. He lives in Denver, Colorado, USA.

## by Andrew Hogan

*Rector Fareburgh*: Hubert Polkingthorne Wrightsom III, you stand before this investigatory panel of the Disciplinary Committee charged with vandalism, committed last Thursday following your Social Studies and Wealth Management Class, whereupon, in apparent response to failing to achieve a B+grade on your mid-term examination, causing you to fall from the Consul Honors Group back to the ranks of the Praetors, you vented your spleen by running the tip of a 1957 Budweiser promotional beer can opener across the Stanley and Harriet Fleischmann etched glass panel of the George and Mona Smithville lacrosse trophy case; you then entered the ArcoTonics Memorial men's lavatory through the Jeffrey Donaldson door after spraying Dupont Krylon magnetic paint on the Dorothy Manion door handle; inside the men's room, you blocked the Fitzsimmons Corporation washbasin drain with paper towels from the Georgina Hawkins towel dispenser and opened the Ira and Phyllis Larkspur burnished brass faucet; after scraping a treble clef on the door of the Drake Exeter toilet stall, you climbed onto the Marsha and Miles Washborne toilet seat, dislodging the Edith Pippinham cistern cover, which fractured upon hitting the floor; you then proceeded to ignite a vintage Po Sing Phantom Cherry Bomb and dropped it into the Clive and Agatha Tortelson toilet bowl, where it shattered the Edna Parkhurst wax sealing ring, allowing water contaminated with fecal matter to discolor the Barconi Family synthetic Italian marble tile floor; fleeing the scene of your delinquency, you ran the keys of your BMW AC Schnitzer ACS7 sports car across the right fender and passenger-side door of Social Studies instructor Delilah Sampsonite's Mini Cooper S Clubman; you were apprehended by the Campus Security in their Dixie Hills Motors Saab 9000CD police cruiser after you decimated the Frederico Quiñones flock of black-neck swans that was crossing the Regina Tillingshire Boulevard on their way to the Peggy and Slim Rankin reclaimed water wetlands. Unless you can provide an adequate explanation for your vandalistic behavior, in addition to full restitution, your family name will be removed from all items donated to the Trent Lockhardt Preparatory School for Aberrant Adolescent Aristocrats, including the Martha Fletcher Polkingthorne Memorial Koi Pedicure Pool located in the Silvia and Thorton Buckingstern Garden of the Ambassador and Mrs. Archibald McPherson Rector's Residence. What response do you submit to these charges?

*HPWIII*: There're bogus. Everyone knows 1950s vintage promotional beer can openers are made of low-grade alloyed steel, rating only a 5 on the Mohs hardness scale. High quality etched glass like that in the lacrosse trophy case rates a Mohs scale of 6.5 and requires tools with carbide tips for a deep scratch like the one I allegedly made on the trophy case. I think the school administration should investigate whether any vanadium burs are missing from the Sarah and Arthur Tendholm equipment locker in the Parkhurst Industries jewelry and gem laboratory. Recent tweets rumor that some of the students in Jewelry for Debutantes 101 class have been misappropriating laboratory equipment.

*1st Interrogator Marley*: Rector Fareburgh, if I might be allowed a follow-up question of the respondent. Master Wrightsom are you claiming you did not attempt to desecrate the George and Mona Smithville lacrosse trophy case? There are witnesses who saw you pass the trophy case and heard a scraping sound.

*HPWIII*: It's true I passed by the trophy case following my Social Studies and Wealth Management class, as did several others of my classmates, and, as Rector Fareburgh noted, I went to the men's lavatory, again with several classmates. Following mid-terms, as is the Trent Lockhardt Preparatory School custom, I and my classmates were provided with a celebratory mid-semester snack catered by the students of the Executive Mansion

Management and Economics class, who were forced to substitute some hinky paddlefish roe for genuine caviar due to the large investment losses suffered by the Trent Lockhardt Preparatory School endowment following the collapse of the investment fund run by Bernie Madoff of the class of 1957. The fake caviar resulted in acute indigestion for me and several of my classmates, causing certain involuntary flatulent emissions that could have been confused for scraping sounds reported by witnesses. A better explanation of the scratch is found in the recent tweet from second-year deb Irandia van Stoelkenberg about Marc Jenkins, captain of the lacrosse team:

"ccksckr had tung in mouth of bitch Viki Lutz. Gonna cut balls off w/ diamond saw nxt time i see him!!"

***Rector Fareburgh***: Irrespectively, you nonetheless desecrated the Dorothy Manion handle of the Jeffery Donaldson door of the ArcoTonics Memorial men's lavatory with magnetic paint...

***HPWIII***: Bogus again.

***Rector Fareburgh***: Be so kind as to not interrupt me while I am speaking to you.

***HPWIII***: But I can explain the paint. Building maintenance was painting the bulletin board in the hallway between the classroom and the restroom so they could use magnets instead of thumb tacks, which the students have been stealing and putting on the teachers' chairs...

***Rector Fareburgh***: You are referring to the Edythe and Jasper Conklin Memorial informational display, now equipped with neodymium rare earth magnets?

***HPWIII***: Right. We all wanted to get to the restroom fast because of the crappy paddlefish caviar. We were running and slid into the fresh paint on the bulletin board. It wasn't just me that put the paint on the door handle.

***1st Interrogator Marley***: A very imaginative story, young man, but my niece Rebecca Anne is a debutante in the Executive Mansion Management and Economics class. I asked her whether anything unusual happened in her classes on that day, and she did not report any cases of food poisoning. I'm sure she would have remembered such an event.

*HPWIII*: Mr. Marley, Rebecca Anne cut the home ec class and was snogging with Rolfe Lindsemere, who cut Ms. Sampsonite's Social Studies class – that's why he wasn't poisoned by the paddlefish caviar. Rolfe has been surveilling Ms. Sampsonite in the faculty parking lot to learn the door code for her Mini Cooper. That's where he and Rebecca Anne were snogging, because he knew Ms. Sampsonite parks her car next to the azalea bushes…

***Rector Fareburgh***: You are referring to the Priscilla Tattenberg azalea grove bordering the Dahlberg Family Vehicle Enclosure?

*HPWIII*: Right. It's pretty secluded, and Rolfe and Rebecca Anne were sure Ms. Sampsonite wouldn't be using her car. By the way, you should talk to Rebecca Anne and Rolfe about the scratch on Ms. Sampsonite's Mini Cooper. According to a tweet I got from Rolfe: "had bitch's bra unhkd but dissed her cup size. elbowed me in balls, made nice scar on MiniCooper leaving."

***Rector Fareburgh***: We shall postpone that discussion until we reach the vehicle vandalism portion of the allegation. Now Master Wrightsom, there is the matter of the Fitzsimmons Corporation washbasin drain which you blocked with paper towels from the Georgina Hawkins towel dispenser and then opened the Ira and Phyllis Larkspur burnished brass faucet, causing flooding in the lavatory. You admit to being in the lavatory at the time the flooding took place.

*HPWIII*: Well, yeah, but I wasn't the only one in there. Several members of the lacrosse team ate the polluted paddlefish caviar and they thought they'd been poisoned on purpose. Irandia has a lot of bffs in the Executive Mansion Management and

Economics class, most of whom have been groped pretty thoroughly by the lacrosse team. One of them, Cynthia Garthwood, is the granddaughter of the Tortelson bowl donors. So the lacrosse team took out their being pissed off on the Cynthia's ancestral crapper. I'm not sure who put the clef mark on the toilet door.

*1st Interrogator Marley*: You're very good about shifting the blame onto others, aren't you Master Wrightsom, no matter how innocent they may be? But isn't it true your father appeared last year on the Antiques Roadshow episode broadcast from Richmond showing off his widely renowned collection of antique fireworks? Or are you saying someone on the lacrosse team just happened to have a vintage Po Sing Phantom Cherry Bomb to drop into the Clive and Agatha Tortelson toilet bowl?

*Rector Fareburgh*: Is your father missing any antique fireworks, Master Wrightsom?

*HPWIII*: Okay, but I can explain.

*1st Interrogator Marley*: I'll bet you can, Master Wrightsom, I'll bet you can.

*Rector Fareburgh*: Please, Mr. Marley, let him finish. We need to get this on the record.

*1st Interrogator Marley*: Of course, Rector.

*HPWIII*: I confess. I brought the vintage cherry bomb to school.

*Rector Fareburgh*: That's a class-one infraction, Master Wrightsom. I could expel you right now, just for that.

*1st Interrogator Marley*: Good. Can we wrap this up? I'm tired to listening to these lies.

*Rector Fareburgh*: Please, Mr. Marley, we have to follow procedure. His father is a corporate attorney. You remember what happened the last time? Go ahead, Master Wrightsom.

*HPWIII*: We've been going over explosive materials in chemistry class; you know, how much plastique does it take to damage an armored limousine? Anyway, Professor Drueckhoeffer had a picture of some Nobel No. 808. He always encourages students to bring in historical items from home to show the class, you know, to make the class more relevant. My dad said it was okay to take the cherry bomb to school as long as I was careful, although he made me sign a release.

*Rector Fareburgh*: Any kind of explosive whatsoever is prohibited on campus.

*HPWIII*: I grabbed for my handkerchief to wipe my face after I'd puked in the toilet, and the Po Sing fell out of my pocket. One of the lacrosse players picked it up, lit it and threw it in the toilet. My dad said he was surprised the damn thing went off; it was over sixty years old. The value of the other half dozen cherry bombs in his collection just doubled because of this test.

*Rector Fareburgh*: There is still the animal cruelty issue, when you drove your BMW AC Schnitzer ACS7 sports car through the Frederico Quiñones flock of the black-neck swans that was crossing the Regina Willingshire Boulevard toward the Peggy and Slim Rankin reclaimed water wetlands.

*HPWIII*: It wasn't me. I swerved around the geese. It was campus security that was travelling at like ninety miles an hour trying to catch me that killed the fowl.

*1st Interrogator Marley*: Again shifting the blame for your actions to someone else. I think we've heard enough, Rector.

*HPWIII*: My Dad told me to give you this, Rector.

*Rector Fareburgh*: What this? "You are hereby served with this subpoena for all images recorded between 2 p.m. and 3 p.m. on 3 March 2009 by the Patrolrecorder 4C installed in the Campus Security Saab 9000CD police cruiser with the license plate REBCOP15." I see. Well, perhaps, we should return to this matter at a later date after consulting with the general counsel.

*1st Interrogator Marley*: Are we finished now, Rector?

*Rector Fareburgh*: Yes, I think so. Hubert Polkingthorne Wrightsom III, you are hereby placed on suspension from the Trent Lockhardt Preparatory School for Aberrant Adolescent Aristocrats until the full Disciplinary Committee has had the opportunity to examine the transcript of this interrogation and the other evidence and vote on your expulsion. Since the full Disciplinary Committee only meets twice a semester and its last meeting was held ten days ago, you will miss the next six weeks of class.

*HPWIII*: I will never be able to catch up after all that time. I'll have to repeat the whole semester.

*Rector Fareburgh*: Yes, that is unfortunate, indeed. Perhaps you would like to consider transferring to another college preparatory academy more suitable for your temperament? I happened to be speaking to Warden Christoffe at the Breckenriver Adolescent Remedial Institute. He told me he has some openings for qualified transferees.

*HPWIII*: I thought you needed to have at least a Class 2 misdemeanor arrest or higher to qualify for admission at Breckenriver?

*Rector Fareburgh*: Yes, but in your case he will make an exception.

*HPWIII*: In that case, my Dad told me to give you this.

*Rector Fareburgh*: What? Another subpoena? "Be advised that Article IX, Section 3, paragraph iv of the bequest agreement between the Trent Lockhardt Preparatory School and the Estate of Martha Fletcher Polkingthorne specifies: 'insofar as there exists a linear descendant of Martha Fletcher Polkingthorne within the fourth degree who is physically capable and willing to attend the Trent Lockhardt Preparatory School for Aberrant Adolescent Aristocrats, such individual shall be assured unconditional

305

admission and retention; failing this, the entire contents of the Martha Fletcher Polkingthorne Memorial Koi Pedicure Pool located in the Silvia and Thorton Buckingstern Garden of the Ambassador and Mrs. Archibald McPherson Rector's Residence, including but not limited to (1) any physical structures other than foundations, pediments or basements, (2) furniture and office equipment, (3) aquarium equipment, including tanks, tubing, filters and aquatic pedicure stations, and (4) all fish, regardless of their descendancy from the original school of donated koi, along with any amphibians and reptiles living in the pool, shall be delivered at the School's expense to the estate of the closest Polkingthorne descendant within fifteen days of the notification of non-admission, expulsion or suspension exceeding sixty days.'"

*HPWIII*: My family is only renting the house here in Roanoke. Our estate is in Tappahannock near Richmond.

*Rector Fareburgh*: Perhaps a warning will suffice until the Disciplinary Committee can make a final determination. We wouldn't want to do anything precipitous that might damage your future academic career or the reputation of the School.

*1st Interrogator Marley*: What? You're going to let this delinquent stay here after what he said about my niece? My son-in-law owns a trucking firm. I'll transport the whole goddamned koi pond for free just to get rid of the arrogant little bastard.

*Rector Fareburgh*: I'm sorry, John, but the koi pedicures make Mrs. Fareburgh very happy. And when Mrs. Fareburgh is happy, well, I can be at peace. You are dismissed, Master Wrightsom. Take this as a lesson to stay out of trouble. You will receive notification of the final outcome of this investigation in late April. Don't be surprised to receive a strongly worded reprimand.

*HPWIII*: Thank you, Rector Fareburgh, for your understanding. And Mr. Marley, I apologize for having to be the one to inform you that your niece is a slut.

[Transcription finished.]

Andrew Hogan received his doctorate in development studies from the University of Wisconsin-Madison. Before retirement, he was a faculty member at the State University of New York at Stony Brook, the University of Michigan and Michigan State University, where he taught medical ethics, health policy and the social organization of medicine in the College of Human Medicine.

Dr. Hogan published more than five-dozen professional articles on health services research and health policy. He has published more than ninety works of fiction in *The Sandscript, OASIS Journal* (1st Prize, Fiction 2014), *The Legendary, Widespread Fear of Monkeys, Hobo Pancakes, Twisted Dreams, Long Story Short, The Lorelei Signal, Silver Blade, Thick Jam, Copperfield Review, Fabula Argentea, The Blue Guitar Magazine, Shalla Magazine, Defenestration, Mobius, Grim Corps, Coming Around Again Anthology, Former People, Thrice, Foliate Oak Literary Magazine,*

*Black Market Lit, Paragraph Line, Subtopian Magazine, Pine+Basil, Festival Writer: Unpublishable, Fiction on the Web, Children, Churches and Daddies, Midnight Circus, Stockholm Review of Literature, Lowestoft Chronicle, Apocrypha and Abstractions, Spank the Carp, Beechwood Review,* and many others.

*The Transcript* was originally published in SPANK THE CARP, Issue 12, September 2015

# Carolina Brimstone

## by B. David Larson

"I do believe the heathen folk would call that *being born under the wrong sign*," said Constance with her grey brows arched to their peak, though her eyelids scarcely rose above her pupils. This, of course, was her trademarked cue for laughter, feigned or otherwise. The three women seated on the parlor sofa across from the old woman willingly obliged their host. The youngest of the gaggle, Betsy – a girlish, red-haired housewife – shifted on her cushion almost awkwardly, perhaps uncomfortable with the conversation, or perhaps uncomfortable with the overwhelming summer heat which covered Darlington, North Carolina, like an unshakable blanket.

"Constance Hennfield, you are so *bad*," said Betsy, attempting to appease her host, drawing out the last word with a smirk to intimate that Constance was not bad at all, though the Devil himself may truly have resided within her. "The poor boy hasn't had the most pleasant of lives, I'm sure. I've heard his daddy beat him something awful, before he skipped town, that is. He never was a brain in school. Then to lose his job at the hardware store... I should say he just had a string of bad luck."

Constance swayed back and forth in her wooden rocker with a perfect tempo. It was her throne, from which she held court every Friday night. Her courtiers varied on a weekly basis, though only a chosen handful were ever invited regularly. No music played. No testimonials spoken. Only idle whispers and unholy snickering could be heard above the rhythmic rocking in the home of the Darlington Baptist Church's Sunday School teacher.

"My girl, there is no such thing as luck," said the old woman in her motherly, southern drawl. "'Do not be deceived: God is not mocked, for whatever one sows, that also will he reap,' says

Galatians 6:7."

"And you know that boy was tryin' to sow his seed all about town," quipped Diane Bibby, a dark-haired young woman to the right of Betsy. "Why I even caught Jeremy on my porch talkin' to my Jenny not a week ago. I shooed his filthy little hind right down the steps before he could get another word out."

"Down your steps and up another set, I'm sure," chimed in the hitherto silent woman seated furthest to the left on the davenport. Julie Myers, closest in age to her host, pursed her lips and adjusted herself upon the cushion. "That boy's nothin' but trouble!"

"*Was*," corrected Constance. "He *was* nothin' but trouble."

"His mama is a wreck!" said Diane.

"Well, if she had bothered to raise him right–"

"Who lets a boy out in the middle of the night like that?"

"Carousin' and boozin', no doubt."

"And then... wham!"

"My stars–"

"Just walkin' down the street."

"No more than a mile outside town."

"I heard the car never even stopped!"

"Out-of-state registration is what I heard."

Betsy twisted her nose at the last line in the hymn. "Who could know all that if nobody ever saw?" she asked, bringing a drastic halt to the sing-along.

The grey host, ever rocking, uttered a deep and knowing hum beneath her breath. She made a point to address each of the ladies, looking them sternly in the eyes, allowing her gaze to fall lastly and most heavily upon Betsy. "Somebody *always* sees, dear Betsy. Even if it is God himself, somebody always sees. Somebody knows

310

your deeds, no matter how secret you think you've been. The sins of the unrighteous will be made known to the world. All will be laid bare before the glory of the Almighty. 'There is no darkness, nor shadow of death, where the workers of iniquity may hide themselves,' so says Job."

Betsy cleared her throat and sheepishly set down to the coffee table her glass of sweet tea, which she had been delicately sipping throughout the length of the latest bout of gossip. The evening was again quiet, save the rocking, for all across Darlington supper was ended. The dishes were done. Newspapers and knitting needles were in disinterested hands, as little unwashed ears were falling to pillows for the night. But the peace and comfort of the stillness was robbed by the air – humid, dense, and oppressive. The citizens had been suffering through several weeks of unforgiving North Carolinian summer with no reprieve at sundown. Clammy hands gripped the daily news. Sticky thighs crossed one another. While upstairs, little legs kicked at the covers, flailing restlessly in the unbearable warmth.

The passing of Jeremy Lawrence only served to heat the town further, as mysterious small-town deaths often do. Foolish accident, drunken mishap... murder – nobody knew, but all would speculate in steamy ignorance over the latest unsolved Darlington fatality.

And in the parlor of Constance Hennfield, hotter was it still, as the atmosphere was saturated with hot rumors and haughty chatter. It was during yet another bout of simmering conversation that the condensation from Betsy's glass slid slowly down the side of the cup, coming to a rest in a cool ring upon her host's coffee table.

"My Lord," huffed Constance, in grave exasperation. The lyrical sweetness of her country accent nearly evaporated. "Do you not see the coaster not a foot away from your nose?"

Betsy held her breath as she hurriedly placed a small doily beneath the glass. Her face turned as red as her amber hair.

"Bless your heart, sweetie," cooed Diane. "This being your

first time in Connie's house, I'm sure you didn't know. Connie is a stickler for coaster use in her home, aren't you dear?"

"Yes," stated Constance coolly. "Amongst other things."

"Your house looks beautiful as usual, Connie," sang Julie. She rarely missed an opportunity to interject a word of kindness to her host – ever the peacemaker, ever the sycophant. "How do you manage this entire place on your own?"

"I wake up at a Godly hour, you know," said Constance. "I don't waste my time in idle merriment, not until the chores are done. The hairdresser can always tend to one's roots tomorrow," she said with an *almost* imperceptible nod toward Betsy.

A ringing silence prevailed. The air in the room closed in tighter around the guests. Constance sat nearly still, save her toes undulating ever so slightly to keep her rocker swaying at its slow and steady pace. Diane and Julie fidgeted with the ends of their respective dresses, occasionally pressing them down upon their laps. Betsy bit her lip. Sweat ran down her forehead and flushed cheeks. She peered blankly out the parlor window, then scanned the faces of the room. Not a single eye met hers, as even Constance's eyes lay shut peaceably, her nose pointed heavenward – a manifest picture of piety and prayer if one had not known any better.

"Oh my," said Betsy, forging counterfeit surprise. "I didn't notice how late it was. I'm sure my Steven will be wondering what's taking me so long over here."

"You can assure him it's been church matters of the highest import," said Julie with a faint smile.

"I will, surely," grinned Betsy. She stood and made a move to the front door, pausing before Constance. "I thank you for a wonderful evening, Connie."

"Please," responded the elderly without opening her eyes, "it's Mrs. Hennfield."

312

"Of course, Mrs. Hennfield. Thank you again."

Constance took a deep breath and exhaled. "Good night, dear."

Betsy looked to the other two one last time. Both donned expressions that thinly veiled their anxious desire for her departure. "I'll see you ladies in church," she said shortly.

The screen door snapped shut with a clap.

"I'm glad that unpleasantness is over with," whispered Julie. She fanned herself with her hand – a fruitless effort to dispel an omnipotent heat.

"She needn't worry about Steven wondering where she is," said Diane. "I'm sure he's *passed out* for the night," she added with a drinking motion from her right hand.

"Always with a beer in his hand," continued Julie. "Mowing the lawn, tinkering with his car... wouldn't surprise me a bit if he showed up to service with a bottle."

"But I suppose anything will do to wash down her cooking."

"Did you eat that potato salad?"

"If you mean tuckin' my tongue to the side and lettin' it *slide* down the back of my throat? Then yes, I *ate* the potato salad."

"Youngsters nowadays..."

"Just like that Jeremy."

"Up to no good."

"Then *wham!*"

"Runned right over."

"Gracious, what has happened to the youth in this town?"

"I don't know. I truly *don't* know. But I'll tell you, this generation is steerin' us down quite an unruly path–"

"Now, ladies," interrupted Constance. She had been listening

313

quietly to the latest flurry of sentiments, basking in the heat of the night and the heat of conversation without a single drop of perspiration to show for it. "Let us not misdirect our enmity for the current state of affairs, for it is not youth which is owed the blame. The Apostle Paul himself instructed young Timothy: 'Let no man despise thy youth; but be thou an example of the believers, in word, in conversation, in charity, in spirit, in faith, in purity.' No it is not youth, dears, which carries us to the precipice. It is ignorance – a blindness cast over the eyes of any who should but stray a little – a pitiful ignorance to which we must assign fault. The devil's greatest tool is convincing a man that he and God Almighty do not exist. For if Good and Evil do not exist, then neither does Truth. And without Truth, then man is free to live as he pleases, seeking out all the desires of his heart and all the pleasures of the world. And that, ladies, is the speediest way to eternal damnation." Constance stopped her rocking for the first time in an hour's passing.

She opened her eyes and solemnly folded her hands upon her lap. "These are the signs of the End of Times, ladies – that false prophets should strike the name of God from our vocabulary and cause our people to follow the teachings and whims of mere men and false idols. Do not be fooled. Guard your minds from such teachings, lest their temptations lead to your demise. Yes, dear ones, safeguard your minds, safeguard your children. And when the Lord calls upon you to act as his instrument of purification, do not hesitate, but rather answer the call with a willing spirit and a righteous heart."

The evening was wearing late. Outside, the sweltering town of Darlington slowly released its accumulated heat up to the moonless night, up into the hazy star-strewn southern sky, even up unto Heaven itself. But within the home of Constance Hennfield, the temperature never dropped, and in fact, seemed to rise as the evening waned. The bleach-white walls of the parlor radiated. Both guests glistened with perspiration, tugged at their collars, and attempted in vain to appear comfortable in the presence of their

314

pious host. Even Julie, who was no stranger to the heat, bobbed her foot in nervous discomfort. All the while, Mrs. Hennfield rocked without a hint of distress, relishing her private inferno.

"Well I suppose we should leave Connie to herself," spoke Julie, breaking what felt like eternal silence. Her fellow supplicant shot up from the couch immediately. Both women retrieved their purses and donned their hats without delay. "Yes, dear, it's best y'all get back to your homes and back to your families," stated Constance in a motherly tone.

The two women each extended their highest gratitude for the pleasant evening as they made their way in file toward the door. "See you at service, Connie," said Julie over her shoulder with a foot over the threshold.

"Oh Julie, dear, that reminds me," called Constance.

"Yes, ma'am."

"Would you and John be so kind as to pick me up on your way? My car is at the mechanics."

"Of course!" responded Julie. "Nothing too expensive I hope."

"Just fixing a dent in the hood," hummed Constance with a subtle smirk of content. "Caught the tail end of a doe the other day," she added after a pause.

Julie smiled and nodded, but the smile quickly melted away as she turned once again to leave.

Constance lifted her head from the back of her rocker and called out to her departing guest, who halted at the beckon. "Remember the Word of the Lord," she stated, leaning back once more. "'I know thy works, and thy labor, and thy patience,'" she began slowly and deliberately. She paused and breathed in deeply, and for the second time that evening she ceased her rocking. "'And I know how thou canst not bear them which are evil,' so says the Book of Revelation."

Julie once again summoned her most polite of smiles and slipped out quietly. The door clicked softly. Constance remained still for a moment. She shook her head in voiceless disapproval. Exhaling heavily out her nose, she began rocking once more. With a perfect tempo she swayed, and to the beat she began to sing, boastfully and heartily. A song of praise – a song of worship – she sang to her Heavenly Father. *Onward Christian soldier, marching as to war. With the cross of Jesus going on before.* But as the song carried on, the volume diminished, and Constance Hennfield began to doze, her mind one with the mind of her Lord. Swaddled by the inferno of her parlor and the fires of her zeal did she drift off to a self-assured sleep, dreaming of Paradise, while envisioning her next act of obedience to her god on earth.

Brad Larson is a happily married father of two, who spends his day time working at whatever he can do, in order to support what he loves to do: write. Brad recently gave up a decade-long career as a teacher of mathematics at the high school level, trading in his chalk and eraser for a hammer and nails as he remodels homes in Charleston, South Carolina alongside his father. But when the workday is over, the kids are in bed, and the dishes are done, the laptop comes out, and the real work begins.

When he's not laboring on the jobsite and clacking at the keyboard, Brad spends as much available time as possible squeezing joy out of life. Aside from day trips to the beach and afternoons at the playground, Brad performs stand-up comedy locally, builds furniture, and records a podcast, *The Zack and Dean Geek Machine*, (available on iPodcast and Podbean).

Website: https://bdavidlarson.com/

# Tripping

## by Paul Lewellan

He emerged from his deathlike sleep with Technicolor memories of chorus girls in gaudy orange and lime costumes, wearing seamed nylons and impossibly high heels. He heard voices outside his room. When he opened his eyes, nothing looked familiar.

He lay in a queen-sized bed in a large stateroom suite. Looking through the glass sliding door to the cabin's veranda, he saw a rugged coastline. "I must be on another cruise," he thought, without knowing where the idea came from. He sensed movement next to him and rolled over.

The naked woman beside him smiled. She had curly dark brown hair streaked with gray. He didn't know her or how she had gotten there, but she obviously knew him. He returned her smile, then rolled back onto his pillow so he wouldn't have to meet her gaze.

Movement caught his eye. On a string hanging from a balloon on the ceiling was a note. *Enjoy Alaska, Joe. Don't forget your journal.*

So his name was Joe. Now he knew that much, and that he was in Alaska. Suddenly he recognized the handwriting on the note. *He'd written the balloon's message.*

Joe scanned the cabin, and there, on top of the mini-bar, was a leather-bound book with the word *Journal* in gold letters.

He rolled back to face the woman beside him. Her smile was more tentative than it had been thirty seconds ago, and she'd covered her breasts with the sheet. "Woo!" Joe said, and shook his head as if in disbelief. "That was amazing!"

The comment reassured her, and the full-blown smiled returned. "That's what I thought, too."

"I'm so glad you spent the night," he told her. It was a neutral line. If the woman beside him was his wife, she'd quickly set him straight, but her expression suggested a proper female caught in bed with a stranger, wondering if it had been a good idea.

He playfully tugged at the sheet covering her. She gave only token resistance. Her toned body told him that she took care of herself. There were no signs of a lift or tuck, but too much golf or tennis had taken a toll on her skin and the lines on her face. Joe guessed early fifties and wondered how old he was. "So-o-o-o?" He moved toward her as if to pull her closer.

"Oh, no, no!" She sprang from the bed, clutching the sheet around her. "There's no more 'so-o-o-o' until tonight after my family is in bed. Last night's gymnastics will just have to satisfy you for a while."

She looked at the clock on his dresser. "I've overslept. I need to get back to my stateroom and shower. My daughter won't mind if I miss the family breakfast, but if I'm late for the shore excursion, there will be hell to pay. My granddaughters must be served."

"I still think you're too young to be a grandmother," Joe suggested. Her reaction told him his instincts were right. He'd said the same thing to her last night, and she never tired of hearing it.

"I have photos to prove it," she joked. She pulled a large purse from under the small desk and hastily stuffed her bra and panty set into it. She discarded a ruined pair of hose, apparently torn off her during last night's coupling. She slipped into a simple black dress and a pair of tasteful Ferragamo heels. They'd probably met for the late show in the main lounge after she'd tucked her grandchildren into bed.

"Are you going to the martini tasting again this afternoon?" she asked, attempting to sound casual.

"Of course." That's probably where they'd met. "Best buy on the boat." The details came to him in a burst. The bartender provided humorous commentary while introducing paying participants to five different martinis. "$20 for five stiff drinks. What's not to like?"

"Chelsea, my daughter, was not pleased when I showed up at Pronto late for the family dinner, drunk, and in the company of a mystery man who disappeared before he could be introduced…"

Joe took a guess. "You certainly couldn't walk there unassisted."

"Yes," she said, as though lost in nostalgia, "that's always been my problem. I can't hold my liquor. Other men might have been tempted by my compromised condition, but you delivered me safely to my family and then discreetly disappeared. Fortunately…"

"Fortunately?"

"I suggested we meet later for cappuccinos. That's when you seduced me."

"I think you were the one doing the seducing." The truth of his statement registered on her face. He rose from the bed, naked and erect, and pretending to scold her. "But now you must hurry or you'll be late."

"But I'll see you at the martini bar?" she asked anxiously.

"I'll write myself a note." He said it teasingly, but immediately wrote the note. It would be the only way he would remember.

She kissed him on the cheek. "Thank you," she said, and then hurried to the door. She hesitated, but didn't turn back. "You know, I've never done anything like this before."

He glanced down to her left hand: a wedding band and large diamond. "I didn't suppose you did. You're not that kind of woman." But of course she was because she had sex with him and spent the night and was planning to do the same thing again tonight.

"Exactly." She left without looking back.

Joe walked into the stateroom bathroom and sat down on the toilet. There was a Post-it note facing him. *Check your cell phone calendar.* On the shelf above the sink a cell phone was charging. The note beside it said *1492.* He entered that number and the phone unlocked. It claimed the date was May 25th. The calendar entry for that day led him to a note he'd apparently written before he fell asleep:

*The woman who spent the night is Marcia White. You met her at the martini tasting yesterday. She is married and riddled with Catholic guilt. Her husband chose to go fishing in Canada with his buddies rather than accompany her on this cruise. Today she's going to take the trolley tour of Skagway with her daughter's family. You are not. Suggest martinis again tonight at five. Write a note to yourself if she agrees. If you take her to supper, avoid the Brazilian restaurant. It's where you met Beverly. That did not end well.*

Joe did not remember Beverly, but found several entries in his journal tagged with her name. Maybe he should read them later.

To the calendar he added the martini tasting date with Marcia and set an alarm to remind him. When that was done, he checked his watch and the daily schedule. It was time for breakfast in the Grand Dining room. He had no idea where that was. There was no map. He found a breakfast note. *Order the crab omelet. You like your breakfast potatoes crispy with lots of butter. Drink coffee to stimulate your brain.* That seemed simple enough. He took a leisurely shower to wash away the smell of sex and alcohol. When he finished, he felt like a new man.

While toweling off, Joe spotted a balloon on the ceiling and a note that read *Enjoy Alaska, Joe. Don't forget your journal.* The handwriting looked familiar.

He dressed before opening the journal. In the section tagged *Begin here*, he discovered his name was Joseph Morgan. He'd been diagnosed with early onset Alzheimer's the week after his forty-third birthday. On his forty-fourth birthday his third wife left him. "Not what I signed on for," she wrote in an email from Brussels. She was content with the provisions of the pre-nuptial agreement they'd made a decade earlier. Six months later, in March, when the divorce was finalized, he left his brokerage firm for *an extended cruise.*

Joe learned in the journal that each month a family member or friend would cruise with him for a week. This cadre of trusted associates would evaluate him and eventually determine when he could no longer live safely on his own. Until then, he managed routine days on the ship with the assistance of his cabin steward Eduardo and a few other crew members that knew of his condition. Their names were listed along with notes about when and how much to tip them. Joe realized he was both a generous and a wealthy man.

In the journal Joe found his daily schedule. He learned that he followed an exercise routine with a personal trainer and loved to go to cooking demonstrations, even though he couldn't cook. The journal documented an ambitious and quirky sex life made possible because the pool of eligible women changed every week, and his wealth of distant memories made him an entertaining date. Apparently, in addition to being able to dress himself, he was also a good conversationalist and a great swordsman.

Ongoing relationships were difficult because he couldn't retain what happened the night before. To compensate, he wrote himself notes after each encounter. Usually though, Joe preferred to start fresh every morning.

There was a knock on his cabin door. He closed the journal and sat quietly. When the knock came again, it was louder, more insistent. "I know you're in there," a woman said. "Open the door, Joey," she pleaded. "It's me, Beverly. I'm sorry about what I said. I'll make it up to you." He didn't move. He didn't know anyone named Beverly. He glanced at the journal on his lap. Maybe she was mentioned in there.

The knocking came a third time, more insistent. "Please let me in. People are staring."

Joe stood up and walked over to the stateroom door in his bare feet. Before he could open the door he heard a second voice – male, more formal, with a Spanish accent. "Mr. Morgan, I believe, has gone on a shore excursion, ma'am."

"Mr. Morgan never goes on shore excursions. Certainly not in Skagway."

There was an awkward silence. "Still, he doesn't appear to be in his stateroom," the man said politely. "I could leave a note for him when I make up his suite. Who shall I say came calling?"

"Beverly."

"And does he know you, ma'am?"

She laughed a wicked laugh. "No way he could forget me," she told the steward. "Not a chance in hell."

After a few moments Joe heard her retreating footsteps, then another knock – softer. "It's Eduardo, sir. Would you like me to escort you to breakfast?"

"I'll put my shoes on," Joe told him.

"Very good, sir."

As he slipped on a pair of deck shoes something caught his eye. There was balloon on the ceiling with a note. *Enjoy Alaska, Joe.* He was relieved. At least now he knew where he was.

While teaching in the public schools Paul Lewellan received the Distinguished Teacher Award by the White House Commission on Presidential Scholars. *Casualties*, his play about a school shooting, was awarded the Iowa Peace Prize by the Grinnell Peace Institute.

Now semi-retired, Paul lives on the banks of the Mississippi River and teaches Communications Studies at a small liberal arts college. He's married to Pamela, his best friend and accountant. They share their home with an annoying little Shi Tzu named Mannie. Paul has recently published stories in *Lodestone Journal* and *Front Porch Review*.

Connect with Paul on Facebook:

https://www.facebook.com/paul.lewellan

# The Finder

by Perry Palin


The first one was a little boy. He was three years old. His name was Charlie. On the radio they said he had been gone for two days and two nights, and they asked for people to come to search the fields and woods near his home. I didn't know the family. They lived on the other side of town. People went to walk shoulder to shoulder through the summer high corn. I felt bad for the boy and the family and I went too.

I walked through the high corn with a gray haired woman on my right and a thin dark brunette on my left. The sun was hot in the late afternoon. I wore a long sleeved shirt to avoid scrapes from the corn leaves, and this made me hotter still, and the sweat ran down my face and neck from under my brimmed hat. There were fifteen of us in our group, led by a firefighter trained in searches. There were a hundred and thirty of us altogether. Other teams were in other fields and searching through the woods and along the banks of a shallow pond. We were desperate to find Charlie.

I knew that the little boy was not in the corn. We weren't going to find him there. I left the line and started back toward the road. The group leader called me back to my place in the line, but I kept walking toward the house where the family lived. It was a half mile. I was challenged twice more by search leaders, but I kept on walking. In the yard the County Sheriff and Fire Chief had formed a command center. They didn't want searchers crowding into the yard, and a deputy told me to go back to my team. I didn't speak to him. I looked at the house and the yard and then walked to a wooded ravine behind the house. The searchers had swept through the ravine repeatedly for two days, but I knew the little boy was there. I went down into the ravine. I don't know what sense or senses took over, but something was leading me to the little boy. I found him sleeping in the shadow of the trunk of a fallen tree. His leg was caught in the branches of the fallen tree. His clothes were dirty and torn. He had mosquito bites on his face and neck and hands. His skin was pale and he felt cold, but his eyes fluttered when I touched him on the shoulder. I pulled the branches free of his leg and picked him up. I didn't know how to carry a child. I put his head on my shoulder and his chest on my chest so he could feel some warmth from me. I climbed up into the yard and when a deputy saw me walking across the lawn he shouted that Charlie had been found. His mother and father ran out of the house, the screen door slamming loudly behind them. The boy jerked at the slamming of the screen door. His mother was crying and trying to take the boy from me, and I let her have her son. Paramedics led the mother toward their truck where they took the little boy from her and put him on a gurney. One of the paramedics said they had to take him in, but it looked like he would be all right. They left in the ambulance with both the mother and father inside.

A call went out to the searchers that the boy had been found and that they could leave, once they had checked out with their team captains. I had left my team, so I walked back to my truck and drove home without talking to anyone.

I still had the searcher's vest I had been given, so I dropped it off at the fire hall when I went into town. I didn't want any special notice of what I had done, except from one person. It wasn't anything special, it was something that just happened, but I wanted Loretta to think it was a good thing that it was me that found the little boy.

When I dropped off the vest the fire chief was there, and he said they knew I was the one who had found the little boy. People wanted to show their gratitude. They wanted to have an event at the school. I said I wouldn't go. I didn't know how I found the little boy. It was an accident maybe, and I was glad that somebody found him. But I would have been happy if Loretta noticed.

Loretta had been in my class at school. She was the only one I asked on a date. I asked her to a dance, and she said no. She lived on a farm too, closer to town, and we rode the same school bus. I got on before her and I tried to save a seat for when she got on. She sat with other kids, and some of the other boys, and she didn't sit with me. She was the only girl I was interested in. She gave me no reason to hope, but I wanted to be with her.

The year after I graduated from high school was a bad year for small farmers, and my parents lost the farm they had been on for fifteen years. They moved south to be close to my older brother, and my dad got a job driving a truck. I didn't go with them. I should have gone to school for drafting or mechanical engineering, but I could not leave the place where Loretta lived. She worked in one of the two real estate offices in town. I rented an apartment above a store and worked at the feed mill. Loretta dressed nice in her office clothes. I was dusty and sometimes greasy when equipment needed repairs.

Our county was low hills and gently sloping farm fields and hardwood forests with some steep and rocky valleys. With a loan from my brother, I bought some rocky pasture land. It was mostly cleared of trees but too steep for crops. I repaired the fences and put up sheds and a pole barn, I had a well dug, and I bought sheep and goats. Over a year and a half I built a three-bedroom house. I did most of the building myself as time and money allowed. It was a family house for Loretta and me. I moved in alone when the house was ready. I bought more sheep, and when the ewes lambed in my third February, I started to pay off the loan for the land. Loretta never seemed to notice what I was doing. When I was in town, when I went by the real estate office, she gave me the same smile she gave to everyone else.

The second one was a little girl. I heard about her on the radio. She had been missing for half a day, ninety miles north of our town. There was a call for volunteers and I drove my truck for two hours to get to her home. It was late March. Most of the snow was gone,

327

but the ground was still frozen. When I was within a few miles of the place, I felt that she had gone to water. I don't know why I thought this. Volunteers were being directed to park in a field across the road from the house. There weren't so many volunteers this time. I parked my truck in the field and walked across the road to the house. A sheriff's deputy tried to stop me, to send me out to join a search team, but I walked past him without speaking and down a long slope to the woods. In the woods I saw brown swamp grass and a frozen pond. I walked through the tall grass and found the girl up to her waist in the cold water at the edge of the rotting spring ice. I had to walk into the water to get to her, and the water was cold on my legs and in my boots. She was blue and her eyes were closed. I pulled her out by the hood on her jacket and I carried her up to the house. The cold was painful on my legs, and I was afraid the little girl would be frostbitten. The paramedics saw me with the girl and came running with blankets. I drove home in my bare feet with the heater turned on high. I heard later that after a few days in the hospital the little girl would be okay.

After the little girl, some people greeted me on the street in town, and wanted to shake my hand. They asked me how I had found the children, they wanted to know my secret, and I told them truthfully that I didn't know. Loretta was one of those who never mentioned it, and her smile for me was the same as it was for everyone.

I bought two dogs to help me with the growing flock, an Australian Shepherd and a Sheltie. I worked long days and nights in lambing time in late winter, and during the spring and summer when I brought in hay from surrounding farms, but the sheep didn't take much time the rest of the year. Coyotes took some of my lambs, and I went to a stock auction to buy donkeys, which were good guard animals for a flock. At the auction few people were bidding on the animals, and I bought four donkeys and a pair of black draft mules. The mules were full brothers out of a Percheron mare. The mules were big and they were smart. I cut firewood trees on my hillsides and used the mules to pull the logs to the farmyard. Then I started skidding saw logs with the mules. I sold the red oaks for flooring and furniture and the hickories to cabinet makers. I used the mules as singles, working with one, and then as he rested, working with the other. One mule was easier to control than a pair when working on a hillside between the trees. I would hitch them together, one in front of the other, to drag a large load across flat ground to a landing or a road. Neighbors asked me to thin the trees on their hillsides, and I trailered my mules to their woodlots and worked carefully to keep from scarring the landscape. Loretta's dad hired me to log a part of his property. Loretta lived with her parents, but she didn't come to see me work with my mules.

The third one was a six-year old boy. It was summer, and the phone rang when I was having lunch. The sheriff called me to a farm on the south side of the county. The boy had been missing for half a day. There was no search party. A group of firefighters and a few sheriff's deputies were waiting for me to arrive. When I drove into the farmyard I knew that I would find him. The ground was flatter here than at home, and the fields were bigger. This was a grain farm with two rows of round steel grain bins. The boy had climbed a ladder on the outside of a grain bin up to the port at the top and fallen in. The bin was half full of spring wheat. When the boy tried to stand he sank in the wheat, so he had laid down flat. I climbed the ladder to look in and saw him lying face up on the wheat, scared and dusty. I went back down the ladder, and a firefighter lowered himself with a rope into the bin to pull the boy to safety. I was glad that I had found the boy, and I went home to my house and my animals without stopping along the way. That week the local newspaper had an article of how I had found another lost child. The city paper from eighty miles away sent out a reporter to ask me how it was that I could find these children. I didn't know how I did it. I didn't know how to answer her questions. Without much to go on, they published a story with my picture, and called me The Finder.

I would see Loretta in town sometimes, on the street or in the grocery. She had a great smile and I enjoyed talking to her. I wanted to ask her out, but she was always so busy. She talked about the plans she had for that evening or for this weekend. She was always busy, but I didn't want to be with anyone else.

Loretta's mom had a nice yard, with flowers and a deep green lawn. I spaded flower beds around my house and planted perennials that would bloom in the fall and then come back green and strong in the spring. I planted annuals in some of the beds close to the front door. I kept seeds from some of my flowers and threw them out in the pastures in the spring. Some of them took hold and grew bright colors until it was time to rotate my stock into that pasture, and the sheep and goats ate them to the ground.

I worked hard on poor land, and my dogs helped. The mules helped too with the logging of hillsides. In the summer the fields and pastures of the neighborhood glowed in the sunlight. I enjoyed the warm rains because I knew it would keep the pastures growing. In the winter we had sharp hard cold and deep snow and short bright days. After barn chores I drove into town for supplies and lunch at the café. I went home to a nice house, but it was an empty house.

Loretta had a baby a couple years after high school. She didn't tell anyone who the father was. I thought hard about that baby, Loretta's little girl. I was getting my farm together then and I thought hard about what I was doing. I decided to go ahead and build the family house. There would be room for Loretta's daughter. I would help raise the little girl, and Loretta and I would have more children.

Then, in the early summer, the next call came. This time it was Loretta's little girl who was lost. The fire chief had not called for volunteers. He called me. That was what everyone wanted him to do. They wanted him to call me. I drove the few miles to Loretta's parents' farm. I wanted to find Loretta's daughter, to bring her back to her mother.

In the front yard the fire chief said he was glad I could come. He said he was counting on me to find the little girl. I had a bad feeling. I didn't know where to look. It wasn't like the other times. Then the storm door slapped shut, and I heard Loretta's footsteps on the concrete and then on the grass, running to me. She saw me from the kitchen window and came running across the yard. She had been crying and her hair was mussed. She hugged me and told me to bring back her little girl.

I turned around and looked in every direction, but I was empty. I knew with the other children that I had something inside that would lead me to them, but now I was empty. People followed as I began to circle the house, but I turned to them and held up my hand, signaling for them not to come.

It was late morning when this began, the circling of the house, the walk through the barn and the sheds and the abandoned chicken coop, the survey of the dusty ground leading to the machine shed. The oats in the field were short so that a child, even lying down, would be seen from a distance. Loretta's girl was not in the oats. The corn was near waist high, and I walked through the corn fields looking for the girl, but the fields were empty. I wanted to find the girl, but where I had a feeling with the others, now I was empty.

After the corn fields I went back to the yard and turned around and looked in every direction. Then I circled the buildings again and walked between the buildings, covering the same ground a second time. I walked into the woods on the west side of the farm, past the sheds and the barns. I walked as far as a quarter mile from the house, and then doubled back a few yards to the side of my first course, and then back out again and again. I circled the farm, searching through the woods, and where I came to the border of the farm, I walked through a neighbor's pasture and cornfield, and I found nothing. The day wore on. I wouldn't stop. I went back to the woods and walked some more. Deputies followed me in shifts.

They gave me water to drink and offered me food. When evening came they told me it was time to stop for the day and go back to the house. I didn't want to stop, but I was exhausted and I was tripping over roots and stumps and tree branches fallen to the ground. I wouldn't stop, but two deputies took me by the arms and told me I had to give it up. It was dark then. The air was cooling and I was getting cold in the evening air and in my dirty clothes. I didn't want to stop, but I was empty.

The two deputies led me out of the woods and back to the yard. The barnyard light cast a bright blue-white light from the top of the power pole, obscuring the stars. I leaned against the picnic table and rubbed my face with my hands. I wanted to go back out to look for Loretta's girl, but I was too weak. One of the deputies gave me a water bottle and a granola bar. I drank half of the water and slowly chewed on the bar. I was shaking from exhaustion.

The screen door slapped shut on the house and I heard Loretta's steps running toward me. I looked up as she approached, and she ran right into me and she was hitting me with her fists. She was crying and hitting me hard and then she began to curse at me. Why wasn't I finding her little girl? What had she ever done to me? She always thought we were friends. I tried to explain to her, told her that I didn't know how I found those other kids. I didn't do those things. They just happened. But she wouldn't listen. She just kept crying and cursing and hitting me with her sharp little fists, and I didn't try to stop her. I just let my hands hang at my sides.

Finally a deputy took her by the shoulders and led her back into the house. I could hear her crying even after the screen door closed.

Perry Palin lives in rural NW Wisconsin with his wife, several barn cats, two horses, a small flock of laying hens, and honey bees. His articles and stories have appeared in local and regional newsletters, journals, and magazines, and he has had two short story collections published by Whitefish Press of Cincinnati, Ohio. A first novel is looking for a publisher.

The short story *The Finder* first appeared in the Winter & Spring 2017 edition of Lost Lake Folk Opera, a publication of Shipwreckt Books Publishing Company.

# Leaving From Gate One

by Kimberly Cunningham

Petite, curled, wispy feather swirls down.
Withdrawn woman lay there as it lands.
Burgundy caterpillar crawls on her bed.
Transformation will be fast and forceful.

Dust mites converge with bed bugs at the zone
where day crosses into lingering night.

Soon she will depart from this station
but not without the rusty clock.
Guaranteed a first class seat,
she puts on her beautiful, sparkly shoes.

Moving day is here but no boxes come.
Proud peacocks march by in a parade.
Light turns black, darkening archways.
Burnt gateway is her entrance and departure.

Kimberly Cunningham has published two books: *Undefined* and *Sprinkles On Top*. Also published in: *Evergreen Journal, NY Literary Mag Tears, Torrid Literature, NY Literary Mag Flames, From The Heart* by International Poetry Press, *Crossways Lit Mag, herstry.com, The Daily Abuse book, Blood Into Ink, Poetry Super Highway, Silver Stork Mag, Diverseverse 3, Poetry for Peace Anthology "Spring", Snow Leopard Publishing Anthology "Strength,"* and other works forthcoming.

This scriber holds a Bachelor's Degree in Education and Master's Degree in Curriculum and Instruction. Her blog is located at undefined1blog.wordpress.com.

You can find her short stories at:

https://www.amazon.com/-/e/B072WNW4XB?follow-button-add=B072WNW4XB_author&captcha_verified=1&

Kimberly's two books can be found here:

http://www.lulu.com/spotlight/kimberlycunningham

# Editors' Note

It is our hope that *The Rabbit Hole* will become an annual Writers Co-op publication. Encouraged by the response to our first call for submissions, both in quality and quantity, we believe that many talented writers are keen to explore weirdness in all its forms, and that many readers are equally keen to partake of the result.

Your honest opinion will help us greatly as we seek to provide readers with a rich and satisfying experience: to this end, please consider writing a review, however brief, of this first volume of *The Rabbit Hole* on Amazon. Not only will this incite new readers to discover it, but it will guide us in our future editorial choices. Thank you.

GD Deckard, Atthys Gage and Curtis Bausse

Made in the USA
Middletown, DE
04 November 2018